Praise for Erin Green:

'Uplifting'   *Woman & Home*

'Full of humour, poignancy and ultimately uplifting this is an absolutely gorgeous read. We loved it! Highly recommended!'   *Hot Brands Cool Places*

'Like a scrummy bowl of Devon cream and strawberries, this is a tasty, rich and delicious summer read laced with the warmth of friendships and the possibilities of new beginnings ... The author has the knack of making her characters spring off the pages so real that you'll care about them'   *Peterborough Telegraph*

'A pleasure to read ... A summer breezes treat'
                                              Devon Life

from Shetland, with love

ERIN GREEN

H

REVIEW

First published in 2021
by HEADLINE REVIEW
An imprint of HEADLINE PUBLISHING GROUP

1

Cataloguing in Publication Data is available from the British Library

ISBN 978 1 4722 8150 0

Typeset in Sabon by CC Book Production

Printed and bound in Great Britain by
Clays Ltd, Elcograf S.p.A.

HEADLINE PUBLISHING GROUP
An Hachette UK Company
Carmelite House
50 Victoria Embankment
London EC4Y 0DZ

www.headline.co.uk
www.hachette.co.uk

To the tiny seeds planted today that will bloom tomorrow

The cold wind in the winter,
The pleasant summer sun,
The ripe fruits in the garden,
He made them every one.

'All Things Bright And Beautiful',
C. F. Alexander (1818–1895)

Shetland Glossary

Peerie – small/little

Daa – grandfather

Crabbit – bad-tempered

Yamse – greedy

Chapter One

Wednesday 31 March

Jemima

My palms are clammy, my breathing erratic and there's a pain developing deep inside my chest. My anxiety grows with each passing minute. I must focus and breathe; I can't lose face in front of these family members. We've never been close. They know nothing of my current situation so I can do without their empty words or fussing, should I feel lightheaded or, even, cry.

Sadly, I belong to a family of liars. Or people who 'tell fibs', as my mum used to say. Honest, I do. A tiny flaw in our bloodline where the variation has resulted in a spectrum of individuals who frequently negotiate and twist the value of the truth.

I'm far from perfect, but I'm truthful. We all tell the odd porky-pie to sidestep a problematic situation. Such as your best friend asking, 'Does my bum look big in this?' when it's kinder to mellow your answer than ruin her self-confidence. But my family are different, very different.

I glance sideways at my aunt and uncle, my mother's older siblings, looking alike in frame and features in their black attire: together with two female cousins, they are seated next to me and making a line of five upon hard-backed chairs staring about the dingy office of Baxter, Baxter and Smyth of Lerwick, Shetland. The aged Mr Smyth sits before us carefully reading the legal document to himself prior to sharing.

How many lies have been told within these panelled walls? Diluted shades of the truth pioneered from this legal office?

I'm not comfortable. I awkwardly shift position, attempting to alleviate the numbness in my left leg caused by restraining my knee from touching the shin of my younger cousin, Pippa. I could move my chair a little to the right – there's plenty of space – but I know such an action will be examined later for a hidden meaning, and incorrectly deciphered.

During my twenty-eight years, I've endured plenty of deciphering, given my likeness to the Button family, my father's side. His gene pool supplied olive skin, dark glossy hair and a curvy frame, unlike the Quinn family who resemble the archetypal Scandinavians long-present here in Shetland: freckled, with blonde hair and pale eyes.

Only Grandpop could have occupied a seat to my right, extending our 'honesty' spectrum. Sadly, we buried him just under an hour ago. Right now, we should be drinking sweet tea and mingling with old acquaintances whilst attempting to balance a paper plate of buffet food in the back room of the Douglas Arms. Sadly, we aren't a typical family, so we're waiting to hear the Last Will and Testament of Thomas Quinn, a true gent and the smiliest person who ever graced my world.

My portly uncle coughs; an attempt to hasten the proceedings.

I can imagine their reaction if I'd opted for a simple church service and a burial just nine months ago, when my own mother succumbed to cancer. They'd provided little comfort or appreciation of my efforts to hold it together emotionally as I'd circled her wake, thanking people for attending. The Quinns even blanked my father for showing his final respects despite their divorce, fifteen years earlier. They probably never forgave his decision to stop living a lie within an unhappy marriage. Though, afterwards, they welcomed his decision to return to Glasgow, from where he'd arrived unexpectedly one summer during my mother's teenage years. The Quinns forget he was totally selfless in accepting that my permanent home was Shetland; he could have caused my mum untold upset in a custody battle. I'd have hated leaving Shetland, I'm an islander through and through. My dad's no different now; he wouldn't cause anyone pain, least of all me – his only child.

The truth is that last September was the final set of lies the Quinns have fed me; despite their promises of 'we won't become strangers' and 'you'll always be one of us' I've seen neither hide nor hair of them since. Only Grandpop kept in touch with 'his little pumpkin' during our weekly brew-ups.

I sincerely hope Grandpop's friends at Happy Days sheltered housing complex are raising a glass or three in the community's hub while I sit here, wriggling in my seat to improve the circulation in my leg.

I can sense their urgency for news of material possessions. I don't need anything. Grandpop provided me with enough childhood memories and smiles to last for the rest of my days. Inheriting his sense of fun is enough for me, though others will disagree. They'll find very little at his sheltered accommodation, considering he sold most of his possessions when downsizing from the family home he once shared with Gran. He wasn't materialistic by nature. The man was thrifty through and through, nothing was ever wasted; he'd purchased nothing new since the millennium, and yet he never went without a thing.

'Is everything in order?' asks my uncle, presuming a duty as head of the family. His sister shuffles in her seat but doesn't comment, seconding his role.

'Quite, quite,' mutters Smyth, looking up before clearing his throat. 'It is very simple; the late Mr Quinn has divided his assets into three equal portions to be received by his children.' He stares along the line of faces before continuing. 'I'm led to believe one daughter is recently deceased?'

Four heads nod simultaneously. I remain still.

'As a result of his instructions, the remaining portion will not be divided between the surviving issue but be received by her offspring. I believe that's you.' Smyth stares directly at me.

'Yes, m-me,' I stutter, fully aware that other faces don't appear happy.

'There are no other parties named in the will, all personal possessions are to be divided as the family see fit. You will each receive a paper copy in due course. Given the nature of Mr Quinn's affairs and accommodation agreement, I think it will be a matter of weeks before we can safely complete his final wishes. Any questions?'

'Jemima gets her mother's third, and there's no mention of us?' asks Pippa, clearly surprised to receive nothing.

'That's correct. A provision was made for you, should your parent be deceased at the time of Mr Quinn's death,' explains Smyth.

'Well, that's that then. Thank you, Mr Smyth ... we'll be on our way,' says my uncle, slapping his hands down upon his thighs before standing tall. He stares down at his daughter, Callie, demanding she follow; she's in her early thirties and isn't following silent orders.

'Jemima inherits as much as my father then?' asks Callie, her mouth tightly pursed.

'That's correct.'

'So, Mima, what's your thinking?' asks Pippa, her wide-eyed expression addressing me.

'My thinking?' I'm stunned. Firstly, by the nature of Grand-pop's wishes, and secondly, by my cousin's outspoken cheek.

'I honestly thought he'd left you each a small bequest, but given the instructions – and Jemima's status as an only child – I don't see what we can do,' mutters my aunty.

'Thank you,' I say, grateful that one relative understands this was not of my making.

'Don't thank me. If it were me, I'd be splitting my share with the other cousins, but that's me. Don't feel you have to.'

I'm gobsmacked. I stare at four woeful expressions turned in my direction.

'Anyway, all that remains is this ... an envelope addressed solely to Miss Button,' says Smyth, offering a white envelope across the desk.

'For me?'

'Yes, it isn't included in his Last Will and Testament but it has been delivered to the offices as a private request from your grandfather. Here, take it.'

I rise, retrieve the offered item and quickly sit back down.

'This is taking the piss!' says Callie, standing up and collecting her handbag.

I slide my thumb under the sealed edge, removing two keys on a wire loop: one a Yale, the other a padlock key.

'What are these for?' I ask, showing an open palm to the family, who shake their heads.

'I have the keys to his accommodation, so who knows?' says my aunt, tapping her own handbag.

'I believe they're for his allotment plot. They were delivered a week ago, with the instruction that they be given to you,' says Smyth, clearing his desk of our paperwork.

'I can explain. I used to pay his annual fees as part of his birthday present. I'll make sure they're returned,' I say, pleased to shed some light on the envelope.

We shuffle from the dingy office into the reception area before saying our goodbyes. Our parting interaction is frosty as numerous lies spill forth: 'it's been good to see you', 'we'll be in touch soon' and 'nip around, any time'.

And that's it. Which feels so wrong. A small funeral, a ten-minute wait, a mere five-minute address and a few quarrelsome remarks put to bed an individual's life – a man who lived, loved and laughed so heartily whilst gracing this earth for eight decades before succumbing to old age and peacefully passing away in his sleep, twelve days ago.

Dottie

The morning sun is shining bright as I cross the stable yard and unlock the side entrance of Lerwick Manor. The green-painted door scrapes upon the cracked tiles, as always, on opening and closing. It needs a fraction shaving from the bottom edge; it'll get done one day. It feels like my private entrance. Others rarely use this route, preferring to use the main doors.

Once through the door, I kick off my boots and slip into my comfy 'house shoes', as I call them, waiting for me just inside, where I left them. It's not that Ned insists, more that I don't approve of bringing the outdoor mud in as it's me that'll have to clean it up. There's enough dust floating about this place without traipsing Shetland soil into the carpets.

The manor is my second home; it shouldn't be, but it is. I've been visiting here since I was six years of age, when my mother was head cook and my father head gardener. I came as a package deal, aged fifteen, once I'd left school and refused to find secretarial work, which was all the rage back in the late fifties. It was the fashion, back then, to desert your roots and hop over to the mainland to seek a new life in the big cities of Edinburgh or Aberdeen. I simply wanted to follow my kin to the big house, though not many families were still taking on staff after the war, except the Campbells. My mum always said they cared about us local folk, had a traditional way about them and would always follow their own moral compass when it came to looking after staff. They didn't hesitate, allowing me to work in the kitchen alongside my mother. I'd never have coped away from Shetland;

there's an invisible thread running deep within which tethers me to these beautiful islands. From cradle to grave – with everything in between – here's where I'm meant to be.

I nip through the aged kitchen, no longer used but still fully functional, with a coal range and water pump, along the warren of narrow tiled corridors to hang my coat up in the boot room. Purely habit, nothing that Ned insists upon. To be fair, there is nothing that Ned insists upon, apart from me noting my hours in 'the book' I've conveniently placed in the boot room, open upon a hard-backed chair, complete with a working pen.

Nobody else uses it, I'm the only one. I've progressed from young scullery girl to an octogenarian who keeps her hand in with a bit of light dusting, three days a week. I get to choose which days, but all the same I never work on Mondays. Ned thinks I don't know that the other cleaning team visit every Monday to blitz the place from top to bottom. I assume they're given strict instructions not to touch, clean or disturb any ornament or mantel that's within my reach, other than the carpets. I haven't vacuumed in fifteen years, yet there's no accumulation of dirt underfoot. As if I wouldn't notice. At my age, I can't lug the vacuum up and down grand staircases to titivate eleven empty bedrooms.

Donning my cleaning pinny, I sign in, before heading for the main hallway and the grand staircase, under which is possibly the poshest cleaning cupboard in Shetland. Home to my neat shelving unit of polish cans, beeswax and yellow dusters; I use very little else, other than elbow grease, white vinegar and lemon juice. You can keep your new-fangled air fragrances with micro-sized abrasive technology that ruins our planet. When I clean, I want clean. Not some smeary, chemical film rubbed upon the surface of every mahogany or oak table, dulling the shine. I want to see my face in it; likewise, so does Ned.

I stand beneath swathes of sumptuous burgundy velvet

competing for ceiling space alongside the drapery of Black Watch tartan, representing the Campbell clan. Each swag of fabric encircles the ginormous chandelier which dominates the central drop of the grand staircase. I tut most mornings on viewing them; they're nothing more than giant duster-catchers which I'd gladly see replaced, as they're only cleaned every five years. I climb the grand staircase, armed with a feather duster, polish can and yellow cloths. I can't help but admire the portraiture smiling down from the walls: the elaborate attire, gentle smiles and majestic poses of generations gone by. They feel like family; I know each of them so well. I enter the first-floor lounge and begin the diligent task of lifting each ornament from every surface, to spray and wipe, before replacing it. There's silence all around, but not in my head; I recall the chatter, the giggling, even the raised voices of yesteryear, as I move about each room removing this week's collection of dust. I sense I'm the first person to enter some rooms since I was last here. Ned hardly uses the manor as he should, simply rattling around a handful of rooms, but I still polish every week; I have a routine which I stick to. I'm methodical.

'Morning, Dottie, I didn't hear you come in,' says Ned, poking his head around the edge of the doorway. 'Any chance of a brew?'

For thirty-five years old, he looks tired today; his hazel eyes aren't sparkling, his complexion is sallow, and he hasn't had the haircut he mentioned yesterday. Why he leaves it longer than he should is beyond me; the salt 'n' pepper flecks appearing at his temples look quite distinguished against the dark brown when neatly trimmed, but unkempt and uncared for when longer. It amazes me how much he looks like his dear father, with that cleft chin and chiselled cheekbones; the Campbell men have always inherited a strong jawline.

'Morning, Ned, as quiet as a mouse, that's me. Sure, I'll bring it along to you,' I say, eager to please.

He's technically my boss, but in reality a dear friend. I still see him as a peerie lad running about the landing in shorts and a school cap – not that he'd appreciate my vivid recall.

'Here you go!' I say, minutes later, nudging open his office door and carrying a tray complete with tea and biscuits. I pride myself on not slopping half a mug's worth upon the tray. Why he chooses this office when the study and library downstairs are resplendent and more suitable for his needs baffles me. Though, given his choice of modern furniture and minimalistic style, I suppose the lower rooms seem stuffy and claustrophobic.

'You are a star!' he mutters, getting up from his desk to join me at the conference table, where I've deposited the tea tray. 'Are you staying for one?'

'No, I've got plenty to do on the first landing.' I never hang about; likewise, he has plenty to do running the estate single-handed. 'I want to revisit the allotment while the rain holds off.'

'Has the spare plot opposite yours been assigned yet?'

'Number eighteen? Not yet. You know how it is with the council, they get notified, receive the keys, and it seems to take ages before they offer it up. It's a right state, mind you. The new people will need strong backs to work that plot towards tidy.'

'Are you still helping out each morning with the chickens on Old Tommy's plot?' he asks, stirring his tea.

'I am, though I expect it'll draw to an end soon. His funeral's this morning, so the young lassie should receive the keys later today.' I'd offered to play my part, purely as a decent friend and a committee member of Lerwick Allotment Association. But if the truth were known, I'll be glad to return to my usual routine. Which doesn't involve chickens.

'I'm sure it's appreciated,' says Ned, grabbing the plate of biscuits and returning to his paper-filled desk. 'Despite the family's refusal for his closest friends to attend the service.'

'Mmmm, we'll see. I just hope she appreciates the allotment that Tommy created. He loved that plot of earth – that and his obsession with noting the weather details in his peerie book. Let's hope she enjoys it too,' I say, heading for the door, before adding, 'and, Ned, get that haircut you mentioned.'

'That bad, hey?' He smiles as I frantically nod. 'I'll do it today, I promise.'

Chapter Two

April

Hiqh: 9°   Daylight: 14.5 hours
Low: 4°   Rain: 12 days
                                  Wind: 16 mph

Note: the bloody fox has nobbled Levi's chicken coop again, last night. The silly
bugger didn't lock the hatch properly. What's he expect? I bet the pregnant
vixen had more than her fair share before delivering more of the little blighters.
No doubt Levi will feed them too!

Jemima

I hook my fingers through the diamond shapes of the heavy-duty wire fencing as I peer through, questioning my own logic. A cockerel crows in the distance – it's barely past dawn and the streets are deserted – yet I stand beneath a morning sky of pink and lilac hues. Is there anywhere in the world as beautiful as Shetland? A morning sky such as this simply reminds me how lucky I am to witness an ever-changing but glorious canvas created by weather and science. I'm rarely awake at this hour, even when I'm working; unheard of whilst I'm on sabbatical. I can't see a single bird, but the dawn chorus trumpets a cacophony of warbling from every direction. I suspect they haven't been awake all night; unlike me, twisting two tiny keys through my fingers like worry beads.

After saying farewell to the Quinn family, my mood hadn't

lifted nor my anxiety lowered all day. I was tempted to nip around to Happy Days to raise a glass in Grandpop's memory, but feared I'd bump into the Quinns sussing out his possessions. Instead, I'd dashed home, showered and changed before spending the night watching TV, which didn't make me laugh, and then emptied the fridge of a cheese selection which I wasn't meant to consume alone or in one sitting. I even went in search of a hidden bar of cooking chocolate – which can be a suitable substitute for comfort eating, sometimes. Sadly, I suspect I scoffed my secret stash the night Grandpop died.

By nine o'clock, I called it a day and sullenly climbed into bed clutching the tiny keys, their edges biting at my skin, and taking comfort in the thought that his fingerprints were rubbing off on to mine. I considered getting a duplicate copy made, enabling me to attach these originals to my house keys. I'm not averse to hoarding objects, another trait inherited from Grandpop. As my flat rightly proves. I live amongst treasured possessions which others would have thrown away: broken clocks, peacock feathers, chipped china cups, decorative perfume boxes and one-eyed cuddly bears. All are safe for eternity, safeguarding my specific memory of time, place or person.

A blackbird warbles. I strain my ears to pick out the distinct call. A wren. Possibly a robin, and the blackbird again.

Grandpop loved to listen to birdsong. I was only seven when he'd dragged me out early one morning to tend his allotment; my lesson for the day, despite it being a school holiday, was to recognise each song. Boy, did I moan.

Reluctantly, I release the wire fencing. Folk will think I'm potty if they arrive to find me motionless and staring at the gravelled car park, shrubbery and drystone wall beyond.

I touch the industrial-sized padlock adorning the sliding latch.

I'd only come to look through the entrance gate; a simple reminder of days gone by.

A large wooden board declares 'Trespassers will be prosecuted' in angry red lettering. I assume this may be a lie; the painted wobbly font mimics a child's handwriting. But still – I've been warned.

I hesitate before inserting the key. I'm surprised by the ease of its connection: no snagging, biting or jarring. Surely you can't trespass with a key? I'm free to nip inside, take a recce, and leave immediately. As long as I secure the padlock, who will ever know?

The padlock springs open. I unhook it from its coupling before sliding the metal plate across, freeing the wire gate. There's plenty of juddering and a vibrating sound occurs as metal signage rattles when I push open the gate.

When did I stop visiting Grandpop here? After Gran died? 'The old bugger wants an excuse to get from under my feet,' was Gran's frequent remark after he took on his plot as a hobby, some forty years ago. She'd have loved him to have sectioned off part of their garden, allowing him to be within hollering distance of the back doorstep, but Grandpop never obliged her.

I sneak inside and secure the padlock, before hastily tiptoeing across the empty gravel car park. From childhood, I know there are two paths around the allotment site – the nearest, on my right, or the other, at the far end – which sweep around and link up to create a figure-of-eight formation on which the allotments are arranged. It's been many years since I last visited but I know which track to take.

A sense of déjà vu washes over me as I take the nearest dirt track. It seems narrower, with its centre line of tufted grass and its borders edged with overgrown brambles and nettles. 'It encourages the wildlife,' I remember Grandpop saying, on more than one occasion.

Ahead, numerous coloured flags are hoisted high upon extendable poles, their fabric unfurling in the gentle breeze. It's like a

United Nations convention amongst compost heaps and water butts. I can name a few – the Norwegian flag, the Union Jack and, of course, the Scottish flag – and yet there are others, such as the blue, black and white, which I've never seen before.

I've forgotten how far along on the right-hand side Grandpop's allotment is, but no doubt I'll recognise it when I reach it. It was always quite distinct, with its dilapidated blue shed and the rain-washed scarecrow I made one bonfire night, and which Grandpop claimed was 'too good to burn'.

I plod along, taking in the view as I pass allotments on either side.

The first two allotments have wire fencing, enabling me to see the symmetry created by block paving and slabbed pathways, neat rows of healthy green plants and furrowed rows of rich brown soil. One has a string puppet made from brown flowerpots, with googly eyes and a painted smile, hanging beside the gate post. Both have brightly painted sheds, water butts, and watering cans lined up like soldiers along their fencing – each plot is neater than my flat, if I'm honest.

The next few allotments are distinct and unique in style and layout. One has a gaudy patterned carpet covering half of the soil. It has wigwams of canes, dotted here and there, but nothing growing up each knotted structure. There are several buckets filled with brown water, others are upended and several watering cans lie on their sides. Another plot has army camouflage netting suspended by metal poles, creating a tent-like structure beneath which two deckchairs and a barbecue are strewn and ... I peer through the fencing. There's a face staring back at me. I'm watching them watching me! I step back, embarrassed to find someone tending their plot while I'm blatantly trespassing, albeit in possession of a key.

The head doesn't move. The eyes don't blink. In fact, much to my surprise, the person isn't anything but a head and some well-positioned shrubbery. There are no shoulders, no body or limbs. It is literally a bald mannequin head, supported on a pole, watching me as closely as I am watching her. How freaky is that? I instantly regret mistreating my Girl's World by cutting her hair and piercing her ears with drawing pins, but never did I shove her on a six-foot pole and display her in the garden.

I continue along the row, amazed by the variety and abundance. Some plots are a gardeners' paradise full of greenery and vitality while others are bare patches of recently dug soil with simple pathways dividing the oblong plot. Raised beds, bird tables, chicken runs, painted bookcases, supermarket bags-for-life, strange ornamental pots and orange traffic cones quirkily decorate others. Perimeter fences are either aligned and secure or lopsided, with easy access via a gaping hole in the side section. It's simply another world. I don't remember it being like this as a child. But what child questions an adult's obsession with collecting ten galvanised burnie bins, footballing gnomes and streamers of weather-worn plastic bunting? It appears that each plot is as individual as their owner. I reckon if I had a line-up of total strangers, I could probably match 80 per cent to the right allotment plot within a five-minute conversation. Though whether I want to meet the owner of the spiked mannequin head is another matter.

Just think, every morning since my last visit, the birds have sung and busy hands have worked these allotments. I feel quite overwhelmed; Grandpop loved being here.

I reach the middle section of the figure of eight and, glancing to my right, catch sight of a view which I haven't seen in years. Not since Gran died and Grandpop couldn't cope with being alone in a three-bedroomed house. Instantly, everything makes sense. I don't need anyone to tell me whose allotment plot this is. Before me is the solid oak front door which had once graced their beloved family home, complete with its brass door number

51, matching letter box and tiny semicircle of glass in the upper section. And a Yale lock.

I presume Grandpop replaced the door before the new owners took possession. I gently stroke the closed letter box, causing it to rattle on its tiny hinges. My crayoned birthday cards, our holiday postcards declaring 'wish you were here!' and, sadly, the hospital's written confirmation of the results of Gran's biopsy had all been delivered through this very slot. My mum and her siblings must each have owned a key; they had probably snuck in after late nights out, on occasions slammed it in temper, and been escorted towards wedding cars by doting parents. Wow, even I was once carried past this door as a newborn to meet my grandpop for the first time.

I gulp at the sentiment; he might have downsized the property but not his memories.

I don't need to go any further; this is the one. I peer through the heavy wire fencing at the plot on which I used to run about, tending weeds with a plastic toy watering can, wearing dungarees with a pretty patch pocket, my favourite red wellingtons and Grandpop's handkerchief knotted on my head.

'It's about bloody time you showed up.'

I'm lost in a world of my own, so his voice startles me.

'Oh!' My hand reaches for my heart as if I were frail.

Behind me stands an elderly gent. His tartan cap of grey, black and red is pulled low, and his smile is as wide as Grandpop's front door.

'I'm not trespassing, honest. I have keys. I can prove it. Call me nosey but curiosity got the better of me.' I jabber on until the old man gently taps my forearm.

'I know, Jemima. It was Mungo who delivered them to the solicitors' office.'

'Yes, Tommy's granddaughter,' I add, for clarification.

'I'm Bill Moffat. I'll show you around.' He gestures towards the door lock and, without hesitation, I insert the Yale key and twist, before taking a tentative step across the threshold.

'It's very early,' I say, reminding myself that a guided tour wasn't part of my plan.

'I'm up with the lark and down here as soon as I can be,' he chuckles, following my lead and closing the front door behind us.

Right now, I should be at home, preparing my usual cereal and deciding how to fill Day 29 of my sabbatical. I slip the keys into my jeans pocket as my limbs adopt an awkward self-conscious stance, unsure how to behave whilst remembering all the times I've played on this crazy paving.

'This way . . . I'll give you the fly-by-night tour – you can discover the rest for yourself.' Bill marches off along the pathway towards the potting shed and polytunnel at the far end.

I scurry after him, afraid to be judged as uninterested or lagging in vitality. For a man of his years, his strides knock spots off my slower pace. His faded corduroy trousers are baggy over his aged frame and are clumsily gathered, held in place by a wide leather belt which he wears over his woolly jumper. His clumpy boots show a multitude of colours and marks: paint splatter, dust and dirt.

'We've done the best we can between us for near on a fortnight, but I'm sure Tommy's up there cursing us for not completing tasks to his standard. He was a stickler for tradition and standards, you know?' He suddenly turns, addressing me, and seems surprised that I'm not a step behind but ten steps away. He continues to walk and talk. 'Anyway, between us, the committee members – that's me, Mungo and Dottie – we've managed to keep it ticking over. Given that the funeral was only yesterday, I'm chuffed to bits that you've shown up straight away. Dottie will be pleased, as it saves her putting them in tonight. I hope you don't mind, she did take the eggs each day. Mungo said it was a token gesture for her time.'

'Eggs?'

'Yeah, from his girls.'

'Girls?'

Bill turns and stares intently at me. We're standing in front of the potting shed with a large polytunnel to my left, which is crammed with objects and potted plants.

'Tommy's girls,' says Bill, unlatching and swinging wide a chest-height picket gate to reveal a large pen hidden behind the shed in which stands a cute little doll's house. There are no windows, just a ramp leading to the front door.

Bill enters the gate, I remain on the path.

With a flick of the catch he lifts the front door and out flood a brood of farmyard chickens. Their heads and necks rhythmically bob in sync with their strutting as they peck and scratch the ground.

'He's got five, though don't ask me which is which,' says Bill, exiting the picket gate and sidestepping around me to enter the potting shed. He busies himself with a large sack that states 'corn' in big black lettering across the hessian weave.

'Names?'

'Yeah – Tonight, Madras, Korma, Roast and Nugget, I think . . . maybe not Nugget . . . maybe Kiev. Oh, I don't bloody know. He called them "my girls" more than anything.'

I'm speechless. I'm hearing his words, but I'm struggling to take them in. I didn't know Grandpop had such a twisted sense of humour, let alone chickens.

Bill re-enters the pen and begins throwing handfuls of corn upon the ground while the chickens peck ferociously at each morsel.

'Firstly, who is Dottie? And, secondly, why's she not putting the chickens inside tonight?'

Bill stops dead in the middle of the enclosure, where he is busily ladling water from a butt using an old tin can. He stares for what seems like hours, until his head slowly begins to bob, much like the chickens.

'I see. Us old 'uns have each spent time doing what we can, assuming you'd want us to keep it ticking over nicely in your absence.'

I'm baffled as to which question he's answering.

'Sorry, I'm not quite with you.'

'No apologies needed. Maybe it's us that should be apologising to you. Your dear granddad bloody loved this allotment. He spent the best part of his life down here amongst us, sharing his time and his experience, making us laugh our bloody socks off, most days. Us old folk shouldn't have presumed that we were actually useful, helping out one of you young 'uns!' he continues, huffily. 'It's not as if you'd asked for our support – let alone our time and effort, trying to fend off the vultures around these plots who think nothing of ransacking an empty one within twenty-four hours.'

I shift uncomfortably under his intent gaze. I'm unsure if this elderly gent has suddenly had an episode or a funny turn; either way, I am out of my depth, struggling to fully understand his mutterings.

We've entered a stand-off, with him staring at me, me staring back. My mouth has gone dry, my palms are clammy. I might need an ambulance for the two of us.

'Hello, lassie, I didn't think you'd be showing up this early,' comes a cheery female voice from behind me.

I turn to view the widest-brimmed straw hat ever seen. The span is wider than her delicate hunched shoulders, with a pink satin ribbon secured beneath her chin. The elderly lady is bird-like in frame and mannerisms. I'm surprised she can carry the weight of such an enormous hat. From beneath the hat two kindly, watery blue eyes take me in.

'Hello,' I muster, more in shock than politeness.

'I wondered if you'd spotted her, Bill,' she says, peering around me to view Bill – the statue still clutching the tin can of water inside the chicken run. 'Bill, are you alright?'

'Morning, Dottie. I won't beat about the bush – this young lady doesn't seem interested or grateful,' declares Bill, shuffling towards the chickens' watering tough to empty the contents of his can.

'Is that so, lassie?' asks Dottie, her tone conveying surprise.

Her watery gaze is directed firmly on me. I can't lie. I hadn't a clue what Bill was rabbiting on about, but now, it's dawned.

I gesture around me. 'This has been somewhat of a surprise. I only came for a look before I hand the keys in. I'm the one who actually paid the council their annual fee for this plot,' I say, triumphantly.

'We know. Tommy used to tell us all the time, "My little pumpkin gives me the best birthday present every year – it lasts the entire year and I use it every day." Didn't he, Bill?'

'At least once a bloody week!' chunters Bill, exiting the chicken pen and securing the picket gate.

'And, between us, he always used to add that the others only ever bought him socks.'

'He did.' Bill strides past us and into the potting shed, from where a sequence of bangs, thuds and dragging noises emerge.

'Is he alright?' I ask, nodding towards the shed.

'Give him a minute. He's a bit crabbit of late. He loved your daa as dearly as a brother . . . he's taken it badly, these past few weeks. It reminds us old ones that we've all got places to go . . . none of us knows how and when.'

A tsunami of guilt floods my senses.

I get where Bill is coming from. It's as painful for me to see the allotment and know that my granddad spent every waking hour up here. His fingerprints are on every item in that potting shed. I visited Grandpop every week in his little flat and we'd talk about my week, his week and the dramas between the other residents in the sheltered housing. And sometimes, not often, I'd ask him about his onions, his potatoes and his pride, come the annual Harvest Festival show's allotment competition.

The potting shed has gone quiet.

'Well, I can't stand here all day, and there's no point crying over spilt milk,' says Dottie, gently rubbing my forearm.

'Mmmmmph,' comes a muffled sound from the shed.

'I'm very grateful for the time, effort and consideration you've given to Grandpop's plot,' I say, fairly loud, so Bill can hear. 'I'm very much like Grandpop in many ways, we both liked to collect things, nurture things and hoarded a little more than we should, but this . . .' I turn to survey the entire plot, as if speaking to every stone, paving slab and water butt. 'Honestly, this isn't what I'm into.'

'Mmmmmph,' repeats the potting shed.

'You youngsters, you're all so busy with your careers, your relationships and hobbies – there's not much time for anything else,' soothes Dottie, in an attempt to ease my embarrassment.

I bite my lip and sigh. 'Someone else deserves the enjoyment that Grandpop had.'

'They'll be fighting over a plot this size, mark my words. Not to mention the quality of the soil, after the amount of compost Tommy dug into it over the years. The aeration, the tilth and the drainage – there's no better allotment plot on the entire site. Bill, I'll lock the girls inside tonight,' calls Dottie, adding an aside to me, 'the fox has them otherwise.'

There's a lengthy pause in our conversation, which I'm grateful to the birdsong for filling.

'Thank you, Dottie. I have enough on my plate right now, without taking on any more.'

'You're welcome. Before you go, would you like a bunch of flowers from my allotment next door?'

I exhale in a gasp, not realising how tense I've become.

This really is too much for today. I should have stayed in bed, made my usual breakfast and then started my usual day. Damn my curiosity! Damn these nice people for caring so much. I've wasted their time and generosity.

'I'd love that, thank you,' I mutter, unsure if I'm worthy, having declined my responsibilities and disappointed people.

Melissa

I patiently await my turn at the Town Hall but, as soon as the smiling desk lady calls me forward, I dash across the council department like a gazelle on heat. I can't help myself; the allotment gods might be smiling upon me.

'Good morning, I'm Melissa Robins. I received this letter yesterday, offering me an allotment plot, here in Lerwick.' I quickly take a seat before her, without being invited.

The smiling desk lady doesn't know it yet, but there's a chance of me performing a solo sit-in and refusing to vacate said seat, should she refuse to honour my notification letter. I've been waiting long enough. Bloody ages, in fact, on some sodding list. During which time, I've phoned three times chasing an update. As of yesterday, I'm next in line for the first available plot.

'Hello, yes, please take a seat.'

I already have. I hand over my notification letter and then lean my elbows on the edge of her polished desk, awaiting the details.

Desk lady reads the notification. I promise it isn't forged: it's authentic.

'Perfect. Let's have a little look on the system and see what's being offered to you.' I buzz with excitement at the prospect of the produce in my pantry having been grown by moi. 'You're being offered allotment number eighteen. It has been vacant for a little while following a short-term occupancy.'

'I assumed everyone kept their plot for years.' You learn something every day.

'Not always. Some people sign up and lose interest within a matter of weeks whilst others stay for decades.'

'Is this why the waiting time is so long?'

'Exactly. Sometimes we offer several allotments within a space of a few weeks, other times it can be months.' She continues to tap at her computer keyboard.

I've been waiting for nearly two years, I won't be giving up within six months. People must be daft. The chance of an allotment for a small annual fee, yet they hand it back due to a bit of hard work. Phuh! Not me.

'Here we are. Plot eighteen is a standard-sized plot, the notes say it has decent soil drainage, secure wire fencing on all four sides, a full-sized gate ...' She reads from the screen, adding, 'The allotment committee retains a set of keys enabling access, should it be needed in an emergency. We supply one set of keys for your personal use.'

I nod along, absorbing the details.

'How does that sound?'

'So far, so good.' I need this outlet, to help my work–life balance. It'll increase my social interactions and channel my energy into a positive pursuit in the absence of my husband, Hamish, who's working away on the oil rigs. Even better when he's at home and can join me. Surely a couple that gardens together stays together?

As much as I wish to support Hamish's new career choice, the impact upon my world is undeniable. Offshore drilling was supposed to have a limited shelf life for us. Our original plan was to endure five years of hardship by being apart during the early years of our marriage, having been childhood sweethearts. Hamish had the skills necessary to net the big money on offer from the Aberdeen oil rigs, to save as our future nest egg. After which, he'd return home and we'd start planning for our family. But how do you return home to an engineering job in Shetland when the Gulf of Mexico offers the same offshore work, but with bigger rewards, securing a larger nest egg? There's a reason why oil isn't one of the traditional gifts for anniversary celebrations; a drop too much and it ruins everything. We're celebrating ten years with tin, but I feel as if we're eternally stuck on paper or cotton. I'd never ask him to leave, but there are days, sometimes weeks, when he's away and our only contact is via Facetime chats. Not the marriage I'd imagined, despite keeping myself busy with teaching part-time at the local art college and my ceramic projects at home.

'The entire site is extremely sought after. They have a pro-active committee who spearhead a lot of initiatives on the site and within the local community.'

'That's nice to know.'

'The original site was donated by the family from Lerwick Manor, aeons ago – you know, an attempt to encourage the average family to be more self-sufficient after the war. These days, it's probably more important to help curb the carbon footprint of goods imported to Shetland.'

'I've never thought of it like that.'

'Mmmm, few people do, but I'm sure the committee will enlighten you.'

'Is it a mix of ages, or mainly the elderly?'

'A complete range of folk on this site – all ages, families, couples – a good mix helps, because it's a community in itself.'

The desk lady hands me a leaflet outlining the allotment's rules and regulations, with details of the committee. She explains the fees, makes a note of the details for my direct debit and suggests I do an annual payment, rather than six monthly instalments, as it works out slightly cheaper.

I sit back in my chair, basking in satisfaction, as the council lady tap-taps at her keyboard, entering my details and confirming my official status as a plot holder at Lerwick Manor Allotment Association.

Within five minutes, clutching my new set of keys and leaflet, I am heading towards the grand staircase leading to the lower floor and the main exit. Before reaching the department doors, I locate my mobile phone and, standing before the two shiny shovels mounted upon the council's interior wall, I pose for a self-conscious selfie as a new allotment holder. Not that I usually waste energy on such things, being forty-two, but hey, I'm proud of my new status. It'll be something to mark the moment and send to Hamish later. I can see the council lady is serving the next person: an attractive dark-haired woman fiddling with a set of keys. I can't help but overhear their conversation as I peruse and delete numerous unflattering selfies.

'I'd like a refund on an allotment please.'

'Sorry, we don't provide refunds on annual fees.'

'My granddad has died and the annual fee was only paid a month ago.'

'I'm sorry for your loss. Can I assume you're returning his keys?' she asks hastily, eyeing me near the exit.

'I might be.'

'Right. Excuse me . . . Mrs Robins! This lady is handing keys in, so you may want to view both allotments before deciding which one,' calls the council lady.

'Do I get a choice?'

'What plot number are you?' the council lady asks her.

'Sorry, but had you finished serving that lady?'

'I had. But since she's still in the building and you're about to hand a set of keys in, it seems only fair that she gets to browse both plots before we offer whichever one is spare to the next name on the waiting list.'

'There's a list?' she asks naïvely.

'Plot number?'

I notice she closes her fingers about the key ring; suddenly, she looks very glum.

'And the plot number is?' asks the council lady, a tinge of impatience in her voice.

'Has she paid her annual fees?' asks the woman.

'I have,' I interject quickly.

'She has . . . I'd just need to amend the paperwork in relation to the plot number if she were to choose your granddad's.'

'I'm not sure of the plot number,' she admits, still clutching her keys.

'Can I take a name?' asks the council lady, tapping her computer keyboard.

'Quinn, Thomas Quinn.'

'I'll take a seat, and wait,' I mutter, pointing towards a vacant seat.

'Ah, here it is. Thomas Quinn and Jemima Button, plot number fifteen . . . it's virtually opposite the other vacant plot,' she says briefly, smiling at me.

'My name is listed?' asks the younger woman.

'Oh yes.' The council woman taps the keyboard. 'Your name was added a little over a year ago.'

I'm blatantly earwigging.

'It was?'

'Yes, and the direct debit is taken from your bank account. Are you still wanting to return the keys?' asks the desk lady.

I watch as the woman ponders her options; her expression is trance-like as she stares into her lap. I attempt to send my own needy vibes across the council lobby: a choice of plots would be wonderful.

'Actually, I've changed my mind. Thanks for your time.' She stands and swiftly leaves the council department.

A welcoming breeze greets me as I quick-step through the Town Hall's main entrance, chasing the dark-haired lady. I have no idea if I'm about to make a huge mistake but gut reaction insists I must ask.

'Excuse me!' I holler up the street.

She turns around.

'Plot fifteen isn't available then?'

'That's right. Sorry.'

'No worries, I'll see you at the allotments,' I say, reverting to my original joy at securing plot eighteen.

Dottie

'Tommy's girl has turned up,' I say, lightly flicking the yellow duster over the mantelpiece in Ned's office. I stop and turn about to watch his profile, busily working on his estate paperwork.

'Really? She's taken her time about it,' says Ned, without raising his head but continuing to write.

'Not really. She only received the keys yesterday. Apparently, Tommy hadn't discussed her taking the allotment on after him, though it's not surprising; he was as fit as a fiddle prior to his passing. He probably assumed he had years ahead of him in which to mention it properly or possibly show her the ropes. Us committee members doing odds and ends in her absence came as quite a shock, so I doubt she'll stay.'

'Met her then, have you?' Ned continues to work.

'This morning, I went to feed the chickens and found Old Bill giving her a guided tour.'

'I'm sure he read her the riot act.' He flips a page and busies himself with more details of his tenant farmers. He's answering but he's not interested, which is a shame.

'He was put out when she mentioned handing the keys back to the council.'

'Did he go into a silent strop?'

'He did. It took him an hour of wheelbarrowing his stockpile of rotting manure back and forth before he could say a civil word to anyone.'

'He's still moving that manure pile?'

'Little by little, each day.'

Ned's brooding features hang low, his back rounded and hunched over his huge paper-filled desk. He didn't attend the barbers, as promised, so his hair curls at his collar. It's not good for him to spend so many hours shut up here: alone. Living alone is all I've ever truly known, which is why I make an effort to mix socially. I connect with as many good people as I can, though I suppose Ned's circumstances hinder him somewhat. What his dear mother wouldn't have given to see him happily settled at this stage of his life. Only thirty-five, yet he's clocked up eight years already in sole charge of this place. It's unnatural for a man to spend his time alone. If his mother, Cecilia, had known how things would be after the untimely deaths of both his parents, in quick succession from cancer, she'd have made him pull his finger out and start courting straight after university. Or she and Douglas would have carried on trying for another bairn after Ned's late arrival, twenty years into their own married life. Having thrilled their social circle with a whirlwind romance, the heartache of such an extended wait for their firstborn seemed a cruel twist of fate. That's the problem: have them late in life and they'll lose you too early, forcing them to shoulder their cares alone. Ned should be settled by now, with a wife or a life partner – even a toddler or two gambolling around the place – but no, he busies himself in this office, working day and night, for what?

'Dottie?'

'Yes.'

'Stop staring as I work; it bugs the hell out of me.'

'I wasn't. I was just saying about Tommy's girl.'

'Tommy's girl and the soon-to-become-unoccupied plot.'

I shake my head. 'The very thought brings a lump to my throat. Tommy had that allotment for nearly forty years ... I can't imagine anyone else plodding his crazy-paving pathways. Honest, I can't, Ned.'

He finally looks up, probably expecting to see me teary; it wouldn't be the first time.

'Nothing lasts for ever, you know, Dottie,' he says, sitting back in his chair.

'Well, some things ought to. Tommy loved that plot. He nurtured and advised half the young 'uns tending the other ones. I still can't believe he's gone.' I twist the duster between my agitated hands. It's upsetting when your friends start passing; reminds you of how swift the years are flying by. That's what's wrong with Ned. In the last six months, he's lost all sense of purpose and fallen into a bachelor life of routine and constant work. He's turned his back on a social life and rarely invites anyone into his world.

'Are you OK?' he says, watching me.

'I am. You won't be a youngster for ever, you know,' I say, sniffing back the emotion that has finally risen.

'You can't class me as a youngster, Dottie – though I'm hardly past my prime at thirty-five!'

'Even so, you're always stuck in here working – you need to get yourself out there and have a crack at life.'

A smile dawns across his tired features.

'And I suppose that's what you think my mother would have been saying to me?'

'Oi, don't start questioning my wisdom. Your mother was a fine lady. The best day's work your father ever did was in marrying her; every eligible bachelor in their society was doe-eyed over your mother. Your grandfather thought he was being hasty, but as Douglas said, "When you know, you know – so what's the point in waiting?" Cecilia wouldn't have put up with half the stuff I stay silent about. She trusted me and welcomed me into this family when I needed it.'

'She valued your opinion, she truly did.'

'Cecilia wouldn't want me to be silent where you're concerned either. We all need to learn from Tommy's unexpected passing.'

'We do, but decisions in life can't always be controlled, can they? If Tommy's girl wishes to hand in her keys, who are we to stop her? The council will take over and offer up the plot where appropriate. Which might be the downside of my great-grandfather donating the land, all those years ago, but there's plenty of plus sides. I wouldn't want to be tied up with allotment duties – or their squabbles – when I've got enough on my plate with tenant farmers.'

'I suppose you're right, though I hear plot eighteen has finally been offered to a newcomer . . .' I pause and he jumps in.

'Excellent. You're in for a busy week – firstly, tracking down Tommy's girl to convince her otherwise, plus a newbie to interrogate.'

'You're wicked to be teasing me,' I say, waving my duster at him in a comical manner. 'I can't help myself.'

'A lifelong hobby, more like.' He shuffles in his chair, before returning to his paperwork.

I resume my dusting as my mind races; if only I'd convinced Tommy's girl to stay for just a week, it might have solved more than one situation.

Chapter Three

Melissa

I peer through the fencing at my neighbour's tidy plot. I assume it's number 16, comprising of designated areas: grass, soil and paving slabs. Every straight line is edged with miniature wooden logs, every cane topped with protective cones and the seating area perfectly situated, ready for a *House & Garden* photoshoot. Even the blue, black and white bunting is perfectly hung, simultaneously mimicking the unfurling flag flying high above the plot. My only dismay is caused by the surprising addition of a complete bathroom suite: a roll-top bathtub, vanity sink unit, bidet and matching toilet in pristine white ceramic, positioned in an arc arrangement, with each bowl and crevice filled with dark soil.

Surely everyone can afford a selection of ceramic pots? Enviously, I divert my eyes from their gleaming chrome taps; puts me to shame, when I think of the limescale at home.

One day, that's how my allotment will look – minus the bathroom suite.

I turn about to view plot 18. There might be several bathroom suites hidden amongst the jungle of weeds. As expected, the weeds are waist height, even shoulder height in some places. I suppose it depends on the length of your legs.

I'm disappointed, in some respects. I never expected it to be as pristine as next door, but surely someone's been in here recently? Weeds can't possibly grow this tall in six months, can they?

My initial inspection took five minutes. I found a number

plaque alongside a sturdy padlock, a wooden structure resembling a shed – despite its slimness mimicking a sentry box – and an overturned water butt. On the plus side, it appears to have four wire fences, a hinged gate and a set of keys, all for the grand price of £26 a year. You don't get much bang for your buck these days, but I was expecting a little less foliage.

'Hello, lovey, are you Melissa?' The woman's hat brim is broader than her height, though her piercing gaze immediately demands your attention. I note her red wellington boots; a potential purchase in the coming days.

'I am. I signed this morning and thought I'd take a look.'

'It's a bit grim but you'll soon have it sorted.'

'You have more faith than I have. I don't know where to begin.'

'With the weeds, lovey.' As if that was helpful advice, she continues. 'You'll find there's a brick pathway criss-crossing the plot, so you won't have to prepare the groundwork with rumble and lay pathways – not unless you plan to relocate them. Which I wouldn't do, but you might choose to.'

I want to laugh. I'm used to quirky teenage personalities, but the older generation speak their mind, whether required or not.

'Sorry, I didn't catch your name,' I say.

'Dorothy Nesbit, Dottie to my friends. You'll find me over there, on plot seventeen.' She gestures across the dirt track. 'I only grow flowers, mainly delphiniums.'

'No vegetables?'

'I'm not interested, lovey. They talk non-stop around here about parsnips, pumpkins and beetroot – there's only so much I can stomach. We exchange goods when I need a cauliflower for my Sunday lunch.'

'That's sweet. I grew carrots as a child so I wanted to try growing a few now – hopefully with better results.'

'No one grows carrots up here.'

'Why?'

'What's the point? You tend them all season and when you dig them up they're usually tinier than a newborn's winky. I assume you proved that as a child.'

I need to toughen my armour if I'm to survive conversations with this sweet dear. I'm taken aback but attempt not to show it, I teach young adults every day, yet their talk rarely surprises me.

'Anyway, Mungo – he's further along on my side – he'll talk you out of sowing carrots. Parsnips is what you'll want, or so he'll say. Old Bill's plot number thirteen is just there, alongside Tommy's plot with the front door, it says fifty-one but it's actually plot fifteen . . . it's now Jemima's, she's recently joined us after her daa died. You need to look out for her, if she stays.'

'I met the woman from plot fifteen earlier, at the Town Hall. She was unsure but decided to keep her keys rather than throw the towel in.' I'd given the plot the once-over as I passed.

'Great news. I was frightened she'd hand them straight back – so many people do. The last occupants for this plot stayed just long enough to dedicate several weeks of back-breaking work, do themselves an injury by pulling a muscle, then leave enough time to elapse before returning, enabling the weeds to grow back to their original height. You're not planning on doing that, are you?'

'It wasn't what I was thinking. I was hoping to buy a small greenhouse this afternoon – but there are so many weeds, that's just not feasible.'

'Not a greenhouse, lovey. It wouldn't last a week with the gale-force winds that sweep around this place. It's fairly open land, despite being protected by the neighbouring manor's wall. A small polytunnel is what you want, though a couple of cold frames will do you nicely for starters.'

'It's fairly daunting, to be honest.'

'Have fun with it. Some might see weeds but others see treasure. You've got plantain growing over there, which makes for a nice cough remedy, and if you boil those nettles down you can have a broth or a herbal tea,' says Dottie, pointing at various spots. 'Don't underestimate that mare's tail, right there – it's a devil to get rid of. You're better off putting chickens on top of it to keep it at bay.'

'Oh thanks, I'll bear that in mind.'

'Most of us along this side of the site have been here for years, so anything you need to borrow, simply speak up. OK?'

'OK.'

'You're welcome to join us at the site's social club, The Cabbage Patch, but don't take offence if people sit in rows, smell funny after one too many beers and linger longer than necessary.'

'I'll bear that in mind,' I say, grimacing at the very thought. 'Where's that exactly?'

'On the cross section of the site's figure eight, you can't miss it. Anyway, I'll be off. I've got slugs to catch. Bye.'

'Bye, Dottie.' I watch her wander across the dirt track. On reaching her gate, she turns to give me a jaunty wave before entering her plot.

I'm delighted by her warm welcome, especially as I haven't any tools or prior knowledge. I'm grateful for any advice available, but that brief encounter has taught me to try before I enquire. Otherwise, I might find myself forced into growing parsnips when my desired crop is carrots.

Jemima

It's a cumbersome process, driving in via the allotment gates. Drawing near, leaving your vehicle in order to unlock, open and secure the swinging gate, clambering back inside before manoeuvring through, then on to the car park before returning to lock the gate. I understand why others might choose to walk or park their vehicle further along the street, rather than use the parking facilities on site. I might start using my old bike; it'll save time and be healthier.

I'm conscious that I left under a cloud this morning; I'd clearly upset Old Bill and left Dottie to sort out 'the girls'. I'm determined to make it up to them. When I explain about my sabbatical from work, I'm sure they'll forgive me. Earlier, at the Town Hall, it was strange how my decision changed. The annual fees are irrelevant in comparison to filling my days with a mindful activity. Though if anyone dares to suggest I'm on 'gardening leave', I'll be correcting them straight away. After my sabbatical, which I chose to initiate, I'll be returning to the tourist office in no time – and, hopefully, I'll be in a better place. Whether I'll ever find a renewed enthusiasm for such a repetitive role is doubtful, but it's all I'm qualified for.

I collect my recent purchase – a pair of new gardening gloves – from the passenger seat, before locking the car and making my way towards my allotment: cap in hand, seeking forgiveness.

Since last September, I've been feeling out of control, penned in by the daily toil of life and shell-shocked after the death of my mum, to the point that my anxiety levels are constantly sky high. I can't sleep, I don't eat and my knotted stomach never unravels. I hadn't realised how isolated I was until I needed a shoulder to cry on. Lifelong friends are so busy with their husbands, homes, careers and babies – I felt selfish denying them their 'family time' purely to listen while I bleated on. I tried to cope, week in, week out, but the raw emotion simply wore me down. Work colleagues are great sometimes, but they come and go with such frequency, despite their best intentions to keep in touch. Grandpop always seemed happy enough. I should probably have spent those months alongside him; he'd have known what to say to cheer me up. He spent the majority of each day pottering around here, but I'm determined to spend only a few hours a week, nothing more. I'll be sensible. I'll take control by growing a few carrots, a row of lettuce, and maybe make a few home-made crumbles, if the rhubarb patch still exists. There's no virtue in busting a gut and failing to produce anything.

I feel nervous, despite having inadvertently been an allotment owner for some time. As I pass along the dirt track, I spot people busily tending their plots. I give a little smile here and there as they respond with a puzzled look or a congenial nod, acknowledging a newcomer.

I make a concerted effort to locate plot 18, a mass of weeds, literally opposite mine. I predict the blonde willowy lady may rue the day I changed my mind. I feel foolhardy, knowing that I nearly gave away a perfectly manicured plot.

Suddenly, I hear the shout of male voices behind me. I spin about to view my front door wide open and two men on stepladders wrangling with my polytunnel. They don't look as if they are maintaining anything – they are removing it!

'Excuse me, what are you doing?' I yell, striding along my crazy paving. Nipping across the soil patch would be quicker but Grandpop would frown upon me for compacting the soil when it isn't necessary.

As I near, the two guys are removing a section of polythene sheeting, which is being carefully lowered to the ground whilst they remain on their step ladders.

My surprise arrival in between the stepladders makes each occupant jump.

'Excuse me, but what are you doing?' I ask again, indignantly glancing between each male and the gaping hole in my polytunnel. I can see there isn't a single plant or pot remaining inside, unlike earlier.

'We're removing the sheeting. You can't move these things in one piece,' scoffs the younger burly guy, his blond hair poking out from beneath his woollen beanie, and his lumberjack shirt heavily soiled with dirt.

'Removing it! Are you joking?'

'Yeah. The keys have been handed back in, so this becomes a salvage job . . . Old Tommy wouldn't want his stuff being left to strangers,' he says, looking down from on high, his pale blue gaze piercing mine.

'Unless . . .' mutters the older gent, grimacing behind his grey bushy, beard before nodding in my direction.

'Ah shit. Yeah, unless . . . the council have reissued this plot quicker than usual. In which case, we've been caught red-handed!'

'Red-handed?' I repeat, unsure what is going on. 'I'm Jemima, Tommy's granddaughter. I was going to hand the keys in, but have decided against it.'

Both men are motionless and eyeballing each other.

'So, what are you doing?' I ask insistently.

'Ahhh, right, decided against it,' repeats the older man, scratching at his wiry beard.

'Yep.'

'And now your plan is to tend the plot like your granddad did?' asks the younger one, his eyes not leaving his buddy's grizzled features.

'Yep.'

'Back it up, Levi,' sighs the older guy.

Both men swiftly descend their ladders, retrieve the nearest piece of sheeting and jointly begin rolling it like a giant sheet of wrapping paper.

'Were you pinching my polytunnel?'

'No!' quips the old boy.

'Not exactly,' mutters Levi, pursing his lips. 'This is slightly embarrassing, Mungo.'

'You're Mungo? Bill mentioned you this morning.'

'Look, love, it's like this. When you say you're handing your keys in, you actually hand your keys in. The rest of us then do you a favour by clearing away any debris that you've left on your plot, because otherwise the new folk come in and take ownership. See?' explains Mungo, avoiding my gaze.

'You were pinching my polytunnel before a newcomer could arrive?'

Levi begins to cough and splutter.

'Not quite. This tunnel frame is a decent size, compared to the one that Levi has, so we were just going to do a swap – no one would be any the wiser,' explains Mungo, looking increasingly embarrassed with each syllable.

'Where's all the stuff from inside? There were long tables, shelving units, plants in pots, and I might have spied some bags of compost this morning,' I say, swiftly recalling the items like a Mensa applicant.

'Ah, right. Well, we'll retrieve those too . . . all of it, I promise,' says Mungo, grabbing the next sheet to roll.

'A case of swapsies too, is it?' I snipe.

'Something like that,' sniggers Levi, unable to keep his face straight. 'Look, love, sorry . . . I mean Jemima, Old Bill said you weren't interested, a definite no-shower, and that we might as well help out who we can before the newbies land. We just didn't bargain on you changing your mind.'

'Obviously not!' I snap. 'I wish someone in authority were available to witness this, though isn't Old Bill part of the committee?'

'He is . . . alongside me,' declares Mungo. 'Mungo Tulloch, head of security for Lerwick Allotment Association.'

'Ironic! I assume you've used your spare key to gain access to my plot?'

'Needs must, in this day and age. I've got keys to each plot, purely for health and safety reasons – working alone can be a risky endeavour on an allotment.'

'Plus events such as these!' I retort, staring at my decimated polytunnel.

'Levi, you'd better call Bill and tell him,' says Mungo, swiftly adding, 'then give the others a call.'

'The others?' I repeat, earnestly glaring between them.

Levi coughs, attempting to compose himself, while Mungo continues.

'If the truth be told, Kaspar is interested in your potting shed, Pa MacDonald has rehomed "Tommy's girls" and a young couple on the far side wanted to lift a couple of rows of your paving slabs,' explains Mungo, as I gaze at each item. The chicken enclosure is eerily silent and empty, minus the wooden coop and the fowl.

I am gobsmacked.

'Unbelievable! It's a good job I came back tonight, isn't it? The plot would have been cannibalized if I'd waited till morning.' A thought strikes me. 'Did the same happen to plot number eighteen?' I know the answer, before they attempt to justify.

'Look, lady, this is how it works on allotment sites. It's a community, we look after our own before we give to the newcomers. Where's the harm in it? If I need a larger polytunnel and there's one going begging, we switch. This one is far too big as a start-up project. I'll get more use out of this than a newcomer will.'

'And me . . . will it be too big for me?' I ask, finding my feet in this conversation. Which would be slightly easier if the younger guy wasn't so intriguing, with his Scandinavian blond hair and mesmerising eye colour. I don't remember him from school so he must be a few years older than me, but not much.

'Is it your first allotment?' asks Mungo.

'Yes.'

'Your first proper garden?' asks Levi.

'Yes.'

'Well, then,' they chorus.

My hands lift to my hips; I'm not impressed.

'But still, we'll put it back together as it was and let bygones

be bygones,' says Mungo. 'I'll fetch a staple gun, a hammer and
new nails while Levi can begin calling people. It'll look as good
as new in no time.'

I feel triumphant. I've embraced my official allotment status
and stood my ground against the pilfering of my inherited possessions. Something tells me the Quinn family might protest
somewhat more when emptying Grandpop's home.

I need to move; I can't stand rooted to the spot as they busy
themselves trying to rectify their error. Should I check out the
water butts? Peruse the perimeter fencing for large holes? Or
make a feeble attempt to seek out the rhubarb plant? Though
without any knowledge of the leaf shape or its growing season
I might be on a wild goose chase.

I spy the potting shed. I'll find a home for my new gloves.

As the two men mutter between themselves, I head for Grandpop's bolt-hole. I smile, recalling a recent conversation we had
over sponge cake and tea. 'The younger generation think they
invented the term "man shed" – I've news for you – us allotment
oldies did that decades ago! They've saved many a marriage
around this area.' I'm sure he was right; my gran always bristled
when he found solace drinking his flask of coffee in his potting
shed.

I reach the wooden door, expecting to find a lock of some
description, but there isn't one, just a simple hook and a bent
nail popped in.

'Have you pinched the lock off the potting shed already?' I
ask, indignantly.

Levi shakes his head and sighs.

Mungo doesn't answer.

'Shocking,' I say, opening the door wide and pining the bottom
edge with a house brick lying nearby.

'See, that's how much you know about this place,' says Levi,
standing tall from his task. 'Nobody has a lock on their sheds.

They might have a wedge or a pin holding the door closed but most are free to open. It's only newcomers who lock their sheds.'

'They proudly put big hefty padlocks on as a sure-fire sign of showing how security conscious they are,' explains Mungo, piling the rolled sheeting into bundles.

'Plus, a helpful signal to any trespassing scallywag that they've got something valuable to nick,' adds Levi, tilting his head as if proving a point. 'So, yeah, go ahead and buy the biggest padlock you can find – they'll only rip the door off at the hinges to gain entry anyway, as that'll be its weakest point.'

'Or leave it how it is and how it has been for decades,' adds Mungo, heading along the main path to fetch the required supplies.

'Oh.' My reply sounds feeble; I have a lot to learn.

'Or you'll do as you wish and learn from your mistakes – all the newcomers do,' mutters Levi, neatening his tools before following Mungo. 'We'll have this back to how it was by the morning. See you.'

'Bye.' I watch as they leave through my front door and turn left along the track. It wasn't the best introduction I could have wished for. Tradition or no allotment tradition, they shouldn't be cheeky enough to take what isn't officially theirs.

I move inside the potting shed and immediately step back in time. The musty smell of dried earth, the sight of blood and bonemeal boxes, wooden dibbers lined up on the worktop, clay pots in various sizes stacked neatly, all Grandpop's gardening paraphernalia which takes me back to my childhood. Above the window, a double row of satin award ribbons are pinned: yellow, red but mainly blue. On the work bench sits his trusty allotment partner, his weather journal, in which he jotted down the daily readings that enabled him to calculate the month's averages for daylight hours, minimum and maximum temperatures, rainy days and wind speed. Earnestly, I flick through the yellowing crinkled pages. Decades' worth of weather details he'd noted long ago from his daily newspaper, then from the nightly TV forecasts and eventually, once he'd mastered a 'mobile telephone', as he called it, from various weather apps. 'The finest thing about Shetland – we have plenty of weather!' was a favoured saying.

The sight of his large loopy handwriting, each letter perfectly formed and sitting neatly upon each ruled line, simply opens the memory flood gates. I burst into tears as the true loss of my grandpop hits home. I stand and openly weep, hugging his weather journal to my chest. For how long, I'm not sure. But when my shoulders stop jiggling, my tears have dried and my nose can't run any more, I take a deep breath.

I feel better; a good cry always works. Today has simply been too much. Maybe tomorrow will be less fraught. I'll make a proper start then.

Placing my new gloves alongside the empty seed trays and wooden dibbers, I turn to leave. That's when I see the figure. Dressed from head to toe in a white bee-keeping outfit, complete with a wide-brimmed hat and hooded netting distorting their features. They stand motionless, a metal object in their hand, alongside the five beehives, like a strange astronaut fallen from outer space, staring at me through the wire fencing separating mine and Dottie's plot. I can't tell if it's a he or she, given their bulging outfit, but still it's rude to stare. I'm embarrassed, knowing that my wailing was hardly silent, more like ugly crying on a grand scale.

'Hi,' I say meekly, raising my hand in a poor attempt to be friendly. It's surprising that, despite the lack of visible facial features or body language, I can still read a lot from their solid, broad stance: they're not smiling, they're not comfortable, and they don't appear to be interested in making friends.

They don't respond with a wave or a nod but simply turn and continue to puff smoke inside the open hive.

Dottie

I don my gardening gloves, grab my wooden trug from my polytunnel and begin my usual trundle through the aisles of sprouting delphinium. I'm not looking for anything particular, more a 'good morning' greeting to each crown mound purely to observe the growth from yesterday's early morning inspection. It sounds unbelievable but I can see a difference each day, be it a tiny glimpse of a shoot, a protruding stem or an unfurling leaf. My eagle eyes might be aging but I can spot new growth. And, more importantly, my enemy: a slug, or the damage caused by one.

I'm always ready to go into combat against my enemy. I don't believe in hurting any creature, but if the slugs take hold they'll snaffle all my delphinium spurs as they show themselves.

'Greetings, Ned,' I call and wave, as I near his beehive collection. As always, Ned's dressed from head to toe in his special suit and veiled hat, with his bee-smoker in hand, plodding back and forth between his five hives. He returns my gesture with his usual nod; he's a man of few words, whether at a distance or not. I never disturb him when he's tending the bees. His time is precious and I'd hate to encroach.

If there's anything to share, we tend to chat when I'm at the manor doing my little bit of dusting. He's not one for gossip or tittle-tattle but he likes to know if there's something local that he should be aware of. I rarely hold back on such occasions; thankfully, he never repeats his source.

I continue my inspection slowly, taking delight in the sure signs that spring is well and truly sprung. I know what I'll be expecting for the season ahead. I've got my cane supports ready to install, once the stems are a fraction taller; they've aged over the years but I scrub them clean at the end of each year in preparation for the next. With the ferocious winds which sweep through Shetland, it's vital that I don't skimp, as years of experience have proven I'll lose to Mother Nature, every time. One bad night and I'll find my entire plot flattened to the ground, and no amount of staking will aid their recovery.

'Hello, Dottie.'

I look up to see Melissa calling through my wire fencing. Bless her, the newbies don't want to overstep the mark but we can't spend all our time answering the gate as if it had a doorbell. I beckon her inside, saving my aged legs for my true allotment work.

'Do you need something, Melissa?' I ask, knowing full well she hasn't any tools or allotment supplies, given her recent arrival.

'I was thinking of ordering some manure to boost the soil before I plant my seeds. Are delivery trucks allowed up the dirt tracks?'

'You need to weed it first, love.'

'That too, but it'll take a week or so to get a delivery organised.'

'Just be careful not to throw away good money on useless stuff.'

'How can manure be useless?' asks Melissa, grimacing.

'You need to buy rotted manure. Fresh manure sometimes contains harmful pathogens which can get into the food source – not good. Plus, the nitrogen can burn the roots, damaging a healthy system,' I explain, seeing her expression instantly change. 'And don't get me started on the straw deposited all over your beds.'

'Bad for the soil, is it?'

'No, it just looks bloody messy, in my opinion.' I laugh, knowing that my personal preference shouldn't affect her allotment choices. 'You'll be picking bits of straw out of your beds forever more.

'Oh no!'

'I suggest you invest in chicken muck if you want the best – or get some layers yourself and benefit with their muck and their eggs.'

I watch as Melissa recoils.

'I'm not one for feathers or fowl,' she says.

'In that case, make sure you give Jemima the heads-up, as you might snag some muck from Tommy's girls.'

'Thanks for the advice, I'll drop her a hint or two.'

'No point, love . . . we ask straight out around here, you won't offend folk.'

'In that case, you haven't got any spare tools I can borrow until I nip into town to buy some?'

'Buy? We don't buy new tools either. Have you got anything in your potting shed?' I've seen it time and time again. Allotment plot allocated and then the newbies blow a small fortune on brand-new tools, all sparkly and shiny, from the local garden centre. What a waste of money! Six months down the line, the tools have hardly touched the allotment soil, the cutting edges remain razor sharp and you could feasibly return each item as unused if you had a receipt.

'I haven't a thing.'

'Leave it with me.'

'Are you sure?' Her expression lights up with delight.

'Sure. There's more unused and abandoned shovels and spades in these sheds than I've cut fresh blooms. For starters, I know Mungo has a decent gardening fork he never uses in his carpet bag.'

'Mungo's got a carpet bag?'

'Lovey, don't ask . . . it's a long story.'

Chapter Four

Jemima

Today feels epic. A Friday morning which actually feels like a Saturday morning from my childhood, when I used to jump out of bed excited for the day ahead. Hours of uninterrupted pleasure, doing as I wish, without a care in the world. I'm officially on a high, having biked to the allotment before seven o'clock. I plan to beat Dottie or Old Bill to letting out 'my girls' – if they've been retrieved from Pa MacDonald's. I've never fed chickens before but, if I follow Bill's demonstration from yesterday, what can go wrong?

I spent the whole of last night Googling anything and everything about allotments. I have a host of elaborate plans in my head and a renewed energy to tackle it all. Locking the entrance gate behind me, I smile, knowing that inside my rucksack, alongside my coffee flask, I have a carefully rolled colour-coordinated allotment plan indicating where each of my produce will be sown. A mood board for vegetables! Last night, instead of downing half a bottle of cheap Chianti, I opted to buy a packet of crayons from the corner shop to complete my diagram. I am going to pin it to the inside of the potting-shed door as a reminder of my master plan.

Birdsong fills the air as I stride along the dirt track pushing my bike. I feel like a true allotment holder, thanks to my wellingtons; I found them thrown at the back of the hallway closet: forgotten and unloved. This morning, after my breakfast, I gave them the once-over with a damp floor cloth, resulting in a gleaming shine to the green toecaps.

Before I know it, I'm standing before my allotment front door, which I plan to keep. It's a painful reminder at the minute but I am sure each visit will get easier and, over time, I'll come to appreciate its presence. For now, I hastily insert the Yale key, twist, and sniff back the torrent of tears threatening to tinge my pride with sadness.

I have a spring in my step. I've got this. I saw no one as I traipsed along the track; maybe I'm the early bird today?

I'm glad to see my polytunnel and chicken coop have been returned to their original condition – contents and all, I hope. The two fellas must have worked long after I'd gone home to reassemble both. It wasn't the best of introductions, but I'll let it go and thank them kindly when I see them. A fresh start and all that.

I enter the chicken enclosure before I've a chance to worry or overthink my actions and their possible reaction. I swiftly lift the coop's shutter. Instantly, a tide of brown feathers streams down the tiny ramp and the girls begin investigating their territory. Such strange-looking creatures, like tiny dinosaurs but with a camouflage of feathers to make them appear less frightening – until you look at their eyes.

I exit the pen and enter the potting shed, searching for the bag labelled 'corn' which I saw Bill grab yesterday. I drag it from behind the door. Boy, what a weight! I can't possibly shift that as Old Bill did, so I grab a tin container from the worktop and scoop out a can of dried corn before returning to the chickens. On leaving the shed, I'm stopped in my tracks; the picket gate is wide open. I scurry inside, clutching my corn pot, and begin counting the occupants. One, two three, four and . . . shit! Where is number five? Madras, Nugget, or whatever your name is, where are you hiding?

My anxiety levels soar as I begin hunting under, behind and around everything, but without luck. I can't find the errant chicken anywhere.

How can one bird have the intelligence to spot the unlocked gate, the nerve to try my patience and the courage to do a runner in less than a minute?

It takes a while to realise that my antics have intrigued the remaining cast of four, who accompany my search like 'follow the leader', encouraged by the fact that I am still holding their breakfast.

Maybe I imagined five and Bill actually mentioned four birds? That thought is swiftly erased when I spy the little bugger scooting along the main pathway towards the front door with the speed of an Olympic gold medallist.

I scatter the corn in a semicircle, watching the girls happily tuck in, then quickly secure the gate and make a dash for the escaped chicken. I have never touched anything with feathers before so have no idea how to proceed. And as for that beak – is it blunt or a highly dangerous weapon?

I dash about for twenty minutes, re-enacting Rocky's fitness scene, before realising how naïve I am. If I dash right, it dashes left. If I tiptoe, it scarpers at top speed. It can also fly, which is somewhat awkward and clumsy but more elegant than me chasing it. In short: I fail miserably. I'm grateful that yesterday's bee-keeper didn't have a front-row seat for this performance. I reckon I can live with a truly free-range chicken wandering my allotment.

I gracefully retreat to the four good girls, praise them and provide them with refreshments from the water butt, as demoed by Old Bill. Within minutes I'm done, though I've mentally logged a vendetta against chicken number five and have irreverently renamed her 'Sunday roast'.

I have no intention of going straight home, I want to accomplish something each day. Chasing a chicken cannot be today's thing!

I want my first task – I'm ignoring the chicken incident – to be pinning my vegetable master plan to the shed door.

I rummage through numerous chests of drawers ranged neatly underneath the worktops, searching for a hammer and suitable nails. Every drawer is a repainted bedside cabinet which Grandpop has rescued from a previous owner who was probably taking it to the refuse tip. It's endearing to see so many delicate brass handles, and intriguing to pull open each drawer to reveal hidden treasures, lovingly filed away in tiny trays laden with folded seed packets and white plastic labels. I can't imagine it would have taken him twenty minutes to find the hammer and nails; he'd have gone straight to them.

Having knocked four tacks into the corners of my master plan, I'm triumphant. It's amazing how satisfying physical work is when the majority of your day is usually spent in a service industry: advising tourists on creating memories while you remain behind a reception desk inanely smiling. Hammer + nails + spent energy = ta-da!

I realise my error seconds later. I push the shed door closed and – *ouch!* I spike myself on one of the four nail points protruding through the thin wood. I'm not changing my master plan, so I immediately grab the hammer and flatten down each nail from the outside. It looks totally unprofessional, but task one is complete.

It's nearing nine o'clock before I look up from my list. On standing tall to stretch my back for the umpteenth time, I notice that there are signs of life on the surrounding allotments.

To my left, Old Bill is busily wheelbarrowing a load of manure the length of his plot. For an old gent, he can certainly shift – and that doesn't look like a light load to me. I imagine Grandpop did much the same when he was here; he was physically strong, despite his age.

They put me to shame; my back is aching after just one morning's work. Though I'm delighted with my efforts. I've managed to rearrange some features on the allotment and tidied the messy areas, giving the plot a more fluid feel. Basically, I've spent the morning applying feng shui to my allotment plot. In my opinion, it looks neater, despite the free-roaming chicken who has repeatedly jeered at me from various hideouts whilst I've worked.

'Hello, Jemima, how are you?' calls Dottie, her straw hat skimming the door frame as she enters. 'I saw the chickens were out so didn't bother nipping around to them.'

'Morning, Dottie – I'm great. I changed my mind.'

'That's allowed, lassie. I hear it caused some confusion amongst the boys.' Her expressive gaze suggests she's heard all about it.

'I've managed to tend the chickens, then I've busied myself tidying the plot,' I say, gesturing in an arc. 'I've emptied a load of stagnant water from plastic buckets which were smelling to high heaven behind the polytunnel.'

'I see. Have you heard of comfrey tea?' she asks.

I shake my head. Comfrey what?

Her watery gaze views my handiwork. 'You've neatly lined up your water butts and watering cans too.'

'Yes, I didn't like them being dotted here and there at intervals along the fencing. I know they look like a pack of tubby soldiers, standing to attention in rank order, but at least they are all together in one patch.'

'And you moved those yourself?' she asks, smiling kindly.

'It took me ages. But once I'd emptied each one, they were quite light and I was able to roll them into position over the bare earth.'

Dottie listens intently. I sense she's about to comment or correct me, but she doesn't.

'And the chopped wooden logs – you've shifted each pile too?' she asks, spying the rows of upended logs lined neatly in front of the polytunnel.

'Why Grandpop had piles of logs scattered here and there, I'll never know – he didn't have a coal fire at home, and he didn't whittle wood. They were covered in creepy-crawlies, but that didn't bother me with my new gloves. They look much neater now.'

Despite Dottie's gentle smile, I don't think she approves of me changing Grandpop's allotment style. I fully understand; some people find change difficult to accept.

'You like it?' I ask, hoping to ease her silent contemplation.

'Did you save the water from the butts?'

'No. I couldn't move them when they were full – they were a bugger to push over, I can tell you.'

Dottie gently nods, her wide brim accentuating the tiny moves.

'And you? Has your morning been productive?' I ask, eager to learn from others.

'It has. I've managed to clear a small area of weeds which I neglected last year after a peerie operation on my wrist. The others kindly helped but it's not the same, you know.'

'I can imagine.'

'When you see what some people class as a weed-free bed, it makes you wonder if they need their eyes testing,' Dottie chuckles in a sweet old lady manner.

'You still have a helper, though?' I ask, recalling my embarrassment from last night.

Dottie seems puzzled, and then her brow relaxes.

'You mean Ned? He doesn't help me – he's usually busy with his bees. You've met him then?'

'Not quite.' I come clean about my shed-induced sobbing, fully witnessed by the aforementioned Ned. 'So, Ned probably got quite a fright, if nothing else.'

'It'll be water off a duck's back, will that. Not much bothers him. Nice chap but very quiet. He keeps himself to himself, even with me – and I've known him for decades.'

'He doesn't garden then?'

'No. He tends his bees a couple of times a week. My plot was the perfect placement, with enough space for the number of hives he has.'

'Aren't you frightened that they might attack as a swarm?'

Dottie gives a belly laugh. 'You need to understand bees a little more, then you'll be fascinated by them.'

'I doubt it. I can't think of anything worse than flying insects buzzing non-stop about your head and dive-bombing your hair. Urgh!'

'Anyway, I'd best be going, lassie. As Old Bill will tell you, "You've gotta do a bit and leave a bit" – I'll see you tomorrow, Jemima.' She nips my cheek in a cute way before tottering out of my front door. I watch her through the wire fencing as she carefully places each step before the next. She's walked a fair distance before she turns around and waves, shouting, 'I'm glad you stayed.'

'And me!' I holler, as a content glow blossoms inside.

Melissa

'And this,' I say proudly, holding my iPad aloft and turning around very slowly on the dirt track, 'is the allotment site. Can you see?'

'What's with the speared heads?' asks Hamish, my stubble-faced husband, via the iPad screen.

'I reckon they're pretty grizzly looking, but Old Bill explained that they'll keep the birds away from produce or summer fruits . . . not that I have any summer fruits yet, but I might have one day.'

'It's slightly twisted, isn't it?' asks Hamish, scratching his auburn stubble.

'I'm sure he said they were rescued from a local hairdressing salon when it closed down.' I continue to walk and talk, allowing

Hamish to view the allotment scenery. Such moments are bitter-sweet; I'm glad I can involve him, but I'd give anything for Hamish to be here in person.

'If bald Medusa does the job of a scarecrow, that's all that matters,' says Hamish.

'Hardly traditional though, are they? Let me put the iPad down so I can undo the padlock.' I nimbly unlock the gate, then collect my on-screen tourist to carry on showing him around. 'And this is mine!'

'Bloody hell, Mel – it's a bit overgrown, love. Are you going to manage all that and your teaching hours?'

'Of course! I only teach three days a week. Everyone's been so welcoming. I only got the keys yesterday and already I've made friends with Dottie plus a couple of old boys, Bill and Mungo. I've got no qualms about getting my hands dirty and making a good start, ready for the planting season. The soil's too cold at the minute . . .' I finally pause for breath, noticing that Hamish is not actually looking at me but chatting off-screen to one of his colleagues. I wait to restart our conversation. Can't his buddies leave him alone just for a minute while I show him what I've been up to? Is it too much to ask? 'Hamish, are you looking or do you need a minute?'

'Nope, I'm back with you, this can wait . . . oh, nice shed – is the lean intentional or for artistic effect?'

'Mmmm, neither, to be honest – it's a tad on the small size but it'll do for now.'

'If it doesn't fall down first,' he guffaws.

No! Laughter is not the reaction I want. I want support and encouragement. I want a husband who is here to dig over a huge section of weeds, rotavate the bare plot and hoe to within an inch of his life. Instead, mine is pitched in the middle of the Gulf of Mexico on an offshore rig drilling for oil, twenty-four seven, for fifty-two weeks, so it seems.

'It'll look very different next time I give you a virtual tour,' I vow.

'Bloody needs to.'

Is he intentionally trying to piss me off? Or are his efforts purely chance, and he's unaware that he's ballsing it up with every negative remark?

'That's smashing, babe. Remember, as long as you're happy, I'm happy, right?'

'Right!' I mutter, my enthusiasm waning – much as it has for our long-distance living arrangements, after ten years of marriage.

'Is there anything else to show me?'

'Not really, this is it. Amongst the weeds, I've found some useful plants. This one here is called plantain – which Dottie says makes a decent cough mixture, apparently.' I fail to mention that Dottie also spotted mare's tail which is a bugger to do battle with, given its rapid growth. 'And from the nettles, I can make—'

'Great!' interrupts Hamish. 'I'll love and leave you, so to speak. Keep on with your weeding, keep out of mischief, and I'll be seeing you in no time.'

'OK.' He hasn't mentioned an actual date for coming home. 'Any news on when that might be?'

I watch as he makes a noncommittal shrug, something that has become a regular habit. I'm sure his brain doesn't register the movement now; it's just an involuntary action upon my asking that particular question.

'Babe, you know how it is. With Jonesy away on paternity leave, Smithy off on his honeymoon – it's all hands to the pump, to fill the gaps, when someone gets ill. I promise, I'll chase it up, leave it with me.'

I've heard that line more times than I care to remember. His 'I promise' is as plentiful as the weeds upon my allotment. I've got a funny feeling that I'll sort my task before he ever does his.

He's been gone for eight solid weeks, without any prospect of a return home.

'I'll let you go then. Phone me. Love you,' I manage, my smile in place.

'Yeah, babe. Miss you.'

In the blink of an eye he is gone. I close the iPad, before pushing it deep inside my shoulder bag. Well, that's that! I tried to involve him; to cajole some interest in my home life, without moaning about my work life.

'Miss you' is his usual sentiment, repeated as frequently as the sea kisses the shoreline, yet it never feels quite enough. He's never been one for throwing bouquets or compliments around, but to hear those three little words now and then would be nice. 'Miss you' – but not enough to relocate or find a job closer to home, or to settle and start a family, or to return at frequent intervals, ensuring that our marriage is a settled, contented one.

I survey the allotment plot with fresh eyes. He's got a point. It's nothing more than a patch of waste ground, with a potting shed poking up amongst a mass of swaying jungle. Which is why someone else bailed on this project as a lost cause. Will I be doing the same? Will someone else be standing here in six months' time, surveying the same view and considering whether I was work-shy?

I turn about to see the numerous mannequin heads staring back in a mocking manner, as if they are reading my thoughts.

'Bugger off, you spineless beauties! Who are you to sneer at me?' That's when my idea strikes. I can go one better than their painted plastic faces and tacky pouts. Besides, I propose to create an allotment plot that demonstrates my individual style and finesse.

Quickly relocking the gate, I stride along the dirt track, my first mission growing in my head. I'm here to stay, and nothing makes home feel more like home than putting your own mark on it for everyone to see. I might not have nice neat rows of bare earth, with tiny labels and windmill flags poking up from the ground. I might not have plentiful water butts, or eco-log piles attracting the wildlife, but if there's one thing I do well, as an art teacher, it's creating unique and expressive textiles. My feet gain pace as my inner pride grows and spreads like mare's tail. My stride quickens to a mini jog and soon, for the first time in years, I am running along the dirt path towards my car, just like a child heading home from primary school.

Dottie

'In all my days, what is that?' I say, as Kaspar, Levi and Mungo struggle to manoeuvre a trailer laden with a long ceramic object along our dirt track.

'Dottie, don't ask – I wouldn't want to cause a lady to blush,' teases Kaspar, as I stare, bemused yet intrigued, as they attempt to turn the trailer into Kaspar's allotment gate. I do love Kaspar's Estonian manner; he's shy and retiring, unlike some of the brash fellas around here.

'Let's say it's for his bathroom collection,' says Levi, putting his shoulder to the trailer's side and pushing forward. Levi might be a local taxi driver but he'll squeeze in a favour for anyone in need.

'Stop staring, it's a ceramic urinal . . . he's not plumbing it in, so you've no need to worry,' says Mungo, stepping back and allowing the younger guys to take the full load.

'Kaspar, never. You can't plant that up – we'll be having complaints from all the ladies, me included.'

The loaded trailer lurches forward through the gate, as Kaspar pops up to argue his case.

'Dottie, it's perfect – with drainage at each end and a solid deep trough – you'll be admiring it once I've planted it with nasturtiums. You'll be begging me to tell you where I bought it.'

'I. Will. Not. That's for certain. Though full marks for recycling where you can, for which I'll award you Brownie points.'

'Where do you want it unloading, Kaspar?' asks Levi, as they trundle the trailer along his path.

'This way, fellas. I want it facing the front of the plot. But can we safely settle it on a brick base?'

'Are you going for mid-thigh height, or lower?' asks Mungo.

We all turn and stare distastefully at his uncouth suggestion.

'Just a thought, no need to get testy!' chuckles Mungo, his eyes dancing and his grey bread quivering.

'It'll be a balls-up if the brick support gives way,' adds Levi.

'I wouldn't joke about such things in front of a lady,' says Kaspar, straight-faced and blushing profusely. 'Sorry, Dottie.'

'I'm glad to see some men can respect a woman's delicate ears.'

'Dottie, we've heard you ladies during your Friday gin session in The Cabbage Patch, you're not as innocent as you make out,' teases Levi, stepping back to assess the unloading of the urinal trough.

'You're talking out of your backside, Levi – us ladies are not the ones who cause the dramas in The Cabbage Patch – we leave that to others.'

'Mmmm, I wonder who you mean?' adds Mungo, raising his eyebrows and nodding towards the far side of our site.

Our committee group like to include all active allotment holders in every decision, but it appears our site has a social divide – not of our choosing, but it exists nonetheless – and The Cabbage Patch marks the spot where both sides regularly meet. Though you have to bring your own booze, as we don't hold a licence.

'Dottie, a question before you go – what would this have been cleaned with, when it was in situ in the pub?' ask Levi, gesturing to the urinal.

'I've no doubt it's been cleaned with strong bleaches and cream cleaners, so best give it some elbow grease to remove any leftover film that might destroy the flora in your soil.'

'Any chance?' asks Kaspar, inclining his head.

'Not on your nelly. I've enough to do on my own plot. Unless you're prepared to help me erect my cane supports over each delphinium crown as they shoot,' I jibe, knowing I'm on to a winner if he agrees. 'And secondly, will you make some more Estonian cookies as a Friday treat?'

Kaspar weighs up the offer. 'Go on, it's a deal.'

'I'll go and fetch some gloves – I wouldn't want to risk putting my hands in there.'

'It's spotlessly clean,' says Levi, flashing me a handsome grin.

'You wouldn't want to eat your dinner out of it!' I retort.

'Too right.'

'Well, you'll be able to once I've scrubbed it, that's for sure,' I say over my shoulder, as I leave the trio of men open-mouthed and staring at the urinal.

Jemima

'Sorry, you've done what?' asks Old Bill, instantly frowning as I relay my productive tasks of the past few hours.

'I said . . .' and I list my tasks again, counting them off on my fingers as I speak.

'Rookie error, my girl,' he says, shaking his head in disbelief.

I'm gobsmacked at his response. I only nipped around to seek some friendly advice, having finished my tasks; I was about to head home but spotted him wheelbarrowing the umpteenth load along his pathway. I didn't expect a pat on the back but I certainly didn't expect this reaction. Old Bill turns away from me, looking towards the perimeter fence on his far side, furthest away from my allotment plot. Has he forgotten which side I neighbour him on?

'Oi, Mungo, are you there?' Bill hollers.

'Yep, old chap.'

'She's only gone and kicked over her water butts and set them in nice neat rows ... can you believe it?'

'I can.'

'You can?'

'I can, Bill. Nothing surprises me, these days.'

Neither of us can see Mungo, but we can both hear him clearly from his allotment plot.

'Talk about wet behind the bloody ears!' calls Old Bill, as if I'm not standing a foot in front of him. 'What the hell would Tommy say?'

'Exactly. What the hell would Tommy say?'

'He'd probably praise me for my effort and handiwork – I haven't stopped all day, I'll have you know.'

'Mungo, she hasn't stopped all day, she'll have you know!'

I hear a roar of laughter.

'What do I say to that, I ask you?'

'I say, she won't have time to stop and draw breath come the height of summer, that's what I'd say, Bill.'

The air is filled with two men belly laughing, with Old Bill sporadically repeating certain phrases to himself, as I stand open-mouthed at their rudeness.

'Can I ask what's so damned funny?' I say indignantly, relieved that I haven't mentioned the escaped chicken.

'Mungo?' splutters Old Bill.

'Nah. Let her work it out. It's always the same with the new-comers, they act before they think.'

'It's so tempting, Mungo,' says Old Bill.

'Be that as it may ... she won't be doing that again.'

'Did you hear the part about neatening her log piles and all the insects?'

'Yep, that too. She'll learn.'

'I wonder if she's found her eggs yet?'

'Not bloody likely, given Tommy's girls and their laying habits!'

I've had just about enough of these two old men rudely chuntering away about me. The younger generation might be lacking in many ways, but at least we have the decency to talk about folk behind their back on social media and not to their face.

I turn on my heel, leaving the allotment without a goodbye. They can both get the silent treatment, if that's how Old Bill prefers it. Grandpop probably gave them endless amounts of his time, effort and experience during his years down here. How dare they pay him back by making fun of my efforts!

'She's stormed off now, Mungo!' calls Old Bill, removing his tartan cap and folding his arms across his rotund belly.

'I'm not surprised. She put the wind up me and Levi with her rant over the polytunnel.'

'Nah!'

'She's a feisty one, she's got Tommy's wayward spirit.'

I can hear every word. Though as I re-enter my allotment I realise their voices are gaining volume, so I am probably supposed to. Well, I'll show them. I can do this allotment business without their help. I have access to the internet, weekly gardening programmes on TV, and gentle Dottie to rely upon. What more do I need? I'm sure Grandpop did his own thing and didn't rely upon the instruction of Old Bill, Mungo or Levi. Why should I?

I feel like the new kid left in the schoolyard at break time, without any friends to eat my crisps with. Though their banter does remind me that I haven't collected any eggs. I didn't give it a thought, first thing this morning. I was more concerned about getting all five of them back. How ridiculous that I can tend a few chickens and not give a thought to the actual reason for keeping them in the first place.

I enter the chicken coop empty-handed, much to the dismay of the girls, and stride to the far end, lifting the wooden flap on the protruding box; I assume it's the nest box.

There's plenty of golden straw lining each of the compartments; their bedding has been moulded into a comfortable shape matching the underneath of a chicken, but there's not a single egg.

Five chickens yet not a single egg! How's that possible? I'm not the world's expert on chickens but I assume they each lay at least one a day – so where are they, ladies? I close the lid of the nest box and move around to search the main coop section. There's a mini door on the side for human entry, rather than the door-shutter entrance favoured by the chickens. I slide the latch across, open it and peer inside. There's chicken shite everywhere: every perch, every wall, the ceiling, the floor, everything is covered in clusters of white-and-black speckled daubing. Great! How can an animal spend all day roaming outside and then choose to crap inside its own bedroom? I'm disgusted to think I'll need to clean this out. Or is it simpler to throw the coop away and start again?

There are no eggs amongst the droppings, which is a relief.

Unless someone has stolen them, which I imagine is very unlikely.

There's not much to their world inside the enclosed wire fence. There is plenty of bare earth, their shitty coop, two large boxes for shelter and a water trough, but nothing else. There's certainly no small cardboard box with six indented compartments and a gentle reminder to 'lay one here, please!' I walk about, my gaze glued to the floor as if I've lost a quid. The girls give me no clues; their heads continue to bob about and peck at the barren earth they've already pecked a million times earlier today.

'If I were a chicken, where would I lay my egg?' I mutter, trying to gain some insight.

Nothing.

I stand and stare in every direction. The only thing remaining inside the fence which they have access to is the profusion of weeds lining the bottom of the wire fencing. It hardly looks comfortable, in preference to their cosy straw beds, but what have I got to lose?

And I'm glad I did.

Within minutes, with the use of a stick to separate the clumps of weeds, I become the proud owner of five perfectly formed creamy white eggs. Why any chicken would choose to plop their daily delivery there is defies logic, but I've known enough parcel couriers who were happy to find the right street if not the correct house.

I pull the hem of my T-shirt out to create a hammock shape, and place the eggs inside; from tomorrow I'll bring an empty egg box.

I carefully exit the chicken coop, not wishing to crack my bounty against the wooden gate post, and tuck the eggs into my rucksack. I'll need to nip up later to ensure the chickens are locked away safely for the night, but now I'll head back home. It's gone four o'clock, and I've been here all day without a bite to eat, or anything to drink – and no access to a toilet, so needs must.

I arrived this morning with a list of tasks and a master plan for the shed door. Day one of allotmenteering, done and dusted.

Chapter Five

Melissa

'I'm so sorry. It'll only take a minute and then you'll look beautiful, I promise.' I slip the cross section through the blouse sleeve, along the back and out through the other cuff, before hammering it into place. The five-foot stake vibrates with the impact of each blow and my new addition jiggles and dances as if brought to life on this Saturday morning. Three final nails into the back post, purely for good measure, and then I down tools. Passing around to her front, I begin titivating her clothing. I can't leave her flashing her lacy undergarments at the passing parade; what would the old boys say?

'She's gorgeous!' cries a voice over my shoulder.

I turn, whilst straightening her petticoat hemline, to see Jemima peering through my fencing.

'Have you made that?'

'I have. It took me a while to get the pattern right, but I'm rather pleased with it. Can you see the family resemblance?' I pose beside Miss Scarecrow and pout, enhancing our differences: blonde woollen hair, cross-stitched blue eyes and an unwavering backbone supporting a willowy frame.

'I can. That's so lovely, Melissa. A girl scarecrow who's a mini-me of you. I love it! It beats having these severed heads on spikes.'

'Exactly, they give me the creeps. I'll make you one, if you like. I've loads of fabric scraps – any particular colour?' I've moved on from wishing she'd handed her keys in, and am open to the possibilities of friendship.

'How wonderful. I'll pay you for it. Any colours – you choose.'

'OK, give me a few days as I've got college assessments to mark, but I'll make a mini-me for you too,' I say, noting her clothing and hair colouring.

'How exciting. You'll have the flowerpot man on the end knocking on your door, asking to date this one. So watch out!'

'He can stay down his own end – my girl's not interested in dating, just scaring away the birds when I eventually plant a crop.'

'How's it going?'

'It's hard work. I can't hack the new growth down because that leaves the roots intact. I can't dig the roots out because the soil's too hard – I've cleared that small spot earlier today and my back is breaking.' I point, purely to ensure she doesn't miss my morning's work. 'And you?'

'My efforts seem to give everyone a bloody good laugh. The two old boys are watching me like a hawk, though Dottie seems a sweet dear.'

'Yes, very knowledgeable. She tried to convince me that weeds are simply plants in the wrong place. Though looking at my patch, it takes some believing.'

'Could you imagine their reaction if you nurtured that jungle, encouraging it to grow higher and healthier?' giggles Jemima, surveying my plot.

'Apparently, I'm already nurturing a supply of decent cough medicine and broth on this plot. I wanted to be boring and simply grow carrots!'

'I've got a rogue chicken running free, so I can't talk. You haven't seen a guy called Levi about, have you?'

I shake my head. 'I haven't come across that name yet, just Old Bill, Mungo and Dottie. He's not from the bathroom showroom, is he?' I say, thumbing in the direction of my neighbour whose ceramic display has increased.

Jemima laughs. 'Nah, Levi's the one with the army camouflage nets on my side – a local taxi driver, or so I'm told.'

'Well, I'd best get on, otherwise I'll need to focus on cough medicine and broth-making to justify my existence here,' I say, collecting my tools.

'Aye, me too. I've got a task list as long as my arm. But I need someone to catch the chicken for me, which is why I asked.'

'Good luck in finding Lenny.'

'Levi,' she corrects me. 'Bye.'

Jemima

I don't manage to locate Levi, despite asking everyone I meet. I stride around the allotment busying myself with tasks, conscious that I have a rogue chicken spying on me. I manage to plant several tiny mint plants along the edge of my main pathway. I'm hoping that, in time, the rainfall plus my brushing against them will release the fragrance, filling the air. I'm carefully stomping one wellington-booted foot around each plant to firm the soil when I hear the tiniest of cheeps. Turning towards the noise, I spot the smallest bundle of mottled brown and yellow fluff that I've ever seen. For there, toddling towards me, having to climb over and navigate boulders of earth, is a tiny duckling. Its orange beak is moving non-stop, emitting a cheeping noise that sounds like a TV special effect.

I remove my gloves and crouch down on my haunches to peer closely at the duckling, which plonks itself down before me, staring upwards. Its tiny head swivels from side to side, taking me in, whilst I peer down like Gulliver in Lilliput.

Cheep, cheep.

I scoop up the bundle of fluff. Its tail feathers wiggle and jiggle, nestling into my palm with room to spare. Its beak, which looks two sizes too big, twists and turns as it stares up at me in the cutest fashion.

'You've taken a wrong turn somewhere, little fella,' I say, striding along the main path towards the chicken enclosure. 'But we'll soon find your mum.' I can just about squeeze along the outside of the enclosure fencing to reach the brook which runs beyond.

There's a tiny footpath edging the brook, just wide enough for me to walk in either direction. I'm delighted to see there's plenty of shrubbery on my side of the bank, quite an idyllic spot, and somewhere within is a mother duck missing a chick. The duckling sits quietly in my palm as I traipse the length of two allotments in each direction, without spotting a single duck, let alone one with a healthy brood in tow.

'Well, you're certainly not frightened, I'll give you that.'

Now, what do I do?

I can't leave it here alone, hoping mother duck will swim by anytime soon. What happens if it drowns? Does it know how to swim at this age?

I sit down on the grassy bank, my gaze twisting back and forth for any signs of life amongst the reeds and brambles. Nothing.

'What are you doing there?' calls a male voice, causing me to jump.

I turn to my left, only to find Levi's piercing gaze directed at me over the rear fence of his allotment. He's wearing a woollen beanie, pulled low over his brow, and his usual checked shirt. His puzzled expression remains fixed.

'I've found a duckling. I was hoping to find its mother.' I raise my hands to show the proof.

'No chance.'

Why is everyone so negative around here?

'She can't be far away.'

'She could be right down the other end of the brook, they

don't tread water all day simply to look pretty . . . they travel a fair distance, you know.'

'So, she's abandoned her duckling – he's alone?' A lump clogs my throat. Join my club, little one. 'What am I supposed to do with him?' My knowledge of fowl is non-existent, but calling it 'he' seems natural.

'Put it down and walk away. I reckon it's a case of survival of the fittest,' says Levi, climbing over his rear fence to join me.

'You'd leave it?' I mutter, as he reaches me.

He nods, crouches down and leans, a fraction too close within my personal space, to peer at the little fella. 'Cute, though.'

'Mmmm,' I say.

'Or you raise it by hand.'

'Do you think?' I say, turning in excitement to find I'm peering at his stubbled chin. I flinch with embarrassment and turn away, unsure if he's being friendly or overly friendly, such is my inexperience conversing with handsome males. In my previous two long-term relationships, I learnt very little other than how to compromise about my every need. Hardly right or healthy.

'You'd need to hand feed it; if it's healthy enough it'll survive. Then see if it wants to go free. If not, you've got a new allotment buddy. Old Bill's done it once or twice.'

'Hmmmph,' I retort, not interested in anything Old Bill has to say.

'Don't mind him. He's as cranky as hell at the minute; he's missing your granddad. He's a genuine sort when you get to know him.'

We stare at the duckling sitting patiently in my palm.

'Thanks for returning all my stuff,' I mutter, careful not to reignite that particular rant.

'No worries. We'd never have touched it but Old Bill said that you'd definitely rejected the plot. It's better to recycle where we can.'

I give him a dubious glance. Who's he kidding?

'Seriously, ask old Bill how he reared his. He likes being asked for advice.'

'Do think he can advise me on how to catch a runaway chicken too?'

'Has one got out?'

'Got out, let out . . . same thing, isn't it?'

Levi laughs and shakes his head. 'Have you tried to catch it?'

I raise my eyebrows in reply.

'Give me ten minutes, I'll have caught it for you. Otherwise Mr Fox certainly will.'

'Are newcomers always useless?' I ask, warming to his manner.

'Yeah, but Mungo reckons some are worse than others.' He gives me a sideways glance.

'That's a bloody cheek.'

Dottie

At the car park, I circle the yellow skip three times, inspecting the jumble of items poking out from awkward angles: garden chairs, fence panels, broken pallets, discarded water butts and shattered buckets. Stashed right on top, as if the crowning glory, is a bundle of wire: heavy duty, expensive and useful.

Who in their right mind would throw something as valuable as that away?

Even on tiptoe I'm four foot too short to rescue such an item from the landfill.

The skip company won't be happy; it clearly states along both sides 'don't fill beyond this level', but already, in only one morning, it's piled high.

I circle one more time, just to be sure there's nothing of suffi-cient length poking out which I can use in a modernised version of hook-a-duck. There isn't. The entrance gate hasn't opened whilst I've been circling. Bloody typical! All I need is one minute of someone's time. It's hardly going out of their way to help one of us old 'uns – not after everything we do for the younger generation. There's never a burly youth around when you need one. Any other day, there's Levi, Kaspar, or the MacDonald trio traipsing towards their father's allotment to give him a helping hand, but never when I need them.

I could leave it until later, but the chance of it still being there is slim. I check my watch: two o'clock already, plus there's a site meeting at four. It'll definitely be spotted by then. The skip hire company will collect before five, they usually do on a weekend.

Suddenly, the wire gate at the entrance to the car park begins to vibrate, indicating an arrival. I shoot around the end of the skip to see Jemima, pushing her bike through before carefully securing the gate.

Nah, I couldn't ask. She's fragile ... but spritely and very nimble ... plus, she's wearing her allotment dungarees. 'Jemima!'

'Afternoon, Dottie, how are you?' she asks, wheeling her bike towards the dirt track.

'Any chance you could spare a wee minute, lassie?' I say, standing beside the overflowing skip.

'Sure. I nipped out to buy a bottle of water. What do you need?' She leans her bike handlebars against the metal skip. There's a wicker cat carrier strapped above the rear mudguard of her bike, which I haven't spotted before.

I'm sure she'll regret asking in less than a minute. I ignore her water bottle purchase for now, but will introduce her to the cold tap inside the social shack later.

'Well, you see that bundle of wire, the one on top ... you couldn't fetch it down for me, could you?'

I watch her smiley expression falter and her eyes widen as she follows my extended arm.

'You want *me* to fetch it?'

'Please. It'll take two seconds for you to scamper up the side. You won't get mucky, because no one's been thoughtless this time and emptied their unusable compost in it – unlike the last time our committee offered a free communal skip.'

Her gaze roams across the overflowing contents.

'I'm not sure it's safe to climb up, Dottie.'

'You won't have to climb, lassie. Look, if you simply pop yourself on the edge here, and then place a hand there ...' I indicate the route, hoping to convince her of her safety. 'I reckon you could reach the bundle of wire very easily.'

Jemima stares, her horrified gaze outlining the discarded items piled up into a junk mountain.

'You'll be fine. I'll make sure you're safe.'

'How? Knowing my luck, I'll slip, fall and break a leg ... it's a bit dangerous, Dottie.'

'Honest, I've done it hundreds of times myself over the years. If I was five years younger, I wouldn't be asking. But since my rheumatics have gone to my hips, there's no way I could heave myself up there,' I explain, tapping the skip edge.

'And you think I can?'

Yes, easily, if you try.

'It looks higher than it is. I'll help you up.'

'Dottie, wouldn't it be better if we ask one of the guys to fetch it down? They're much stronger than I am – Levi would jump up there in a second. I'm useless at supporting my own body weight.' Jemima dangles her arms, as if proving her lack of strength.

'We don't need the guys; they'll simply complicate matters. You know what the boys are like, they'll start mooching about and emptying stuff they think they need, or even deciding that they'd quite like the bundle of wire – when I saw it first. Us girls can do this without them, I'm sure.'

My God, I didn't think she'd need convincing. I thought she'd be up and down like a jack rabbit. She's definitely got Tommy's stubborn streak, that's for sure.

'That's just what I need for my delphiniums,' I wheedle. 'It would cost me an arm and a leg if I needed to buy that out of my pension money. Pension money doesn't stretch too far nowadays, you know.' I hate tugging on their heart strings, but sometimes it's necessary with youngsters. 'Please. For me.'

'Dottie, it wouldn't have been thrown away if it was decent quality, would it?'

I lean in close and whisper. 'Some folk around here don't know their arse from their elbow, lassie. They've got more money than sense, and it burns a hole in their pocket. That's forty quid's worth of wire sitting pretty up there.'

Jemima looks at the prize, glances towards the entrance gate and then back at me.

'Honest. Possibly fifty quid's worth if the skip man gets his hands on it first, when he comes to collect. Don't tell me they don't remove the good stuff before they reach the council tip.'

'Go on then.'

Bingo!

'I'll hold your bike, it won't fall over,' I say, knowing perfectly well that it's securely propped against the side of the skip.

I watch as Jemima tugs at the legs of her dungarees, easing the fabric about her hips and giving her more room for movement.

'Now push on your hands to heave yourself up,' I instruct, as if I'm an expert.

She firmly grasps a corner of the skip and raises her body weight, as if exiting a swimming pool, swinging the inside of one wellington boot to meet the metal edge.

Good girl, she's a treasure.

Jemima hovers on the edge, puffing and panting, her three limbs pinned and one leg trailing. A tiny wobble occurs before she steadies herself.

'Hold tight!' Lord knows what I'll do if she comes a cropper and lands on the car-park gravel.

'Are you sure about this, Dottie?'

'I'm sure. Where there's muck, there's brass, believe me.'

'Now tell me where to go from here,' she says, drawing her left foot up on to the edge whilst raising both hands to hug a sturdy water butt wedged firmly in place before her.

'Stand on the corner section if you can, not the straight-edge bit,' I warn. 'Or you might fall off.'

'Do you think!' hollers Jemima, looking down at me from her precarious position.

I hope not, but there is a bloody good chance.

'Ignore me. I'm being overprotective. Your daa would have shimmied up that skip in a heartbeat for a bundle of wire such as that.' I see Jemima roll her eyes. I can't help it: everyone mentions her granddad at the most inappropriate moments, but it's true. He was a bugger for a freebie, was Tommy. 'Come on, you could be down in a minute or two.'

I watch as she gingerly clambers towards my treasure, her hands feeling their way across the jagged mountain of junk. The odd item moves as she places her weight upon it for support, only to quickly let go again and reach for another more secure and stable object from which to propel herself forward.

'You're nearly there!' I'm so grateful to her, she's such a trooper. A true asset to the allotment association.

'What the hell are you pair up to?'

The voice makes me jump, let alone Jemima.

I turn about to see Ned hurriedly crossing the car park from the direction of the dirt track. I didn't realise he was here.

'Hello, Ned, we were just . . .' I cease talking.

He looks annoyed. 'Get down from there, this instant!' His tone is deep and gravelly; he looks like a fisherman in that jumper.

'Ned, she's quite safe, she's nearly got it.'

'Got what?'

'That bundle of wire, there on top.'

'Bloody hell, Dottie – all this for a bundle of sodding rusty wire. Here, let me.' Ned swiftly heaves his body up alongside Jemima's quivering frame and snatches at the bundle, sending it flying towards my feet.

'You've saved the day,' I coo.

'And you, stay there!' he barks, pointing at Jemima, before leaping down from the skip to stand beneath her trembling frame.

She had more courage when Ned wasn't present; his tone isn't helping matters. Though she can't complain that his silent staring is a fault on this occasion.

'Thank you, Ned. Look how much wire there is – definitely worth saving, don't you think?'

Ned shakes his head and proceeds to help Jemima awkwardly negotiate her way across the pile of junk to reach the skip's corner edge. It wasn't the pathway she'd originally taken.

'It'll be easier to lift you down.'

Jemima's face blushes as Ned reaches up, wrapping one arm about her back and placing the other beneath her knees, before lifting her down from the metal edge. Oh, to be young again. Despite the dungarees, she's so feminine; he has such breeding and manners.

'There you go.'

Ned gently returns Jemima to her two feet, and she thanks him profusely.

'Have you pair been introduced?' I ask coyly. 'Ned, this is Tommy's girl, Jemima. Jemima, this is Ned Campbell, the bee-keeper.'

I watch as they exchange pleasantries, each with their gaze locked upon the other's face. Her cheeks colour some more, if that is at all possible, while Ned drags his hand through his uncut hair. I bet he wishes he'd nipped to the barber's now.

'See, I said it would be easy.'

'Easy? I'd have got stuck if Ned hadn't turned up,' retorts Jemima, straightening her dungaree legs over her wellingtons.

'No worries. Dottie, next time, can you think twice before you fancy a bit of skip diving . . . it might save us all from harm and potential injury,' says Ned, his tone verging on authoritative.

'Skip diving?' repeats Jemima, a comical expression on her face, addressing both of us.

'Yeah, when one person throws stuff out and someone else dives in to smuggle it out. It happens all the time around here – no names mentioned, eh, Dottie?'

'It's been ages since the committee hired a skip for communal use, so don't go blaming me.' I sound terse, but I'm not taking the blame for others.

'Mungo usually devours every skip we have. He must be feeling ill, or something.'

'Oi, less of your cheek. For that, you can carry this up to our plot and be done with it,' I say, wagging my finger. I love the chap to bits, but sometimes he pushes his luck, even with me.

'As if I wouldn't offer, anyhow,' he says, lugging the wire from the ground to carry it across his shoulders. 'It's too heavy for either of you to carry – or collect from a skip!'

'Pah! She was doing just fine.'

'Am I OK to go?' asks Jemima, collecting her bike from where it's resting against the skip.

'Thank you. I'm sure you'd have managed without the muscle turning up. But now, at least you've been properly introduced,' I say, over my shoulder, as I usher Ned towards the dirt track. 'I'll catch you later at the meeting, don't forget.'

'Bye,' calls Ned, as we begin to walk.

Jemima trails some way behind, pushing her beloved bike.

'You were naughty asking her to climb up there,' he says in a hushed tone, after a brief silence.

He's annoyed with me, which is unusual.

'She's fit, healthy, a peerie young woman . . . she's very capable,' I mutter, conscious that she's a short distance behind us.

'I've got eyes in my head but, regardless, she could have fallen and broken her neck – then what would you have done?'

'She was quite safe. Jemima has a will of her own and a backbone to go with it.'

'Has she now?'

'Hmmm, you seem overly concerned about her safety and welfare.' I eye him cautiously, knowing I'm pushing the boundaries of our friendship.

'Well, it appears you have little regard for her safety.'

That told me.

We fall silent for the remainder of our walk; I sense we are consumed by similar thoughts.

I hastily unlock my allotment gate, holding it open for Ned to pass through, before issuing my instructions.

'If you could stash it behind the polytunnel, away from prying eyes.'

Ned strides along the path, doing as requested. Past my prepared flower beds and on towards his beehives which sit alongside my polytunnels, he carries the wire bundle with ease upon his shoulder. I don't know what I'd do without him. Like the son I never had, yet wished for.

As I close the gate, Jemima reaches her own allotment door and clumsily juggles with the Yale lock and her bike. The handlebars turn, twisting free from her grasp and falling to the ground with a clatter, dislodging the wicker cat carrier.

Ned wouldn't go far wrong in life alongside that one. His mother might not have approved immediately but his father definitely would have. Cecilia was always wary of those from outside her own social circle and yet, once she trusted you – like she did me – you couldn't ask for a truer ally. Whilst Douglas would have seen the natural attraction before observing any faults. A man of few words, but a true believer in his son's future happiness being the sole purpose of his life.

'Be careful,' I say, as she quickly pulls the bike up by its handlebars.

'Thank you, Dottie, I'm fine.'

You certainly are, and I'm not the only one to notice.

Jemima

'Excuse me,' I say politely, squeezing through the chattering crowd blocking the entrance to The Cabbage Patch. I have no idea what to expect from my first allotment association meeting, but Dottie insists I attend.

'You'll never get a true account, if you don't. Be there, or spend the next two months listening to twisted tales of inaccurate accounts,' she said, when I mentioned committee meetings 'aren't really my bag'.

Once inside, the social shack is cavernous, rather like a Tardis: a vast wooden structure consisting of bare beams, joists and floorboards. It is decorated with untidy notice boards detailing long-forgotten urgencies, and a strand of red bunting scalloping the front of the tea counter, complete with a hissing urn and a coffee machine. On entering, I see a horde of people seated on row upon row of white patio chairs and the occasional low-slung deckchair. I don't recognise anyone at first, so I'm grateful when I spy Melissa sitting in the corner. I trundle across to form an alliance of newbies.

'Hi,' I say, settling beside her. 'Not sure what to expect from this, are you?'

'No. I didn't want to attend but Dottie made me ... she reckons hearing it from the horse's mouth is always best.'

'She said the same to me. Do you know anyone else here?' I ask, gesturing towards the influx of chattering bodies.

'You, the committee trio seated over there, and the helpful guy you mentioned earlier . . . the good-looking chap, what's his name?' I follow her gaze to see the three aforementioned members seated behind a small trestle table, and Levi seated nearby.

'Levi?'

'Yes, Levi . . . he popped by after we spoke, to introduce himself. I think you'd nipped off on your bike.'

'I nipped out to buy a cat carrier and bottled water . . . I'll explain later. He caught my AWOL chicken too.'

'Did he?'

'Yes, he had to lunge at it a couple of times, but he caught it in the end. I was quite impressed.'

Old Bill walks, huffing and puffing, along the rows; he hands out a yellow flyer to each of us. It doesn't appear as if refusal or lack of interest qualify as an excuse not to receive the literature. 'Thank you,' I say, before scanning the committee's agenda of discussion items: annual festival date, bonfires and waste disposal, prohibited keeping of cockerels, stolen tools, security/personal safety, rules and regulations and, finally, AOB.

'Have you anything you want to bring up?' asks Melissa.

'Me? No. You?'

Melissa gives me a quizzical glance. 'Not in front of this lot. How many allotments are there?'

She's got a point. There must be seventy people squeezed inside this shack: sitting or standing around the edge, waiting for the meeting to begin. I need to have a proper walk around to gauge the size of the site. Embarrassing to think I've only met six people. You'd think, living in Shetland, that you'd know everybody, but I don't.

Ting, ting, ting. A teaspoon is rapidly tapped on the side of a mug by Dottie, and the raucous chatter fades to silence.

Old Bill stands tall behind the trestle table to address his audience.

'Welcome to the Lerwick Manor Allotment Association's first meeting of the year. I realise we've many newcomers, so I'd like to start by introducing ourselves: Bill Moffatt as chairman of this committee, Mungo Tulloch as treasurer, and Dorothy Nesbit as secretary. We have many more committee members, who you can rely upon in our absence. Now let's get down to business.'

Bang on cue, the shack door nosily opens, admitting a solitary male in a chunky knitted jumper and heavy walking boots; his fleeting nod towards the top table is taken as his apology to the entire room. I blush as Ned swiftly strides across the remainder of the wooden floor, finding space to casually lean against a wall on the opposite side as people's attention reverts to Old Bill.

'As I was saying ... by tradition, we always hold a meeting in April despite it being a no-goer month for us while we await finer weather. But this month gives us ample opportunity to get ready for the growing season ahead and plan for the festival. The first item on the agenda is to choose the date of our annual festival. Now, I need a show of hands in relation to dates. Is there any objection to a public vote? We can organise a secret ballot, if folks prefer, but you know me, I hate wasting time on the unnecessary. Anyone?' Old Bill's gaze scours the room for an indication of a hand or a twitching eye. I doubt I'd have the nerve to raise my hand. 'Good, that settles it – a public vote. Last year, we held the festival later than usual, on the twenty-sixth – so think on, what's it to be?'

The audience watches as Old Bill collects his diary, then quickly flips through the pages before addressing us. 'There's four weekends, so the first vote is to decide which section of September – the beginning of the month or the end? Raise your hand for the end of the month, like the previous festival.'

September will be one year since my mum died; I can't associate it with anything else. I stare about the room; I have no bloody idea what's best. There's little movement to indicate assent, just a tiny cluster of seven votes by the entrance. My hand remains static in my lap.

'OK, so a show of hands for the first half of the month, please?' asks Old Bill.

A sea of hands rise; mine alongside Melissa's. I feel ridiculous, but instantly become part of the proceedings.

'Good, good. I suppose it makes sense to align our festival date with Shetland's various agricultural shows – us locals should be supporting each other. The next two votes determine the exact date: the fourth or the eleventh?'

Old Bill swiftly counts hands for each of the offered dates, but there's a clear winner.

'That's agreed then. Saturday the fourth of September is officially our festival date – I'll be circulating a brochure outlining the specific categories and awards. It goes without saying that we'd like a hearty bunch of volunteers alongside the committee members supporting the day's proceedings. We did well last year in terms of attendance from the locals – people outside of our allotment community – it'd be great if we could encourage even more this year. Dottie, are you OK with folk coming to speak to you about specific activities and the mash-up?'

'I certainly am,' says Dottie, cheerily smiling at the audience.

'Fine, that's settled. Item two . . .' announces Old Bill swiftly.

My concentration drifts from the all-important proceedings. I don't understand half of their concerns, the queries asked by numerous allotment holders, or the answers offered by the committee table. Instead, curiosity gets the better of me, and I find myself watching the audience. I never imagined that my grandpop mixed with such a diverse group of individuals, certainly more than I have ever socially encountered, despite working in the tourist office.

My relaxed gaze travels along each row in turn, taking in the variety of the human race. I've never seen so much corduroy in my life – obviously the favoured material of the allotment holder. My gaze lingers upon the latecomer; there's something different about him from earlier. A stocky, solid frame for one so tall – some men are inclined to look willowy and hunched with such a stature – and not wearing corduroy, either. My body didn't rest against a doughy torso when he rescued me from that towering pile of junk; he's solid under that jumper. How embarrassing for him to pluck me from the side of that skip! With such ease, and very little effort. I felt like a small child again, when Grandpop would carry me up the wooden hill during holiday sleepovers. I didn't flinch, I knew he wouldn't drop me: neither Grandpop nor Ned. It takes a second to realise that I'm openly staring, whilst lost in thought. I rapidly blink as I become aware that his dark gaze, those chiselled cheekbones and cleft chin are squarely facing me. He doesn't attempt to avert his eyes. His gaze is direct and intent, staring at me as I stare back at him. That's when I realise: he's had a haircut.

I instantly look away, to focus upon the proceedings. My brain instructs me to listen intently, to concentrate and ignore the other side of the shack. Mungo stresses the importance of locking the main gate, preventing scallywags from entering our site. I find myself nodding, agreeing with every word, despite having no experience of such matters. I'm conscious that my every move is being watched.

My eyes take on a defiant nature, disobeying my brain to sneakily attempt a sideways glance with my peripheral vision. My eyeballs are strained to an extreme degree, attempting to look over my own right ear. In spite of the blurry image, I can see that his stance hasn't changed; he's still facing me. I forget myself and twist my chin, to glance up. Yep, eye to eye. I witness a fleeting lift of his brows and a twitch of his lips. Damn it, he saw me pretending not to look.

I reposition myself, turning my shoulder slightly to block the bee-keeper from my view. I must focus on Mungo's expectations for security, it's the only reason I'm here. That and to impress Dottie, should she quiz me later. Not that it matters, but I feel the need to please her by reinforcing my dedication to maintaining Grandpop's allotment.

'Are you alright?' whispers Melissa, touching my forearm.

'Fine, just listening,' I answer, realigning my gaze with the trestle table trio.

'Huh, I can't be bothered with all this nonsense ... I'm only here to show my face.'

I fight the urge to shush her but know that would take feigning interest to another level.

Before too long, Old Bill is wrapping up proceedings.

'Can I ask that no more is placed in the communal skip – if needs be, we'll arrange for another one next week, if it keeps the site cleared of unwanted debris. We do have a delivery of wood chippings on order, which will need barrowing by interested parties. Please don't be greedy. And now, finally, any other business?'

An elderly chap wearing a green wax jacket raises his hand, requesting attention. 'Could everyone observe the site regulations by encouraging natural habitats for the much-needed insects. I'm reliably informed that some newcomers are dismantling the piles of chopped logs provided on each plot, in the name of conformity and neatness . . .' He pauses, adding, 'Such diligent housekeeping destroys the valuable eco-work we've undertaken in recent years.'

I nod along to his suggestion, until I realise that all eyes are upon me.

Logs. Insects. Neat lines. The penny drops. That is aimed at me!

His neighbour, a plump chap dressed in yellow waders, adds, 'I'm Kaspar, and if anyone's throwing out their comfrey tea, please throw it in my direction – it might resemble rancid water, but it's the best plant food I know of for nasturtiums.'

Buckets of stinking water. Plant food? Argh, that too.

Afterwards, I don't feel like lingering for a social cuppa once the tea counter is manned and an orderly queue starts to form.

I hurry from The Cabbage Patch, eager to collect my duckling and head off home, though maybe a touch of personal embarrassment propels me along the dirt track too.

So, I've made a mistake. No one gave me a copy of the allotment regulations. Maybe Old Bill should have done a better job on his guided tour. He shouldn't assume that I understood anything about log piles and stench-filled buckets!

If the whole site is sniggering behind my back, then let them get on with it! I'm not here to socialise, I'm here to plant a few rows of cabbages, maybe a pumpkin or two, while I'm on sabbatical. Nothing more.

I enter my potting shed to gather my belongings. The tiny duckling is nestled inside a small Tupperware box lined with straw, which I carefully place inside the wicker cat carrier, securing the door using the tiny leather strap and buckle. Crispy duck immediately stands and pokes his fluffy head and body through the wicker door grille. Wow, you're smaller than I thought! I carefully scoop him up and over my shoulder, plopping him inside my jacket hood; the cat carrier can wait until he's grown. I jiggle my shoulders, feeling the gentle weight of his body and a paddling sensation as I imagine he's getting comfy for our bike ride home.

Chapter Six

Melissa

'Ta-da!' I say, whipping off the white sheet which I've artistically draped over Jemima's scarecrow in her absence.

Jemima's eyes widen and she squeals on seeing her mini-me version propped up against a water butt.

'I thought lacy dungarees and a knotted headscarf represented you perfectly.'

I've taken my time in creating this scarecrow, adding decorative embroidery stitches to the denim bib and T-shirt, which I'd dreamt up since creating my original girl's petticoat.

'That's definitely me! Maybe I should add a line of frilly lace to my dungaree hems too. Melissa, I love her.'

'Good, I'm glad. Mungo let me in, knowing you'd be returning to lock your girls away for the night. I thought you could choose the spot you want, then give me a hand hammering in her wooden stakes. She'll be happy and secure in no time.'

'Mungo and his security duties by any chance?' she says, shaking her head at the principle.

'Aye, with a spare key – *hush, hush* – *wink, wink* – *say no more.*' I try to impersonate Mungo's rough manner but fail.

'He's a law unto himself, it's a joke. He used a spare key when attempting to switch my polytunnel with Levi's.'

'I forgot my own keys the other day and there was hell to pay when I asked to borrow his spare key for my own plot. He refused to hand it over, insisted on walking me to my locked gate, then opened up and walked off with the spare. It's not worth the hassle. Next time, I'll drive back home to collect my mine. So, you like her?'

'Like her? I love her! Have you named yours?'

'Nope. She's a scarecrow.'

'So? I'm naming mine Minnie – as in mini-me.'

I laugh out loud.

'I'm not joking. I think you're on to a winner with these.'

'Mini-me scarecrows?' I repeat, unsure how I feel about a brand-new enterprise created on the off chance.

'Though if you make one for Mungo, please fill his hands with bunches of spare keys.'

We both fall about in a fit of laughter.

Jemima securely locks the girls inside their chicken coop for the night, before choosing Minnie's new home in front of her potting shed, and we begin hammering. It's far easier and more enjoyable having two people to complete a task than relying on my solo efforts.

'How are you enjoying your plot?' I ask, as we work.

'It's made me realise how long I've sat around feeling sorry for myself, when I should have been doing stuff or achieving something. Which is why I didn't hand the keys back, that day,' explains Jemima.

'I'm with you there. Boy, if I could turn the clock back, I'd certainly do one or two things very differently.'

'Mmmm, I'm currently on a sabbatical and I haven't used that properly, until now.'

'You've spent most of the day up here recently – has it helped?'

'To some extent, but I think I need to start broadening my horizons and taking some risks in life.'

'You and me both, Jemima.' I put down the hammer, straighten the scarecrow's headscarf and we stand back, admiring our handi-work. 'Happy?'

'Absolutely. She brightens up that entire patch of ground. Wait until tomorrow – everyone will want one,' says Jemima, smiling at Minnie.

I think Jemima could be right; my scarecrow creations may well have legs.

Dottie

'Here you go, and don't say I never give you anything,' I tease, putting a roast beef dinner with all the trimmings before him, as Mungo quietly sips a dram of my best whisky.

'Dottie, you're something else, d'you know that! Them there tatties are off my allotment, the parsnips are probably from Bill or Levi, and the winter cabbage is left over from what Kaspar gave you! I don't see anything on the plate that you've grown!' says Mungo, pointing with his knife at his dinner plate.

'I provided the beef, and the produce was surplus to requirements,' I say, settling opposite him, as is our weekly ritual. 'Let me know when you'd prefer roasted delphiniums and I'll smoother those in gravy instead.'

'Phuh!' says Mungo, tucking into his mashed tatties.

The old bugger never ceases to amaze me. He can moan for Scotland yet still turns up on the dot every week, without invite or confirmation. He thinks I was born yesterday, but I sussed him out years ago.

He was a good-looking chap in his youth, many a Shetland lass tried fluttering her eyelashes at him, but he wasn't game. He was always choosy, was Mungo. Not that I'm saying he chose right by laying his cap at my door. I was too naïve to reciprocate his attentions, despite knowing him from school.

I begin cutting my sliced beef, aware that Mungo is tucking in faster than a starving dog. It'll be a one-sided conversation until his plate is scraped clean. But I'm used to that, after forty years of our Sunday roasts.

'The new ladies have settled in nicely, don't you think?' I don't need an answer, he's listening, so I continue. 'Tommy's girl is on sabbatical from the tourist office in Lerwick's main square, reckons she's at sixes and sevens with anxiety since her mum died, and then low and behold – Tommy follows suit.'

Mungo looks up, nods and returns his focus to his dinner.

He'd have made a fine husband, given the chance. I should have paid attention, got to know him as well as I know him now. But having male friends back then wasn't an option – and definitely not after my Albert's accident, anyway.

'Yesterday, she did me a peerie favour regarding the communal skip. Though I was pleased when Ned turned up, offering her a helping hand.'

'He's finally had his hair cut,' mutters Mungo, between mouthfuls.

'He did. Pretty sharpish too, if you ask me.'

Mungo continues to eat and then stops dead, his cutlery suspended above his plate, staring at me. 'You aren't meddling again, are you?'

'Me? Never? Purely observing.'

Mungo resumes eating.

'You said yourself, she's a feisty one. I think that'd do him some good. Bring him out of his shell – he works too hard.'

'I thought being inside his shell is what he's opted for. All this walking in late to meetings, never mixing with the rest and steering clear of additional responsibilities. I doubt he'll blow his cover now and join the committee.'

'I don't mean at the allotments, I mean at the manor. He needs to start socialising, meeting decent people, if he's going to make a success of that place.'

'Not like that last one,' scoffs Mungo.

'Exactly. I think we all got wind of her intentions . . . but mark my words, if he doesn't, he'll need to start selling off the land to pay for the upkeep of the buildings.'

'Or sign it over to a trust.'

'Mmmm, that's my biggest fear. Life will never be the same again, if he does. We'll be overrun with tourists for a start.'

Chapter Seven

Jemima

'Hello, Dottie,' I call, from the step of my potting shed, as she makes her way along my pathway. It has been a quiet couple of days, simply plodding along with my new routines – chicken feeding, weeding and pottering – but I'm still smarting from the weekend's meeting.

'Hello, my dear, how are we?' Her hat brim wobbles as she totters towards me.

I pause before saying anything, not sure if her loyalties extend to me after such a short time. Her watery blue eyes smile kindly upon me as I shade my eyes from the sun.

'I've had better days, if I'm honest.'

'Tell me more.'

I spend the next fifteen minutes recalling my embarrassment following the association's meeting at the weekend. As I talk, I continue to brush the cobwebs from the various piles of flower-pots I've found in the shed, and pile them into size order.

'I feel slightly deflated, to be fair, which isn't why I came here,' I explain. 'I've enjoyed it so far, but if treading on eggshells is the name of the game, I'll call it quits.'

'Don't say that. I'd miss you terribly.'

Bless her.

'You're right, I know how it is around here. Mungo told me about how he and Bill laughed at your rookie errors. As for Ned's gruff tone at the skip, well . . . he's never been one for socialising.

Word simply gets about – spreads across the site – and, yep, others can't help adding their two penn'orth, as you heard at the meeting.'

'Folk around here are weird,' I mutter, quickly adding, 'present company excluded.'

'Of course,' agrees Dottie, adjusting her hat to avoid the bright sunshine.

'I can't see me doing longer than the year, if I feel like this.'

'Now that would be a shame, because I have a distinct impression that some . . . well, most . . . have taken a liking to you.'

'They've got a funny way of showing it.'

'Folk are set in their ways. They don't expect the unexpected to walk in and enlighten them, do they?'

Enlighten – what is she on about?

'Trust me when I say everyone has their own agenda. Old Tommy being replaced by a younger, prettier version wasn't on the cards for this season, so we must give them time to adapt. And who knows what may come of it?'

I shake my head. I guess she's being kind. Nurturing, in fact – but surely grown adults can accept that change happens in life? If they grasp the concept that the seasons continually change, I don't buy the idea that they need time to accept my arrival.

I stand up, collecting my neat piles of plastic pots, and begin stacking them inside the doorway of the potting shed. I can use them now that I won't find dried spider carcasses and cobwebs inside each one.

'I'm not convinced, Dottie, but thanks for trying. Anyway, was there something you needed?'

'I wanted to invite you to a tête-à-tête, along with Melissa. The men tend to congregate in The Cabbage Patch for a quick half most afternoons, so why can't us ladies?'

I'm taken aback that Dottie would frequent the social shack, it doesn't seem the place for her.

'I'll reserve a tiny table in the quiet corner, and maybe we could enjoy a G&T one afternoon and a few nibbles. How does that sound?'

'I didn't realise they had a booze licence,' I say, having only spied a coffee machine and tea urns at the weekend.

'No, we provide our own – I'll bring the necessary, it's all very civilised. There's usually ice in the freezer. What do you say?'

'That's very kind of you, but surely you have better things to do than play nursemaid to me?'

'I love fussing over the youngsters down here, and even more so when it's two spritely young ladies,' she chirps. 'It gives an old hen like me something to look forward to.'

'In that case, yes. I'd love to join you and Melissa one afternoon – just say when.'

'That's settled then. I'll nip across to Melissa and have a word. I'm thinking of Friday.' Dottie quickly stands, with a renewed energy. 'Bye for now, I'll see you tomorrow – and, Jemima, don't let these men get under your skin.'

'Thank you, I won't, Dottie.'

'Chin up, lassie – it's not all bad news around here.'

I watch as she collects herself, checking she has keys. I wonder what I'll be like at her age, if I get there. I doubt I'll have the same spirit or energy she exudes.

She stops as she sees me watching her. My next question spills from my lips without a conscious thought.

'Dottie, how long have you known Ned Campbell?' I blush as soon as the words are airborne.

'A fair few years.'

I notice she doesn't elaborate. Most people say a little extra when asked a question. So why's she being so concise with her answer?

'He seems a decent sort, would you say?' Suddenly, I feel the need to tread carefully once more.

Dottie straightens her straw brim and smiles softly. 'He

does – whatever a decent sort looks like nowadays. In my day, even a decent sort caused more trouble than they're worth, my dear. Anyway, if there's nothing more, I'll be off. Bye now.'

'Bye.'

I watch as she totters away, her straw hat quivering at the edges with each step. I wonder what keeps her spirits up, as if she's the eternal smile for the rest of us. Dottie turns and gives me a little wave on closing the front door. I wonder.

Melissa

I surf the TV channels for almost an hour before finding anything of interest. I'm curled up beneath a cosy fleece, savouring a very large glass of wine. I've had an enjoyable day teaching art classes – my final teaching day for this week – and now I'm free to spend my time at the allotment. I had a brief chat with Hamish before his meal was served, though he didn't have much to say. Poor bugger was probably too hungry to focus on the banality of my day.

I survey the quiet lounge. I've got the basics: I'm fed, clothed and very much loved. I've got a nice home, all the bills are taken care of, and I have the freedom to come and go as I please.

What more do I need in life?

My gaze drifts to the other end of the empty sofa, where the cushions remain pristine, placed at a jaunty angle in their plumped position when I tidied earlier. Was it yesterday, or the day before? The vacuum lines remain crisp and clear on the carpet – the only section disturbed is my plodding pathway from door to sofa. The gleam across the TV screen is as shiny as ever; there's only a light film of my daily dust to be removed.

It seems a long time since I had to deep-clean this room rather than 'tickle it with a duster'.

I'm OK. In fact, I'm grand. I have what I want. I want a happy husband, who's doing the job he loves, spending his time how he wishes. We've survived ten years of marriage pretty comfortably, considering we started married life in a cramped bedsit in Lerwick. We'd never discussed a specific time frame for our future, because we reckoned that it would simply begin on Hamish's arrival back home with our nest egg. In fact, our wedding plans seemed overly complicated, with plenty of in-family bickering about dates, times and bridesmaid duties, despite their continued support over the years. But surely we didn't leave the years ahead open to chance? I hadn't expected his work to take him to the Gulf of Mexico but now, five years on, maybe I should have given it more thought. Were our wedding photos to be the first and final images of a happy family? Our plans for bubble baths crammed with smiling faces and rubber ducks, or sunshine picnics with a back seat filled with niggling or dozing toddlers, all depended on his offshore drilling.

I sip my wine, then flick through the channels on the TV for the umpteenth time, before surveying the room again.

How different would this lounge look with a box of toys in the corner, an array of moulded plastic on the rear lawn, and a family dog? Would I be sitting here clutching a large glass of wine? Possibly – but it would be a welcome treat after completing bathtime, the nightly bedtime struggle and succumbing to the pleas of 'just one more' story. How different would life be if there were two tiny heartbeats upstairs, and another alongside me on the sofa?

I'm brought back to reality by a rolling tear landing on the back of my hand.

Do I really have what I need?

I sniff back another tear.

I have an unmet need . . . an unwavering desire to nurture. I'm not entirely sure when that thought crystallised but it feels right, admitting it to myself. Planting carrots and tending an allotment may be my first steps but, at forty-two, I'm ready to nurture my own children rather than other people's.

I allow the thought to settle for a moment.

There's no immediate panic or rush of guilt; I'm ready.

Question is: when do I tell Hamish?

I grab the remote again to distract my thoughts, happily finding something on the TV to fill the next hour before I retire to bed. It's been a long day; an early night will do me good.

I've been asleep for ages when the tinny ringing sound wakes me from my slumber. I flick open my iPad cover, expecting the screen time to read three o'clock in the morning; its only eleven o'clock.

Hamish is calling on Facetime.

I press the screen to accept.

'Hi, babe, how are you?' His voice is too high, too jovial and too drunk for this to be a worthwhile call.

He takes a swig of his Guinness whilst I wipe sleep from my eyes. How many pints has he had tonight?

'Grand. You?'

'We're just having a break from a poker game – just thought I'd give you a quick call to check you were OK. You seemed a bit down earlier.'

'Did I?'

'Yeah, all mopey and moany. Has someone pissed you off at college?'

Mmmm, as if.

'Not at all. I just didn't have much to say – it's been one of those kinds of days.' I watch the screen, waiting for a soothing response. It doesn't arrive. Hamish is looking my way but his gaze is lifted above the screen, obviously interacting with the other guys.

'That's nice, Mel,' he says, adding, 'yeah, in a second.'

That's *nice*? What the hell! He's woken me up yet isn't even listening because the drunken crowd beyond the screen are more interesting than my crappy day. And here was me, thinking I could be honest with my husband!

'Right, I'll let you get off, Hamish.'

'OK. I just wanted to check on you. Night, love.'

'I'll speak to you . . .'

The screen connection goes blank from his end. Great! He couldn't even wait for me to finish my sentence.

I close the iPad screen, placing it on the duvet on Hamish's side of our bed. I take my irritation out on plumping my pillow before settling back to stare into the darkness, imagining the pimpled ceiling above.

Is this as good as it gets? Frequent early nights, eagerly accepted invites from new friends, and interrupted sleep thanks to offshore poker games. He'd better not be gambling with our nest egg!

Dropping off to sleep will be a challenge, given that I've already had two hours. How ridiculous am I, a grown adult ending her night at nine o'clock purely to escape the silence downstairs?

Shall I make a cuppa? Run a hot soothing bath? Do I have any more art assignments to mark?

I fling the duvet back, escaping its warmth, grab my towelling dressing gown and plod downstairs to the kitchen. Whilst waiting for the kettle to boil, I spread my fabric samples and scarecrow pattern pieces upon the kitchen table and begin selecting contrasting textures and colours. I can easily fill an hour by designing another mini-me scarecrow; it might stop my mind from meandering like earlier.

Boy, what an exciting life I lead.

Chapter Eight

Dottie

'Melissa! Jemima!' I holler, as loud as I can, from the dirt track. It has been a harmonious and productive morning at the allotments, one of those days where everything's right in the world. I know both women are here, but I haven't time to politely nip to each gate or front door to pass on the invite. Around the allotments, a chorus of voices is calling out names in haste.

'What?' says Melissa, running to her wire fencing.

'Yes, Dottie,' answers Jemima, popping up from beside her nearest water butt.

'There's an orca whale near the harbour – are you coming?'

'Lerwick harbour?' asks Melissa. Her excitement is instant.

'Yep, that's what they're saying – look, everyone else is shooting down there too.' I gesture towards various allotment holders who are appearing on the track, locking their gates before scurrying off towards the car park.

'I think I'll give it a miss,' shouts Jemima, returning to her hoeing.

'Are you serious? I thought you used to work for the tourist board.'

'I did . . . I mean I still do.'

'Shame on you! How many orca whales have you ever seen?'

'Errr, none.'

'Well then, put down your tools and get yourself in the rear of my car and act like a tourist. You're in for a treat.' I turn to view Melissa, who is hastily locking her gate. No need for any encouragement for her. 'Nice to see someone appreciates the beautiful environment of Shetland.'

'Come on, I can't wait. I've never been in the right place when the shout goes up,' says Melissa, beaming with joy.

'Sometimes it's gone by the time we arrive, but it's a bonus if it hasn't. Come on, Jemima, get a wiggle on!'

'Dottie, I'm happy to stay here and wait – I have the duckling, remember.'

'How dare you, lassie! Old Tommy would have been leading the troops, ensuring he got a good view. Now, let's be having you – and the duckling, if needs be!'

There's always one, isn't there? The one who dawdles along, unsure and unaware that nature has thrown them the chance to experience something beautiful.

The two women unfold themselves on stepping out of my tiny Mini. I take delight in having found the last spare parking space, which others couldn't squeeze into.

'How many people are there?' says Melissa, registering the gathering crowd standing about the harbour edge and staring out to sea. Most are armed with binoculars or mobile phones.

'I told you, it happens every time there's a sighting. People dash from everywhere, local offices or shops, purely for a chance sighting,' I explain, whilst making our way to join them.

'We'll never get a decent view with this crowd,' says Jemima, cradling her tiny bundle of fluff. Crispy, I believe she's called it.

I flash Jemima a death stare; has she not given up moaning yet?

'Follow me, ladies, I'll get us the perfect position.' I beckon them to follow as I elbow my way through the crowd. 'Excuse me, coming through. I'm eighty, you know. Thank you.' The sea of bodies splits, allowing me to pass. I drag Melissa and Jemima in my wake until I reach the safety barrier. 'Perfect view. See, I told you.'

'Dottie, you are naughty,' giggles Melissa, trying to hide her own embarrassment.

'I'm not eighty, though, am I?' says Jemima.

'No, but you are my carers for the time being, so please change your expression. And look, over there!'

In the distance, a mass of black and white blubber lifts and banks in the glistening water at intervals. The observing crowds' cheers ebb and flow with each appearance. How can a creature so large be so graceful, providing the most beautiful display in the middle of the day?

'That there is why we reuse hessian sacks and avoid polythene bags on allotments.'

Jemima gives me a fleeting glance; she's learning, slowly.

'I can't believe how large it is ... has it lost its way?' asks Melissa, as a photographer snaps multiple images using a long lens.

'Not necessarily, orcas sometimes come nearer than expected whilst feeding. Some get disorientated or lose their way, which gives us plenty of chance to study them by grabbing a photograph or two,' says the photographer, showing the impressive snap he's just captured. Jemima stares at the tiny screen; I notice she looks enthralled.

'It's amazing, isn't?' I ask, nudging her arm. 'Your daa loved days such as these. He always made the effort to join in. Whether it was the dolphins, porpoise or a humpback whale – he'd dash along if there was a hope of spotting them. One time, he drove us down to Sumburgh Head, took us over forty minutes, just in time to see a huge pod of orcas cavorting in the sea for all of five minutes!'

'He told me about those! He'd have taken great pleasure in telling everyone at his sheltered accommodation all the details.'

'Exactly, especially as many of the residents aren't physically able to make it down here to see for themselves. Old Tommy

brought pleasure to others whenever he could. Remember that,'
I say, as her eyes begin to glisten. I don't wish to upset the young
woman, but she's knows I'm right.

Jemima

'Hi, Mima!'

I look up to find Pippa, my cousin, waving at me through the
wire fencing.

The last person I was expecting.

'Hi, Pippa, come on in,' I holler, knowing the door is ajar. I
ease myself up from my kneeling position on the crazy paving,
trowel in hand, where I am making a poor attempt to dig a small
furrow for seeds in the tilled soil. My knees ache as I straighten,
whilst my thighs suddenly prickle with pins and needles – the
painful sensation will fade eventually.

'You need one of those kneeling pads,' she says, embracing
me and delivering an exaggerated air kiss. 'I like the scarecrow,
by the way.'

'How are things?' I ask, unsure what's brought this little surprise to my door. I upend two wooden crates and take a seat,
prompting her to follow.

'Nothing much. I didn't expect to see you here on a weekday.'

'I didn't mention it, but I'm taking a wee break from work –
I haven't coped too well since September, so I thought it best.'

'And you didn't hand the keys in, I see,' says Pippa, staring
around the plot.

'No. I probably should have informed the family of that too.
Sorry.'

'I used to come down here all the time with Granddad, you
know. I spent hours down here helping him dig, weed and clean
out his chickens.'

Did you? He never said.

'Anyway, that's why I've dropped by. Granddad's place is empty now, they've handed the keys back, and my dad has a few things they thought you'd like. Trinkets and stuff you gave him for birthdays, mainly.'

'Oh, right.' No one has been in touch since the funeral, so how would they know what I'd like? 'And you?'

'So-so, to be fair. Nothing ever changes for me, does it? Same old, same old.' I hear her despondent tone. 'Not like some.'

My defensive radar flickers to life. Is that a dig at me?

'Such as who?' I ask, buckling up my emotional armour before I'm even sure it's necessary.

'Callie, for one. She had to hire a removals van for the amount of possessions she nabbed from Granddad's place. I don't think it's fair. Regardless of family ties, we're not all treated the same, know what I mean?'

'Sure.' I refrain from airing an opinion. 'Did she claim anything you wanted?'

'No, but it's the principle, isn't it?'

Oh, yeah, principles, I know all about those in this family. I don't answer, which she takes as the signal to continue rather than cease the conversation.

'I said to my mum, just because Callie's the eldest of the cousins, that shouldn't mean that she gets to keep everything – I mean, you would have liked something other than your own gifts back, I'm sure.'

'Not really. I was surprised by the legacy I received, so I wouldn't want to take anything else, especially if others wanted it.'

'You're not bothered that she's taken the army medals then?'

I shake my head.

'What about Gran's sapphire engagement ring?' mutters Pippa, leaning forward, watching me intently.

I sigh. 'If that's what she wanted, then fair's fair.' Secretly, I would have liked such a treasure from my grandparents' marriage. Since Gran's untimely death, I'd almost forgotten how she used to smile, prior to her battle with cancer. We'd never been as close as Grandpop and I were. But still, I know she loved me to bits.

'It was the first thing she asked for – crowing that she was Gran's favourite, she was. It doesn't even fit her, so what's the point?'

'Did you want it?'

'No.' She screws up her features, as if I've offended her taste. 'You?'

'I wouldn't have said no. It was such a beautiful ring – Gran loved it.'

'Nah. It's not my thing, but I thought you might want it. Well, Callie's got it. We won't be seeing that again . . . you know what she's like.'

I don't comment. I know what they are all like: materialistic and self-centred.

Pippa stands and pops her wooden crate back to its original position.

Is that it? She's only been here for five minutes.

'Are you off then?' I ask, unsure if I'm reading her correctly.

'Yep, I just thought I'd drop by and say . . . in case you were bothered . . . but as you aren't, then that's that.'

She sounds cold, uncaring towards me and Grandpop's memory.

'It's not that I'm not bothered, more a case of being happy with what I've been given – and to ask for more seems a little greedy. I am bothered, he was my granddad, but I recognise that he was also yours.'

Pippa chews the inside of her cheek, which gives her a sulky expression. 'Anyhow, see you.'

She's off before I can check she's alright with Callie's bounty or my response. I watch as she walks along the pathway towards the front door. I feel a bit mean not showing her the girls or my cute duckling, but I can't imagine she's interested. What was the point of that fleeting visit?

'Pippa?' I call.

She stops and turns to face me.

'Are you OK getting out of the entrance gate?'

'Yeah, I've got a key.' She digs into her pocket and holds aloft a key ring.

'OK. Bye then.'

Within seconds, she's out of the front door and passing along the wire fencing, heading towards the exit. I return to my kneeling position on the hard pathway, and continue turning the soil with a trowel.

How has Pippa got a key?

Melissa

I stare in amazement, watching as the rear door of the trailer is lowered to meet the gravel car park. It's not a delivery that I'd ever imagined receiving – but needs must, in desperate times. I've spent an entire week weeding, with very little to show for my efforts, apart from my non-existent manicure.

Inside, the tethered nanny goat, a blur of shaggy brown and beige, bucks and cartwheels in every direction, scattering its straw bedding into the air.

Suddenly, the prospect of keeping this live wire for a week has lost its appeal. Given her appetite for constant grazing, my initial idea seemed foolproof, but not now! What the hell I was thinking?

'Make sure she has plenty of water, the spare leash is pretty lengthy, so I'm sure she'll happily munch away to her heart's content,' says Henry, a helpful chap with whom I'd spoken after Saturday's allotment meeting.

A deep sense of dread envelopes me as I grasp the offered lead and accompanying rucksack, in which I assume I'll find the spare leash.

'She can be a handful, so you'll need to take charge. Any problems, just give me a bell,' are his parting words.

'Cheers, I think,' I say, through gritted teeth. My entire body is forced to jiggle about as the nanny goat continues to frolic at the dangerous end of the lead. I'm grateful that she hasn't a set of horns.

Earlier, I'd imagined gracefully walking my hired weed killer along the dirt track to my allotment, much like a calm alpaca during a birthday treat afternoon. Sadly, that prospect has been shattered.

I've paid £25, cash in hand, to be dragged at high speed along the dirt track one minute, only to be forced to put my shoulder to the goat's hind quarters and push when she refuses, the next minute, to be dragged or cajoled towards allotment number 18.

I might not be a biology teacher but I soon realise that a donkey and a goat share similar personality traits. Neither will walk if they choose not to; input from the fraught handler is of little consequence.

It takes me ninety minutes to manoeuvre the goat from the car park to my gate. Every morning, it takes me no longer than six minutes to walk the same distance. I'm sure I could attempt fairy steps and still make it in less than the time taken with my tethered friend.

I'm mortified by the barrage of remarks and watchful gazes from every allotment we pass; the world and his wife come to watch the spectacle. Mungo belly laughs out loud, Old Bill simply waves us on with his tartan cap, Kaspar mutters in his native tongue, and Dottie peers out from beneath her wide straw brim like a rabbit caught in headlights. Only Levi and Jemima appear to have missed the proceedings.

Eventually, I manage to unlock my allotment gate, having conceded the fight, and Nanna randomly charges through. I swiftly kick it shut behind us.

Henry can collect his belongings from my allotment. I won't be doing that walk of shame again.

'You, girly, had better chomp my weeds down to the ground, rotavate every inch of soil, *and* plant my carrot seeds, to make up for the fuss you've just caused me,' I manage to say in a breathless manner.

I've reached the limits of my energy and patience, but I manage to switch the short lead for the longer leash, allowing her to roam freely amongst the weeds once I've safely secured the end to something other than my blistered, aching palm.

A while later, I've almost recovered when Levi wanders over. 'I thought I'd see if you need a hand, I hear she's a wild one.'

'Not easy, but she's a motor-mouth for sure,' I brag, leaning against my fencing. How sweet of him to ask. Thankfully, Nanna is consuming weeds and grass at a faster rate than an industrial lawnmower. She hardly stops for breath, but when she does it's heads up, a majestic look around, before taking another bite. 'She isn't daunted that breakfast, lunch and dinner are laid before her in one go!'

'Her bottom jaw seems robotic – has it stopped munching since she arrived?'

'Nope, but that's why I invited her over; nettles, brambles and weeds, she'll scoff the lot, apparently. Her leash is a bit long, I'm frightened it might snag around her leg, but at least she can move freely around the whole plot.'

'Where's she going to sleep?'

'I've thrown a layer of straw on the floor of my shed. It's just

big enough, though whether she stays inside will be another
matter.'

We stand in silence and stare at the creature who is inadvertently preparing my allotment for planting. She ticks every box
for green issues; she's almost carbon-neutral and, having been
in her presence for the duration, she seems methane free too.

'Their pupils freak me out. They're oblong. Urgh!' Levi shivers,
grimacing simultaneously.

'Get away with you!' My tone is jovial, possibly too familiar.

He gives a cheeky grin, before squeezing past me and striding
towards a chomping Nanna. He shows no fear in approaching
her, though she reacts with a start as he grabs the leather strapping alongside her muzzle and turns her head to face him. His
brow puckers immediately, before a look of bewilderment is sent
in my direction. 'Eyes of the devil, if you ask me ... they look
like letter boxes!'

I rapidly nod, in agreement. I hadn't noticed.

Having inspected her weird pupils, he gently cups her face with
both hands, pushing back her overgrown brows, before slowly
tracing his thumbs along her thin profile towards her chomping
mouth. Such gentleness offered from one creature to another.

What I wouldn't give to have his undivided attention. If
only ... what the hell am I thinking? I pull myself up sharp,
before my mind descends any further and reaches depths from
which I can't recover.

When is Hamish coming home for a holiday break?

By the time Levi returns to the gate, I'm in a different frame
of mind, shy and embarrassed by my thoughts. The previous
relaxed atmosphere and exchange between us has dissolved. I
become rigid and haughty, thanks to my own discontent with life.

Chapter Nine

Jemima

Gin o'clock can't arrive quickly enough for me. I've spent the last few hours hunched forward, kneeling on a folded scrap of carpet, trowelling the main bed on my plot. My lower back is aching, my right hand has a definite callous and my nails are shorter than ever.

I raise the door latch, slightly nervous to be entering alone, and hope that Dottie is early too. If she isn't here, I'll head for the tiny corner table and assume my seat – I doubt there'll be a plastic reserved sign in place.

I'm not disappointed.

The corner table is decorated with a tiny blue gingham cloth, three bulbous glasses and an array of nibbles in decorative bowls. Dottie is proudly holding court and chatting to the other tables, a single woman amongst the men and their selection of hip flasks, miniature bottles and cans.

'Here she is,' squeals Dottie, excitedly turning to her nearest observers. 'I told you all I wouldn't be stood up!'

It's the first time I've seen her without her wide-brimmed hat; I hadn't realised her silver hair was wound into intricate plaits and twisted into loops about her ears. Slightly Victorian-looking in style, but elegant and befitting her generation – pretty chic for tending an allotment.

'Certainly not, this is my treat of the week,' I answer, settling beside her and attempting to be heard over the neighbouring chatter.

'Melissa will be along in a while, she's running a little late. Shall we wait for her or indulge?'

'There's no harm in waiting.'

'Unlike this lot – these fellas don't wait for anyone,' says Dottie, offering me some nibbles. 'Kaspar's made us these delicious cookies – his own special Estonian recipe using condensed milk. They're very moreish; you might only want a couple of little ones.'

As I nibble the proffered cookie, I glance around the shack; every table is filled, with additional chairs drawn up to each, and rowdy cheers erupt as newcomers join.

'It's a weekly tradition, though some would prefer it to be a daily one, which is taking it a bit far in my opinion.'

'Are all these people allotment holders?' I select another condensed milk cookie, I can't help myself.

'You're not allowed on site unless you're an owner, though some folk attempt to smuggle their mates in for a swift nip of whisky,' Dottie says, before adding, 'we'll be leaving if the table in the far corner start smoking their strange roll-ups.'

I'm shocked at her suggestion, immediately staring in the gestured direction. The group of four middle-aged men are currently enjoying a selection of cans alongside their buoyant conversation, not a roll-up in sight.

'Are they allowed to smoke in here?'

'No, they're part of the Far Siders. They'll each disappear outside for a crafty one, linger by the doorway, and the dreaded sweet smell comes back inside with them.'

'And here's me thinking that allotment folk are all staid and respectable.'

'Chance would be a fine thing . . .'

'Sorry, sorry, sorry,' gushes Melissa, dashing towards us through the narrow pathway of chairs.

'Welcome, Melissa, first things first,' says Dottie, grasping the neck of the gin bottle and stealthily cracking the seal.

Melissa seats herself, dropping her handbag next to her chair. I eye the dish of cookies; would a third be classed as greedy or moreish? I refrain, hoping Dottie will offer me another alongside Melissa.

'Phew, now this is a welcome treat – I didn't expect so many to be in here,' says Melissa, glancing over her shoulder, before waving to the table of Far Siders in the opposite corner. 'Hi, Henry, Nanna's doing great, thanks.'

'Do you know them?' I ask, surprised by her choice of acquaintance, given Dottie's remarks.

'Yeah, Henry – the guy who waved – has lent me a goat for my allotment. She's busy chomping weeds like there's no tomorrow. He introduced himself after Saturday's meeting.'

'Oh,' is all I manage, unsure if birds of a feather flock together. Or can they be trusted to be different?

'No sign of Levi?' asks Melissa, looking about the shack.

'No, he'll be out taxi driving tonight, so he never comes near here,' says Dottie, pouring a generous amount of gin into each glass. 'Jemima, can you pour the tonic, please?'

'I see.'

I note how Melissa's eyebrows flicker on hearing the information, as if stashing it away for future reference. I carefully pour the mixer as Dottie complements each glass with a few chunks of ice, causing the bubbles to hiss and rise to the lip of each glass before dying back.

'Cheers, my dears,' chuckles Dottie, raising a glass and chinking it against ours.

'Bottoms up!' replies Melissa.

'Here's mud in your eye!' I cheekily add, knowing it was Grandpop's favoured toast, before taking a long-awaited sip.

Silence descends on the three of us, allowing the men's chatter to fill the air.

'So, Melissa, what's your news?' asks Dottie, sitting back in her chair, refreshed and relaxed by her first sip.

Melissa puts down her drink and leans forward, a coy smile adorning her features.

'I've decided I'm going to enter produce for the festival show. Do you enter, Dottie?'

'Every year. And I'm proud to say that I usually . . . actually, I *always* win the prize for the best bouquet. I've no fresh produce to enter, so I have to excel in my chosen category.'

'Sure. And you, Jemima?'

'Me? Oh no, it's not my sort of thing.'

'Oh, come now, Tommy was known for his pumpkins. Many a year he scooped first prize for the weightiest beast – some years, the men struggled to manhandle it into position without dropping or damaging it.'

'He never said.' A pang of sadness strikes my heart. How come Grandpop shared so much with his fellow gardeners yet rarely mentioned his achievements when his own Little Pumpkin visited him? We talked so freely, I laughed heartily at his weekly musings – but never once did he mention prize-winning pumpkins.

'Didn't he?' Dottie seems as surprised as I am. 'Each year, he'd germinate several plants in the hope that one of them might develop into a strong enough specimen, capable of supporting one prize-worthy pumpkin.'

'Might develop?' I repeat, sipping my drink.

'It can be very hit and miss for the best of them. Tommy was always disappointed if his pumpkin plants failed to thrive. But the years when they did, boy oh boy, no one else got a look-in on the big day!'

'You should try it, Jemima – in honour of your granddad,' adds Melissa, her excitement growing.

'Surely not! It's taken me a week to clear a patch of weeds, clean out a chicken coop and spark rumours by making rookie mistakes tidying logs, wasting water and throwing away plant feed.'

'So, show 'em what you're made of, have a go and see what happens,' continues Melissa.

'And you'll do it too?'

'Sure, I have every intention of entering.'

'Sounds like a plan to me, ladies.' Dottie raises her glass, gesturing for us to do likewise. 'Here's to healthy seeds and long hours of sunshine.'

We gently clink our glasses, toasting in agreement.

I know nothing about pumpkins, their growing conditions or the weighty size necessary for festival entry. But I do know that each time the shack door opens, there's a sweet smoky fragrance that lingers about the individual returning to the Far Siders' rowdy corner table.

Chapter Ten

Melissa

'I'm not sure, owning an allotment seems so complicated,' I say, embarrassed by my naïvety.

'We each help each other in the early days. It's how it is here,' says Levi, leading me along his turfed pathway towards the polytunnel. His lumberjack shirt and woollen beanie appear to be his allotment uniform. 'At least have a look, then decide.'

I don't like to refuse, so follow his lead. He seems so obliging, always ready with a cheery smile and a helping hand. It must be lovely to be able to encourage others; I get satisfaction from supporting the students at work, but being selfless enough to do the same for adults is a generous gift. Nothing is too much trouble.

'There's nothing wrong with it. It isn't damaged or anything; it just proved too small for me to use for any of my crops, so I've collapsed it down and stashed it in here.' He holds open the entrance flap, allowing me to pass through.

Inside, the air is filled with a glorious warm smell which greets me, along with the luscious sight of healthy plants, of various heights and species, arranged in rows. The bottom end of the polytunnel houses his benches and worktops.

'You've grown all these?' I say, utterly impressed. The larger ceramic pots are free-standing, inside frying pans, their handles turned in the same direction. 'Frying pans?'

'Yeah, it doesn't take long to establish yourself if you put the effort in. Why throw anything out just because its primary use is no longer feasible? The Teflon coating is damaged on all of those, but they hold water as good as any pot holder.' He makes his way to the rear of the tunnel, and begins pulling sections of metal tubing from a stash below a worktop table. 'The majority of the frame is folded up near the back. I'll grab it later if you want to borrow it.'

'It wouldn't be for long. I don't want to lay out a load of cash only to find I join the previous owners by giving the plot up in six months' time. It'll seem a waste if I did.'

'Exactly. Though I'm sure you'll prove to be very different to them. They kept themselves to themselves from day one. We all knew they were heading for the exit with a set of returned keys.'

'Was it that obvious?'

'Yep, you can tell that sort a mile off. Ignoring all offers of help, advice and freebies which are going begging.'

'Freebies?'

'Yeah, we all grow too much. It's a shame to waste it, so you end up walking the dirt track asking the other allotment holders, "Do you need a cabbage for your tea?" or, "You got any swaps going begging?" Everyone does it. You have to – unless you're going to eat cabbage soup three times a day.'

'And folks just swap?'

'Yeah, all the time. It won't just be veg – it could be seedlings, flowers, even spare manure – saves it going to waste. Anyway, my spare polytunnel measures seven by six by six, but it'll get you started before you invest.' Levi gestures, using the retrieved metal frame.

'That's very kind of you ... I want to start off with a few carrots, some beans and maybe try peppers,' I say, enthusiastically.

'Perfect. I'll sort out the rest of the tubing and I'll get it over to you in the next day or so.'

'Are you sure?'

'I'm sure.'

Jemima

'Bill, how many keys are there for each allotment?' I ask, through the fence, on spotting his tartan cap traipsing back and forth.

'The council issues one on allocation of the plot. Why?' He pouts, resembling a disgruntled gnome pushing a wheelbarrow.

'Just asking.'

'It doesn't sound like a "just asking" kind of query – what do you know?'

'Nothing. Honestly.'

'Why the interest?'

I wish I hadn't asked.

My silence ignites his curiosity further. He's looking at me quizzically.

'Just in case I lost mine, that's all – I only have the one set.'

'Best get a spare copy cut then, hadn't you?' he mumbles, trundling his barrow towards his muck pile and breaking our conversation. 'Yours is a Yale, so it's easy enough to copy.'

'I will.' I scurry away from our dividing fence but instantly return. 'Bill, did my grandpop ever have regular visitors helping him out?'

'Nope. Never. Your granddad tended his veg single-handed.'

I watch the vigour with which he digs and fills the barrow with manure. For a man of his advanced years he's certainly fitter than most.

I return to my chicken enclosure with the aim of deep-cleaning every inch of the inside before I can establish a weekly cleaning regime that's easy to maintain. I have no idea what I'm doing, but surely everything comes clean when you mix elbow grease and plenty of water? Within minutes, I've found a scrubbing brush, a blackened coal shovel and a plastic bucket stuffed in the rear of the potting shed – which appear to be ideal implements for mucking out.

I'm double rubber-gloved, wearing goggles plus a decorating mask, with chicken poop splattered on my exposed forehead, leaning inside the coop, when the nest box flap is lifted and Mungo's face appears. It scares the living daylights out of me.

'A quiet word,' he says, in a hushed tone.

'Yeah, sure. Just give me a minute to finish this.'

'No need, I'll talk while you scrub – I must say, these perches are in a bit of a state. Have you been neglecting the basics of chicken husbandry?' His stern expression indicates I'm being unfairly judged.

'Neglect? Are you serious? I think I've done well to get a handle on this chicken malarkey – I suggest those who babysat the allotment might have shirked their duties when it came to scrubbing shite from perches . . . now, I wonder who was that?'

'I wouldn't know about that . . . that was down to Dottie.'

'Aye, I bet it was. Anyway, what's with the chat, Mungo?' I say, my yellow gloves blurring with the speed applied to my scrubbing brush.

'I was just wondering if you'd heard anything about spare keys?'

Is every conversation repeated around this place?

'Nope. Not me.'

'Oh.' He's utterly thrown by my answer. 'I was just wondering if you'd mentioned anything to Bill, that's all.'

'Nope. Not a word. In fact, I haven't spoken to Old Bill today. Have you?' I can guess the answer but it adds to my fun.

'It was just a passing thought I had about you and spare keys . . . well, in that case, if anyone mentions such a thing, not that they are likely to, but you'll let me know who, won't you?'

'Sure. I'll do that, Mungo. But why?'

He visibly flinches at my question. 'Sorry?' He mumbles, his brow creasing deeply, as if offended.

'I asked why?' I focus on my scrubbing brush, to avoid witnessing his cogs whirring.

'I'm concerned about the security of the whole site. I have a duty of care to everyone.' His ingenious answer helps him recover. 'We can't have scallywags loitering about the place, you know. They're as sly as foxes, and things get stolen around here.'

'Do they now. Such as what?' I'm rapidly losing interest; more concerned that the particular perch I'm scrubbing is not relinquishing its inch of dried droppings despite my best efforts. Who'd have thought that mucking out chickens could be so absorbing?

'Dottie's favourite secateurs went missing during the winter months. Kaspar had his prize cucumber stolen last year. I've lost numerous spades and shovels over the years – decent ones taken from my shed. Even Ned's had his bee-keeping suit lifted before now.'

'I thought you kept your tools in a carpet bag?'

'I do. And nothing's ever been touched since I have.'

'Well, then, your belongings are safe and sound.'

He eyes me cautiously before a smile creeps on to his lips. 'Do you even know what a carpet bag is?'

'Yeah. How old do you think I am? I've seen *Mary Poppins*, you know – though I doubt you fit as much in yours as she manages!'

He gives a knowing nod, before continuing. 'Anyway, just refer folk to me if they have spare keys going begging, OK?'

'OK. Good day to you, Mungo!' I say, climbing backwards out of the confined space within the coop's doorway and stretch my back.

He closes the nest box flap, tacitly accepting my dismissal, but stops short and points at my jacket hood.

'And who is this little fella?'

'That's Crispy. He wandered on to my allotment a few days ago.'

'Did you look for the mother?'

'Of course. What do you take me for?'

'Not everyone does.'

'If you don't believe me, ask Levi; he spotted me walking along the brook searching.' Why does this guy always rub me up the wrong way within fifty seconds of speaking? 'I won't be offended if you do, honest.'

'So, did Old Bill advise you on how to feed it?'

'No. I went on the internet and searched for suggestions. Though it seems somewhat cannibalistic feeding a duckling a hard-boiled chicken egg,' I say, my inner disgust revealing itself in a grimace. 'Which he gobbles down in seconds – simply wrong, in my opinion.'

'You're not feeding it solid chunks?'

'No. The website advised I mash it through a tea strainer, creating strange wiggly-worm shapes. Which takes me longer to do than to boil it.'

Mungo gives a curt nod. It's as if he's marking my answers each time I speak to him.

'Have you put him in water yet?'

I shake my head. I'm embarrassed to admit I'm scared in case he drowns.

'Haven't you got a bath at home?'

'Yeah, but I didn't know if he was strong enough; he's only tiny.'

Mungo gives a throaty snort which develops into a chuckle.

'What?'

'You're scared he'll drown!'

'No, I'm not!'

'Go on then ... make him a pond,' says Mungo, pointing towards my nearest water butt.

I cradle the duck into my chest. 'I've got work to do,' I bluff.

'It'll take all of two minutes.'

I give him a doleful look.

'Come on, get a grip, woman. It's a bloody duck; he's born to swim.'

I really wish the older generation would allow me the space to do things in my own time.

My heart rate lifts. My palms begin to perspire. And my breathing becomes staccato.

'Bloody hell, Jemima! Tommy would be having a fit waiting for you to follow instructions. He wasn't one for wasting time – or slacking off, you know.'

'I don't need folk reminding me every two days about Tommy. I am nothing like him, nor do I have his talented green fingers. Whether I'm feeding his chickens, cleaning them out or sweeping the bloody path – I'm constantly being reminded that I do it all wrong,' I rant, my words spilling over each other as I follow Mungo's instructions. I lower the duckling on to the surface of the chickens' water butt. I fall silent. Crispy duck glides along the surface like a plastic toy afloat in my bubble bath. I'm amazed as this tiny creature twists and turns, flapping his wings and causing droplets of water to fly like diamonds about his wiggling bottom.

Suddenly, he dives under the water and is gone from sight. My knuckles turn white as I grab the edge of the water butt, peering inside. Mungo follows suit in a calmer manner. As quickly as he disappeared the duckling resurfaces and proudly shakes his tiny head, sending water droplets flying from the end of his orange bill.

I sigh with relief, like a proud mother.

'What did I tell you ... though he'll be expecting this every day now!'

'Isn't nature incredible?'

'It is. I've got an old tin bath you can have for him.'

'I'm not sure I'm having second-hand for my first,' I say cheekily.

'Recycled, Jemima – it's what we do here.'

'I'm joking, Mungo. Some people around here need to nurture a sense of humour.'

'Mmmm, chance would be a fine thing.'

Within seconds, I'm alone and Crispy is returned to my jacket hood.

I'm sure our terse conversation will be instantly repeated to a third party, regardless of involvement or interest.

I empty the dirty water from the plastic bucket into the weeds growing against the perimeter fencing. All I did was ask an innocent question, trying to figure out how Pippa could have come by the keys. Obviously, I've opened a can of worms.

I leave the chicken enclosure, to collect clean water, and immediately spy the top of two heads over the fencing in Old Bill's allotment. Bloody hell, Mungo, did you have to report straight back? It'd be laughable if it wasn't so sad for grown men to act with such pettiness.

As I turn, I come face-to-face with Ned through the other wire fence. He's dressed in his bee-keeping gear, with his smoking can suspended from his waist.

'Hi,' I shout in a friendly manner, hoping to build on our brief interaction the other day.

Nothing. He stands stock-still and stares straight through me. I turn about, expecting to find something of interest behind me. Nothing. Maybe he didn't hear me. I repeat my greeting, with a little more volume. Still nothing. What the hell is wrong with folk around here? I must look a sight in my yellow gloves and a decorating mask, but he can hardly be misled by the disguise and not know who is waving at him from the adjoining plot. He speaks one minute, all chatty and charming, lifting me down from a skip. The next, he stares me down in a frosty manner, as if he's never seen me before.

No wonder newcomers to the allotment come and go like the wind. If I didn't have my family links to this plot, plus my sabbatical, maybe I'd have already thrown in the towel too. I watch as Ned continues on his way, as if I hadn't acknowledged his existence.

I quickly retrieve my fresh bucket of water and reluctantly return to my cleaning task. My mind continues to swirl. A swift 'hi and bye' would have been sufficient. I'm not asking for his life story over the allotment fence – though chance would be a fine thing, given his brooding good looks. I giggle to myself whilst I scrub, causing the chickens to congregate and stare inquisitively.

'Girls, he can ignore me as much as he wishes. He's self-conscious because I know that he knows that I know that his sudden desire for a haircut was in response to our skip-diving introduction. Who dashes into Lerwick town on a busy Saturday afternoon purely for a quick trim and tidy? Exactly, girls, a man trying to look his best!'

Dottie

'You look very pleased with yourself,' I say, spying Jemima strolling along the dirt track.

'I am. I've just cleared some sacks from the plot, as another communal skip has arrived.'

'A tidy plot equals a tidy mind. What did you chuck?'

'Chicken poo which I'd bagged from cleaning out the coop, plus another bag stashed behind my shed,' she says, before seeing my expression.

My face always lets me down.

'What's wrong?' she asks.

'You've thrown chicken manure in the skip?'

'Yes. I was told I could dump anything I wanted in there.'

'Bloody hell, Jemima ... you need to fetch it back; it's the elixir of manure,' I say, tugging at her sleeve. 'Come on, we can't waste a minute.'

'What's the rush?' she mutters, as I drag her along.

'All my days, you newbies will be the end of me!' I release her arm, leaving her behind, and march as quickly as I can, muttering with each step. I know what to expect before I even arrive at the car park; it's too late. A duo of Far Siders are manhandling polythene bags as I turn the track corner.

'Ya alright?' says the smaller one, hitching a bulging bag the size of a sack of spuds into his arms.

'Yes, thanks, have you just nabbed that from the skip?'

'Aye, two bags of chicken crap – someone's made a rookie error,' chuckles his mate, cradling his bagged treasure.

Jemima won't be doing that again. There's no point trying to stake a claim, everyone around here knows I grow flowers and nothing else, especially not chickens. I turn about and slowly walk back as the men depart, each with a jaunty stride.

'Don't ever ditch chicken manure again – it's the best you can get, and you get it for free,' I scold her. 'The Far Siders will be offering to carry it away for you if they find out who was daft enough to ditch such goodness.'

'Sorry, I didn't know.'

'And what's more unforgivable is that you're using polythene bags, not hessian – how long d'you think they're going to lie in landfill?'

'Again, I'm sorry. I have no idea what I'm supposed to use. There's so much that no one mentions but expects you to know around here.'

I hear her complaint; I just don't know the solution.

'Don't worry, just start thinking about the environment – in time, you'll be advising others of the "dos and don'ts" – we've all been there, lassie.'

She gives a weak smile in reply; Tommy's girl's spirit is definitely waning.

'There you go, a nice bowl of beef and tatty stew,' I say, entering Ned's office carrying a tray.

'Dottie, you didn't have to do that,' he says, surprised by my entrance, as it's gone seven o'clock. 'Though I'm glad you have.'

'I assume you haven't eaten, as your kitchen hasn't been touched or dirtied. I made it for my tea, so I've brought you a portion. There's no point us both eating alone. Here, eat it while it's hot,' I urge, setting two places at the conference table.

Ned does as he's told, flopping into the chair opposite me without objection. He's knackered. I can see it in his eyes and the way he slumps down.

'That bad?' I say, offering him a hunk of fresh bread, before buttering my own.

'There are days I can't see the wood for the trees, Dottie. The tenants are great, they ensure they stick to their agreements, the flow of capital is steady, but each week brings me nearer to making a decision. I don't want to be the generation that has to fold, when every other generation has found a way through the mire.'

I've heard it all before: the repair costs, the designated acres of farmland, pastures and woodland. Nothing changes – except his weariness. I have no ideas or suggestions so do the only thing I can: I listen.

'Anyway, what's new with your allotment neighbour, Jemima?' he asks, after ten minutes of venting between mouthfuls. 'I saw her scrubbing her chicken coop earlier. She was donning her yellow Marigolds, a decorating mask and goggles, and she had the duckling poking its beak from her jacket hood. She did look a sight; it took all my self-control not to laugh out loud.'

'Tommy's girl? Well, it looks like she's wilting under the constant criticism of her rookie errors. She threw chicken muck into the communal skip. Can you believe it?'

'A second skip?'

'Yes, delivered today and it's full already. The amount of junk that litters our site is unbelievable but, hey, the committee are happy to organise skips if they're used.'

'I bet you gave her what for?'

'I did, but I felt bad afterwards. Her face crumpled and her chin went a bit wobbly. I think she needs a lift, otherwise she'll be upping and offing.'

Ned sits back from his empty plate and stretches. 'Don't we all. Though upping and offing isn't much of an option for some of us.'

'Mmmm. The other woman, Melissa, is getting along nicely. She's hired a sodding goat to clear the weeds. What a palaver!'

'From the Far Side guy?'

'Yes, sadly. Henry.'

Ned shakes his head. 'I'm not fond of the likes of them,' he mutters. 'They aren't your typical allotment holders, are they?'

'No, there's something about a couple of them. Friday, they were smoking that funny stuff again. It gives me a headache by the end of the night, despite them doing it outside.'

'Is that not the double gins you favour?' teases Ned.

'Oi, less of your cheek, please. I was busy talking the new ladies into entering the festival day. Melissa is all for it, but again, Jemima seems less taken with the idea.'

'Look at you, taking them under your wing.'

'I am. We need fresh blood to join. It helps everyone when all the plots are occupied and our community comes alive.'

'You're right. You are the epitome of a mother hen, Dottie.'

'Mmmm, any chance of you helping out more?'

'I doubt it. I'm happy staying in the background, without others knowing my history or my connection. Leave me with my bees, Dottie – it's the least you can do.'

'Do me a favour then; start being a little more social when you attend. A word or two of encouragement goes a long way.'

'Deal.'

Melissa

I struggle to unlock the padlock and fiddle with the gate catch. My arms are filled with odds and sods generously given to me by Old Bill. I'd only gone to ask him what comfrey tea was – everyone here swears by it and mentions it on a daily basis. I suspected the locals were drinking it, not feeding it to their plants. I never expected he'd give me a ball of string larger than a football, dozens of unopened seed packets and several wooden dibbers. Finally, I ease the gate open with my foot before squeezing through to bump it closed with my arse.

I freeze at the sight before me: an empty allotment. Dropping my armful of goodies to the ground, I dash around my partly weed-free plot, hoping to see a shaggy brown and beige back. I don't; Nanna's not here.

'Nanna! Nanna!'

No answer. Not a chomp, a hoofed tread or a curious narrow face inquisitively popping up amongst the nettles and brambles. 'Good grief, I've lost Henry's goat, he'll kill me.'

The long leash.

I squat amongst the remaining weeds, blindly feeling for the length of tethered leash to which I hope she is still attached. The leash is lifeless. There's no tugging, jolting or snaking as it lies, slack and abandoned, amongst the foliage. What I wouldn't give to have a lively goat cartwheeling on the other end! In a half-bent doubled-up stance, I continue to search, calling her name as I follow the leash here, there and everywhere through the dense bush. Has she strangled herself while I was away? Am I going to find a weighty goat collapsed in the semi-jungle? The panic in me is rocketing sky high as my head bumps into the wire fencing separating my plot from Kaspar's. I follow the leash along the wire fencing . . . until I reach the hole. A hole! I didn't know there was a hole in the fencing. Let alone one big enough to allow a fully grown goat through, without a set of allotment keys – such a breech in security, Mungo will go mad! And there she is, in the middle of Kaspar's allotment patch, standing amongst his bathroom suite. Nanna plunges her face into Kaspar's bidet to begin nibbling at his colourful pansies – which probably taste better than my offerings. How do I get her back? Thankfully, Kaspar never comes here at this time of day; I have only one option.

'Oh no, not his pride and joy! Please stop or he'll string me up alongside his flag!'

I'm stunned to see the goat stop chewing, turn about and view my ungainly position, poking my head through the gap in the fence.

Ah bless, she's listening to me. 'Good girl, come to me.'

At the sound of my voice Nanna slowly trots towards me, only to be tempted by the passing produce. She buries her muzzle determinedly into the urinal trough and its fresh offerings: Kaspar's freshly planted nasturtium plugs.

Crawling on all fours, I carefully squeeze my shoulders through the gap. My aim is not to spook her but to gently draw nearer, employing a hand-over-fist motion and keeping low to the ground, until I manage to grab hold of her bridle strapping.

My animal rescue starts well as I attach the leash and give it a firm pull. My plan appears to be working as Nanna staggers sideways, her mechanical mouth still chomping. It's so simple, it's laughable! Nanna draws closer to my plot by taking a fourth and fifth sidestep – only three more steps needed, and she'll be home and dry. Kaspar need never know. Or rather, he might spot the chewed damage but he'll never know it was my fault.

Suddenly, Nanna stops munching. With a jerky head motion she surveys the surrounding patch, taking a liking to foliage a little way off. 'No!' In seconds, my excess of coiled leash is slipping through my hands like a child's kite taking flight in a hurricane.

'Nanna!' I shout, my frustration getting the better of me. 'No, you can't have a free-for-all buffet selection of Kaspar's winter produce!'

I dig the toes of my wellington boots into the hardened soil and yank as forcefully as I can. She instantly counteracts my force with her own. Sadly, there's a huge difference in strength, with an additional advantage being the leverage afforded by Nanna's hooves. Obviously, four hooves are better than two legs!

I am unceremoniously dragged forwards through the hole in the fence to land with my chin upon the bare earth and my arms stretched from their sockets. 'This is crazy, you're not winning this battle, Nanna!' I yank the leash ten times harder than previously, thrusting my body backwards and reversing at speed, with the horrifying result that my shirt hem snags on the wire fencing above my back and, as my frame bolts backwards, my snagged shirt remains firmly attached. The end result being a complete disrobing of my torso. My arms are stuck fast in my sleeves as my shirt is wrenched forward over my shoulders and head, and pulled partway along my forearms, trapping me inside a fabric tunnel of my own shirt turned inside out.

Good grief, which bra did I put on this morning?

I'm praying it's the new white lacy number – which was a 'costly but I'm worth it' bra – but sadly, I know it's the freshly washed greying white bra, long overdue for being turfed out but 'hey, I'll keep it for my allotment days' bra. Boy, what a mistake that was.

I attempt to free myself but simply make matters worse as the wire snags at various other points. I release the goat leash; Nanna has won. Having revealed my underwear to all and sundry, I might as well go the whole hog and yank my hands free – but for the cuffs, which are tightly buttoned. I daren't move for fear of impaling myself on the jagged fence wires protruding near my skin.

Give me strength, this can't be happening! I want to be at home baking cookies, nursing babies and creating a happy family life. Instead, I'm on all fours, arse in the air, in just my second week at the allotment. The council woman certainly didn't mention the likelihood of this happening when I paid my annual fees.

I have no option but to yell.

'Help!' I squeal like a pig.

'What the hell are you doing?' says a male voice, approaching me from behind.

'Does my arse look big in this?' I say, instantly regretting my reliance upon humour.

'Errr, from this angle, yeah!' he says, before furthering my humiliation by laughing.

'Levi?'

'Yep, that's me.'

I'm relieved that someone has answered my wailing but want to curl up and die just a tad more. Why could it not be my lucky day? Mungo or Old Bill – better still, if it were Dottie or Jemima.

'Can you untangle me, please – Nanna's got through the fencing.'

'I can see that. But worst still, so can Kaspar . . . here he comes.'

I look up and peer along the tunnel of fabric to see our very own bathroom expert storming along his pathway in his yellow waders, yelling in his mother tongue. I don't understand a single word, but I gather from his wild gesturing that he's not a happy bunny.

'I'm sorry,' is the only phrase I utter for the next fifteen minutes as two men manhandle a kicking goat back through a hole while I grapple with my shirt, covering my greying bra – which will definitely be going into the dustbin tonight.

'Thanks for your help,' I say to Levi, once the drama has passed.

Kaspar has returned to his usual polite self, and a hefty knot has helped to shorten Nanna's leash.

'I suggest you return that goat asap.'

'But what about the weeds? She's made a huge difference in just a few days. I can't borrow your polytunnel until my plot is cleared.'

'Don't worry, I'll make some arrangements. Simply get her returned to Henry. You might think about owing Kaspar a favour,' says Levi, preparing to leave.

'It was unfortunate, but it was an accident – I didn't do it on purpose.'

'Seriously, folks around here don't forget. You might just want to make him an offering of some kind – bake him a cake or, better still, compliment him by asking for his condensed milk cookie recipe.'

I'm bemused. An IOU favour – really?

'Are you joking? Doesn't my impromptu striptease count for anything?'

'Nope. You'll learn how it is around here – all the newcomers do, eventually.'

Chapter Eleven

May

Highi 11°
Low: 6°

Daylight: 16.5 hours
Rain: 10 days
Wind: 15 mph

Note: The tourists have arrived, yet again! As always, they're shocked to find
we've actually got Shetland ponies! You'd think they were related to unicorns,
the way some folk act. Walked the cliff top early this morning and the sea pinks are
like a carpet in full bloom — like confetti strewn amongst the craggy rock. Beautiful.

Dottie

'Jemima!' I call, knowing she's tending to her girls.

'Morning, Dottie, you're here bright and early.'

'Yep, we've got a mission. Levi has requested that everyone donates an hour of their day to help Melissa with her weeding. Are you up for it?'

'I thought she'd hired a goat last month.'

'Mmmm, least said soonest mended, methinks. What do you say? One hour? Two hours? It'll help her out no end,' I say, tugging on her heart strings.

'OK, I can do that. When?'

'Today – now, in fact. She's providing bacon butties at ten o'clock, so make sure you're around, otherwise you'll miss a well-earned treat!' I turn about, with not a minute to lose; I've got so many allotments to visit.

'It's only just gone seven o'clock, Dottie.'

'I know, we're trying to rustle up a weeding party for the day. Head on over as sooner as you can. I'd take your gloves with you. Bye.'

Swift, sharp and sweet is how it needs to be. Otherwise, allotment folk start asking questions and making excuses about their busy lives, their commitments and family responsibilities. The truth of the matter is, you need to repay the help and guidance you've received since you arrived on this site. End of.

I swiftly close Jemima's front door and move to the next plot in search of support.

After numerous hours, my fingers are aching and my back needs stretching, but we're getting there. I pause to admire the growing patch of earth creeping along Melissa's plot. The goat may have started the job, but it looks like us allotment holders will finish it.

The usuals are helping out: Levi, Mungo and even Old Bill are scattered amongst the many other helpers. I'm pleased to see so many have volunteered their time.

'Kaspar, what have you brought?' I ask, spying a new arrival sneaking through Melissa's gate at half nine.

'I had spare nasturtium plugs and some unopened seeds, which I thought she might like,' says Kaspar, offering them to Melissa, who is bent double yanking at a dandelion root.

'Bless you, especially after the goat incident,' she says, straightening up and blushing profusely.

'You're welcome. Levi keeps stressing that Nanna's escape was an accident. I can finally laugh about it. Now, where is it you need me?'

I can't help but smile. This is the very fabric of an allotment site. I cajoled eleven people into giving up an hour of their day to help another plot holder, though many should have left by now. In time, I'll expect Melissa to do the same when she's established.

'Kaspar, can you start over on the far end, bagging up what others have pulled up?' I instruct, knowing that the quicker someone starts composting this foliage the better.

'Dottie, does everyone always share excess produce on the allotments?' calls Jemima, a short distance from my weeding spot.

'Always. Why keep something purely for the sake of keeping it? It'll go past its best before you know it. Kaspar has always been pretty good like that. You wait until the peak summer; folk walk about offering up cabbages, broccoli, even tubs of vegetable soup, in an effort not to waste what they've grown.'

'Why isn't there a central hub then . . . like a swap shop?' she asks, a quizzical expression upon her brow. 'Wouldn't that save people time walking the site offering their goods?'

Why has no one suggested that before?

I stand tall, stretch my back and say the only thing that comes to mind. 'You need to show us how that would work then, Jemima.'

'To me, it makes sense to have a central point where folk can drop off their excess, be it seeds, plugs or comfrey tea. Some people might even choose to donate a few pennies for what they receive. Wouldn't that be a worthy system?'

She's got her head screwed on, for sure; I can hear Tommy's common sense coming through.

'Do you know I found large two pumpkins stashed inside my shed?' she says.

'I'm not surprised. Your daa used to store his veg well, to help preserve its lifespan.

'All week, I've been Googling to see what I could make. I didn't know you could make pumpkin chutney, did you?'

I shake my head.

'If I make jars of pumpkin chutney, I could walk the site offering it to people or, if we had a central hub, they could drop by and pick it up. Either way, the concerted effort Grandpop put into nurturing those pumpkins will be valued and eaten, rather than wasted.'

I want to cry. In forty years of attending this allotment, we've never had someone offer such a constructive and creative idea!

'Why don't you ask Mungo about the old shed which sits alongside The Cabbage Patch?' I offer, not wishing to dampen her enthusiasm. 'It hasn't been used in years but he'll have keys for it, I'm sure.'

Jemima's face lights up. 'I might just do that,' she says, wrenching a weed, complete with roots, from the compacted soil. 'Though given the size of my kitchen, it'll take me a month of Sundays to make jars of chutney.'

'Phuh! Don't let that stop you. I can organise a kitchen or two for you, I'm sure.'

'Really?'

'Yeah, I've got my sources,' I say, giving her a wink.

Instantly, her spirit lifts – I've accidently tapped into something which brings Tommy's girl alive before my eyes.

'Is Mungo on site?' she asks, eager to proceed.

'Probably, but I wouldn't go looking now, I think the bacon butties are on their way.' I nod towards Melissa, collecting her car keys to drive the short distance to the local café.

'Kaspar got his timing right,' she says, rolling her eyes to the sky.

'Funny that. Ask Mungo about keys and I'll ask about kitchens,' I say, fearing her enthusiasm may fade. Though it won't hurt for me to ask Mungo too.

Jemima

'I'm not sure about this idea, young lady . . . it seems a bit free and easy for the likes of us,' says Mungo, having difficulty undoing the padlock on the shed positioned near the social shack.

I don't answer. I feel I've explained my request most eloquently. Dottie seems game, so why not Mungo?

'Anyway, this is it. As I told you, it is hardly large,' says Mungo on releasing the padlock and, finally, opening the door.

'It's much bigger than my potting shed, and that holds loads,' is my only remark. I peer inside, to be greeted by large cobwebs, an inch of dusty soil and a selection of junk leaning in the far corner. 'It'll be perfect after I've cleaned it out and begged some shelving from the others.'

'From who?'

'I don't know, but someone will have spare shelving – I've got no intention of paying.'

'I doubt you'll get shelving donated.'

'Mungo, you and I know that there's loads of wood hoarded on this site – can you put the word out that I'm looking for wood, shelving brackets and someone handy with a drill?'

'I don't know if—'

'Mungo, will you just do your thing, please? Otherwise, I'll pin a request on the notice board in The Cabbage Patch,' I say, continuing to recce my new project. 'Can I also get a spare key for this place?'

'That might be tricky. Old Bill wants a tighter inventory on keys.'

'Seriously?' I whip round to stare him out. How bloody ridiculous! I have a legitimate reason, and he's stalling. 'In that case, can you please make sure you're here each morning at six o'clock to open up, and then return at seven o'clock each evening to lock up for me. Cheers.'

Mungo's expression drops, before he makes a stuttering protest, but I continue to talk.

'I could do with an offcut of lino too – so if you hear of any, let me know.' I enter the shed, striding about my new domain. 'I'm thinking of naming it The Veggie Rack – for which we'll need a sign. What do you think?' Not that I'm interested in Mungo's opinion; it's obvious my new idea is grating on his nerves.

'Here.' He pushes the padlock and inserted key into my hand. 'Don't lose it – and don't give anyone else a copy.'

'Cheers, Mungo.' Result!

He shuffles off towards The Cabbage Patch, probably to complain about my curt manner.

I spend all day sweeping, scrubbing and nailing things into position inside my new shack. Crispy duck sleeps in his straw nest, secure inside the wicker carrier now that he's grown a little and can't readily escape. By the time Kaspar arrives carrying a roll of red lino, I'm fit to drop but his arrival renews my energy.

'I heard you needed flooring – I was wondering if this might do the job?'

'Perfect. Any chance you're offering to spend thirty minutes laying it?' I give my sweetest smile, then chuckle at my own cheekiness, but if you don't ask around here you don't get anywhere.

'I hadn't planned on it but . . . go on then.'

I pull the same stunt when Ned strolls past later.

'Ned, do you own a drill?' I call after him.

'Yes, thanks.'

'Great. Can you spare fifteen minutes helping me to put these shelves up?'

Fifteen minutes was a definite understatement – it took him twenty minutes to fetch his toolbox, but still.

'Dottie mentioned that you're interested in using the large kitchen at the manor,' he says, unpacking his tools upon his return. I didn't expect conversation, given his usual temperament.

'I want to make pumpkin chutney, then offer it for sale in here,' I say, pleased that Dottie is as true as her word. 'I didn't realise you had links too.'

'Yeah, as the estate manager. Dottie cleans a couple of days a week, so she asked me earlier. She mentioned this was entirely your idea.'

'I'm proud to say she's right there. Why walk the site offering produce when this saves time? And people can donate a handful of change, if they choose. I'm happy to donate the proceeds from my chutney, making it a community project,' I say, adding, 'I promise to clean up after myself, the family won't even know I've been.'

His eyebrows lift as I fall silent.

'I can't promise anything.'

'Cheers, I'd appreciate it. I imagine their ovens are huge.'

'Yep, old but huge.'

Within the hour, Ned has secured numerous brackets and I've loaded each one with the donated shelving which has been dropped off throughout the day.

After nearly ten hours, I'm giving the new lino a final wash before going home. On all fours, creating soapy circular motions, I glance up to view a fully functioning allotment shop – without it costing a penny.

'Wow! You've been a busy bee!' exclaims Melissa, from the doorway, a look of surprise etched on her face.

'I can't believe it either, but I used Mungo's talents to get what I needed – and ta-da!'

'Are you opening tomorrow?'

'I imagine so. There's no point delaying it, is there?'

'Anything you need?'

'Only a frontage sign, but that can wait.'

Melissa leans back to view the shed's small window, before speaking. 'I'll make you a ceramic sign to sit along the window ledge.'

'That would be great, if you could.'

'Think of it as my contribution. What's with the plastic tubs on each shelf?' asks Melissa, lingering in the entrance.

'Honesty boxes: you deliver your spare produce, and later that day nip by to collect the offerings left by those who've purchased anything.'

Melissa gives a knowing smile.

'What?' I ask, grabbing my handbag and flicking the light switch off.

'And you think folk are going to be honest?'

I close the shed door, Crispy inside my jacket hood, and begin fiddling with the rusty padlock.

'Yeah, I do. Look how many people have dropped by today to donate wood, old screws, brackets and even the tubs. I have faith that there remains a level of honesty and decency in this community. It'll be fine, you just watch.' I withdraw the key and give the padlock a tug, ensuring it's secure.

Melissa

'Can you just tell me what to do?' I ask, as Levi finishes erecting the small polytunnel which he's kindly lending me. I can't believe the transformation since the weeding party worked their magic.

He walks the patch of prepared earth for the umpteenth time, shaking his head. It has taken weeks to weed, dig and hoe this section – not to mention Nanna's heroic contribution – to reveal pristine bare earth. Sadly, Levi doesn't seem impressed. Whereas I'm overwhelmed by the effort required; it has changed my hands from an artist's soft fingers with a French manicure to the calloused hands of a seasoned labourer with ragged cuticles.

'It's not that easy, Melissa.'

'Not. That. Easy,' I repeat, slow and terse.

Levi looks up and pulls a face.

'Right, please stop pacing and listen ... I have waited two years for this allotment and all because I had a little dream in my head. And that dream started as a child when I watched the *Blue Peter* garden and saw the presenter make a little drill with a plastic dibber into carefully weeded soil. Now, correct me if I am wrong, but this is definitely weed-free soil, isn't it?' I say, pointing dramatically at the patch before us.

'It is.'

I lift my palm, gesturing; he resumes his silence.

'Now, after making the long drill, the adult on TV opened a packet of tiny seeds and, after showing them to camera, pinched them and scattered them along the waiting drill line – and then guess what they did?'

Levi nods slowly, following my dream instructions.

'They covered the tiny seeds with soil and watered them in. Now, is that something I could do on my allotment?'

'It is, but not if you're wanting prize-winning carrots.'

'What?'

Levi opens his mouth to explain but thinks twice about it.

'Who said I want prize-winning carrots? I don't. I just want a row – no, make that two rows – of regular carrots which I can slice, dice and grate for a salad, a roast dinner or crunch just as they are. That's all I want. I don't want freaky metre-long ones, tabloid-humorous shaped ones, or even purple, yellow, red or white ones!'

Levi smiles.

'Yes, believe me, I've done extensive homework on this subject. I didn't even know carrots came in other colours, let alone with a range of names. At forty-two, I've finally learnt all about carrots. Is there anything else I should know?'

'You'd be better off growing something a little more—'

'I give up. Seriously, what is the problem with carrots? Mungo reacts in the same way each time I mention them.'

Levi smirks and then attempts to straighten his features.

'Come on, spill the beans,' I urge, watching Levi attempt to stay silent by rolling his lips together and forcing the words to remain inside.

'You promise, you won't say a word.'

'Pinky promise,' I say, grabbing his little finger and awkwardly shaking it; I'm frantic to hear a smidgen of gossip about the Mighty Mungo.

'I don't know exactly when this was, probably decades ago, as I've been here since I was a child, and it was before then. Anyway, he entered a bunch of carrots in the allotment festival, and the judges duly awarded him first prize. But an altercation occurred when another entrant objected to the award, claiming that Mungo had switched his carrots with their display. Apparently, a naturally occurring notch on their carrot proved it was theirs. Mungo was stripped of his prize, and so began his lifelong objection to carrots.'

'No way! An identifying notch? What the hell!'

Levi nods.

'Excuse me, sir, but that natural notch there belongs to my allotment – honest, I can prove it!' I mimic, holding a pretend carrot up for Levi to inspect before tugging my forelock.

'It's not funny, they take it very seriously.'

'Obviously – his dislike of carrots has lasted a lifetime.'

'The Far Siders have paid the price.'

'The objecting plot holder was a Far Sider?'

'Well, not a current one, that complainant is long gone, but yeah, their allotment was on that side of the site. That's when the battle lines were drawn, and have remained firmly entrenched ever since.'

'It's too funny for words.'

'You should be grateful to be given an allotment on our side and not theirs.'

'I'm so relieved. Do you think he did it?'

'I couldn't possibly say,' mutters Levi, withdrawing from our sharing experience.

'Come on, you must have a theory.'

Levi shrugs again.

'Ah ha, that's not on. I reckon he switched the carrots. Mungo might be an upstanding man of the allotment committee now, but we all do stupid stuff when we're younger – and he's spent a lifetime reliving his mistake.'

'The only thing Mungo regrets is not chancing his luck with Dottie when they were youngsters.'

'Noooooooooooo!'

'Yeah, they're still dancing around each other at eighty-odd. It's cute in one way, but bloody annoying in another.'

'I assumed he was a widower?'

'Nah, neither one has ever married. She had a fiancé once, but he was killed in a motorbike accident. We're talking over sixty years ago.'

I give Levi a wry smile.

'You're asking for trouble, messing with the committee trio – you know that, don't ya?' His voice is stern.

'Yeah, but we won't let that stop us, will we?' I say, giving him a cheeky wink.

Chapter Twelve

Dottie

At the entrance gate, I'm greeted with the commotion caused by an allotment freebie: wood chippings. The delivery truck is positioned at the far end of the car park, tipping its load. An amazing whooshing sound fills the air as the pile spills like a torrent of water on to the gravel patch. A short distance away, not far back enough for my liking, is a line of eager allotmenteers armed with their shovels and wheelbarrows, ready to nab their allocation. I've no problem with their eagerness, more their judgement. In the past, some people have proved to be utterly selfish with what is essentially a free gift from the local tree surgeon.

'Afternoon!' I holler, approaching the group. Their expressions drop somewhat on seeing a member of the committee arrive. 'Now, remember, we'd all like a fair portion, so I ask that you be generous with your neighbours. Not everyone has the opportunity to be here in the middle of the afternoon.'

'Fair's fair, Dottie. I suggest we each take a barrow and then deliver one elsewhere, before taking another for ourselves,' shouts Kaspar, eyeing the others cautiously.

'That's very generous, Kaspar. A sensible solution which I believe everyone can uphold.'

Kaspar squares his chest and shoulders, as the others give him sideways glances.

The driver gives a big thumbs-up before jumping into his cab and pulling away from the mountain of wood chippings.

I smile politely, knowing what's about to occur. I appreciate the generosity of donating their waste product; its biodegradable and makes excellent mulch around our produce. But boy, does it cause us issues each time we accept a delivery!

The assembled crowd doesn't wait but surges forward, circling the base of the mountain and beginning to shovel the chippings as quick as you like. Within minutes, the first wheelbarrow is full and its owner happily trundles off towards the far side of the site as another person jumps into his standing space, to shovel at speed.

Before heading off towards my allotment, I note who's present; they've all heard Kaspar's generous suggestion.

As I walk, I phone Mungo and Old Bill.

'It's me . . .' I explain about the delivery, the frantic shovelling, and Kaspar's excellent suggestion benefitting absent parties.

Mungo complains that the delivery is early. Old Bill moans that others shouldn't be organising solutions, only committee members. I don't argue; it seemed reasonable to me.

I continue busying myself with my own tasks. There's not enough hours in the day at present. I haven't changed my allotment patterns or dusting hours, and yet everything seems to be slipping – not that anyone else would notice. I'm usually ahead of the game, but this year I seem to be three tasks behind and playing catch-up. Maybe it's the committee involvement, the newbies taking up my time, or perhaps I'm beginning to feel my age. I chuckle to myself; *phuh!* That'll be the day!

Today's main task is to add a little extra compost and manure to each root mound, which'll nourish the developing shoots. However many years I have been doing this I still feel such satisfaction and anticipation for my beautiful blooms.

I look out across the young green foliage and imagine a glorious sea of rainbow petals, like every previous year. I'll be happy to welcome such sights again. If I close my eyes, I know what September will look like – if I can get my jobs done.

'Dottie, do you want a barrowful?'

I turn to find Kaspar at my allotment gate with a wheelbarrow of chippings.

'I wouldn't say no!' I call back.

'Here you go then ... I'll go back for some more.' Kaspar manoeuvres his barrow in and along the path. 'Where do you want these dumping?'

Bless him.

'Just there is fine, thank you.' I gesture towards a central position which will save my legs when I get around to that task.

'If you're sure,' he says, tipping up the load where specified. 'If I get time to bring you another, is that alright by you?'

'It certainly is, though make sure others get their fair share too, Kaspar.'

'Dottie, you worry too much.'

I nod. If he'd been around here for close on forty years, he'd know what I know about human beings: they're yamse. Some want to harvest more than they sow!

I've been gardening longer than planned, so I'm just taking a minute to admire my handiwork when Mungo charges through my gate, bouncing it off the hinges.

'I thought you said the delivery had arrived!'

'It has.'

'Where?' Mungo spreads his hands wide; his annoyance is sky high and his rudeness not far behind.

'Mungo, you must be blind, man. Seriously, you must have walked through the car park to get this far.'

'Where, I ask you?'

'What?'

I march him along the track faster than my legs have moved in years. I'm fuming. My annoyance is growing with each step – because if what I think has occurred again has actually occurred, then I am going to be the committee member who performs a hissy-fit in the middle of The Cabbage Patch.

On reaching the car park, I understand his confusion.

The corner of the car park is empty. Gone is the mountain of wood chippings: no allotmenteers armed with shovels, and not a wheelbarrow in sight.

I stand open-mouthed.

'See what I mean?'

'Unbelievable!' I search the gravel for any evidence to prove that I'm not going around the twist. 'The pile was up there and out to here,' I gesture. 'And the vultures have devoured it in less than ninety minutes; not a single speck remains.'

'You had me worried there.'

'This is past a joke!' I say in disbelief.

'I hear you. Can you remember who was present?'

'Me, Kaspar . . . quite a few from the far side, a couple from our side – the usual afternoon crowd.'

Mungo nods, he knows them all.

'I'm not having this, Mungo. Seriously, I'm not. The likes of Jemima and Melissa haven't even got a look-in – nor Levi, come to think of it – and they could probably do with a small pile of mulch to start off their plots. It's shocking. I've got a good mind to . . .' I cease chattering as words fail me, but actions don't. 'Come on. Let's take a stroll.'

It doesn't take long to wander the track, clocking numerous piles of wood chippings decorating various plots on our side. Outside a couple of locked gates there's a small pile delivered by a kind soul who took Kaspar's suggestion to heart.

'That's nice to see,' I say, pointing as we pass.

As we wander along the far side the evidence is clear.

'Look at those hessian bags,' says Mungo, gesturing to a corner of one plot. 'Stashing it for future use, do you reckon?'

'It's evident that they've take multiple barrowloads.' I'm disgusted. 'What's fair about that?'

'I'm not surprised.'

'I am. If I thought they'd be this yamse, I would have stayed to witness what they each had. I bet Kaspar didn't take more than his fair share. Some folk give to this allotment site whilst others just take, take, take.'

'I'll give the tree surgeon a call and ask if we can have a second delivery for those who have missed out, but that's all I can do.'

'Is it, Mungo? As a committee member, I don't think that's good enough. We need to take action.' We circle the allotment site and arrive back at my gate.

'Dottie.'

'Don't you "Dottie" me. I mean it. Just because I'm fragile, older than most women here. I'm offended by their yamse behaviour. And it happened on my watch, while my back was turned!'

'There's not a lot you can do, other than appeal to their better nature.'

'Humph! Some people around here don't have a "better nature", from what I'm seeing. Mungo, I'll be dealing with this one. I'll show them what true recycling is, you mark my words!'

Jemima

Crispy duck and I arrive at the allotment site thirty minutes earlier than usual; I can't wait to open The Veggie Rack. I haven't a thing to sell – but still, someone is bound to provide a small offering to grace the shelves. Last night, after arriving home, I'd typed, printed and laminated a set of instructions on how to be a seller or a customer, highlighting the use of the honesty boxes.

'Morning!' calls Dottie, as I approach. She's holding three bunches of fresh flowers, and a plastic bucket sits at her tiny feet. 'I was wondering where you were. Can I offer these gerberas for sale?'

'Of course, you can. I'm early, I'll be with you in a jiffy.'

Within seconds, I've unlocked and Dottie has arranged her flowers in the water bucket.

'You'll need one of these,' I say, offering her an honesty tub. 'Make sure you drop by later today and collect what's been left. It might not be much but it'll be something towards your efforts.'

'I'm not expecting much, Jemima. A few coins will cover it for me. I simply relish the idea that anyone can have my flowers in their lounge, without me having to traipse the site offering them to everyone I spot.' Her apple cheeks are flushed, adding a sparkle to her watery blue eyes.

'Even so, you'd pay a fiver for a bunch that size in most florists, Dottie – a couple of quid won't go amiss, will it?'

I'm thrilled to bits that Dottie is my first vendor. I wedge open the shed door and pin my laminated instructions upon it. Within minutes, I find Kaspar eagerly reading every word.

'I brought spare garlic bulbs,' he announces on entering, pulling several intricately plaited strings from his bag.

I show him to a shelf, offer him a plastic tub and leave him to unload his produce.

Within half an hour, there's much coming and going as various allotment holders bring packets of unopened seeds, small bottles of comfrey tea and balls of twine. Each one sets up home for the day on a shelf – and within no time, there's the sound of change being dropped into plastic tubs. I stand in the corner and marvel at the speed with which the shelves fill as allotment folk, many of whom I've only spied at the meeting or in the car park, enter for a mooch around and leave after delivering a small donation.

'I needn't ask how's it going,' says Ned, drawing me from my dizzy trance.

'I'm shocked, just look at it. I couldn't have asked for a better turnout, could I?'

'Any chance of leaving a few jars of honey?' he says, indicating the cardboard box he's carrying.

'Sure, find a free shelf and away you go – make sure your honesty box sits directly in front, if you're sharing a shelf.' Despite watching the flow of traffic, I hadn't realised there is very little empty space remaining.

While he displays his goods, I take a walk around and view the honesty boxes. I'm delighted to see that people haven't been miserly – which I'm sure will delight the vendors. Dottie's flower bucket is empty but for the water – she'll be thrilled when she sees seven £1 coins gracing her tub.

Melissa

'Here we are,' I say, entering The Veggie Rack, my arms bulging. 'Scarecrows of various sizes, colours and, I'm proud to say, genders.'

'That's quite a surprise,' says Dottie, greeting me from her sturdy chair.

'Not really, Dottie. We have girls, boys and gender neutral – I like to please everyone.' I drop my goodies on to the counter and hold each aloft as I speak. 'There's one large, several midi and quite a few mini ones at knee height. Priced at twenty, ten and five pounds accordingly.'

'Regardless of gender?'

'Yeah, everyone's equal in my book, Dottie. I've used far more fabric in the frilly petticoats, and several skeins of wool for the plaited hair, but let's keep life simple!'

'I suggest you claim the corner spot. They're not likely to fit on a shelf, are they?' instructs Dottie, moving a mop and bucket from said spot. 'Let me give it a sweep before you begin displaying your goods.'

I stand by, as proud as a new mum, while she hastily stands up and tidies the corner spot, collecting the minuscule pile of dirt in a shiny new dustpan.

'There, that's better. I'd empty your honesty pot as often as you can. With one or two sales there could be a fair bit for you to take home,' warns Dottie, as I stand my crowd of scarecrows in a pleasing arrangement.

'I'm sure they'll be fine. Folk around here give away so much to each other – I doubt anyone would rob me of a few quid.'

Dottie gives me a knowing look.

'Ah no, Dottie, even the Far Siders are OK, really – they wouldn't touch anything that wasn't theirs.'

'Mark my words, if certain things aren't nailed down around here, they'll go walkabout.'

I need to make a stance; I need to believe in the innate goodness of people.

'I'll take my chance – if they steal from me, they're obviously desperate and need the cash more than I do,' I say, voicing my stance on human nature.

Dottie says nothing, but grabs a spare honesty box and places it before my assembled crowd.

'Morning, ladies,' calls Mungo, entering The Veggie Rack. 'Are these new today?'

'Yes, for those of us who prefer a traditional approach to crow scaring,' I say, making a flourishing gesture towards my corner display.

'Damned silly idea with those heads – looks like a load of guillotined convicts from the olden days, if you ask me.'

'I have your approval then?' I say, sashaying across the floor to squeeze the old bugger's arm.

'Well, not that I'll be buying one. I have my own methods

regarding bird control, but for those that haven't – they might prove useful.'

'Do you hear that, Dottie? Mungo thinks my scarecrows are great!' I say, pulling a comical expression.

'Mungo has a heart of gold, I'll let you know,' says Dottie, tidying the worktop. 'He won't have a bad word said about many folk around here.'

I notice Mungo's cheeks flush a little as he glances towards Dottie, who misses his gesture, too absorbed in her cleaning duties.

Oooo, do I detect a little something between the pair? Well, good luck to them, that's all I have to say.

'I'll be leaving you good folk to your busy day then,' I announce, after several moments of lingering silence.

Chapter Thirteen

Dottie

'Morning!' I call, in a brighter tone than my usual, as I enter The Cabbage Patch for my elevenses, to find several of the Far Siders drinking from lager cans. Haven't they got allotment beds to dig? 'Everyone happy today?' No one answers me; they're miffed, and I know why. 'If anyone knows who owns the hessian sacks littering the car park, can you ask them to collect their belongings, please? I don't want someone having an accident if they snag in a car wheel.'

Silence. I'll bide my time; one of them will answer.

I grab a glass of water from the mini kitchen, knowing that every eye is watching. All mouths seem to be zipped tight. I finish my drink, wash my glass, dry it and replace it in the communal cupboard, before anyone speaks.

'Dottie, do you know how the hessian sacks got there?' asks Henry.

'I'm not entirely sure. They weren't there last night when I left for home.'

'No, but neither was that pile of wood chippings – the car park was cleared yesterday afternoon,' chirps a second fella.

'It was. Mungo has ordered a second delivery.'

'We think the current pile of chippings is the original delivery, collected from allotment plots during the night and unloaded back on to the car park, is that right?'

I shrug. 'I have no idea, fellas. I just know that there was a huge delivery yesterday, and yet by five o'clock there was nothing left.

Now, if you're telling me that the fairies have made a midnight visit to reorganise the distribution of wood chippings, then it's news to me.' I eye each male slowly. These men are naïve about many things in life; thankfully, their respect towards my age and experience isn't one of them. 'But should you find out any information that concerns you, or offends your sense of fairness, please bring it to the committee and I'll be all ears.' I linger for a second, before waving goodbye and leaving The Cabbage Patch. My ears will be burning in no time but I'll survive.

I nip along to Levi's plot as I'm passing.

'Morning, Levi, how are we today?'

'Can't grumble. You?' he says, unfolding a sheeting of black tarpaulin.

'I'm on my best behaviour.' I give him a wink. 'Just wanted to say the Far Siders aren't happy – it appears the wood chip fairies have upset them.'

Levi shakes his head. 'They shouldn't be such greedy sods then. Though if they catch sight of the way Old Bill's staggering today, they'll put two and two together about how he's pulled his back. Those hessian bags weighed a fair amount, and they hoarded them good and proper across several plots.'

'And you?'

'Me? I'm fine. It was worth losing sleep to get one over on the cheeky gits. We made sure you, Jemima and Melissa received an extra barrowload too.'

'And Mungo's had all his spare keys returned?'

'Of course – I daren't not.'

'Thank you, anyway. I owe you one, Levi.'

'No worries, Dottie – you've helped me out enough times.'

'Just mind yourself, because they'll be trying to figure out who and how.'

'Hardly difficult, but they can't prove a thing.'

'Bye now.'

Jemima

Pushing my bike, I reach the car park to find Dottie and Melissa standing stock-still in the middle. Neither woman moves or changes her expression as I draw near; both are fixed as if turned to stone.

'Are you OK?' I call, not wishing to be nosey.

'Shhhhh!' whispers Melissa, her finger drawn tightly to her lip. 'An owl.' She gestures towards the perimeter wall, where a speckled and white owl is perched in broad daylight.

I do a double take – surely that can't be right?

'I've never seen anything so beautiful in my life,' whispers Dottie, peering from beneath her wide brim.

It seems amazing that an exquisite bird of prey would sit calmly and watch us as intently as we watch it.

'Can you believe it?' says Melissa, speaking out of the side of her mouth. 'It must hunt across our allotments each night, yet we didn't even know that it exists.'

'Amazing how nature can exist in such harsh environments – survival and breeding, that's their only aim.'

I'm speechless, frozen in time beside the other two. I stare at the owl; its large orange eyes stare down upon us. Does it sense we won't hurt it? Is it injured?

'I'm taking a photo,' says Melissa, slowly raising her phone.

I need to go home, but if I take a step forward I'll ruin the moment. I sense the deep connection that Dottie is experiencing and Melissa's delight, being at one with nature.

'What's up?' asks Ned, appearing behind us.

Turning in unison, we noisily '*sssshush*' him and point.

'The owl?' He's not impressed.

I glance over my shoulder to witness his quizzical face, complete with knotted brow.

'How long have you all been standing here?'

'Fifteen minutes,' says Dottie, her face beaming.

'Same,' utters Melissa, not averting her eyes from the owl.

'About five minutes,' I add, unsure if my expression matches their delight.

Ned's confusion is clearly apparent.

'I've taken a photo or two,' adds Melissa, tapping her phone. 'I'll print and pin them up inside the social shack.'

'I'm sure everyone will be overjoyed to see them,' mutters Ned sarcastically.

'Ned, it's not every day you see such a sight,' retorts Dottie.

'Every day for at least six months!' he quips. Then adds, 'It's plastic. A fake. I believe it contains the lens for the CCTV cameras.'

Three shocked faces turn in his direction.

'Seriously. That owl has been perched there for months – you can't have seen it move since you've been watching.'

'I swear it has,' says Melissa indignantly.

'You can't have done, it's plastic. Look.' Ned marches to the wall and raises his arm, calling to the owl. '*Tttttchhhhh*, nice birdy, don't peck now.'

The owl doesn't flinch as Ned raps upon the front of its chest, making a resounding sound much like an empty watering can.

'Ladies, I hate to say it, but you've failed your audition for *Springwatch*,' he teases, making his way towards the gate. 'But don't worry, I won't tell a soul!'

'I bet!' calls Dottie.

'I knew it,' splutters Melissa. 'Since when do owls appear in daylight?'

'Come off it, you were suckered in as much as I was,' retorts Dottie.

I remain shtum. I hate to admit, I swallowed it: hook, line and sinker.

Chapter Fourteen

Melissa

'You can have these old dustbins – they've seen better days,' says Mungo gruffly, as he drags two more aluminium bins to join the two he's already delivered to my plot. 'You see, the secret to winning with prize parsnips is the straightness and whiteness of the flesh. There's no point presenting wobbly, knobbly ones which might look humorous but are as tough as Old Nick, once cooked. I presume you'll be donating them afterwards for the evening mash-up.'

My head is spinning. I never asked him to produce four empty dustbins, unwanted advice about parsnips – and now, something about a mash-up.

'Sorry, a what?'

'The mash-up happens on festival night. All the prize-winning produce is cooked and served to the public as soups, curries and hotpots – to show our appreciation for their attendance. Though some people – I won't name names – refuse to contribute. I hope you won't be joining that crowd.' He stares at me indignantly.

I shake my head for fear of the repercussions.

'Fill each of these bins with sharp sand, compact it firmly, so there's very little give or shift.' He is staring intently, making sure that I'm listening to information I don't need; I'm planting carrots. 'This is the tricky bit … you'll need lengths of plastic piping – Levi already has some cut to size from a previous year, though maybe the less said about his parsnips the better.'

Noted.

'Anyway, plunge the piping into the sand and—'

'I'm confused, why aren't they going into the ground?'

Mungo gives me a look of utter contempt, as if mine's the stupidest question ever asked.

'Were you not listening? You're aiming for straightness – that's key! Growing in the ground doesn't offer straightness.'

'What?'

'Phuh! I'll ask Levi to demonstrate. I'll not compromise my standing on the committee,' he explains, before hollering, 'Levi, Levi!'

I stand stock-still; I'm mortified that an older gent would wail like this. But Mungo's method works; Levi comes running along, peering worriedly through my fencing.

'You called?' he asks, taking in the dustbins as he nears.

'Can you show this lady here how to plant prize-winning parsnips?'

'Sure . . . I thought you wanted carrots?'

My doleful expression is begging him to save me.

'Have you got parsnip seedlings to hand?'

I shake my head. The situation is becoming more ridiculous by the minute. I'm about to receive a prize-winning demo about something which I don't eat or want.

'That's a stumbling block,' mutters Mungo.

'Do you think?' I blurt out, wishing I could continue with my allotment tasks.

'I could lend her some . . .'

'Nah, she'll be disqualified if anyone finds out she's borrowed seedlings.'

'Who would ever know?'

Mungo repeatedly taps his chest slowly yet very firmly.

'Fair dos. Melissa, get yourself some seedlings on the go and when they're about this big,' Levi gestures a three-inch size, 'shout and I'll show you what to do with the sand and piping. I've got some cut to size, which you can borrow.'

'See, I told you, didn't I?' adds Mungo, his face glowing with pride.

'You did,' I mutter, wondering how I'm ever going to get three-inch seedlings if I'm not left alone long enough to plant what I wish to. 'Thank you, Levi.'

'No worries. Right, I'll be off.'

The second Levi leaves us, Mungo begins again.

'Get yourself a couple of seed trays on the go – you'll need a variety called "Gladiator", there's no point planting anything else.'

Yet again, I'm nodding like a fool. These folks must think I am utterly stupid; I say very little in their presence, and absorb every word. I want help – I desperately *need* help – but give me the chance to complete a few tasks before bombarding me with more information.

'Right, I didn't realise that you hadn't even started yet. You'll need to get a wiggle on if you want a decent growing season before the festival.'

'I will.' There's no chance any of you will allow me to do anything of my own choosing upon my own allotment. Is this why the previous holder left so quickly? As Mungo bids me goodbye, I chastise myself for being so ungrateful.

I spend the next thirty minutes turning the soil inside the polytunnel, layering it with chicken muck gained from Jemima and, secretly, begin to sow a row of carrots. I'm not telling anyone, not even Levi.

Strange, yet comforting, how the cycle of life quietly evolves and rejuvenates us at each stage. How many years have I been blind to the passing seasons? Each year, moaning about the arrival of a frosty winter; we don't get thick snow in Shetland, but the blustery winds make up for it. I should be embracing the elements as preparation for the coming spring. I complete my sowing, label the row, and am just hunting for my new watering can when my next visitor arrives.

'Hello, how are you today?' calls Dottie, her floppy hat bouncing with each step as she crosses my plot.

Don't stop working! I haven't time to stand and chat any more this morning.

'I'm great. I'm going to carry on as we chat, Dottie. I haven't got a minute to spare.'

'Absolutely, I don't blame you. There's a lot to be said around these parts for never standing still while others talk. Some folk have so much to say, you'll take root if you stand and listen to them all day!'

Isn't that the truth.

Jemima

'Ned!' My fingers curl tightly, holding my wire fencing. I'm sure he can hear me through his bee-keeper's veil. But so far, despite repeating his name, he's not responded. 'Ned!'

I can't imagine it brings Dottie much joy, working alongside him on a shared plot. No wonder she comes across to me and Melissa for a daily chat.

I don't want to start hollering like a market stallholder, so my only other option is to nip around. He can't ignore me then. How can one person blow hot and cold as readily as he does?

I swiftly leave my position and traipse around to Dottie's gate. The sight of her allotment always raises a smile; it seems novel, seeing her cane wigwams and cages waiting to support and protect the delicate tendrils and new shoots. At present, each of her delphiniums has a pile of sand creating a strange molehill and increasing the root ball at base level. I don't understand the whys and wherefores, but I respect Dottie's experience – she knows what's best for her prize-winning blooms.

I approach Ned whilst his back is turned. I don't bother calling again as I stride nearer. Ned's lifting and lowering frames from the open hive, examining each before returning it. I won't give him another chance to blatantly ignore me.

He jumps when I finally tap his shoulder.

'What the devil are you doing?' he snaps, pushing me backwards away from the open hive.

Ned quickly replaces the hive's roof before walking away from the area.

I follow, trying to speak to him. 'I was calling you, and you ...'

Once we're a fair distance away, Ned removes his headgear, dropping it to the ground, and takes out a set of earplugs before staring at me indignantly.

'Oh, I see ... earplugs.' My voice is a whisper, almost apologetic.

'Did you want something?' His dark gaze is glancing between my face and the beehives behind.

'You repeatedly ignored me, so I thought it best to walk around and ... I didn't realise you were wearing those.' I indicate the earplugs.

He turns away, paces a step or two, then doubles back on himself.

'I merely wanted to ask if the arrangements have been made for me at the manor house ... I just thought I'd ask.'

'But that's the problem – you didn't think, did you? You can't just stroll up when the bees have been disturbed, expecting it to be safe. They might be docile, given the smoke I use, but you could have come to serious harm if they'd stung you. I'm fully protected in my bee-keeping suit, and yet you approach without so much as a pair of gardening gloves. That was foolish, Jemima.'

His brooding expression and tone are both stern, as if chastising a small child.

How dare he raise his voice to me!

'Ned!' My heartbeat is racing, my palms are clammy and I'm feeling incredibly warm. Is this another anxiety episode, or a symptom of my growing infatuation with this guy?

'Jemima, I appreciate that you thought I was ignoring you, but I clearly wasn't. I use earplugs to block out some of the distractions that occur down here. But regardless of my manners, you didn't give the bees a thought, or have a care for your own safety. Apologies for sounding terse, but you startled me – and you could have startled the bees.' His tone and expression soften with each sentence he utters.

'Sorry, I just wanted to ask about the arrangements.'

Ned turns away and stares intently at my vacant allotment. I follow his gaze, viewing my own allotment with fresh eyes. My hard work is clearly visible. I cringe, witnessing the clear view afforded of my potting-shed door; any sobbing woman would be visible at all times.

'Ned?'

'Look, I've clarified the details with the family. They're happy for you to spend as much time as you need for the chutney making. I'll gladly accompany you – it'll give me a chance to harvest and jar my honey, emptying some of these frames.'

'You'll be there too?' I say, feeling relieved. That will make things simpler regarding keys and access. But I'm still uneasy and awkward in his company.

'It makes sense if the kitchen is to become a hive of production. I might as well pitch in and nab a corner with my own product. If you don't object, that is.'

'Object?'

'You might. The last thing you planned for was making polite conversation with me all day.'

I'm stunned by his concern.

'That's settled then. I suggest we spend the day there on Friday – I'll call by to collect you and your equipment, it'll save taking two cars.'

'Thank you, plus it'll save time and effort loading up my little car.'

'No worries.'

An awkward silence descends between us, again. The drama seems to have passed; all is calm and peaceful, apart from my racing heartbeat.

'So.' I shuffle on the spot.

'So.'

'I'll be getting back to my own plot. Apologies for disturbing you and your bees. And I'm pretty grateful that they didn't attack me. Next time, I'll be more careful. I promise.'

'Thank you, my bees and I will appreciate that.'

'Bye.'

'See you.

I hastily sidestep him and leave as swiftly as I arrived.

Maybe I misread his signals from our first meeting? He might simply want to be left alone to enjoy his beehives. As I enter my plot, I exhale deeply; I need to sit down. I stride to my potting shed, as casually as I can muster, enter and close the door before sinking down on to my haunches. I assumed I was coping better since arriving here. I hadn't meant to surprise him – but he ignores me at every opportunity, otherwise. I close my eyes tight and focus on steadying my breathing.

One thought concerns me: how are we ever going to get through a day sharing a kitchen together, if every conversation contains such damned awful silences?

Dottie

'Is Jemima on board with the festival?' asks Old Bill, as we gather at my dining-room table, making our annual arrangements.

'She's planted six pumpkin seeds, of which three are strong, healthy and ready to be transferred to her chosen bed,' I say, hoping he's pleased with the detail. 'Levi helped her. Isn't that right, Mungo?'

'Ah, he did that. His laddish good looks seem to be getting him on the right side of all the new ladies recently.' Mungo chuckles at his ribald suggestion.

'Mungo, there's no need!' I quip. 'That's exactly what's wrong nowadays; males and females aren't allowed to be genuine friends without others starting rumours. That's not how it was in our day.'

'In our day, us lads acted like true gents in the presence of young ladies. That's gone out the window, nowadays. Even here on Shetland, the youngsters have reverted to the ways of the mainland. We never did.'

'We never did a lot of things from the mainland, I'll give you that,' jibes Old Bill, tapping his notebook with his pencil.

'Back to it please, fellas, otherwise we'll be here all night,' I say, knowing we can have this festival wrapped up within no time.

I don't need reminding that our youth was spent here in Shetland. I don't regret not leaving – who wants the dust and dirt from city life? But occasionally I marvel at the possibilities which never came my way – or theirs, for that matter. Shetland feels like Mother Nature herself, the ultimate matriarch within my world, and that umbilical cord was never going to be sever-ed. Despite the glorious tales from afar, I was never tempted, anyway; the folk at Lerwick Manor relied upon me to keep their daily lives in order.

'Ned says we can pitch the marquees beside the manor's driveway, like last year. Dottie, can you organise a catering team for the evening mash-up bash, to be served on the terrace patio? I'll organise the beer supply for one of the marquees, plus the entry forms and awards ribbons. Mungo, will you secure three judges via the Scottish Allotments and Garden Society, offering the usual expenses and requirements, please?' Old Bill sits back, ticking tasks off his list. 'Well, that's sorted then.'

'Record time of six minutes, Old Bill ... any chance we can organise next year's too?' I ask, conscious that it took me longer than that to make our mugs of tea.

'I'd rather have a discussion about the Far Siders' antics. To my knowledge, they're harbouring a cockerel and smoking wacky baccy outside The Cabbage Patch. And I hate to point fingers, but we've got tools and equipment missing left, right and centre.'

'I suggest we give them until the festival to change their ways and then push for evictions,' says Mungo, glancing between us.

'I'll second that,' says Old Bill. 'Dottie?'

'I'll go with the committee's decision,' I add, as the peacekeeper of our trio.

'Hee hee, though I'll congratulate them if they ever locate my carpet bag!' quips Mungo, sipping his tea.

'Are you still keeping your tools hidden in that roll of shag-pile?' asks Old Bill.

'Oh yeah, half of these youngsters don't even know what my carpet bag is,' says Mungo, chuckling at his ingenious idea. 'Some of 'em imagine I'm copying old Mary Poppins.'

Chapter Fifteen

Jemima

I waited by my lounge window for ten minutes prior to Ned's arranged collection time. It was a conscious attempt to control my anxiety and avoid unnecessary conflict; I can't imagine him being slapdash with his timings.

He proves me right, swiftly bundling my two sacks of supplies, various cardboard boxes and Crispy duck's wicker carrier into his Range Rover's rear door. I've packed everything I might need minus the kitchen sink.

Lerwick Manor looks surprisingly grand when approaching along its lengthy driveway. The red sandstone reveals rich warm hues and depth to its intricate masonry. The facia of each archway is highly decorative, with floral carvings and gargoyles observing us from the high keystones. Ideally situated against a backdrop of vast open space, there are luscious gardens and traditional drystone walling. I'm conscious that behind one high wall sits our allotment site, where others are busy tending seeds.

A sinking feeling consumes me as we drive round the side and into the cobbled stable yard. What happens if I burn, rather than roast, the pumpkin? What if my chutney making is a waste of his and the family's time? Potentially, I'll be sneaking down this driveway cringing with embarrassment.

We're surrounded by closed stable doors, laid out in a horse-shoe shape and interrupted by an orangery at the far end, beyond which I spy a manicured lawn.

'Are there any horses?' I ask, as he parks the vehicle in front of a painted side entrance before we climb out, Ned opening my door like a true gent.

'Not any more. There used to be riding and working horses at one time – plus Shetland ponies, of course. It's been a long time since anyone rode around here.'

'I hope they don't mind me trespassing like this,' I say, as we empty the car of my belongings, Ned stacking my two boxes into my outstretched arms.

'For the umpteenth time, I can reassure you – you're not trespassing,' says Ned. 'If you carry those, I can manage the rest.'

'Are you sure? Haven't you got equipment to unload?' I say, grateful that he's saving my legs and back.

'Mine's already here, I delivered it earlier. Where do you want the duckling?'

'There's no fear of him escaping, so anywhere safe, but away from my cooking.'

'I suggest the boot room, this way,' says Ned, balancing the wicker carrier under one arm, grabbing the final sack and nudging the rear door shut, before heading to the side entrance.

I feel selfish insisting on bringing Crispy, but I can't leave the poor thing alone all day.

'This bloody door,' he mutters, forcing it open when it sticks.

I follow in silence, stepping into a myriad of tiled corridors, linking numerous storage rooms and servants' quarters backstairs.

'This place is something else, don't you think?' I ask, after we've visited the boot room to deposit the duckling.

'Do you reckon?'

'There's such artistry in every stone block. Look at that ceiling cornice ... and there on the newel post of that staircase. Such detail is beautiful – and unexpected, in the servants' quarters. The family were lavish with their money when this was built.'

'Most likely, but not now,' is his only remark.

On reaching the kitchen, I'm transported back to a bygone era. It reminds me of TV dramas, but I gladly deposit my two boxes upon the centrally positioned scrubbed table. I'm relieved to spot a modern cooker slotted between the worktops; it's older than I'm used to but if I can't manage the range ovens, then I'll switch to cooking on gas.

'You sound very knowledgeable,' says Ned, dropping my boxes and sacks to the floor beside the cooking range.

I notice a pile of equipment and other boxes in the far corner: I assume they're Ned's belongings, delivered earlier.

'A passing interest, really. Traditional arts and skilled trades are falling by the wayside ... many of the features displayed in the masonry couldn't be replicated by the locals any more. Which is sad, don't you think?' I say, unpacking my ingredients upon the table.

'I do, but I haven't met many young people who wish to become stonemasons. I thought they all wanted to be footballers or media influencers.'

'You're right, but there's definitely a small revival in certain skills, preventing them from dying out completely.'

'Is there?'

'The stained glass in the Town Hall, for example – you must admit that it's stunning, thanks to the meticulous renovation work. It was painstakingly cleaned and repaired by hand, using traditional methods to ensure each panel looks pristine.'

'I'll give you that, but surely that's a specific one-off project?'

'I can't imagine there were many companies tendering for the project, it's such a specialised trade nowadays. If those skills die, then we lose our heritage over time. You could hardly clean each of the coloured panes with a bowl of mild soapy water and a toothbrush!' I grimace. 'Or would you?'

'My heavy-handedness would cause enough damage.' He gives a hearty chuckle.

I like how his temples crease with laughter; his dark eyes are closed for a fraction of time as he openly roars.

'I'd have been sued for irreparable damage to Shetland's fine heritage.'

'Working at the tourist office, I frequently advised visitors to view the stained glass at the Town Hall. So many of them thought I was pulling their leg when I explained that our history is depicted in those windows – plus, it's totally free. Simply walk in and climb the stairs to the second floor.'

'Are you missing your work?'

I grimace. 'Not really. I miss the people, of course, but there's only so many times you can repeat the same conversation each day to a different family. Some groups are interested in exploring everything; others just want to shelter from the rain. I suppose every job has its down side.'

'It sure does.' Ned sighs heavily.

'There, I'm ready!' I say, observing my unpacked equipment laid out neatly upon the scrubbed table.

'I'm happy working over in that corner, you can have the remainder of the kitchen to yourself, OK?' he says, gesturing to the equipment I've already spied.

'Sure, I've brought everything that I need ... but you'll need to show me how the ovens work.'

'I've filled both with coal and lit them earlier, so they should be ready to use—' He ceases to talk on seeing my surprised expression. 'I did mention I'd already been up.'

'You did, but I didn't realise you'd prepared the ovens too.'

Ned shrugs, as if it were a given. 'The large baking trays are kept there ... and there ... you'll squeeze a fair amount on to each, in one go. These cloths are heavy duty and will hopefully prevent you from burning yourself.'

'You've thought of everything, cheers.'

'No worries. Thank Dottie, not me.'

It's hardly believable, but this morning I was dreading spending the entire day alongside Ned, for fear of a deafening silence. But just maybe, it won't be too bad, after all.

My progress is slow. The pumpkin rinds are much tougher than I was expecting, so chopping and sawing each one has taken some time. I've spread my ingredients out in preparation for the next stage, only to discover I've picked up turmeric instead of the curry powder stated in the recipe. Never mind, it'll do. I'm definitely more organised here, given the amount of space and the range of surfaces, than I could be in my cramped kitchen at home. At least here I can complete one task at a time without having to switch back and forth, repeating steps and processes.

Ned's been busy on the opposite side of the kitchen with a pile of wooden frames, each grotesquely bulging with a waxy substance. He's sitting in a large wooden chair, a cloth laid across his lap, scraping the wax covering from both sides before hanging the wooden frame inside a small machine at his feet. He's arranged various buckets before him into which he drops the scrapings from his knife. He's been so quiet, I quite forgot he was here at times. Our chatting faded, once we both became absorbed in our tasks.

'How long have you kept bees?' I ask, wanting to show some interest after my faux pas the other day.

'Since I was a teenager. My grandfather always kept bees, so I grew up with them really.'

'Oh.'

He smiles to himself.

'What?' I ask.

'Nothing, except that "oh" sounded like a full stop, end-of-subject type of "oh".'

'Sorry, I didn't mean that. I just don't get the fascination with bees. They live in a big box, buzz back and forth, yet Dottie's forever praising your bees. I think she talks to them at times.'

Ned nods slowly, watching me intently, his knife suspended over the current bulging frame.

'There's an old custom of telling the bees first before telling others of any news,' he says, breaking the silence.

'I see. Sorry, but I just don't get the bee thing.'

'Do you class the allotment site as a self-contained community?' he asks, as I continue to chop a wedge of pumpkin into cubes.

'I'd say so. I haven't been part of it for long, but I recognise the community spirit which brings everyone together, such as the meeting the other weekend and The Cabbage Patch Friday sessions.'

'Exactly. Do you reckon the allotment community works well?'

'At times. When Melissa was stuck, Levi and Dottie organised a weeding party on her behalf. We got the job done in record time, and now she can think about planting her seeds, which she couldn't before.'

'Precisely. But aren't there anomalies within the community – people who don't pitch in?'

'You mean the Far Siders?'

'Maybe.'

'From what I see, they do their own thing. They were definitely smoking something dodgy the other Friday afternoon, outside The Cabbage Patch . . . none of them attended Melissa's weeding party either.'

Ned agrees. 'Not perfect, is it?'

'Nope, but there will always be individuals who stand out and buck the trend.'

'Not in a beehive, there aren't,' says Ned, a broad smile animating his features. 'Each bee has a job, each bee knows their job, and each bee will give up its life ensuring that it does the necessary for the sake of the entire hive, its community.'

I listen carefully as he explains. I watch how he turns the bulging frame over in his hands, his eyes admiring every inch of it, before he looks up at me.

'It's the perfect community – one us humans try to emulate but never quite achieve.'

'Is that true?'

'Yes, it's true. Their sole existence relies on keeping their community as healthy as possible, with enough food for all. A mini allotment inside a "big box", as you called it. Some fifty thousand bees: workers, drones and a queen – each with a job to do.'

'Can they have more than one queen?'

Ned pulls an expressive face.

'They can, if one is being nurtured towards maturity by the workers and the older queen is being forced out or past her prime. The queen is the dominant female, she's usually the mother of most bees in the hive, if not all – depending on when a new queen was created.'

'Dottie's like our queen bee on the allotment!'

'She certainly is. There are days when she plays the same role here,' says Ned, a soft chuckle escaping as he shakes his head.

'Wow, I've learnt something there.'

'I'm glad to hear it.' Ned puts the frame down before standing, asking, 'Tea?'

'Please, though I can't see a kettle,' I say, viewing the nearest worktop for an electric one.

Ned crosses the aged flagstones to lift the blackened kettle from its hook beside the range.

'Surely not from that,' I say, looking up from the scrubbed table.

'Why not, if it works?'

'Does it?' I say, watching him near the butler's sink, blackened kettle in hand.

Ned dramatically wrenches the pump handle beside the butler's sink.

'And you'll have me think that the water pump works too?' I joke. 'Surely the cold tap would be more reliable.'

'Wait and see.' Ned continues to pump the handle with force; the muscles in his shoulder ripple beneath his shirt.

I'm speechless.

Who the hell is he kidding? I assumed he was a level-headed guy, on the evidence of our limited interaction, but watching him now suggests otherwise. I guess it's been decades since ... My thoughts are quenched as a deluge of water pours from the pump head into the blackened kettle.

Ned flashes a wry smile in my direction as he replaces the kettle's lid. 'I assume it is "yes" to tea then.'

'Please,' is all I can muster, before adding, 'How did you even know that pump still works?'

Ned turns around from the range, where he is hanging the kettle on to the large hook over the fire. 'Sorry?'

'I said, how come you knew that the water pump still worked ... it wouldn't have entered my head to even try it, but you went straight to it.'

Ned shrugs, looking bemused, before his expression relaxes on spying a visitor. 'Dottie! Come and join us for tea.'

I turn swiftly, in time to see Dottie tottering across the flagstones.

'I wouldn't say no, Ned. Though I'll remind you both that I expect this kitchen to be spick and span when you finish playing *MasterChef* – it isn't on my cleaning rota for another week or so.'

'It will be, Dottie. I didn't know you'd be here too.'

'I work several days a week, young woman ... it might be just an hour or so, but it suits me,' explains Dottie, drawing up a chair opposite me at the table. 'How's the chutney going?'

'Slowly, but I intend to begin roasting the first batch of pumpkin after my tea.'

'Have you enough jars?' asks Dottie, viewing the nearest worktop where I've lined up fifty jars.

'Plenty, thank you. Though I'd like to buy gingham fabric to decorate the jar lids – they'll look more appealing.'

'Very fetching, I'm sure,' calls Ned, leaning against the brick-work and waiting for the kettle to boil.

'A watched pot and all that, Ned,' jests Dottie, observing his manner.

'Did you know that the water pump still works perfectly well, Dottie?' I ask, returning to my original musings.

'Everything in this house works. Why, are you expecting it to be dilapidated, in rack and ruin?' says Dottie, glancing at Ned whilst answering me.

'Not at all, but I certainly didn't expect that. Is the rest of the manor kept as well as this?'

Neither Ned nor Dottie answer.

I glance between the two to find they are staring at each other – each waiting for the other to respond.

'Have I put my foot in it?' I ask, unperturbed by their silence.

'No, but I don't suppose the family have given it much thought, would you agree, Ned?'

'For sure, I think they've simply got on with their lives and modified the rooms they use – without servants and such like, what's the point in throwing money down the drain?'

'Literally!' I squeal at his pun.

'That wasn't intended, but it works,' teases Ned, as steam lifts from the kettle's spout. He grabs the nearest cloth and removes the kettle from the fire, placing it on a trivet before discarding his protective cloth.

'Can you imagine being a scullery maid working in here all day, every day, running up those backstairs, carrying jugs of hot water for washing and bathing?' I ask, seeing their intent gaze. 'I wouldn't last a day.'

'I can assure you, I once did. It's tough enough carrying hot water for the cleaning, given the number of stairs around here,' jests Dottie, taking the offered teacup from Ned. 'She'll be nabbing my job next, Ned.'

'I doubt it,' comes his reply. 'There's only room for one queen bee around here,' he adds.

Melissa

'So, as you can see, there's been a huge difference since the last time I showed you around,' I proudly declare, holding the iPad and slowly turning a full circle, allowing Hamish to view the allotment plot.

'I'm impressed, babe. You've really stripped it back to the bare essentials. I was fearing you'd jack it in as a bad idea after two weeks of weeding.'

'I nearly did. The hired goat did well but the other allotment holders have proved to be troopers, donating their time to help with some of it,' I add, not wishing to venture there, for fear of dropping certain names.

'That's my girl – always a fighter, never a quitter!'

I nod in agreement, basking in his praise. He does care. I know he cares. So why do I feel so sodding down about the fact that I am here and he is there? Am I being selfish by wanting what I want? Or am I maturing into a grown-up, at last, to want what I want?

'Melissa, are you still there?'

'I'm still here.' Isn't that the truth! Still here, still waiting, still being the good girl and not complaining.

'I thought I'd lost you. What are you planning to grow over the coming months then?'

I begin to walk the plot, explaining and pointing out where I intend to plant potatoes, radishes, courgettes – and hopefully, more carrots.

'The committee want me to enter parsnips into the annual allotment festival.'

'Just do it! What's the harm in trying?'

He's right, as always.

'I suggested growing carrots, but the old folk mentioned I should try parsnips. I suppose I can withdraw nearer the festival date, if I wish.'

'Exactly. What date is that?'

'Saturday, the fourth of September. Do you think you can make it home?' I ask, my voice as eager as a child promised sweets.

'Babe, you know how it is . . . there's been so much illness and crap happening this year, who knows what the rota will look like by then?' His features appear pinched and tired on the screen.

'Huh, it's always the bloody same, isn't it? Me here, you there, regardless of what the event or occasion is. Will this ever change, Hamish?' I can't help myself, it spills from my lips before I put my brain into gear. This wasn't my plan for our screen time conversation today.

Hamish looks shocked. 'Melissa, now come on. I'm breaking my back out here for you and me, babe. Every day that I'm away from home, I'm missing us being together, but it has to be done if we're to have the nice things in life.'

'At what cost, though?'

'Sorry, I don't know where you're going with this.'

'I said, at what cost? What price are you prepared to pay to secure our future? What if, and I'm only speculating here, the family we once dreamed of doesn't become ours because we left it too late to start trying. What if we need more support than most to conceive? Or there's an issue which needs medical appointments, screening or lengthy and costly interventions. I'm already forty-two, Hamish! Are you on call to dash home so we can achieve our dreams?'

'Melissa! Now hang on a minute—'

'No, Hamish, you bloody well hang on. I think I've been hanging on long enough.'

Silence.

I might have raised my voice just a tad. I swiftly glance over the dirt track towards the opposite plots. Old Bill is a statue mid-stride with his blessed wheelbarrow in hand, Mungo's head is motionless, popping above his hedge, and Dottie is standing stock-still with her secateurs in hand. I think I'm right in saying they have all just overheard my private conversation with my absent husband.

'Anyway, I need to go. I've got things to do, people to see – so you have a think on, and we'll chat another time.'

'Melissa, are you really leaving our conversation there?'

'Yep, to be honest, I am, before I say more than I should. Have a nice day, chat later . . . or sometime convenient to you. Bye now.' I tap the screen, ending the connection.

I feel like crying, but that really isn't an option. I've disturbed the peace and at least three fellow plot holders are currently tuned in. I'll plod about, looking busy, and hopefully folk will think they misheard us, or rather me, washing our dirty laundry in public.

I pop the iPad into the potting shed, grab a hoe and begin tickling the earth as fat tears run down my cheeks and drip from my chin into the parched earth before me. There I go, multi-tasking by watering my seedlings too.

'Melissa, are you OK?' his voice calls, through the wire gate.

I look up, aiming to appear surprised, but I'm not; I knew Levi would show up. The jungle drums are healthy around here.

'Me? Always fine and dandy me. How are you?' I stop hoeing, stand upright and rest my elbows on the wooden pole in a casual pose, reinforcing my words.

Levi enters the gate before traipsing over. His gaze doesn't leave mine; he knows.

He stops right in front of me, leaving a space of two feet between us, for the sake of decency.

'How are you, Levi?' I say, my voice raised slightly louder than usual.

'They've all gone home so they aren't listening.'

'Like hell they're not listening! No one misses a sodding detail around here – overhearing stuff, while pretending to garden.'

'Can I fetch you a coffee or some water?'

'No. Who called you? Old Bill, Mungo, Jemima?'

'Dottie, actually. I was taxiing folk around town, but I came as soon as I was free.'

I stand up as straight as I can, rock the hoe's wooden handle back and forth between us, creating an invisible barrier, but inwardly I acknowledge I'm failing big time. He's scrutinising me, intently. Waiting for me to crumble. And I will crumble. I can feel it surfacing with each second that he stands before me. I gulp once, twice. Look away, feigning interest in the bare earth to my left. I gulp some more before hot tears spill over my lashes and stream down each cheek.

'Come here,' he whispers, stepping forward, his arms open wide to wrap about my juddering shoulders.

Instinctively, I drop my forehead on to his right shoulder and sob uncontrollably.

'Are we good to go?' he asks after a rather long time, when my tears have dried, my hiccupping has been silenced and I can't justify standing in this cradled embrace for a moment longer.

I nod, as his embrace relaxes. My hands briskly wipe the remnants of tears and blurred make-up from beneath my lashes.

I don't apologise as I step back, away from his solid frame; I sense I don't need to.

'That'll give them something to yap about in The Cabbage Patch, won't it?'

'We might have fooled them into thinking we were probably a new double scarecrow installation.'

'I doubt that very much,' I say, looking around my plot.

'If they're yapping about us, they're leaving some other poor sod alone,' says Levi.

'Hamish should be doing this alongside me, but he's not ... he's choosing to be stuck in the middle of the Gulf with a bunch of colleagues drilling for oil.'

'Melissa, it is his job. He can hardly drill for oil up the allotment plots, can he?'

'I know, but when's it going to change for us?'

He gives a tiny shrug. 'I don't know what to say; I'm not good with advising folk, especially about marriage and stuff. But surely you should be happy, living the life you have? I'm sure he wouldn't want you to be feeling like this.'

'He doesn't get it.'

'You only get one chance in this world, Melissa – it's wrong that you're feeling this way, when life could be so different.'

My gaze meets his and sticks fast. He's so lovely, so patient with me. His mesmerising gaze begins to drift about my features: from eyes to lips, to temples and back to my eyes. When was the last time that Hamish listened so intently or looked at me in such a manner? Too long ago, that's for sure.

'Do you fancy a day trip?'

'An away day? Where to?'

'Wherever you like ... a picnic and a day out might do us both good.'

'Let me know when you're free from work and we'll take off.'

'Perfect. Seeing that you've cheered up, I'll get back to my work. Catch you later.'

I watch as Levi swiftly leaves: a friend to everyone, enemy to none.

Chapter Sixteen

Jemima

It takes five hours for me to chop, dice, roast and mash two large pumpkins but I'm satisfied with the end result: fifty glass jars filled with a deep orange chutney. It might not be produce grown by me but it saves wasting Grandpop's final season as an allotment holder. I'm sure it's worth fifty pence a jar in the allotment shop. Likewise, Ned has filled thirty jars with golden honey prior to us cleaning every surface and sweeping the floor. My energy is finally zapped as we lug each cardboard box back to his Range Rover.

'I hope the kitchen's cleaned to Dottie's high standards,' I jest, fearing the repercussions if it isn't.

'She'll have no complaints. Are you ready to leave?' asks Ned, securing the rear door.

'Certainly am. Let's hope each jar gets sold. And you?'

'Yes, quite ready. Though I was thinking maybe you'd like to tour the rest of the manor before we leave.'

'Are you sure the family won't mind?'

'Not at all, they'll be impressed that you're even interested,' he says, retracing our steps to the side entrance.

I don't linger. I'm following his strides like a faithful Labrador as Ned leads the way back inside, through the warren of tiled corridors. We take the exact same route as this morning, leading us back to the aged kitchen. This time, we exit via the door through which Dottie appeared earlier. There's a short corridor where the scrubbed flagstones change to a distinct geometric tile

pattern, defining the change of status. Likewise, the walls trans-
form from basic emulsion to wallpaper of a rich burgundy velvet,
with swathes of navy and green tartan hanging tastefully from the
decorative ceiling and a huge chandelier plunging into the abyss
created by the grand staircase. Looking up from the foot of the
stairs, I see gilt-edged frames depicting long-forgotten fashions
and resolute stares, glaring down upon my upturned face.

My heart is pounding, my palms are tacky and my anxiety
levels are rising faster than the tide when the moon is full.

I can't do this. I dearly want to, but I can't impose myself
on others when they've been generous enough already. I'm not
viewing a stately home which is always prepped for visitors –
those families are aware that the public are wandering about. I'm
not like the others; I can't lie. This feels wrong. I can't pretend
to be blasé and simply go mooching around, uninvited, imposing
myself upon strangers.

'Are these the family ancestors?' I ask, distracting my thoughts.

'Sure. I doubt they'd have sat so patiently if they knew how
long they'd be suspended from a picture rail,' jests Ned, striding
up the grand staircase.

'Ned . . .' I cease following him, I can't go any further.

'What?'

'I don't feel comfortable – it's as if we're snooping. They've
been kind enough to allow me to use their kitchen, but this feels
as if I'm taking advantage . . . I'm sorry, I can't do this.'

'Are you serious?'

I nod repeatedly.

'They won't be offended.'

'Perhaps not, but my moral compass isn't happy – and now,
I'm beginning to feel quite light-headed.'

His eyebrows lift in surprise.

'I'd happily tour the stables instead . . . I think I need some
fresh air.'

Ned pauses, glancing up the staircase, before slowly turning to me and gesturing that we should retrace our steps.

'Stables it is then, Jemima. We'll collect the duckling at the same time. This way.'

Dottie

A gentle walk around my plot, inspecting each plant as it grows, is the greatest joy I have. You can keep your meditation or yoga sessions, for me this is the meaning of life. Watching healthy shoots, and eventually a flower spear, bursting open over successive days and displaying their full glory makes my heart sing. I get to enjoy the freshness of the dew upon vibrant stems, and nab the odd slug here and there before he has a hearty supper munching my plants. To any observer, I might look odd – wandering up and down each row, ferreting amongst the leaves every now and then – but over the years, I've learnt that it pays to know on a daily basis how my beauties are doing and . . .

I stop short, having reached the end row where my particular favourites grow: the genus Guardian Lavender. It'll produce a superb display of double flowers, in a pale blue and lavender, densely populating each spur. You get your money's worth in blooms. I could name three florists who would gladly buy each bloom every season, but I refuse to become a commercial grower.

I bend down to take a closer look at the crown of shoots, not believing my eyes. There are four shoots sprouting from the mound of earth: those on the left are healthy, but the other two have a brown frazzled edge along each delicate leaf.

I run my fingers along each one, as if a magic touch can restore my scorched leaf to a healthy specimen.

Chemicals!

I look towards Jemima's allotment, peering at her semi-naked plot. She wouldn't have, would she? She's made some rookie errors, but surely she knows not to use pesticides or chemicals on her allotment.

'Are you OK, Dottie?' calls Ned, entering our allotment and finding me crouched amongst my beauties.

'Come and have a look at this,' I urge, wanting a second opinion.

'What have you found?'

I stand and step back, giving him a full view of my injured plant.

'There. Do you see?' I gesture at the damage.

Ned kneels, before peering at the leaves; his expression darkens and he immediately stares back at me.

'Someone's used chemicals.' He fingers the leaf, much as I did. 'That's chemical scorching, which has blown across from . . .' He glances up at the wire fencing of Jemima's plot. His brow furrows tightly. 'Surely not!'

'That's what I thought. Old Bill will have mentioned it when he was handing out advice. Mungo definitely. Me, errr, maybe not directly – but the younger generation are so clued up regarding the environment. Aren't they?'

'Well, she bloody should be!' he says. Then adds, 'If it's affected the shoots and leaves, it'll affect the flower spears too. Is she up here?'

'I haven't seen her, but the minute I do I'll be asking her.'

'Look here,' he says, pointing out another crowning mound displaying similar signs. 'And here. These too.' Ned is on his feet, bent double, inspecting my beauties and pointing to each blighted crown nearest Jemima's fencing. 'It's obvious what she's done.'

'These were my prize winners at last year's festival; I wanted a repeat entry, come September, alongside a new variety.'

I'm trying my hardest to remain calm, to conceal how upset I truly am, but her one error – the damage she's caused – could mean the difference between me entering the festival in September or ripping up the entire row and not being able to replant anything in this soil for the rest of the season.

'You are going to mention it, aren't you?'

'Sure. I might wait a day or so, when I'm feeling more ...' I don't finish my sentence; Jemima appears on her allotment, closing her front door.

'Evening!' she calls, bright and breezy. I can see she has the duckling nestled in her jacket hood and that giant smile that reminds me of Tommy.

I raise my hand to wave, but my voice has gone.

Ned looks at me, then looks at Jemima. He steps nearer the wire fencing, calling her across.

I can predict his tone before hearing it. I recognise the Campbell anger, a trait passed from generation to generation.

'Have you been spraying chemicals?' he says, not waiting for her answer before continuing. 'Weed killers, pesticides or any other chemical? Because look what you've done to Dottie's beautiful plants – you've half killed them. Look!' Ned pulls a damaged leaf from the nearest crown and thrusts it over the fence towards Jemima's surprised features. 'And not just this plant ... but this one ... and these as well. You do know the damage caused to the environment by chemicals, don't you?' Jemima goes to speak, but Ned jumps in. 'How selfish can you be? I get that you're new to the allotment site, but the council provide literature and I'm certain Old Bill and Mungo will have mentioned it to you during their mini tours. Have you any idea how much distress you've caused to Dottie? Have you? I've yet to check my beehives for internal damage, but will my honey be laced with chemicals and pesticides too?

Jemima's chin begins to wobble. She glances at me, trying to get a word in edgeways, but Ned's not having it; for a man of few words, he's got enough to say on this matter.

'I'm so s-sorry, I didn't m-mean to cause ...' she stammers, before the tears fall.

Ned storms off to inspect his bees.

I can't pacify her, knowing how upset I am, but I can't stay angry for long, not when the young woman is crying as wretchedly as she is.

Chapter Seventeen

June

High: 13°
Low: 8°

Daylight: 18.5 hours
Rain: 9 days
Wind: 13 mph

Note: The Simmers Dim Bikers Rally has arrived — boy, what a sight, seeing them pour off the ferry. Old Bill reckons he might join them next year. I said not unless he adds an engine to that squeaky barrow of his. Dottie agreed. He stropped and sulked all afternoon.

Jemima

I hear Mungo before I see him. I've got my head and shoulders thrust inside a filthy chicken coop, attempting to clean a week's worth of chicken droppings. I can do without any more upset, given Ned's recent outburst over my genuine error. I'd even cried when I phoned Dottie's landline to apologise for the damage caused to her prize-winning blooms. I'm surprised she could understand a word I'd said, though my numerous 'sorrys' were pretty clear amongst my sobs and sniffing.

'I told ya, didn't I? I knew it. I told you to be careful. I said it would go tits up, and it has.' He's leaning over my chicken-pen fencing, attempting to open the gate, but is struggling due to his irate state.

'Mungo,' I say, faking a cheery mood, whilst reversing in a very undignified manner out of the tight opening, complete with my face mask protection, goggles and dropping-infested rubber gloves. 'How are you?'

'You should have listened to me. I told you it wouldn't work . . . and it hasn't.' He continues to struggle with the gate, much to my amusement, before it pings open and he pretends he's unlatched it.

'Are you referring to my pumpkin seedlings, my reluctant chicken duties, or my lack of pesticide and chemical know-how – what?'

'The honesty boxes . . . they've gone!'

My expression darkens. 'You had better be joking!'

'Uh-uh! Not a single tub remains, or the cash they contained.'

'You might consider me to be thick, but I assumed that.'

'So, what do you say?'

'Say?'

'Yeah, what am I to tell the allotment holders?'

'The truth, Mungo. Tell them that some sneaking lowlife has had the audacity to pinch, steal, thieve – whatever term suits your mood – their little bit of change from their plastic tubs. That some thieving git must be that hard up, they would steal from a community that would happily give to others, rather than have anything stolen from them.'

'And that's the end of it then?'

'Other than offering a reward for information so we can confront the culprit, what else can I do?'

Mungo begins to pace up and down, before muttering, 'I think you need to close it.'

'Close it?'

'Yeah. As a new venture, it hasn't worked.'

'Jog on, Mungo! I don't know how you've got the gall to say that straight to my face. Behind my back, yeah, but not directly to me. It's brought people together by giving them a chance to share their produce and get rid of seeds and equipment they have no use for. But from now on, we'll need a mini rota system to ensure that our little Veggie Rack is manned at all times. Could you announce that in The Cabbage Patch when you're passing? I'll make sure I'm there tomorrow.'

Mungo stands and stares at me, puffing out his chest much like my chickens after feeding time.

'Is there anything else, or would you like me to assist you with viewing the CCTV footage?'

'No, thanks. I'm quite capable,' says Mungo, turning to fumble with the gate.

Cheeky bugger. I'm offering to give up my own time to support his security role, and it's flatly refused.

'On second thoughts, I'll gladly view the footage – after all, it's my project they've discredited with their actions. Give me a shout when you do.'

'What?' Mungo turns abruptly, his expression and tone terse.

'I'll give you a hand – two viewers will be far better than one.'

'I don't think the committee will allow that – it's not as if you know everyone who attends this allotment site.'

'I've heard it all now, Mungo. Thanks a bunch! Forget it, I'll ask for permission from Old Bill, and then I'll join you whenever you view it. OK?'

'I don't think ...' chunters Mungo, slamming the enclosure gate.

'Bye, Mungo, I'll catch you later.' I've heard enough for one day.

I reposition my protective gear and return to my scrubbing. The bristles of my cleaning brush bend under the force of each anger-induced movement.

If I'd known then what I know now, I'd have handed the allotment keys straight back to the council on that very first morning. I'm supposed to be on sabbatical and taking things easy. Gradually coming to terms with adult life without my mum and my beloved Grandpop, yet all I get is hassle: left, right and centre! People who I think are my friends misunderstand me. Those who I thought were taking a genuine interest and getting to know me better think they can rant and shout at me whenever it suits them.

I stop scrubbing as hot, angry tears spill over my lashes before steaming up my view and collecting at the rims of my goggles. And now, I'm crying again! And. I. Can't. Even. See. Properly!

I throw down my scrubbing brush in frustration, sending a splatter of wet chicken poop up my jacket sleeve and across my cheek.

I hear the gentle click of the enclosure gate behind me.

'Mungo, do me a favour and bugger off! I've just about had all I can take of this place for one day,' I holler, resuming my task.

He doesn't answer, but I sense he's standing behind me.

'I mean it, Mungo. If you've got another complaint or gripe, I suggest you save it for tomorrow. I might reopen for business at The Veggie Rack by installing my own complaints box, purely for those disgruntled with me. I'll even make a mini-sign, "The Jemima Button complaint box", complete with a notepad and tethered pencil! How does that sound?

'It all sounds very intriguing, but I was wondering where the "Jemima Button Apology box" might be found?' says a male voice.

'Ned?' I quickly reverse out through the confined doorway of the chicken coop. I whip aside my decorator's face mask and remove my steamed-up goggles to find him standing there, a bemused expression etched across his chiselled cheekbones and cleft chin.

'Sorry to disturb you. I can see you're busy, but I owe you an apology ... for the other day. It seems that I might have over-reacted. I'm not used to having to correct or advise others ... not on the spur of the moment, anyway. Having said all that, it still doesn't excuse the gruff manner or aggressive tone in which I spoke to you. I was rude. Incredibly rude, in fact. I sincerely apologise for that, it truly wasn't meant to upset you. I assumed you understood about pesticides and the associated damage, when clearly you don't ... didn't – that was wrong of me. My error entirely. Sorry.' He falls silent and waits. His dark gaze and brooding features remain fixed on mine. He's deadly serious. Genuinely sorry. He means every single word.

I won't cheapen his sincerity with futile banter, despite this scenario feeling somewhat intense and in need of an injection of humour.

'Thank you. I appreciate the sentiment, Ned. I was upset. Actually, I'm still very much upset but ... well, now I realise the error I made ... though I didn't do it on purpose and would never knowingly upset Dottie or her flowers. I have apologised to Dotty too. I won't be using chemicals again. But thank you for coming to speak to me. A lesser person would have simply let the incident slide and then we'd be tiptoeing around it for ever and a day.' I give him a bright yet teary smile, unsure if there's any more to be said on the matter.

'Thank you for hearing me out. I didn't want there to be any ... awkwardness between us ... now or ... whenever. But now I'm rambling, when really ... I should leave you to be cracking on with your cleaning task.'

I can see his mind whirring; his hesitation ends.

'Take care, Ned,' I say softly.

'And you, Jemima.' He turns, exiting the chicken enclosure.

The gate mechanism clicks softly shut behind him.

I remain in situ for a moment longer as my mind replays his apology, in slow motion, several times. I smile to myself; if he's humble enough to apologise, he's definitely my kind of guy.

I wipe and replace my goggles, dislodging a large clump of dried chicken poop from my left cheek. Oh great, so attractive!

Dottie

I wasn't surprised when Jemima arrived early. The poor lassie still looks fragile; treading on eggshells and apologising for mistakes is never easy. She probably didn't want to risk Mungo excluding her from the viewing. When he arrived in The Cabbage Patch, minutes later, his face was a picture.

'Hi, Mungo,' I say, giving him a wave to ease the tension as I sit between Old Bill and Jemima, in front of the mini-TV and recording device.

'What's she doing here?' asks Mungo.

'She's every right – it's her project, Mungo. Take a seat. There's a lot to get through,' answers Old Bill.

Mungo draws up the nearest chair and settles behind me, creating a second row. I suspect he wanted a prime position to reflect his role on the committee.

'Mungo, you discovered the empty boxes at half past two, so we've got nearly eight hours of footage to view. Jemima, grab the clipboard and pen to write down the names of each person who Dottie, Mungo and myself will identify.'

'Yep.' Jemima does as she's told; she's not likely to argue, given that Old Bill has granted her wish.

I wasn't against her attending, either. There's no doubt Mungo is miffed by her presence.

'Dottie and Mungo, shout when you recognise folk,' instructs Old Bill. 'We're looking for anything suspicious, or an unknown face.'

Mungo and I gaze at the tiny screen.

'I'll play it in fast forward so we don't waste time. Any questions?'

'What happens if we identify someone?' I ask, not wishing to wrongly accuse.

'We'll see who it is first,' mutters Mungo.

'I hope not!' snaps Jemima, looking between our three startled faces. 'If we identify who the culprit is, they need speaking to . . . immediately. Theft is theft!'

'But some people – they can't help themselves,' I explain.

'And some people make a bloody habit of helping themselves to everything that isn't theirs,' she snaps.

I think she's taking this too personally. I know it's her venture, but still.

'Let's just see what we see first, then we'll discuss it,' says Old Bill.

'I don't believe this,' mutters Jemima.

'Ready?' asks Old Bill, his finger lingering above the remote controls button.

The TV screen bursts into a life, showing a grainy sequence of images in three boxes: the main entrance gate, a section of the right-hand dirt track and a section of the left-hand dirt track. A time and date stamp are shown in white font across the bottom of the screen.

'Is that it?' I exclaim, making the others visibly jump.

Old Bill pauses the screen.

'What were you expecting? A zoom lens positioned on The Veggie Rack door?'

'Not quite, but I expected something more specific than this,' I proclaim, eyes wide and mouth agape.

'Sorry to disappoint your highness, but this isn't MI5,' scoffs Mungo.

'Ha ha, very funny, Mungo.' I nod curtly, slightly miffed that Mungo's tone isn't as pleasant as usual.

Jemima pipes up. 'Dottie's right. The view is limited, so I'll need to write down the name of every person who enters the site.'

'That's why you've been assigned the clipboard – you won't recognise that many faces, will you?' explains Old Bill.

'So, I'll need to mark them off as they leave the site too – if you're to identify who was on site and who wasn't?'

We exchange glances.

'OK, then cross or tick each one as they leave the site,' instructs Mungo.

'Ready?' asks Old Bill, before restarting the recording.

The screen shows all three camera views, each giving a grainy picture of the early-morning light at the time stated: 05:03.

Within seconds, a vehicle draws up to the locked gates and we watch in silence as a male climbs from the driver's seat, leaves his car door wide open, walks to the padlock, fiddles for a second, swings the gate wide, returns to his car, settles back inside and slowly draws his vehicle through the entrance gate before parking and returning to close and lock the main gate. What a palaver.

'Limping Angus, he's early,' calls Mungo.

Old Bill and I nod. Jemima adds 'Angus' to her list.

'Eh, he's not limping either – which is a bloody disgrace, as he's been claiming disability money for near on a decade,' scoffs Old Bill, his eyes not leaving the screen.

We all watch Old Angus's strong, healthy stride propel him along the left-hand dirt track towards his plot.

'Last year, Levi and I dug his bloody spuds up because we felt sorry for him, not being able to manage. I won't be doing that again,' tuts Mungo.

'Especially as he's half your age,' I say.

We sit for an entire hour. It's a weird game of bingo but the set-up seems to be working.

At regular intervals, a name is called out and Jemima hastily writes it down. Having watched the routine of the car drivers, it's no wonder many choose to walk to the allotments.

'I suggest we break for a cuppa,' I announce, pushing my chair back and scraping Mungo's toes.

'You get the kettle on then, old gal – we'll continue,' teases Mungo, rubbing his foot.

Having gone AWOL with the kettle, I notice the men aren't as quick at recognising and calling out the names. Several times, the individual gets through the locked gate and is already appearing on one of the other dirt track screens before the chaps call out.

'My God, that's me!' cries Jemima, watching the grainy image of a woman. 'I look tiny compared to those gates.'

'You look as if you don't understand the mechanism of a lock, either,' mutters Mungo, as the picture clearly shows her struggling, whilst holding her bike.

'Oi, sometimes my key doesn't turn smoothly, it snags in the lock,' she snaps, glaring over her shoulder at Mungo.

He's pressing her buttons, that's for sure.

'Write your own name down then ... quick, quick, the main gate's getting busy,' says Old Bill, prodding her clipboard.

I deliver our teas and resettle myself before the screen.

'You just missed Jemima's entrance – the padlock bamboozled her,' says Mungo.

I grimace, I swear some men never grow up. Wait till he spies himself.

My wish is granted within ten minutes.

'Here we go, Mungo arriving!' I call excitedly. 'There's no mistaking that quick step, eh.'

Jemima adds his name.

The image is getting lighter as the sunlight becomes stronger. We can clearly see Mungo undo the lock, open the gate, stride through, turn to close the gate but then stop, look up towards the open roadway, and wait. And wait.

'What are you waiting for, mate?' asks Old Bill.

'Yeah, I waited yesterday,' mutters Mungo, staring at himself. We then watch as three men approach the main gate and, without taking their hands out of their pockets, are admitted by Mungo without using their keys.

'Hang on a moment . . . who are they?' asks Jemima, pointing out protocol to the head of security.

'The MacDonald lads, come to visit their old man . . . who, if you check your list, arrived an hour ago. They regularly help him out on his plot.'

'That's allowed, is it? Three men who aren't plot holders are allowed to wander about the allotments at . . .' Jemima peers at the screen time, indignantly adding, 'Seven fifty-eight a.m. Did you escort them to their father's plot?'

'No, I didn't. I've known them all their lives. They'd never steal a few quid from plastic tubs. Watch what you say about the MacDonald lads . . . they'll never see you stuck for a helping hand.' Mungo's crabbit nature is beginning to flare; his patience is as short as a cold spell in mid-August.

'Enough!' roars Old Bill, glancing between the two of them. 'Quite enough. Granted, Mungo didn't escort them, but Dottie and I can vouch for them – they wouldn't touch a thing that doesn't belong to them. Right, Dottie?'

'Lovely guys, they really are. The youngest one's still single, Jemima,' I say, testing the waters to see if she's interested in anyone and everyone – or just a certain someone.

'Dottie, I couldn't care less who's single. I can now see how it's going to be, if we ever do manage to identify the culprit.'

Chapter Eighteen

Melissa

I can't help but watch him driving; his handsome profile is intriguing as he concentrates, his pale blue eyes fixed upon the road ahead. It reminds me of those halcyon teenage days, windows down and music blaring, when you have a boyfriend who can legally drive. I foolishly thought it was such an achievement in life!

'I hope it doesn't feel like a busman's holiday?' I say, breaking the lengthy silence.

'Not at all. I love driving, and the chance to get out of the usual routes makes for a nice change.'

'I'll happily drive back, if you wish.'

'No, thanks, no one drives my taxi.'

I get it. I wouldn't allow anyone to use my paint brushes or pencils – the very toolkit with which I've built my teaching career. Urgh! Just the thought gives me the heebie-jeebies.

'So, where we heading?'

'Anywhere. If we head towards the northern peninsula, we can pick and choose as we drive. I'm in no rush to get back.'

'Sounds like a plan, Stan!' I like Levi's go-with-the-flow attitude – so different to Hamish. If we were out for the day, there'd be a minute-by-minute itinerary, cramming in as much as we can for fear of wasting a moment.

Instantly, I feel guilty. Hamish can't afford to waste time; he's rarely home from the Gulf. Would I want him to be any other way? Chilling so much that we accomplish nothing together, come high days and holidays? I wouldn't want him to spend his week cooped up inside when I know he has restricted access to services, places and people during his work shifts. It's not as if he can nip off the oil rig to go to a different pub. I chastise myself for being so selfish. I should be more understanding of his situation.

'Shout when you see something of interest,' says Levi, as we weave our way through purple heather-clad hills, the verges covered with dense bracken, each contour meeting the distant horizon and pale blue skies.

'I'm happy to be out and about with company,' I say, mindfully contemplating the light and shade of the surrounding landscape. 'I hope I don't cramp your style by tagging along.' There's a decade between our ages – which some men might feel uncomfortable about. I hadn't expected him to mention his suggested day trip again; I assumed it was meant as a comfort when I was upset after arguing with Hamish. I can't always cover up my loneliness when I'm upset about life.

'Not at all. Taxiing folk around sounds very sociable, but they simply ask me the same questions. "You been busy?", "What time are you clocking off?" and even, "Had any trouble tonight?" so any variation in the conversation suits me just fine.'

'Mavis Grind!' I holler as we travel along the A970; until this point I've been enjoying the surrounding views and silent company.

'Really, you fancy throwing a stone or two?'

'I've never done it. How absurd is that for a Shetlander?'

'Embarrassing, I'd say,' Levi pronounces, indicating a natural off-road layby footing the huge craggy rock that fills the view from my passenger window

He's got a fair point.

He gently pulls off the road and sweeps into the layby. My seat belt is off before he kills the engine. I hear the driver's door clunk behind me as I dash towards the tourist information board placed by the side of the road.

'I've lived here all my life, but have never stopped to attempt the stone throw.'

'Not even as a kid?'

'No, my dad would never stop. He always promised "next time", but we never did,' I say excitedly, as my eight-year-old self resurfaces. 'Now, listen, I'll read it aloud.'

'I'm listening,' says Levi, pulling a face.

I skim-read the information, not wishing to bore him.

'Basically, it says that Mavis Grind is the only location in the UK where you can toss a stone across land, known as an isthmus, separating two stretches of water. That is the North Sea . . . and over there is the Atlantic Ocean.' I turn and gesture appropriately at each expanse of water.

'I've done this before, unlike you!'

'Humour me, please. I'm pretending I work alongside Jemima at the tourist information office.'

'Phew! I doubt she'll be working there for much longer.'

'Oi, she has choices now, thanks to her granddad's foresight. She needs a job she can love. She'll be on the right track, once she conquers her anxiety.'

'If you say so. I reckon the allotment suits her. I wouldn't go back to an office environment after weeks in the open air.'

As if he knows everything about Jemima's employment prospects.

I back away from the tourist information board. I know what's required, but I doubt I can throw a pebble the thirty-three metres necessary to cover the gap between the sea and the ocean.

'Choose your weapon,' says Levi, searching the ground for suitable missiles.

I scour the ground. I want the perfect two stones. If I'm doing this, I'm doing it properly. It's like marriage: my plan was to do it once and once only, so I wanted to do it right. The jury inside my head is still out regarding that particular matter. Then I spot them, side by side: one beige and the other grey, with a pinkish fleck. Totally different in appearance, unique, yet so alike in their ordinariness within this stunning landscape.

'I've found mine!' I shout, snatching them up. Both pebbles are smooth and incredibly tactile, nestled within my palm. I'd happily hold on to them as a keepsake of a good day out but where would the fun be in that?

I can't choose between them, so I close my eyes, switching them about within my palms, before blindly separating them into my left and right hands. Decision made. I open my eyes to see the beige pebble in my left, the grey in the other, determining their final locations.

'Are you going first, or am I?' asks Levi, juggling the two stones he's selected.

'You. I doubt mine will reach their intended locations,' I say, staring between the two stretches of water; how weird nature is, to create such a phenomenon.

Levi doesn't hesitate; having sussed his throwing position between the two stretches of water, he wangs his first stone deep into the North Sea and, after hearing a satisfying plop, launches the second into the distance towards the Atlantic Ocean. We hold our breath until a satisfying splash of water confirms his success.

'Well done!' I cheer, dancing on the spot, but knowing the excitement will be short-lived.

'Simply throw as hard as you can, from the shoulder not the wrist.'

'The shoulder?'

'Yeah, put your whole body into it. From here –' he taps my upper arm, before tapping my wrist – 'not just here.'

'I know where my body parts are.'

'You might want to limber up.'

'You didn't.'

'I'm not as tetchy and as physically uptight as you.'

My jaw drops wide open. 'You cheeky sod . . . I'm not tetchy.' I fall silent, rolling my throwing shoulder just a little, making him laugh.

I ignore him, positioning myself on the sloping shale beside the North Sea. Levi stands a little way off.

This won't be difficult, I'm barely three metres from the water's edge. The North Sea . . . where my hubby once resided for five years, day and night, year after year, before traipsing off to the Gulf of Mexico for this second stint.

I throw the beige pebble.

I do as Levi instructed, forcing the effort through my shoulder.

The pebble lands with a crunch amongst the shale near the water line.

'I missed!'

'That's an understatement,' says Levi, suppressing a belly laugh.

'That's your fault. "Throw from the shoulder" and look what happens – that's crap.'

'Better luck with the Atlantic Ocean, which is way over there,' says Levi, as if I can't see into the distance.

'No, I'm doing that again.'

'That's cheating.'

'No, it's called doing it right.' I plod down the slope in search of my beige pebble.

'Melissa, you'll never find it amongst the rest.'

'I will. It was beige and round, similar in size to this one,' I say, raising my clenched fist with the grey pebble snug inside.

'You haven't a hope in hell!'

'Defeatist!' I holler back on reaching the shoreline. He's right, there are thousands of tiny pebbles beneath my feet: cream, beige, grey and opal coloured, all begging to be chosen for my second attempt. 'Here it is! I've got it.'

'In your dreams.'

I return to our throwing spot on the embankment.

This time, I plant a kiss upon the pebble, before rolling my right shoulder like an Olympic athlete and launching the pebble into the air. And this time, there's definite effort, determination . . . and a satisfying plop into the North Sea.

'I did it!' I squeal. 'Now for this little beauty.'

Levi stands aside, shaking his head at my hopeful naïvety. I'm not put out; I know he's right. The chances of me wanging this one and hitting the bull's eye is pretty slim, despite the huge target. 'Are you watching . . . this is how's it's done!'

'I'm watching.'

I repeat my sequence. Kiss, roll and launch. As the pebble leaves my hand our joint gaze is fixed upon its journey as it flies through the air, crossing the A970 towards the Atlantic Ocean.

'Wooh!' calls Levi, as we race over the road, eager to see the result.

We are greeted by the sight of concentric circles, radiating outwards in satisfying ripples on the ocean's surface.

'Bloody hell, you did it!'

'I did it!' I say, stunned at the confirmation.

'I thought it was totally beyond you, when you threw like that . . .' he demonstrates a particularly bad technique. 'Wonders never cease!'

'I'll take that as a compliment.'

'You should – because you sure as hell couldn't do it a second time.' Levi is bent double, shaking with laughter. Such a happy sight, such energy and life.

A wave of sadness sweeps the smile from my face. I should be doing this with Hamish – husband and wife enjoying the hilarious antics of life. The piss-taking and banter should be shared with him, not Levi. The moment has passed; the magic is gone.

Chapter Nineteen

Dottie

'Can you stop arguing with me and simply rewind. Something happened in the background that I want to take another look at,' says Jemima, leaning nearer and tapping the screen where something has caught her eye.

'We haven't got all bloody night, you know!' sighs Old Bill, clutching the remote control.

'It'll take seconds, just go back a little way . . . but watch over here, and not the main entrance gate.'

Mungo, Old Bill and I exchange a glance.

'What? Have I asked for the impossible?' Jemima sounds exasperated with us.

'No, it's probably the wind blowing some plastic about – you know how there's always a rogue plastic bag drifting across the site.' I am trying to soothe fraught nerves.

'Honestly, it wasn't. Go back and I'll point it out.' She fixes us with a stare, refusing to be deterred by our three blank faces, sensing our reluctance.

Eventually, Old Bill rewinds by a fraction.

'Watch that spot there,' she says, tapping the screen again.

The image shows the entrance gate on the far left, but at the extreme edge you can just make out the stone boundary wall. Within a split second, there is a sudden movement and a shadow looms on the far side of the wall. 'There . . . did you see it?'

'Nothing.'

'Just shadows.'

'You're imagining it.'

The three of us chime in at regular intervals.

'Stop, rewind and I'll show you again. Watch the shadow appear on this section of wall . . . just here. It's like a figure has entered . . . but through the wall,' Jemima insists. 'Press play.'

'Now you're seeing ghosts, are you?' teases Mungo.

'It's nothing, let's carry on,' I urge.

'Probably the shadow of a tree blowing in the wind,' offers Old Bill.

'It's not, go back again,' demands Jemima.

'No.' Old Bill sounds curt.

'Why?'

'We're wasting our time,' I say.

'We're not. It can't be tree shadows, because there are very few trees on Shetland. And don't say it's shrubbery, because the foliage isn't that tall on the far side of the car park. It's bare stone wall and gravel down there.'

I can hear her confusion, and I know where this is going. Damn it.

'I feel like I'm telling my grandpop how to grow tatties, but I'm right,' states Jemima, adding, 'and I'll prove it.'

Without notice, she jumps up, pushes through the tiny gap between mine and Old Bill's chair and is striding towards the door of The Cabbage Patch before anyone can stop her.

We follow at a slower pace.

It is pitch black outside, just a sliver of moon lights the way. I stumble along the right-hand dirt track, following Jemima's outline. Old Bill and Mungo call out her name. I don't bother calling.

When my feet crunch on the gravel of the car park, I know exactly where she'll be.

Down at the far end, where the edge of the car park meets the boundary, and there are no trees, nor any tall shrubbery, just as she said. But something of interest, which goes unnoticed by many – it becomes like wallpaper, the longer you visit this site. Despite the darkness, I can see it in my mind's eye: the forbidden gateway with its iron-ring handle, nestled into the archway of the wall. Forbidden from use by all allotmenteers but one.

Jemima stands before it, touching the peeling paintwork and proving to herself that it is real.

I hear three sets of feet upon the gravel before me.

'See, I told you there weren't any trees!' she shouts, not bothering to turn and face us. 'Someone came in this way and the camera didn't pick them up, but their shadow crossed that section of wall.'

No one answers her, which probably confirms her theory. I don't know what to do. I could carry on standing here, staring at a wooden gate, or I could return to the shack and resume viewing the CCTV.

She grabs the iron ring and twists with force.

My heart is in my mouth.

It doesn't budge. Not an inch.

I exhale slowly.

It's locked.

Mungo and Old Bill are standing shoulder to shoulder when she turns around.

I return to The Cabbage Patch; they can answer her questions, I won't be there. I slump into my original seat and wait while they make their way back. The screen is frozen on pause, just as we left it. I can imagine their conversation; bickering between themselves about whatever secret Jemima has uncovered. It takes an age before they each reappear and join me, taking their seats.

I'm determined to be the first to speak, but Jemima jumps in.

'I don't know what it is, or who it is that you're covering for, but I have just proved that at six minutes past ten, someone opened that gate and entered this allotment site. Fact! I assume the gate connects to Lerwick Manor.' She sits back and stares, before continuing. 'Don't make out that I'm a fool, because I am far from it. Now, can we continue?' She retrieves the clipboard from the floor and enters a large question mark under the list of names.

Obviously, when she's given a task, Jemima does it properly – everyone needs to be accounted for.

There's an uncomfortable atmosphere, as Old Bill resumes play and the grainy images flicker to life.

I'll bide my time and say my piece when we're alone.

I'm grateful when a slim blonde female arrives at the entrance gate and has difficulty opening it, fumbling with the padlock.

'Melissa!' I say quickly, before the others can react.

Jemima adds her name to the list.

Chapter Twenty

Melissa

I circle The Veggie Rack, inspecting each shelf and having a nosey at the new produce offered for sale today. I like that someone's kind enough to offer a bundle of old flowerpots for a pound. For a newbie like me who is trying to scrimp by on the basics, that's a bargain. The buckets of fresh flowers provided by Dottie are simply beautiful. I love how she mixes fresh foliage with a few simple blooms for an interesting bouquet.

I check my own shelf and pocket the five £1 coins in my plastic tub: the sale of one of my scarecrows yesterday. I check the row and find the mini girl scarecrow has disappeared – interesting that my novel idea was the first to go! I make a mental note to create more females – obviously, the gender gap no long exists in the world of scarecrow duties. I tidy a few jars of comfrey tea, realign the fallen packets of half-used seeds and straighten tubs of bonemeal.

I get a whiff of something as I pass a shelf of jam jars and do a double take. I select a jar and inspect the handwritten label: 'Jemima's pumpkin chutney'. Looks interesting, I might buy some for tonight's tea. I take a sniff at the lid: nothing. I replace the jar, take a step or two back and retrace my path past the shelf to recreate the moment: nothing. My imagination must be playing tricks on me.

Through sheer boredom, I busy myself by sweeping the shed's floor. Moving each tub, basket and trug aside, I sweep beneath and behind each item properly, not just around the front. When

I empty the dustpan and stand in the doorway, the morning is bright and warm – just what the soil needs to germinate my secret tray of carrot seeds.

'Hello!' calls Dottie, seeing me leaning in the open doorway. 'How are we?'

'Ask me in three hours' time – I might find a suitable answer,' I reply, my expression like a slapped arse.

'Quiet, is it?'

'I've checked the duty rota three times to ensure I'm supposed to be here: Melissa from eight till eleven. I'd love it to be a genuine error and I'm free to dash off. I wouldn't complain at the inconvenience. It's just gone nine and, apart from you, not a single person has dropped by to look, purchase or drop off their produce. It's going to be a long shift if it stays like this, Dottie.'

'It won't. You should have brought some crafting with you.'

'Now that sounds like a plan. Being here would have given me an hour or two to hand-stitch or stuff a scarecrow.'

'Essential for next time, eh?'

'Anyway, less about me, how are you?'

'I mustn't grumble, but I will. Have you noticed any strange behaviour from the Far Siders after hours, so to speak?'

I shake my head rapidly. I know where this is leading but I'm no grass. My inner goddess immediately wishes to giggle out loud at the Freudian slip – but thankfully, Dottie can't read my thoughts. She stares at me; I think she has spied my cogs churning behind the facade.

'Anyway, if you should hear anything – whether it's the tiniest sniff, or as wacky as it may seem – let the committee know. There's something going on around there, and we need to get to the bottom of it.'

I nod enthusiastically, avoiding her pan-faced expression. Dottie might feel she's wide of the mark, but she's closer than she thinks to sussing out the Far Siders. With a cheery goodbye, she scurries along to her allotment. I stand in the doorway, watching her. I can't imagine how many years she's done this for; will that be me in, say, thirty years' time? Scurrying down to my allotment early each morning, in the hope of finding new growth, fewer slugs and a willing ear to listen to my gripes. Bless her, she's the life and soul of the committee, but surely there must be other things in life worthy of her dedication than row after row of delphiniums.

A sudden but gentle hissing noise behind me causes me to jump and spin round. I'm half expecting to confront an intruder: a cat or, worse still, a snake. My eyes scan the empty floor: there's nothing. I listen intently: gone. There are no gas canisters or inflatable objects for sale, so what the hell was that noise?

This is going to be a long three hours. I check the rota once again to see who relieves me: Levi. I'll certainly be chuffed to see his smiling face. I might ask him if he's got any free time to do me a small favour with that polytunnel he lent me.

Two hours pass incredibly slowly, with very little human inter-action.

'Morning!' calls Mungo, entering to find me slumped in a wobbly deckchair, absorbed by the task of inspecting my nails.

'Morning, Mungo, can I interest you in . . .'

'Pah! I'm not here to purchase goods.'

'Oh.'

'I want your honest opinion on the security of this set-up – the overnight security, mainly. How did you find it this morning?'

'Wouldn't it be best to ask Jemima? She's organising everything—'

Mungo coughs, covering his embarrassment.

'No, no, there's a method to my workings.'

A method in his madness, more like.

'It's never locked, is it? You know that. We'd have to introduce a key handover each night for whoever is opening up in the morning, and that complicates matters. You know Jemima wants it to run as smoothly as possible ... she's told you that. I'm sure she did.'

'Maybe ... she may have said something or other. And how busy is it?'

I hesitate.

'I've been rushed off my feet all morning, in fact; lots of folk dropping by to browse, and some made purchases. Kaspar delivered a batch of his home-made condensed milk cookies for sale, and he was delighted to find his surplus flowerpots had sold for a quid,' I lie, spying Kaspar's shelf, quickly adding, 'Dottie's nipped in twice for a quick chat on passing. See, it's not all about buying or selling, Mungo; social contact and interaction are what some people need around here. This little Veggie Rack is the equivalent of the Post Office in most rural communities.'

'Mmmm, there's far too much social interaction happening around these parts, if you ask me!' he says, pausing to stare at me for a split second before surveying the shelving units and making a mental note of their current stock.

What's that supposed to mean? I watch him as he closely observes the nearest shelf; his eyes narrow, his wattle throat trembles like a pelican's pouch under his grey beard. How does a small chat with Mungo make me feel like confessing to robbing all the potting sheds, starting illegal bonfires after dark and smoking weed outside The Cabbage Patch? He's definitely got a way about him. I suppose that's what comes from living on your own; the sound of your own voice is a rare occurrence. I instantly feel bad for lacking patience; that could be me one day. One day soon, if my Hamish doesn't pull his finger out and start spending more time at home; I'll be a Mungo, chomping people's ears off for the slightest misdemeanour and obsessing about spare keys.

'Anyway, don't be afraid to have a word on the quiet – I'm happy to raise any issues in an anonymous fashion, if needs be, to the committee.'

I bet you are.

As if on cue, the hissing starts up.

'Actually, there is one thing.'

Instantly, Mungo's ears have pricked up; I've got a new best friend.

'Can you hear that hissing sound?'

'What?'

Mungo and I both fall silent and listen.

Mungo's manner instantly changes. His head tilts this way and that as he slowly paces the shed, peering into crevices and corners, listening intently.

'It sounds like a snake.'

'I've already been down that route, rechecking every corner since I've swept the floor.'

'So, what the devil is that . . .'

Suddenly, the contents of the front jar of pumpkin chutney begin to ooze from beneath its screw cap and slide down the glass jar to pool in a sticky mass upon the wooden shelf.

'Oh . . . look!' I gesture to Mungo, just as a second jar follows suit, with a mass of orange chutney escaping the jar to merge with the contents from the first jar.

'Ping!' A plastic lid shoots from a jar at the rear of the shelf.

'What the hell!' cries Mungo.

'She has a mixture of screw caps and plastic snap-on lids – something's not right with her chutney.'

As I speak, other jars begin to ping or ooze, forming a growing slick of thick sticky gunk which overspills the shelf and begins dripping on to the shelves below.

'Quick, get a box or a tub before it spills on to Ned's honey jars and ruins his labels,' I say, turning about in confusion and looking for anything I can use. There's nothing at hand. 'Quick, Mungo, take them outside!'

Mungo grabs the first two jars, which are now rapidly foaming like cream from a spray can on to the surrounding shelves. I reach for the second pair of seeping jars and follow his lead. Mungo takes two shuffling steps towards the door, before slipping on a deposit of chutney. He dramatically crashes to the ground as his jars lift gracefully into the air, spiralling in slow motion, before smashing upon my newly swept wooden floor and spilling their contents everywhere. I, in turn, panic. Not knowing what to do first: dispose of the oozing goods through the open doorway, or help the elderly gent sprawled upon the floor and covered in orange gunk – which, I'll probably mention to Jemima later, has a beautiful aroma. Mungo's limbs are waving like a newborn during a nappy change.

'Mungo, stay where you are,' I instruct, as I launch both my jars through the doorway on to the grass, where they smash and continue to bubble ferociously. Re-entering The Veggie Rack at speed, I find Mungo attempting to stand up – shame on me for laughing, but it's the funniest thing I've ever seen. As he attempts to place one foot on the floor, he slips and slides on the now wet floor, smearing the chutney in all directions. He looks like Bambi on ice; his limbs repeatedly attempt to gain a solid, slip-free footing from which to hoist himself into a respectable position. Before I reach out a hand to help him, I know I'm not going to be as graceful as Thumper. The kindest thing I could do would be to leave The Veggie Rack, allowing him time to get himself upright and retain his dignity, before sauntering back in ten minutes. We could possibly both act like adults and pretend that this unfortunate accident hadn't happened, and promise never to refer to it again.

That's what I should do, but I don't. I barge in, all guns blazing, attempting my best 'I'm a first aider at college' demonstration. I finally grab hold of the slippery bugger as he falls down for the umpteenth time. But my solid hold doesn't last; my hand slips, covering me in a deposit of gunk and making my rescue attempt more difficult but definitely time critical, given the flight path of the pumpkin chutney, which is now randomly landing on neighbouring shelves and their goods.

'The bloody stuff is fermenting – she should have made sodding wine, not chutney!' cries Mungo, attempting to stand . . . and failing.

'Stop trying to stand! You're not helping the situation. Mungo, get on all fours!' I instruct, seeing his wasted energy.

Mungo's expression conveys utter horror at my uncouth instruction, swiftly turning to dismay as I slip on the growing orange puddle and crash to the floor. Never in my life would I ever have imagined barking such orders at a man, let alone someone as elderly as Mungo, before falling on top of him like a *Carry On* film gone crazy. If my Hamish gets to hear about this little scenario, my marriage is definitely over.

'What the devil is going on here!' exclaims Dottie from the doorway. 'Mungo Tulloch, I know there's still life in the old boy, but you've got some explaining to do!'

I can only imagine how it must look from the doorway: some kinky sex session with a fetish for orange lube. I simply want to die! Right here, right now, on this very spot, and never have to face these folks again. Someone, anyone, please scoop me into a wooden box, secure the lid at all four corners and get me out of here, never to return!

'Don't just stand there – go and fetch help!' shouts Mungo.

'No, don't!' I cry, as Dottie swiftly disappears. The very thought of another pair of eyes witnessing this live-action debacle, or attempting to untangle my womanly curves from the bones of an elderly gent, quenches my last flicker of dignity.

In two heartbeats, though it feels like an eternity, Dottie returns with two healthy, virile men from the far side. Two pairs of strong arms, with well-flexed biceps, pluck me and Mungo from the floor, depositing us on the grass outside The Veggie Rack.

'You need to let the rest of us know what time these sessions begin!' quips one male.

'I agree, I wouldn't mind a taste of that!' replies his buddy.

'Thank you kindly, gents, but we'll be having less of that talk around here,' remarks Dottie, dabbing Mungo's forehead with a tissue, which makes little difference. We must look like overgrown Oompa Loompas escaped from Willy Wonka's factory. 'That'll be all for now.'

One Far Sider gives me a cheeky wink as he proceeds to take his cue from Dottie's tone, and strolls off alongside his mate.

'I suggest you shut up shop for the day and both get yourselves home. I'll get this sorted and report back to Jemima. Though how I explain it is beyond me.'

'Simple. Tell her she's crap at making pumpkin chutney!' retorts Mungo angrily.

'Dottie, just tell her it must have fermented in the jars.'

'Mark my words, she'll be desperately upset,' mutters Dottie, giving up on the task of sorting Mungo's forehead out.

'Not as upset as she'll be when I catch up with her!' snorts Mungo, finally clambering to his feet, shaking the front of his tartan jacket as globules of pumpkin fly in all directions. 'Even more so, when I send her the cleaning bill!'

I remain seated, staring after the two retreating figures, before attempting to gather any tattered remnants of my self-respect which may be lying in the surrounding dust.

Jemima

I collect three watering cans brimming with cold water from the nearest butt, measure out a generous serving of my bottled comfrey tea and pour it into each, stirring well with a stick.

It sounds ridiculous, but each morning I'm eager to see how

much the tendrils on the pumpkin plants have grown. I reckon if I pitch a chair and watch, I might see them visibly growing with the naked eye. It's not surprising that Grandpop showed such enthusiasm. I wonder what he'd think to his 'Little Pumpkin' discovering the same joy and sense of achievement.

Weeks ago, if anyone had foretold that I would be motivated to rise early to perform such a task, I'd have laughed. But now it's the most natural thing in the world.

Some mornings, the sun has barely risen before I'm venturing up here to my allotment.

Admittedly, my pumpkin plants look slightly strange amongst a mass of flowering forget-me-nots – but in some respects, given Grandpop's untimely death, they seem quite fitting. Though Dottie titters each time she spies them, reminding me of yet another rookie error.

Crispy duck waddles around, pecking at the ground as I feed the pumpkins. My arms are stretched by the weight of each watering can, as I stand and patiently direct the spouting rose towards the roots. There's no need to soak the giant leaves and risk mildew or rot developing. Old Bill's already said that I can use crushed aspirin or apple vinegar to combat signs of either developing.

Grabbing the second watering can, I adopt my sturdy pose, feet apart, back straight, and pour. I scan the surrounding area as Crispy duck toddles off, his orange feet flip-flopping about, along the earthy furrows.

Quack, quack, quack. I hear his sounds of delight, scurrying free and nibbling at the earth.

It's hard to believe that he's almost fully grown in size, if not maturity. My bundle of fluff now has sleek brown and beige feathers, though I'm still waiting for his emerald plumage. If not, Crispy was a girl all along. I can't imagine not having his constant company as I tend this plot, or at home. I continue to watch as he moves about, and that's when I spot it: a boot print.

Not unusual for an allotment plot, but definitely unusual in size and breadth, considering my wellington boots are a size five. I cease watering and stride across, my eyes fixed upon the imprint.

I place my own boot alongside; the imprint's toes go way beyond mine. That's not my footprint!

I've had plenty of support and advice since my arrival, but no one has helped me to dig, weed or hoe this section. Someone has visited my allotment in my absence; I spy a second, third and fourth imprint, all of which cut across from the main pathway towards my pumpkin plot.

Firstly, who's been visiting my allotment? And secondly, that proves someone's definitely got a spare key!

Dottie

'Don't look at me like that, Ned Campbell, I have my principles,' I say, wagging my finger at his grumpy expression. He is eating breakfast while I clean his kitchen, the modern one.

'Wouldn't it have been easier simply to order a second delivery of bark chippings?'

'We have – but they'll never learn their lesson if we accommodate their yamse natures, will they?'

'I suppose not, but I worry about you at times. All this involvement, running after the younger ones, and still overseeing situations such as this. Are you sure it's not getting too much for you?'

I scowl at him. What's he heard?

'Certainly not!' I spit, vigorously wiping the kitchen counter to prove my point.

His eyebrows lift, reinforcing his concern.

'Don't you dare write me off yet, young man. There's more life in this old gal than you imagine – I could give you a run for your money.'

'You've got an incredible amount of stamina, but petty situations such as these should be dealt with by . . .' he pauses, shakes his head. 'Maybe I should step up more than I do. Play a part in the running of things.'

'How's that going to keep you in the background, if you begin appearing in the foreground?'

'It's not what I want, but maybe it's time.'

'Phuh! I think that will go down like a ton of fresh manure laden with straw!'

'What?'

'Unwelcome and useless!'

'Any joy with the CCTV and the honesty boxes?' he asks, ignoring my joke.

'Not really. We named everyone passing through the entrance; Jemima made a list, but there was a moment in relation to the walled gate being used. Jemima seems to think someone entered that way. I told her it hasn't been used in years.'

'Would the estate manager not use it for a late-night walkabout?' asks Ned.

'Not if he's smart about keeping himself to himself, he wouldn't.'

We exchange a glance. He knows what I'm saying. Who's ever heard of an employee having the free run of an entire manor, along with all the associated privileges.

'She won't take kindly to being lied to. Anyway, we didn't spot any unknown scallywags entering. Who knows . . .' I say, choosing my words carefully.

Ned sees me eyeing him. 'I think they're keeping a cockerel,' he says.

'Do you?'

'Yeah, I can hear it each morning – it doesn't shut up crowing. Though I haven't spotted it when I've nipped down to search. There'll be complaints galore if the local residents can hear it as clearly as I can.'

'Their list of misdemeanours is growing. I don't like it.'

'Nor me. Maybe we need to start a surveillance crew.'

'Levi and Old Bill didn't spot anything whilst retrieving the wood chippings, but that was just one night.'

'Mmmm,' says Ned, finishing his breakfast and putting his crockery in the dishwasher. 'Leave it with me. Any news from The Veggie Rack?'

'Mungo got the thrill of his life, thanks to Jemima's exploding pumpkin chutney and Melissa's rescue efforts.' I spend the next few minutes attempting to describe the incident, but I can't get to the end without laughing. 'Poor Jemima was mortified when she heard.'

His ears prick up at the mention of her name, and his stance straightens somewhat. If I didn't know any better, I'd suspect there's a flicker of interest there; maybe his outburst and subsequent apology have heightened the attraction.

'With creative ideas such as hers, she'll survive a knock-back or two.'

'For sure, she will. She takes after Tommy.' I leave him with that thought and get on with cleaning the cooker.

Chapter Twenty-One

Melissa

'Morning, morning,' I call on entering The Veggie Rack, cradling a box of products. I wasn't sure who'd be manning the counter but am pleased to see Levi slouched in the communal deckchair, half asleep. 'Late shift last night, was it?'

'Don't ask! I had to take a group of youngsters up to Boddam, and within twenty minutes I had to double back because they wanted to return to Lerwick, only to be called back out thirty minutes later to be taken back to Boddam. What a sodding nightmare! I was sure they were about to do a runner, given the cost.'

'But they paid up?'

'Eventually. A dodgy little crowd of wind-up merchants.'

I shake my head at the very thought. 'Can't you refuse jobs?'

'I can, but how's that going to help me in the long run? I'm knackered now, though. What's new with you?'

'Bless you. Well, look what I've made.' I proudly draw a wind chime from the box by its plaited loop, allowing the brightly coloured ceramic tiles to tingle and clang. 'I thought people might want them to hang up – it might help to scare the birds away from their crops.'

'Nice one – how many have you made?'

'Ten, though I've enough tiles to create another ten if these sell well. I'm asking for eight quid. Do you think that's too much?'

Levi shakes his head, his tired eyes struggling to stay open.

'Your scarecrows are selling like hot cakes, you've got the Midas touch.'

'Ah, I hope so. I'd much prefer to be upping this side of my business, rather than taking on another half day at the college,' I say, unpacking my wind chimes and placing each one on the nearest empty shelf. 'That's not the right way to display them, is it?'

'Here, keep an eye on the counter while I fetch a handful of nails and a hammer,' says Levi, peeling himself from the chair. 'It'll take two minutes to knock a few nails into that beam there.'

'Ah, bless you, you can hardly stay awake and yet you're still helping others.'

'I've never been any different, it's what we do around here.'

Jemima

It feels strangely dangerous, unlocking the allotment gate at ten minutes to midnight. I've never dressed head to toe in black before – like a cat burglar – and I spend five minutes fumbling blindly with the padlock. A flashback of the grainy images witnessed the other night on the CCTV fills my mind. Finally, the bolt slides aside.

As expected, the car park is empty. I glance towards the walled gate before swiftly taking the dirt track. I hitch the rucksack high on to my shoulder and hotfoot it to my allotment. I'm not scared; I'm well equipped with a torch, a set of replacement batteries, a flask of coffee and five Mars Bars – an embarrassing amount of chocolate, but no one need know. I'll read Grandpop's weather journal if I get lonely and need company in the wee small hours.

I stumble along, falling into the deep ruts as I attempt to walk along the grassy middle section. Everything is distorted by the darkness; the distance I walk seems double that in daylight. The sky above is scattered with tiny twinkling stars, mimicking the white solar lights scattered upon some allotments.

I jog the final section, before reaching my plot and scurrying towards my potting shed. It doesn't seem much of a hideout, but it'll offer more cover than my polytunnel.

The allotment looks serene, bathed in moonlight. In the daylight, I see an endless list of tasks, a jumble of untidy possessions collected by Grandpop, and the bare earth which Mother Nature keeps threatening to take over.

I still don't feel like the true owner, given the constant references to Grandpop. It's not that I get upset when he's mentioned, but it knocks my confidence each time. I'm doing my best – literally giving it my all – yet no one's impressed with my efforts.

On approaching the potting shed, the bent nail which I use is missing and the door is slightly ajar.

Caught you!

I tiptoe the remaining few steps before wrenching the door open, to be greeted by an outlined figure reclining in my low-slung deckchair.

'Are you OK?' asks a male voice from the darkness.

'Ned?'

'Who else were you expecting?'

'I wasn't expecting anyone to be hiding in my shed!'

'I assume you're on a secret mission too, so please close the door before you ruin my plan.'

'I'd like to catch whoever is visiting my allotment.' I quickly step inside, pulling the door to. I'm unsure if I should be thrilled or suspicious. 'How long have you been sitting here?'

'Fifteen minutes or so.'

I shuffle past his knees to collect my second deckchair from beneath the counter. Rearranging and positioning it isn't the easiest task in a confined space. When I eventually settle, my eyeline is level with the window ledge. Hardly conducive to a surveillance job.

'Why are you here?' I ask, venturing to challenge him.

'I wondered when you'd ask. If you must know, I'd planned to sit next door. But the position of Dottie's polytunnels makes it a useless surveillance spot. This is much better. I can see the track's figure of eight.'

'It didn't enter your head to ask me?'

'What – and spoil the surprise!' he teases.

I can't see his brooding features in the dark, but I guess that he's smirking.

'Are you narked?' he asks.

'No.'

'You sound it.'

His habit of watching other people's behaviour and determining their mood is spot on. I can't argue with his accuracy.

'Do you want me to go?' He pushes the shed door open with his foot and the moonlight reflects a portion of his face, turned towards mine.

'Will you shut the door, please?'

'I'll take that as an invite to stay.'

His mood switches like the weather. His barometer points to thunderous outbursts one minute, warm apologies the next – and smooth talking, brightening the outlook, when he chooses. Interesting.

'I'm curious. I don't take kindly to thieves preying on this community.'

'Theft happens everywhere, Ned.'

'Not here, it doesn't.'

'I can assure you, it does. The first time I met Mungo and Levi, they were pinching my polytunnel.'

'Recycling, actually.'

'Phuh! You're as bad as them.'

I haven't even clocked up fifteen minutes, yet already I'm bored rigid. I want to open my flask and enjoy a Mars Bar – good job I brought extra.

'Who's that?' Ned rises from his deckchair to crouch before the window.

I struggle from the deckchair to crouch beside him.

'Shhhhh, Jemima.'

Ned's right. There's a figure striding along my pathway.

'Didn't I lock the front door?'

'Yeah, but there are spare keys all over the place – who knows who has what?'

'Well, that's bloody great!'

'I'm trying to watch.'

The figure then hotfoots it across my vegetable beds towards the sprawling tendrils of my prize pumpkin plant, retrieves a bottle from their pocket before crouching to pour the content on to the roots.

'What are they doing?' I snap.

'They're either feeding your pumpkin or destroying it.'

'What?'

Ned looks at me, shaking his head. 'They're either cheating on your behalf, without involving you, or nobbling you from the competition.'

'No way!'

'The festival makes everyone so competitive – some people get pretty fierce in the jealousy stakes.'

'Whoever it is obviously thinks I'm bloody useless too. Give me strength!'

'Not necessarily. They might be sharing a trusted potion, knowing you haven't the expertise or knowledge.'

'It's a pumpkin. How much attention does it require?'

We finish yapping in time to view the stranger leaving my pumpkin and striding further across my allotment towards my compost heap.

'Now what? Am I not turning my compost properly?'

Ned begins to laugh. 'You might wish to step away from the window for this one.'

'I want to see exactly what my midnight caller is doing on my plot, thanks very much. I've got a good mind to go out there and catch them in the act.'

'I'd stay where you are, unless you want to embarrass yourself.'

I'm totally confused. 'Aren't we going to confront them?'

'Trust me. Stay where you are and watch, if you must, but at least we know the mystery caller isn't Dottie.'

'How?'

'She hasn't the equipment for the next task.' Ned can hardly speak for laughing. He raises a hand to cover my eyes, but I push it away. 'Seriously, you might not want to watch.'

'What's happening?'

I press my nose to the grimy window to view the goings-on. The stranger stands before the compost heap, unzips their trousers and . . . I swear I see a jet of water.

I whip around to stare at Ned's barely visible features before turning back to confirm my observations.

'Are they doing what I think they are doing?'

'Yep. He's having a slash on your compost heap.'

'What?'

'They reckon it improves the quality of your compost.'

'No way!'

'Yes, way.'

'I've a good mind to go out and give them what for. How dare they pee on my compost – I've got to put my hands in that!'

'Not without gloves, you won't be.'

'Well, not now.'

'Shhhh, look.' Ned gestures towards the window.

The stranger has finished his business and is exiting my plot.

'That's it? They came, they literally went and then buggered off!'

'Yep, it looks like it.'

We sit in silence. I'm fuming.

'What gives them the right to think I want their help nurturing my pumpkin or improving my compost.'

'I'd stay shtum if I were you because ... ay-ay, who's this?'

'What?'

Ned gestures towards the window again.

I watch open-mouthed, as a shadowy figure shuffles along the pathway, crosses my carefully dug vegetable patch, virtually in the footsteps of the previous visitor, heading towards my pumpkin plant.

'Is it the same person?'

'I wouldn't say so, not with that gait.'

We watch as this visitor empties a large bottle of liquid on to the roots of my prize pumpkin.

'What the hell!' I mutter in annoyance.

'You need to take it as a compliment.'

'Well, I don't. Quite frankly, they must think I am a gardening imbecile.'

'Jemima, calm down. That isn't their intention.'

'I've been breaking my back, watering it three times a day, and now I find that my effort really wasn't necessary. What a waste of my time!'

'And now for part two,' chuckles Ned, as we watch the unknown shuffler make their way towards my compost heap.

'Are they having a laugh at my expense?'

'Again, you should be honoured.'

'Well, I'm not! Have you been doing that too?'

'Call me selfish, but I can safely say I have never nipped around in your absence to use your convenience.'

'It appears that every other male has.'

I'm lost for words. Here I was thinking that the allotments had a natural routine, from dawn till dusk. Tonight's viewing has blown that theory.

'That's it, I don't trust this lot as far as I can throw them,' I say, grabbing my rucksack filled with provisions. 'Do you want coffee?'

'I'm impressed – were you planning to stay for the long haul?'

'I was. And aren't I glad, given what I've witnessed tonight! Though I only have one flask cup.'

'No worries, there'll be a jam jar in here somewhere.' Ned blindly searches, as I settle back in the deckchair, unscrew my flask and retrieve two Mars Bars from my horde.

'Urgh!'

'If you've never drunk out of a jam jar, you've never lived,' he jibes, as the clinking of glass and a definite sniffing sound repeatedly occurs until he returns to his seat.

'Did you just sniff inside that jar?'

'Yep, I can't risk ruining my coffee,' he replies.

'Or your health,' I add.

'I doubt it; I've the constitution of a bull,' mutters Ned.

'Have you now!' I jest, feeling for the edge of his jam jar before pouring his coffee. Blind within the darkness, our fingers briefly touch and a buzz of excitement raises goose bumps on my skin. My free hand digs into my rucksack, attempting to cover my reaction. 'Here's a Mars Bar.'

'Full marks – you think of everything.'

I hear him slurp his coffee. Any second now, I'm expecting him to spit out a dead fly or a foreign body. We sit in a comfortable silence; it's as if a ready-made connection exists. I listen to his steady breathing, accompanied by sporadic sips and gulps, as I eat my chocolate. It's been so long since I enjoyed or experienced male company, platonic or otherwise. Having annoyed him the other day, who'd have thought we could revert to this after our first argument. Our first argument! The very thought pulls me up sharp. I want to laugh out loud at such a Freudian error, but daren't, for fear of having to explain myself.

'Actually, I was thinking about Lerwick Manor the other day.'

'Really?'

'If I owned such a place, there's no way I'd leave the stable yard empty.'

Ned's outline turns from viewing the window to stare at me.

'Slightly pie in the sky, but my ideas aren't always logical. Anyway, you said there were sixteen stables, including the forge, and all are a decent size, which would create sixteen rental properties for small businesses. The family would need to invest in the refurbishment – but that's never wasted, if you own the land and the deeds.'

Ned continues to stare.

'It's none of my business, but it takes my mind off things—'

'And?' he interrupts.

'And what?'

'And what were your thoughts?'

'They should invest in their own project before a tourist trust does. You know what happens. They create a coffee shop come gift shop, before organising historical tours and professional talks relating to the area or the building. I don't get why the family don't attempt it first. There's a decent number of tourists visiting Shetland, and it's increasing year on year, with the recent investment from the local authorities.'

'And what kind of businesses did you imagine?'

'Well, hear me out. Take Melissa, she works part-time at the college, spends some time down here, but once home she spends hours making her textiles or ceramics – and yet, she's got very little chance of selling her goods or of them being seen by the public. If she can't display her goods, the public can't buy; and if they don't buy, she can't generate enough money to renew her supplies – she's almost flogging a dead horse. Her dearest wish is to make more, sell more and create more – but how can she do that, if her products aren't always on display?'

'Doesn't she use the internet?'

'Yes, but once she adds the postage and packaging on to the price of a ceramic jug, which might get damaged in transit, the price goes through the roof. Plus, not everyone wants to buy something that they haven't touched or seen – there's a connection when you spot an object, fall in love with it and want to buy it.'

Ned is following what I'm saying, but at the same time seems lost to another world.

'Textiles, ceramics, what else?'

'Blacksmith, weaving, wood carving, knitting wools and stained glass. The amount of space in the courtyard would allow visitors to mill around and view each vendor working their craft – and there'd still be plenty of space to display finished goods for sale. As a collective gallery dedicated to traditional arts, it could be marketed as a unique visitor attraction, maintaining the heritage of Shetland, without treading on the toes of established businesses already trading in Lerwick.'

'Locals might benefit from it too.'

'I suppose so. More goods for sale, a wider range of products – and visitors can observe the traditional methods, so it's educational too.'

'You'd be calling them all artists?'

'Well, yeah, they all create from bare materials, don't they?'

'I see.'

'Plus, the family could open a coffee shop, given the size of that traditional kitchen – which you admitted is rarely used nowadays. Though they'd need to offer toilet facilities.'

'What, like you do for the allotment holders?' teases Ned.

'Ha ha. Anyway, that's what I'd be doing if I owned the stable yard. The bricks and mortar are already there, so they need to invest time, effort and some additional money – who knows, if it takes off, they might never need the tourist trust!'

'Maybe you should visit the manor and elaborate on these ideas?'

'I'd love to.'

I sip my coffee; it's cooler than I like.

'And you think all these thoughts whilst weeding?'

'That and a lot more,' I say, struggling to stand up from my deckchair.

'Sounds ominous.' There's a cheeky twang, almost flirtatious, to Ned's tone.

I shuffle past Ned's position, ease open the shed door, and am about to throw away my cold coffee when I spy our third visitor. 'Oh . . . look.'

I crouch down, pushing the door a little wider, enabling Ned to see: Mr Fox. We watch in silence as the fox trots along the length of the perimeter fence between mine and Dottie's plot. His nose is high, his ears pricked and rotating, whilst his thick bushy tail proudly quivers.

'Good job you put your chickens away each night,' whispers Ned, his warm breath tickling my neck and ear lobe.

'How's he got inside my allotment when the front door is closed?'

'He's probably got a spare key like everyone else,' jokes Ned. 'You'll scare him off.'

'He's the only legitimate visitor I should be having.'

'Don't let the others catch you saying that.'

'They've a right to be angry at him; he kills their chickens.'

'He's surviving the best way he can – just like the rest of us,' says Ned.

I turn to face him; that last comment sounded deep and meaningful.

Ned's gaze flickers from the fox to my intent stare. For a split second, neither one of us exhales. His pupils are huge black holes. I break the spell by averting my gaze, in an attempt to hide the obvious, but I sense our connection has increased.

We watch as the fox performs an honorary lap before slinking off along the side of my chicken enclosure, heading towards the footpath that runs alongside the brook.

Chapter Twenty-Two

July

High: 15°

Low: 10°

Daylight: 18 hours

Rain: 10 days

Wind: 13 mph

Note: Wild otters, orcas, puffins and seals — the sea and cliff tops are thriving with wildlife. The Cabbage Patch could do with a change of wildlife; the wacky baccy Far Siders need to cull that habit before it gets out of hand. Mungo wants to try a roll-up but Dottie would kill him. Repotted my pumpkin seedlings — good steady growth on each one — there's sure to be a festival prize winner amongst them. My Little Pumpkin is visiting later today, I've bought a sponge cake ready for her.

Jemima

I follow the driveway delivering me to the main entrance of Lerwick Manor, parking alongside Ned's Range Rover, as he instructed.

I'm a few minutes early, so I hope the family aren't offended by my eagerness. My smart appearance doesn't ease the anxiety bubbling beneath the surface and threatening to disable me as I ascend the stone steps under the watchful eye of carved lions. I'm fighting the negativity which advises me to swiftly turn about and go home. Even more so, when I stand before the huge wooden door, decorated with iron studs, complete with an old-fashioned bell pull. I'll be one hour, if that. If Crispy duckling can manage being on his own, I can explain my idea to the family.

The door slowly opens.

'Good evening, welcome to Lerwick Manor,' says Dottie, her smile widening as she opens the door, revealing a hallway of black and white tiles.

'Thank you,' I whisper, entering hesitantly. Surely her dusting duties are finished for the day?

I'm all eyes; the grand staircase and plunging chandelier appear more impressive when viewed from the main entrance, after putting an end to my previous visit.

'This way, please,' instructs Dottie, leading me through an ornate archway towards a series of wooden doors.

My nerves are jiggling in my stomach. I haven't jotted down my idea, because Ned said it wasn't worth doing – but what if I go blank and forget everything?

Dottie stops short before a doorway, pauses and then opens the oak door, leading me inside. The bookcases span floor to ceiling on every wall. I follow, expecting to be greeted by various faces, but there's no one waiting in the library. Dottie leads me towards the French doors, which stand wide open with the lace voiles billowing in the breeze.

I didn't imagine we'd be outside. My anxiety levels are rising as I'm thrown by the labyrinthine trail, but my fixed smile is in place for whenever the family appear.

The paved terrace is dotted with potted ferns and lichen-encrusted statues . . . but no people. A drinks trolley is centre stage, with a large jug of iced pink cocktail alongside two martini glasses.

I look about the terrace in surprise. What the hell is going on?

Dottie has disappeared.

Ned is standing right behind me when I turn about, questioning what I'm doing here. 'Evening, Ned, what's going on?'

'Shall we have a drink and I'll explain?' He touches my forearm, before drawing the drinks trolley nearer and busying himself pouring me a drink. I watch the ice bob in the sculpted lip of the jug, before he offers a glass to me.

'Thank you.' My voice is stilted, my mind whirring, whilst my anxiety is firing on all four cylinders. This is all very nice, but unexpected.

'Cheers, Jemima,' says Ned, clinking his own glass against the side of mine.

I don't react or move to accept his gesture; my brain is fogged with the actions of the past few minutes. I've imagined shaking hands, politely exchanging names with members of the family by now. I'm confused.

'Ned?'

'Sadly, the family can't make it, so I've agreed to walk you around. I hope you aren't too disappointed.'

'I quite understand – busy people, busy lives,' I say, unsure if a cocktail is suitable compensation, given that I'm driving.

'We'll make notes as we go, and I'll feed back. I'm sorry if you feel cheated.'

'They've probably decided that I'm chatting bubbles and have changed their minds.'

'No. Not at all.' He leans forward, gently patting my hand. Ned sips his drink.

I automatically follow, gazing at him over the rim of my glass.

My heels click rhythmically on the brickwork as I walk the length of the terrace, drink in hand, admiring the view before me: a vast expanse of lawn, edged by neat borders and sturdy pergolas supporting bare woody vines, beyond which the garden extends further than I can see, edged by the boundary wall.

'So, what's the agenda?' I ask, determined to push on rather than lose the thread.

'I understand that you're currently on sabbatical, and I was wondering if you intend to return to your old job or whether you fancied a new one?'

'Doing what?'

'Managing the stable project. I figured if you could envision it, you could deliver it too. What do you reckon?'

I'm dumbstruck. Things like this never happen to me!

'What do you think?'

'I think they must be out of their tiny minds, trusting me to establish a new project when they know very little about me or my work ethic.'

'I can vouch for you. I've seen enough in recent weeks, especially from your input into The Veggie Rack. You can have time to think, if you need it – there are no conditions attached.'

'I'm tempted, but can I come back to you?'

'In the meantime, let's walk and talk, and jot down some of your ideas.'

Ned grabs a pile of paper from a desk drawer in the study while I stare from the sofa at the extravagant sight before me: navy and green tartan everywhere, curtains, carpet – and for an additional touch, swathes of tartan fabric draped either side of the great fireplace.

'I take it they're proud of their tartan then?'

'Do you think?' jests Ned, following my gaze. 'Generations of the family have paid homage to the clan colours. Haven't you the same tradition?'

'My surname is Button – are you seriously telling me that some poor soul has had the gall to choose colours, let alone weave a specific pattern, for a bunch of Buttons? They are out of their tiny minds, if they have.'

Ned laughs.

'Exactly. The name's laughable, isn't it? All the connotations of being cheap, plastic, mass produced – and possibly, insignificant.'

'Surely not,' he counters. 'Some might say small, perfectly

formed and pretty vital in certain circumstances, would you not agree?'

Who is he trying to kid?

'No?' he questions, raising an eyebrow. 'I reckon your vision for the proposed gallery may prove pretty vital for the future of Lerwick Manor – so we'll adopt my definition for the time being, OK?'

'Vital?'

'If the gallery generates enough to prevent the tourist trust being brought in, then yes, vital.'

I feel queasy; I hadn't thought the situation was as dire as that.

'The family have always been asset rich but cash poor – if you get my drift.'

I nod, confirming my understanding. Basic economics defines their situation as untenable as a long-term prospect.

Melissa

'You did buy 'Gladiator' parsnips, didn't you?' Mungo questions me sharply, the moment he sees the dustbin corner.

'Yes.'

'And Levi showed you the correct way to plant the seedlings?'

'Yes, just as you told him to.'

'And you're watering, as he said?'

'Mungo, I'm nurturing and monitoring those parsnips to an obsessional level, above and beyond the requirements of a new-born baby, OK? Now please can you give it a rest? I asked you over to look at my carrots – they've got black and yellow bugs on them,' I say, pointing towards my carrot bed.

'You've got carrots?' says Mungo, tearing himself away from my dustbins to inspect the flourishing carrot tops. 'Mmmm.'

'What's that supposed to mean?'

He doesn't answer but moves along the line, inspecting others – his downturned mouth frowns ominously as he stands tall.

'Carrot root fly.'

I'm waiting for his input regarding a vital bottled remedy, or a natural cure. It isn't forthcoming.

'Mungo, what do I do?'

'Did you cover them with fleece?'

'No.'

'Did you thin them out after planting?'

'Errr, no, Levi didn't tell me to.' This brings a small smile to the stern features. 'So, how do I get rid of it?'

'You'll need to move the badly affected ones and then dowse everything with soapy water – plenty of it, mind you. You planted them too shallow, that's the problem – or you may even have planted them on the same patch as last year!'

'Mungo, I wasn't even here last year! How would I know who planted what and where?' I give up trying to convince folk that I'm not a blithering idiot.

'Next time, plant them in a deep container like the dustbins,' he mutters, rechecking the carrot foliage.

'Why anyone has an allotment is a mystery – everything seems to grow better in a sodding dustbin!' I grumble, not caring when Mungo shoots me a warning look over his shoulder. 'I'm just saying.'

'This is what happens when newbies don't follow instructions … these carrots are literally covered – you've got a job on your hands now, that's for sure.' He straightens his frame and shakes his head like a mechanic surveying my car engine. 'Good job you're not putting these in for the festival, or you'd be laughed out of the marquee.'

'Thanks for the vote of confidence.'

'I'm being honest; there's no point telling you otherwise.

Whereas those parsnips over there seem to be coming along nicely – now, you did a good job on those.'

'Have you got an issue with carrots?' I ask.

His features twist, as if to snarl.

'Since day one you've been against me growing them. And now, you seem pleased about the carrot root fly ... had a bad experience, did you?'

'What's Levi been saying?'

'Err, nothing.'

'I'll tell you something for nothing, folk around here need to stop with the gossiping. I'm on the committee here; I've earned my place, fair and square. If folk have got anything to say about me, then they can say it to my face.'

'Mungo?'

'Don't you Mungo me, young lady – I can recall every detail about those carrots, and no one around here can say anything different. Don't you forget that, you hear me?' Mungo exits my plot at the fastest speed that I've seen him shift. He slams my gate shut and snorts as he marches along the track to his own plot.

I'm wide-eyed and open-mouthed. I was only joking – but bloody hell, I'll make sure I warn Levi. Mungo's on the war path.

Chapter Twenty-Three

Jemima

'Incredible detail and foresight, Jemima. Is there anything I've missed?'

I scan the sheaves of paper on which he's jotted down everything I mentioned during our tour of the stables. There are numerous 'To-do' lists regarding building alterations, suggestions for interiors, maintenance tasks and installations involving the stable yard, the neighbouring orangery and the aged kitchen.

'You'll need to contact the authorities, to make sure there are no surprises regarding commercial projects and any insurances.'

He scribbles additional notes.

There is so much to do, yet the project has come alive in one evening. What originally seemed a feasible suggestion now has definite growth and potential.

'The family must really trust you as their estate manager,' I say.

'Absolutely. They trust their own.'

'You're related? I should have guessed. That explains your fondness for the tartan colours of the Campbell clan.'

'Blood's thicker than water, don't you think?'

'Not really, my family aren't. I rarely see them – and we hardly know each other. If it works for you, then great. Cheers to keeping it in the family, so to speak.' I give a yawn. 'Sorry, it's getting late.'

'It's quite stuffy in here, how about a breath of fresh air before you need to drive back?'

'That sounds wise.'

Within seconds, we're in the cramped boot room, overflowing with footwear, jackets and outdoor sporting equipment, having dashed through a maze of corridors and cold flagstones from the warmth of the study. My orientation suggests we aren't far from the old kitchen, used for my chutney making, and I remember that Crispy duck enjoyed spending the day sleeping in here.

'Here, it might be too big but pop this on,' says Ned, handing me a wax jacket, grabbing another for himself.

The corduroy collar is soft against my cheek, while the shoulder seams hang from my frame.

'Here, let's do up these press studs, it'll save you from getting cold.'

I freeze as he pulls the front placket together, swiftly connecting each fastening. My gaze watches his dark features. His fingers are tracing their way down my body, carefully inching from my collarbone . . . to my breastbone . . . and downwards to my fluttering naval. I've never been attracted to a strong jawline before, let alone a cleft chin, but it's incredibly alluring and sexy.

'Jemima?'

I come to, feeling quite undone by the fleeting moment. I notice that the fastenings on my wax jacket are secure.

'This way!'

Leaving the boot room, Ned unlocks the top and bottom bolts of the nearest door. The chill of a damp night greets us, along with a blinding security light.

'Where are we off to?'

'You'll see . . . I don't think you'll be disappointed.'

Ned takes my hand as we dash across the paved terrace decorated with potted ferns and lichen-encrusted statues, on which we'd stood earlier. How long ago that seems, and yet it is only a matter of hours.

I'm conscious of his fingers interlocking with mine. I'd have held hands, palm within palm, one wrapped around the other. But entwined? Better, worse – or simply a clumsy mistake by my potential boss?

We rush down the steps on to the manicured lawn and continue down the slope, following the line of the drystone wall on our right and into a wooded area, a fair distance from the manor. My eager steps begin to slow; my heart rate quickens. Where is he taking me?

'Ned?'

'Shhhhhh,' he whispers. 'You'll like it.'

How can he know for certain? His grasp is tight around my fingers, his stride remains firm as the ground underfoot changes from lawn to a spongy bark surface, and haunting branches twist above our heads.

'Ned, I'm not sure I like this.'

'You're quite safe.'

I lower my head, not wanting to view the silver moon through the naked limbs of ancient trees. It looks like the backdrop for a fearful thriller – and I'm playing the lead role. This is not what I'd imagined, back in the study, when he suggested a breath of fresh air. I wish we were back inside.

'Ned, seriously, I'm not feeling . . .'

Before I can finish speaking, we come to the end of the woodland copse and its spongy surface underfoot, which opens out to reveal a garden of low-level box hedging, no higher than my knees. My shoes crunch upon the gravel pathway as Ned leads me through the geometric knots, teased and trained towards the centrepiece: a large raised ornamental fishpond, complete with a central fountain.

'See, you were quite safe. You worry too much.'

Ned releases my hand, allowing me to lean upon the stone wall of the fishpond, resting my hands upon the thick sturdy rim. The reflection of the moon is fragmented upon the dark water by the constant fall of the fountain's droplets. Slowly, from the depths, appears the ghostly movement of gold and white fish as they surface to greet us with gaping rubbery mouths.

'What are they?'

'Koi carp – I've had them for some years. You wouldn't think they'd survive in Shetland, but they do well, given the depth of the pond.'

'Is this another hobby?'

'Sort of. My grandfather would take me fishing as a lad. We'd kill our catch, gut it and have it for tea, which was the thing to do – and teach a growing lad, but it was never really my thing. I'm not into killing or hunting, as a rule. I enjoy the beauty of these creatures, their finesse, their grace – and oh, look there, the white and gold carp is nearly twenty-five years old.'

'No way! You lived here with relatives then?'

'When I was younger, yes. Honestly, that fish was the first one I purchased. I thought it best to test the conditions, before investing in the others.'

I watch as the koi carp glides below the surface, its glistening scales reflecting the moonlight like a mythical creature. Ned walks around the perimeter, removing a stray weed here and there from the stonework.

'They're beautiful.'

'I thought I was being conned when I enquired with the supplier. The rough weather of Shetland isn't an ideal environment, but they can thrive if I tend to their needs. I've got a polytunnel for additional protection, which covers the pond during the winter months.'

'That's amazing.'

'My granddad always said, "You won't know until you try,

laddie", and he was right. Do you see over there?' Ned points into the distance, across the darkened lawn towards an area of trees. 'That was my granddad's attempt at an apple orchard, but the wind is too harsh. Look at the stumpy twisted growth. He never harvested much more than a few basketfuls, but it kept him satisfied most years.'

'At least he tried.'

'Exactly. Though I don't tend to it, nowadays; I've left the windfalls for the wildlife.'

A sudden wave of sadness overwhelms me at the thought of the decay.

I settle on the edge of the stone wall, listening to the gentle cascade of the waterfall. Being here feels like paradise; a beautiful garden lit by moonlight is verging on Eden-like. And to think the allotment plots are only a stone's throw away, over the interconnecting drystone wall.

'Relaxing, isn't it?'

'It certainly is.' I watch as he continues his stroll. He's fit and healthy, doesn't appear to have a care in the world, thanks to his family connections, and yet he's as ghostlike as the carp emerging and disappearing into the depths of the water.

Like the carp, is he surviving or thriving in this environment?

'We all need something to motivate us to prise our backbones off the mattress each morning,' I observe.

'We do. Mine being the responsibility of acting as warden of all this. Maintaining the estate as a whole, looking after the tenant farmers and respecting the generations of Campbells who have gone before. Which is why your suggestion is vital – and it comes at precisely the right time for us to implement it.'

'I'm honoured.'

'I reckon if we crack on with the refurbishment in the coming weeks, you could see your gallery open by October – ready for Christmas.'

'This Christmas? What about planning permission, the local council, contractors and building work?'

'You just focus on gaining access to the traditional artists and crafters who might be interested in renting each stable. I'll make a few phone calls – recoup a few outstanding favours from the builders and established connections in Lerwick.'

'And marketing?'

'Leave that to me, I've got a company I use in the town who are a dream team.'

'Dream team! As if we aren't?' I scoff.

'Mmmm, as if we aren't,' repeats Ned.

I look up on hearing the poignancy in his tone.

He's barely a step away, gazing intently at my face. Suddenly, I'm aware of a shift in our situation, an intensity which wasn't present a matter of minutes ago, yet now is pressing down upon our shoulders.

'Anyway, I need to make a move towards home.'

Ned comes to; he averts his gaze from mine. The spell is broken.

Chapter Twenty-Four

Melissa

'Hi, Jemima, how are you diddling?' I call out, arriving early and spying her kneeling upon the bare earth tending her seedlings.

'Fine, fine. It's quiet up here this morning. I've hardly seen anyone. No Mungo or Old Bill – even Dottie's deserted her patch before the usual time.'

'There's no telling who will be where, some days. You suss out their routine, only for them to switch the next week.'

Jemima gives a polite smile and returns to her work. She's not one for gossip, I've learnt that. As I fiddle undoing my padlock, I notice she's watching me.

'Are you OK?' I ask.

She grimaces.

'Jemima?'

'Can I have a word, on the quiet like?'

I feel obliged to relock my gate and enter her allotment. That wasn't her happy face, and now I can see she's uptight and nervous.

She gets to her feet and gestures towards her potting shed.

'The plot thickens!'

'Mmmm, not quite,' she mutters as I follow her and settle in one of the two deckchairs she keeps in the shed. 'I'm just going to say it the way I've heard it but . . . well, the thing is . . . I just wanted to check that . . .' She hesitates.

'Spit it out, love.'

'Dottie's mentioned it to me, because Mungo and Old Bill mentioned it to her, because Kaspar made a comment in The Cabbage Patch that . . .' She stalls again, and I gesture her to carry on. 'That you and Levi might have a thing going on . . .' That grimace appears again, as she falls silent. 'There . . . I've said it. Please don't be mad at me for approaching you. If it's true, then you need to know that others already know . . . but if it isn't true, you should know what others are saying behind your back. I really didn't want to broach the subject, but if it were me I would want you to tell me and . . .'

'Sorry, come again?' I say, bewildered at the turn this is taking.

'I wanted to mention that Dottie has said . . .'

'I heard that bit – what about me and Levi?'

Jemima gulps; this is obviously not going to plan.

'Someone has said . . . that you pair have something going on . . . and I wanted to be the one—'

I cut her short. 'You wanted to be the one to blow the story wide open, and then you can confirm that we're shagging like rabbits in the potting shed! Is that it?'

'No, not at all! I just wanted you to know what they are saying.'

'Who's they?'

'The allotment holders.'

'Specifically?'

'Dottie told me – she said that Old Bill and Mungo have both heard it from Kaspar, and he mentioned hearing it from one of the allotmenteers off the far side.'

'Basically, I'm the talk of the site just because I've asked Levi to do me a few small favours over recent weeks. Because my own husband is not around to do the heavy work – which I can't possibly do. Is that it?'

Jemima lowers her head, viewing me askance. 'I'm so sorry. I'd want someone to tell me.'

'That's fine, absolutely fine. I now know the kind of folk I'm dealing with. Thank you for saying. Please don't feel bad about it, unless you're one of the ones spreading such gossip, in which case . . .'

'Melissa, why would I?'

'Well, just saying. I'll be off, plenty to do on my plot, "You've gotta do a bit and leave a bit" – isn't that what folk say around here? I'll see myself out.' My words flow in one extended breath, as I swiftly leave her potting shed and navigate her pathway. My steps are powered by my anger.

Dottie

'Excuse me!' I call to the jeans-clad figure striding along the dirt track.

My legs are sturdy for my age, but they only truly have three speeds: slow, slower and reverse. Unlike a few years ago, when I seemed to gallop about at a steady pace with such ease. I daren't try that nowadays; no doubt I'd tumble and break a hip.

I call again, louder, 'Hello, I say, can I have a word?'

The woman stops walking and turns, her head lolling to the side as she answers, 'Yes.'

She stands and waits, watching my approach – nice if she'd met me partway, but she doesn't move. I have enough time to take in her attire: smart jeans, feminine cotton top and a bobble hat hanging from the pocket of her padded jacket. She doesn't look suitably dressed for gardening – or maybe she wears overalls, which many of the Far Siders do.

I don't speak until I'm standing in front of her.

'Hi, I'm Dottie, I've been meaning to introduce myself.'

'Pippa.'

'Lovely. Are you new to the allotments?' I ask, unaware of any newcomers since Melissa and Jemima joined the association.

'No, I'm with . . .' She points over her shoulder towards the far side. 'I sometimes take a walk around this way to see if there's anything interesting that we could start doing on our plot to help ease the workload.'

There's a prickly demeanour emanating from her; I much prefer warm and open personalities. Perhaps she's none too keen at being accosted as she makes her way along the dirt track.

'I see.' It figures.

I don't recognise her face, and the men on the Far Side rarely bring their wives or girlfriends up here. They seem more interested in their lager cans and funny smokes in The Cabbage Patch.

'Well, it's lovely to see a new face – do you know many on this side?'

'I know Jemima, she's got the plot with the front door.'

'That's right. You know her?'

'Yes, very well. I've visited her on her plot several times in recent weeks.'

I'm taken aback. Jemima hasn't said she's made friends with the folk from the Far Side. I'm slightly surprised to think they share much in common, given this woman's surly attitude. Obviously, Jemima is getting to know people around here quicker than I am.

'I've got my own keys,' she says, lifting her index finger.

Two keys hang from a key ring. I'd recognise the main entrance key anywhere.

'I didn't doubt it; you wouldn't be able to gain access otherwise.'

She's totally legit, which makes me feel awful that I was slightly suspicious seeing her strolling along the dirt track.

'Right. Is that it?' she asks, half turning to be on her way.

'Well, it's nice to meet you – please shout if there's anything you need, and maybe we'll see you in The Cabbage Patch one afternoon.'

'Cheers.' She mumbles something as she turns and strides away, it sounds very much like, 'I doubt it'.

I watch her stroll ahead. When she reaches Jemima's plot she peers through the wire fencing before taking the left turn and wandering around to the far side.

Regardless of my age, I really must learn to be slightly less judgemental of others.

Melissa

I enter my tiny shed, close and lock the door before bursting into hot angry tears. I'm mortified at the very thought that I am the talk of the allotment site. Who the hell do these people think they are? Have they nothing better to do with their time? Surely, they've got veggie plots to tend – or am I fair game, just for being a newbie.

Is this their idea of a warped initiation test to see what I'm made of? I can count the handful of folk I speak to each and every day. I go out of my way to talk and be pleasant, yet some mealy-mouthed person insinuates I'm having an affair. Or conducting a full-blown knocking shop from my potting shed!

I get it; I'm easy prey. A husband away working, I bet they think that's a ploy to get Levi to feel sorry for me. No doubt they think I'm innocently asking loads of allotment-based questions to waste his time. Folk have been offering to help, suggesting ways to improve my plot, whilst they're all too quick to share my misdemeanours and rookie errors.

All putting their two penn'orth in at every opportunity, yet twisting the situation behind my back to suit the site gossips. Well, no more. I've learnt my lesson. I'm up here to be the happy me that I am, not to be upset by the dirty minds of others.

I look about the inside of my potting shed – there's hardly

enough room to stash a folded deckchair, let alone perform some sordid affair or energetic sexual gymnastics! There's a sodding window, for God's sake! Someone must think I'm a right exhibitionist if this is my place of choice for frolicking.

My angry tears begin to subside, but the fire in my belly has been lit and will softly smoke until I've had my say. And if I find out that Levi is the one fuelling such speculation, he can go to hell.

My shed door opens slowly and Jemima's face appears.

'Hi . . . I thought I'd come over. I assumed you'd be upset and I didn't know if you fancied a cuppa.'

I want to lash out at the injustice but wisely bite my tongue. I wipe my cuff across my cheek to hide the evidence of tears.

'I'm fine. Though be careful and watch yourself. I might make inappropriate advances to you and invite you to step inside my potting shed!'

Jemima pulls a face and steps inside anyway, allowing the shed door to close.

'Clearly, you're not fine. And neither would I be, if a friend had just informed me of the word on the street.'

'The word on the plot more like,' I haughtily retort.

She has the grace to smile at my crap joke.

'Sorry, but when I think about how pleasant I've been to everyone. And now I realise that all their welcome offers were simply to lull me into . . . what a gossip trap this place is!'

'Melissa, I don't think they've lulled you in, purely to be spiteful. I don't believe it for one minute.'

'Seriously, don't you? Don't you believe that me and Levi are arranging sordid shagathons in here . . . me propped up on the rickety workbench over there and him squashed in between the sodding window and my new paraffin heater!'

The words spill forth in anger, chased quickly away as Jemima's face cracks into a smile.

'I can just imagine it, though I suggest you focus a little more on comfort and ambience: a few candles and a swathe of rich fabric might enhance the boudoir effect for both of you.'

I start to chuckle at the very idea.

'I'm sorry,' I say, when we each gain control of ourselves. 'I'm so sodding angry that those who don't know me would suggest such a thing. I'm a good person. I'm faithful to my Hamish – and anyone who knows us, knows me, knows that I would never cheat.'

Jemima nods.

'Lone female trying to be friendly – why do people always jump to the wrong conclusion? Can't men and woman simply be friends?'

'Ach, some people's minds are in the gutter.'

'Exactly. Thank you for being straight with me – you're right, I'd prefer to be told and know what's being said than to walk around entertaining folk.'

'Hello, hello . . . what's going on here then?'

Levi opens the shed door – the last person I want to see at the moment.

'Choosing cushions and candles to refurbish my shed,' I chide, eyeballing Jemima.

'I'll catch you tomorrow, Melissa,' she says. 'Give me a call if you need to.'

'I will – and thanks again.' I give a weak smile as she retreats to her own plot.

'What's up with her?' asks Levi.

'Nothing, why?'

'I thought for a minute there, she'd caught wind of what folk are saying about her and Ned.'

'The bee-keeper?'

'Yeah, Mungo was saying that he's heard in The Cabbage Patch that those pair are "up to it" after hours in her potting shed.'

I stare at him as he spills the beans, my lips pursed in sheer annoyance.

'And you believe that, do you?'

'Ned doesn't chat to anyone around these parts, other than the committee members – and that's probably to moan about the rest of us disturbing his sodding bees. But have you seen how much time he spends chatting to her? Why are you staring like that?'

'Well, Levi, I've got news for you.' I spend the next five minutes outlining the gossip about us. 'So, I suggest you might wish to stand outside my potting shed in future. And that isn't a euphemism, OK?'

Chapter Twenty-Five

August

High: 15°   Daylight: 15.5 hours
Low: 11°   Rain: 11 days
                                   Wind: 13 mph

Note: Surveillance shift alongside Mungo — three consecutive nights sat in his
potting shed. Someone's running amuck by burgling sheds. Saw nothing, except for
prowling fox and the new bloke — Kaspar — installing his new toilet. He'll be having
a fitted en suite next, complete with a curtain rail! Mungo's worried about Dottie,
says the dusting at the manor is too much for her. It's no good talking to her and
telling her to stop, she loves that young 'un to bits.

Melissa

I'm fuming. It has been a tough week. I came in here for a quiet
drink and a chat with my friends, yet all I'm observing are the
dark looks and snide remarks muttered by folk as they pass
our table. Jemima has looked up, bewildered, several times in
the last twenty minutes, though Dottie seems oblivious now
she has a double gin in her hand. I sip my drink and hold my
tongue as I listen to Dottie chatting about her dilemmas with
her delphinium display. Mainly the pros and cons of flower
height and harsh winds. My focus drifts from her conversation; my gaze keeps wandering across the room, taking in the
numerous groups, the unexpected chuckles, the glances over the
shoulder. Even Levi's table appear to be joining in, despite him

sitting with them, sipping his can of lager amongst so-called friends.

With each minute, my heart is racing a little faster, my blood pressure is climbing, and I'm becoming miserable knowing that they are all talking about me. Me and Levi. Levi and me. Have they no morals? Is that why they believe I'm capable of acting like an alley cat? Guilty consciences pointing the finger at others before they themselves become fodder for gossip.

I didn't plan it; I certainly didn't think it through. I was up on my feet, interrupting Dottie's delightful conversation, before my next heartbeat thumps in my chest.

I rap my knuckles upon the wooden tabletop, causing Jemima to jump and poor Dottie to clutch at her chest.

'Ladies and gents, especially the gents' corner . . .' I'm unsure why I've singled out the Far Siders crew. I'm not sure they're known for their in-depth gossiping between spliffs. 'I'd just like a word. I'm fully aware of the rumours circulating this allotment site. I wish it to be known that I have never contemplated – and, more importantly, *will* never contemplate – cheating on my husband. I am a happily married woman, despite what some of you may think. Levi and I have never shared anything more than the time of day, let alone a kiss, a snog, a smooch – or whatever else some dirty-minded folk want to call it. There have been no lewd gymnastics in my potting shed – have you seen the size of it? I mean the shed – not Levi!'

There's a gasp of horror from wide-eyed allotmenteers as they turn en masse and stare in Levi's direction.

'Oh no, I didn't mean that. What I'm trying to say is . . . we, Levi and I, have never done anything untoward in my potting shed . . . or anywhere else, for that matter, such as in his potting shed or polytunnel . . . in fact, no one's potting shed or polytunnel, so you're all quite safe. Not that anyone needs to be safe when I'm about – except probably right now, with me speaking to you all in such a frank and open manner. Which isn't something I usually do, is it, Levi?'

The stunned faces which have turned back to me swiftly return their attention to him. Levi is scarlet. This should be a sign for me to shut up and sit down. I don't.

Sadly, I continue. 'Not that Levi knows that much about me, do you, Levi? Just a few small favours, now and then – but without payment of any kind. No IOU favours being issued like the one I offered to Kaspar ... though he kindly refused.'

The open-mouthed crowd switch their glance to Kaspar, who splutters his drink across the table at hearing his name mentioned.

'So, you see, I am trying my very best to get along with everyone on site, and trying not to fuel the fire ... folk gossiping about affairs ... or sexual innuendos ... because that's just not happening on my turf. Is it, Levi?'

It's like a game of tennis as spectators' heads swivel back and forth with each shot. Why I included him again, I really don't know. His flushed face and awkward manner do nothing to convey the truth to those who are judging me. I should leave the poor guy alone, but I can't – I need him to justify my words.

'Levi, we're not up to anything, are we?'

'No. We're. N-not,' stammers Levi, his chin sinking towards his chest, and looking as guilty as a choir boy caught scrawling graffiti on the church pews.

'Levi, hey, they need to know the truth. Because if not, they're going to carry on yapping about us.' I cajole him to speak up, to speak out in my defence.

I watch in horror as his reluctance to say a word ignites their interest once more. There's guffawing, elbow nudging and rapidly nodding heads, which I need to do battle with. I need to eliminate their incorrect ideas, put a stop to their sordid tales and, most of all, restore my reputation across the allotment site. 'Levi, please speak up for us. It just isn't fair, what they are saying about us behind our backs, when it isn't true!'

'I think the lady protesteth too much!' calls a heckler from the Far Siders' table.

I whip about, ready to answer them, when Levi abruptly stands up, collects his can of lager and walks out of The Cabbage Patch.

There is a stunned silence as everyone watches the door close behind him.

The sea of faces turn towards me and stare a little more: waiting for my reaction.

I don't know what to say. I don't know what Levi's sudden departure is supposed to mean. I just don't know!

'What are you all staring at?' I holler, my arms gesturing towards the closed doorway. 'I'm just being honest so that you guys will lay off spreading rumours about me.'

There's a little tug on my skirt and I see that Dottie is clasping the fabric.

'I'd sit down if I were you ... his actions have just erased everything you've said,' she whispers from the corner of her mouth.

'What?' I say, confused as hell.

'Sit. Down!' urges Jemima forcibly.

I slump into my seat, staring wildly at the crowd, and replay the last scene in my head before uttering a weak, 'Oh!'

Jemima

Pushing my bike, I peer around the stone archway, almost fearful of entering the empty stable yard. From today onwards, this is my new office, complete with quirky cobbles, split wooden doors and aged masonry. Gone for ever are my reception desk at the tourist office, the artificial cheese plant which was dusted twice a year, and the influx of ruddy-faced tourists seeking local knowledge. Instead, it's just little old me, with a promising vision and a communications book shared with Ned, my boss. It feels strange to think he's relying upon me to deliver such a project. My new uniform is comprised of green wellingtons, khaki combat trousers and an old fleece gilet over a long-sleeved T-shirt – all in the name of comfort, warmth and ease of movement. Not to mention easy-clean and machine-washable; I'm expecting grime and plenty of it.

I have no reasonable explanation for my nervousness, other than viewing it as a sidekick to my recent anxieties. Ned has provided keys for the side entrance and another for my newly furbished office – though I doubt I'll lock it, given the staff tally around here. He's said I can come and go as I please; he'll be busy with his estate duties. The impression I have is that when he's at work he stays focused on the job in hand until the task is complete – there'll be no long lunches or staff jollies.

Cutting across the yard, I glance at each stable door and envisage the giant cobwebs lurking behind each. I've no idea how much effort each stable will require to give it the once-over, but I've sixteen to complete.

I lean my bike against the first stable door, unhook the storage box from the rear bracket and proceed towards my new office. I've made a colourful plan for my wall and a 'To-do' list; a hot cuppa is top of my list.

It feels wrong to be entering the manor alone, but emptying my personal provisions and making myself cosy feels right. I like what Ned's done. I suppose this must have been a storeroom for the old kitchen, located next door. He's tidied out the junk, given it a lick of paint, dragged in a scrubbed table and a couple of hard-backed chairs, and fixed sturdy notice boards to each wall. There's a tiny skylight window at the far end, delivering a limited view – but at least I'll always know what the weather is doing. I've splashed out on a new kettle, new mugs, matching containers for my tea supplies and even a biscuit barrel – not that I intend to spend much time dunking Bourbons.

'Hello, settling in OK?' Dottie's voice makes me jump.

I spin around to view her head, minus the broad-brimmed hat, peering around the door frame.

'I spotted you biking along the driveway so thought I'd come down.'

'I'm fine, just making a brew. Do you want one?'

Dottie shakes her head. 'I need to crack on, I want to be gone within the hour. Ned's upstairs if you should need him, though he'll be out all afternoon, apparently.'

'No worries, I've got plenty to do. Do you know if there's access to hot water from the old kitchen?' I ask, indicating the room next door.

'There is, if you use the butler sink in the corner. It'll need to run for a fair while before it comes through, eventually.'

'Excellent, it'll save me boiling pans on the stove.'

'The water pump will give as much cold as you wish, though it can be hard work. Unless you want to try the hosepipe connected to the far side of the yard. I'm not promising it'll still be fit for purpose, after all these years.'

'Thanks, Dottie. How are you keeping, anyway?'

Dottie lingers for a minute or two, explaining about the plans for the forthcoming festival, before returning to her own cleaning duties. I won't be making a habit of chatting, but I'll be glad of some company, if I'm working alone.

Having made my tea, I pin my weekly plan to the wall. It's simple. Week one consists of nothing more than clearing, cleaning and scrubbing the interiors of each stable. Ned has contractors booked for next week to plaster the interiors and install suitable lighting.

I grab my mug and swiftly exit, heading for my first task.

*   *   *

Having wrenched open the door of Stable One, as I'm calling it, I stare in dismay at the actual size of the cobwebs. I was being delusional earlier; they are twice the size I remember. Every wooden beam is covered with a thick layer of dust and then decorated with the grimiest grey webs. The only blessing is that each web appears to be empty. There's very little light by which to work, but I can see that the grime extends to the supporting trusses, the interior of the door and the brickwork. Lord knows how long this block has been empty, but I certainly have my work cut out. Let's hope that all the weeding and digging in recent weeks has strengthened my back for this task.

I take a final sip of my tea before grabbing my mobile phone to snap a couple of 'before' shots as a memento. I sense that my first sweep with a stiff broom might be the equivalent of laying the ceremonial foundation stone.

By lunchtime, only three stables are spotlessly clean, with their 'after' photographs taken. I've dragged miscellaneous heavy items out of each stable, swept and hosed down the interiors, and eliminated clouds of dust. I'm filthy from head to foot and I've vowed to add a headscarf to my uniform.

'Morning, how's it going?' asks Ned, striding across the cobbles from the side entrance and heading towards my collection of mystery metal.

'Fine. Though I've found all this stashed in various stables. I haven't a clue what any of it is – or what you'd want to do with it,' I say, consciously standing downwind of him after my physical exertion of the morning.

'Well, that's an old horse plough ... those are possibly the grass-cutting attachments for the tractor rigging ... and the rest is a combination of rusty tools, all long forgotten and misplaced for generations. What I'll do with them heaven only knows, so leave them there and I'll organise their clearance.'

'Oh.' I wasn't expecting an immediate answer, but I'm liking his style.

'Is there anything else, as I'm shooting out for the afternoon to visit tenants?'

'No, nothing I can think of. I have keys to lock up. I found the hosepipe, which made scrubbing each stable far easier than I'd first imagined, and my office is suitably furnished, thank you.'

'And the duck?'

'I've left him at home.'

'I imagined you'd bring him along.'

'You really don't mind?'

'It's a duck. What harm can a duck do?' teases Ned. 'He might become an attraction in his own right, once we're open.'

'Really?'

'There are enough hiding places he can dash off to, if the visitors annoy him.'

'I'll see how it goes over the coming weeks,' I say, appreciating yet another side to his nature: he's happy to accommodate others' needs.

'And lunch – you've brought your lunch with you?'

'Yes, I'm catered for, thanks.'

'That's good to hear. Shout, if there's anything you need,' mutters Ned, his expression faltering, before he retreats back inside.

'Cheers.' I raise my hand in a half-wave as he retreats.

He seems miffed, almost disappointed by my ability to fend for myself. Or am I reading into his behaviour more than I should? He probably feels a duty of care; he's been conscientious enough to talk me through each detail of my employment contract prior to this morning's start.

I do have my lunch with me, but I intend to snaffle my sandwiches as quickly as possible, then bike home to check that

Crispy duck is OK after spending the morning alone. The poor love, we've never been apart for longer than a toilet break.

'Are you still ... oh, I didn't realise the duck was here?' says Dottie, popping into my new office just after three o'clock. She stands pointing towards Crispy, who is settled and asleep in his straw-lined wicker carrier under the skylight. I know that the manor is empty, so she gave me quite a fright appearing in my doorway.

'Hi, Dottie. Likewise, I thought you'd gone home.'

'I had. I've just nipped back to bring Ned a reestit mutton pie I've made,' she says, lifting a deep ceramic dish from her shopping bag. 'He says I make it the way his gran used to. Between me and you, love, that was always my handiwork too. But I never let her down; I won't begin now, either.'

I love it when the older generation show such loyalty; as if their life depends upon it.

'Gran's the word,' I tease, tapping my nose.

'Anyway, how come the wee bird is here?'

'I nipped home during my lunch break and brought him back. He's happy enough in his box so I thought, what's the harm?'

'A bit of company. Ned's got his dogs lounging about his feet when he's in the office.'

'I won't be taking liberties, Dottie – I promise. I have no intention of slacking off or shying away from the task at hand. I've scrubbed five stables today. "You've gotta do a bit and leave a bit," as Old Bill says.'

Dottie raises a hand to wave away my remarks.

'You don't have to tell me. I've seen you grafting on Tommy's allotment. If you put half the effort in here with this new venture, you'll save Ned contemplating bringing in the tourist trust.' Dottie shakes her head fiercely. 'And mark my words, I don't want to see anyone take over Lerwick Manor . . . it deserves better than that. Anyway, lovey, I'll leave you to it. I'll nip this upstairs for his fridge. Get yourself off home, when you can.'

'I will. Night, Dottie.'

I listen to the fading sound of her shoes on the flagstones as she navigates the downstairs corridors before entering the main house. How strange to think she's walked these tiles for so many years. Even funnier to think Ned's gran passed off Dottie's skills as her own; that is a gem of a family secret.

Dottie

I unpack our sandwiches, laying them on the wooden bench slats between us, like a picnic, while he faffs with his old camera.

'I don't know why you don't buy yourself a new one, given the age of that thing,' I say, knowing my suggestion won't be welcome.

'It's perfectly good, thank you,' mutters Mungo, fiddling to insert the film canister.

'And always black and white. I don't see the need – why not bring a bit of colour into your life?'

'Do I tell you what to do when you're preparing your butties, or arranging your delphiniums? No ... well then,' he chunters, closing the back of the camera. 'I like black and white, life's simpler that way.'

In more ways than one.

'Here, get your chops around that and be away with your moaning,' I say, offering him half a cheese sandwich complete with my home-made chutney – which I won't mention, for fear of reminding him of his incident with Melissa and the exploding jam jars.

'Thank you. I reckon these puffins had better play ball this year, unlike last.'

He's right. We make this trip every year, come mid-August, to watch the pufflings take their first steps towards flight from Sumburgh Head. Some years, we're lucky and he captures a couple of photographs; other years, we sit here all evening and miss the best shots. Either way, it's become a tradition for the pair of us, much like our weekly roast dinner.

'How can you complain? Look at them all,' I say, gesturing with my sandwich towards the colony of black, white and orange bills, nesting amongst the turfed soil edging the cliff tops.

'There's thousands of them – surely you'll capture one or two taking flight.'

Mungo chomps his sandwich before answering. I knew he'd answer; he can't help himself.

'It's the close-ups I want, not some black dot in the distance flying in an awkward fashion, all podgy body and short wings.'

'Well, you'd best get up close and personal if you want David Attenborough close-ups,' I say, knowing how he wishes he could clamber across the barrier and the stone walls edging the cliff faces, to gain a better view.

'We'll have to visit one night, after dark, to watch the pufflings actually take flight and leave,' he says, after finishing his sandwich half.

'You say that every year. Like thieves in the night, trespassing where we're not wanted, you mean?'

'Phuh! The adults will have left, the youngsters make their own way when they're good and ready ... we'd be disturbing nobody by sitting here.'

'In the dark!'

'It's not my fault that they choose to leave undercover. I can't imagine they'd make it safely in daylight ... too many predatory birds waiting to feed upon them.'

'Tell me, how's your photography in the dark without a flash?'

Mungo glances towards his camera, currently resting upon the bench slats.

'Exactly. No bloody good. We'd see as much at night as we'd see from my front window. Naught. Here, have some Hufsie cake.' I thrust the Tupperware box at him, knowing he can't resist.

That's the thing, after all these years, I know him as well as he knows me. Like the puffins, we've mated for life in a strange kind of way, returning to the same spot each year to witness the success of those who manage to raise young. Though, together, the pair of us have raised plenty of youngsters at the allotment site.

Chapter Twenty-Six

Jemima

I hear the Range Rover reversing into the stable yard, so I dash out into the pouring rain to catch Ned's attention before he nips out on estate business. He brings the vehicle to a halt with its rear end yards away from the side entrance, before jumping out and glancing my way, as I jog over in a 'I'm getting soaked' manner.

'Are you OK?' he asks, opening the vehicle's rear door to rearrange numerous boxes and create space.

'I am, thanks – except have you seen Crispy?'

'Not since first thing this morning; he was on the terrace pecking at the steps. Why?'

'I've looked everywhere but can't find him.'

'Don't worry, he'll show up; he's probably napping in a quiet corner to get away from this damned weather.'

'Surely this is the perfect weather for ducks,' I say, laughing at the idea of fowl protesting at getting wet.

Ned attempts to hide a wry smile.

'What?' I say, slightly irked by his expression.

'You. Being the concerned mum about her little one. He has to grow up and fly the nest. You can't wrap him in cotton wool for ever.'

'Ha ha, if you'd hand-raised him, you'd be the same.'

'It's a duck, I'm sure he'll be fine.'

'Phuh! I'd like to see you if one of your dogs went missing,' I tease, knowing I've aimed at his Achilles heel.

'Ah now, that would be something of a disaster.'

'Well, touché.'

'Fair deal. If he hasn't appeared by the close of business, let me know, and we'll search all the outhouses. I'm only nipping out for an hour or so, to visit the accountant.'

'I was hoping to find him before that.' I sound whiney and am instantly annoyed with myself.

'Why not take a break and do a full search.'

I cringe at pointing out the obvious.

'I haven't brought a coat, which was stupid of me.'

'No worries, grab one from the boot room. The wax jacket swamped you that one night you wore it, but it's probably the smallest fit in there. Don't think you have to ask to borrow stuff around here – if you need it, use it. Right?'

'Thank you, Ned. I just don't like to assume. I wouldn't want to overstep the mark, that's all.'

'You won't . . . honest. Is there anything else? I've got a couple of boxes of files to collect from the office before I leave. I'm cutting it fine, to be fair.'

'I don't want to keep you. Thanks.' I head towards the boot room.

Ned follows me through the labyrinth of corridors. It feels like a game of 'follow the leader' until I swiftly take the door to my left while Ned glides by, heading for his own office.

'Bye!'

'See you later!' he hollers en route.

Once inside the boot room, my mind flicks back to the discussion the night Ned showed me the koi carp. How stupid I was, expecting to be introduced to the lord and lady of the manor? It now seems obvious that they wouldn't waste time returning to the estate, simply to hear my suggestion. But little old me – with my naïvety and enthusiasm – was suckered in, without any questioning.

I flick through the various jackets, coats and scarves bulging from each metal hook. There's every kind of coat material: tweeds, waterproof, cagoules, padded, quilted. Finally, I find the green wax jacket I'd previously borrowed. It's too big but it did the job; I'm not complaining. I draw my arms into each sleeve and hastily popper the placket along the front. There's no point doing up the zip; I'll only be making a quick search in this miserable weather. Unlike Crispy, I have no intention of getting soaked, especially when he's probably sitting beneath a bush, cosy and dry.

I pull the hood up to save my hair and make my way back outside. The rain is now streaming down and the Range Rover has gone. I didn't hear Ned walk past the boot room laden with his box files.

I take a quick peek into each stable, knowing full well that each door is securely closed so Crispy couldn't possibly be inside. But still, I look. After no joy, I quickly make my way around the orangery, which still needs clearing, heading for the paved terrace from which I'll have a clear view of the lawns and borders. The raindrops are deafening upon the jacket's hood. I lose half my face each time I turn my head, peering left and right, as I jog along the terrace. Still, no joy.

The wind catches me as I change direction and flings the droplets against my skin. How can anyone claim to like being outdoors when you have to contend with this? Urgh, never!

'Crispy duck, you are grounded when I find you,' I call aloud, knowing no sane person searches for a duck in torrential rain such as this.

I trot to the far end of the terrace, before the French doors, and peer about in the hedgerows. I gaze out across the manicured lawn which looks beautiful in the rain, a deep shade of emerald green.

Dare I risk a lengthy walk, as far as the carp pond on the

other side of the copse? I might as well. I don't want to churn up the beautiful lawn with my boots, so I nip down the terrace steps, scurry across the edge of the border, and walk the length of the stone wall. I'm scouring under the large bushes as I walk.

When I emerge from the wooded copse, the fountain display is being blown sideways, which ruins the effect completely.

'Crispy!' I call, through cupped hands; it feels necessary during a search party, even a solo one. My fingers are freezing. Who'd have thought rain could make you feel so damned miserable?

I circle the pond. No sign of Crispy. I perch on the edge of the stone wall, watching the carp swim in their elegant but ghostly fashion before disappearing into the depths. I doubt the rain bothers them either.

The view looks so miserable, but the last time I was here with Ned, everything looked so wonderful and blessed beneath the moonlight. I could have stayed here all night, enjoying the opportunity to talk and learn more about his life, his family, his work. And now, I want nothing more than to be back inside my office; Crispy duck can fend for himself, if he's content to be out in such weather.

I clasp my hands together. My fingers are red raw and wet, making them appear claw-like and evil looking. I swiftly undo the flap on each pocket and thrust my hands deep inside, in a poor attempt to stay warm. That's when I feel it. In the right-hand pocket. It's solid – metal, I'm guessing. I recognise the shape, as any female would, before I draw it out to inspect.

A large decorative butterfly hair clip, with pretty enamelled blue detailing.

Expensive.

Classy.

Feminine.

I can't remember feeling an object inside the pocket that night – or was I distracted by the moonlight?

My heart rate accelerates as my breath snags in my chest. Suddenly, I feel incredibly hot and clammy – I haven't felt like this in weeks.

I come round, to find I'm sitting on the paved walkway encircling the carp pond. My back is pressed hard against the stone wall and I'm clutching the butterfly clip.

How long have I been sitting here?

My heart rate and breathing feel relaxed. The sky has been grey all day, but now it is definitely late, given the darker hues beyond the clouds. My hair is drenched, hanging like rat's tails, but I don't remember the wind pushing my hood backwards.

I must get back to the office and then home. My bike will betray the fact that I'm still here.

I stuff the enamelled butterfly clip back where it belongs; it has a greater claim to this jacket than I have. I won't mention it; Ned has every right to his privacy, as have I.

I should be happy with my lot in life. A bloody allotment, a missing orphaned duck, and now a gallery manager's role – which will no doubt become stressful and awkward, knowing that I must suppress such a hopeless liking for my boss. Aargh! Why must this happen to me?

I pull the hair clip from my pocket for one last look, as a thought strikes me like lightning: this belongs to his chosen queen bee. My heart plummets to depths far greater than his koi carp pond. How immature am I, being jealous of an unknown woman?

I gingerly pull myself up to standing, using the stone wall as support. I feel utterly drained, physically and emotionally; I can explain the former but not the latter. I can't remember an anxiety attack feeling this bad – maybe a trip to the doctor's is needed, after all.

So what if he has a lady friend? A secret lover? He's a decent guy, good-looking in a rugged man's man kind of way, financially stable, with secure family connections and their legacy to fall back upon.

The rain stops as I head back towards the stable yard. Despite my damp appearance, I haven't got the energy to rush, so I take my time and plod. I might need to stop if I feel faint again. All this over a bloody duck – what is my life coming to?

Ned's leggy strides propel him across the stable yard as I round the corner of the orangery from the paved terrace.

'Any luck?' he hollers, unlocking the Range Rover and jumping inside, lowering his window to speak.

I shake my head, not trusting myself to reply. I have no right to be narky with him, or jealous of her. He's never actively encouraged my feelings. She's obviously not a local woman, most probably a long-term girlfriend from the mainland. She probably flies over for long weekend breaks filled with candlelit meals and intimate conversations, declaring their devotion for each other.

'Hey, don't be upset. I'm sure he's having a whale of a time.'

'Probably,' is all I can muster, as I head towards the side entrance, dragging an invisible green-eyed monster behind me. The droplets of rain upon the red tiles signal my route, as I wrench the wax jacket from my shoulders and vow never to wear it again. I've left the butterfly clip in the pocket; I don't wish to cause him an issue, if she notices it's missing. My stomach twists as I recall how he gently secured each press stud that night, ensuring I didn't get cold. I bet he was imagining her, that night; probably wishing she was here with him, and not me, the allotment girl.

I retreat to my office and grab my belongings; I'm justified in calling it a day. As I lock the entrance door, I curse the missing duck and pray that he's awaiting my arrival tomorrow morning. If not, I'll feel as guilty as hell about leaving early tonight, forcing him to fend for himself. Just for good measure, I leave Stable

One's door slightly ajar, wedging it with a random stone. At least he'll have somewhere safe and dry, away from any prowling fox.

Melissa

'Couldn't you have backed me up?'

'What?' Levi glares at me from beneath his woollen beanie.

I've stormed along his pathway, to find him sitting on an upturned bucket whittling a piece of wood with a knife.

'I said—'

'I heard what you said, Melissa. We all heard what you said – and no one's likely to forget it for some time.'

'Levi, I'm not having folk chatting shite behind my back.'

He looks up. His usually handsome stare cuts straight through me. 'Would it be so bad?'

I frown. I don't understand his question. 'Sorry?'

'I said, would it be so bad to be linked with me?'

'Levi, it isn't true. We aren't a couple. We're not having an affair or getting jiggy in my potting shed!'

'But if it were true? And don't say the age gap matters, because it doesn't!'

'Levi!'

'If things were different.'

'But they're not. I'm married. I have been for ten years. Have a little more respect for yourself, and me.'

'I think we'd be good together.'

My mouth falls open. Coming to chat was obviously a mistake. 'It's you who's been feeding them the false news then?'

'Nah! But folk have got eyes in their head, Melissa. They can see when two people get along perfectly well together, have a connection and are content in each other's company.'

'I'm married.'

'Mmmm, are you really?'

'Yes, really ... vows, long white dress and confetti – you know, the usual stuff for the big day – and the end result was this ... a gold band, which never leaves my finger.'

He lowers his gaze to his ringless hands and reworks the wood.

I'm waiting for a response. He has no right to question my intentions. Who does he think he is, aiding the gossips against me? All I've tried to do is be a friend to everyone I meet – and get my plot cleared of weeds, so I can grow a few sodding carrots.

He suddenly looks up, bites his upper lip before speaking.

'I don't think you are married. He'd be here, living each day beside you, if he really cared. I think you're a dating habit that he married, and you accepted the ground rules as his wife – a long-distance relationship via a screen. A marriage should be two people living side by side, sharing the same life, not hundreds of miles apart and communicating via a screen. You aren't married, Melissa, you're a single woman who wears a wedding ring and can't go on dates because she repeated vows before an altar. You're no more married than I am.'

'How dare you?'

'It's true, so I dare.'

There's no point explaining. I take two strides towards the path, but swiftly turn about to answer him.

'It might not be what other women would have accepted, but I did, because it's what Hamish wanted. He's devoted to his career, he's worked hard to climb the ladder and get where he is today – nobody gave him an easy time of it, his basic qualifications weren't up to scratch, but he's made it. He's worked hard to get where he is. And he'll be coming home, once he's secured our nest egg. And then, we'll build our nest, plan our babies and welcome family life with open arms.'

'I'm not questioning his work ethic, more his morals as a husband. He should be here devoted to you, working at creating the marriage and family life you secretly want, right now. Trying to forge a decent existence where both of you are happy doing what you do each day, without you having to fill your time as best you can with teaching, textiles and now nurturing an allotment. Because, if the truth be told, Melissa, you don't want to be here pulling up weeds – or even teaching teenagers how to master a sketch – but at home, nursing a bairn or two, baking cakes and assisting with homework. I'll give you your dues, you handle it well. But you shouldn't have to handle it, Melissa, your husband should be right here, not gallivanting on some oil rig in the middle of the Gulf, probably playing poker and drinking with the lads.'

I don't need to hear this. He has no idea what I need in life. He doesn't know me or Hamish.

I say the one thing that springs to mind. 'What the hell would you know about it?'

This time, my strides take me right to the allotment gate. Keep walking. Don't turn back. Don't even look back. Levi knows nothing. As long as Hamish and I are happy, what should it matter to others? They're just jealous. Jealous that they spend each night alone, waiting to find the right person to spend the rest of their life with. I'm not like Jemima, Levi – or Dottie, for that matter. That's not me. I've found my match. I'm happy with my lot.

Chapter Twenty-Seven

Dottie

'Are you OK?' I ask, peering into Jemima's office whilst she takes her lunch break. I didn't mean to catch her off guard; she's spooning her yoghurt and staring at the bright blue sky through the office's slim skylight.

'Me? I'm fine.'

I scrutinise her before pulling a sulky expression. 'Are you sure? Because the first thing I was asked today, by a certain someone, was if I knew of any reason why you would be upset. Now, I'll ask again, are you OK?'

'Ned asked that?' Instantly, she perks up.

'Mm-hm, and he's not one to notice such things,' I say, adding, 'He reckons you were wet through yesterday, after searching high and low for that duck. You went straight into the office, and then you were off home within minutes.'

I continue to stare at her. She focuses on scraping the remainder from her yoghurt pot, before licking the teaspoon clean.

'Well? What's up?'

'Nothing.' She throws the yoghurt carton towards the bin, missing completely.

'Uh-oh, now I know there's definitely something wrong. Out with it, young lady.'

'Nothing's wrong. I don't know what he's talking about,' she says.

'Well, let me tell you this. I want you to know that I know that there is definitely something wrong with you today – something that wasn't wrong with you yesterday morning. And I want you to know that – whether it takes a day, a week or a month – I will find out what is wrong with you today, despite you denying there's anything wrong. Old Dottie here can sense it. Right? And I sense that there's something up with you today. Deny it as much as you like, but I'm right. You can't fool me. Got it?'

'Got it. But there's still nothing wrong.'

'She protesteth too much, m'lord.' I give a wee wave and disappear, but not before hollering, 'A day, a week or a month – remember that, Jemima.'

'I will. And there's still nothing wrong.'

Jemima

My nerves get the better of me whilst walking through the house in search of Ned. I've spent ten minutes in the office mustering up the courage to go wandering, having never needed to visit his office before. I contemplated waiting until he next strolled by and then grabbing him unexpectedly for a business chat. I even hoped he was out and about, but he's definitely home; his Range Rover is parked outside. As I cross the threshold, transitioning from downstairs kitchen to main house, my nerves quadruple in my stomach. Instinctively, I glance down at my wellingtons; it wouldn't be good to clump mud about these floors. I wrench my foot from each boot and continue on tiptoe in my socks, solving one issue. This is ridiculous, I just want to show him a sample from the printers to gain his approval. Yet I'm totally flustered at the thought of speaking to him. Get a grip; it's business.

I traipse up the grand staircase, clutching the bag of printed goodies, knowing that I'm heading for the third floor, after which

I have no directions.

I daren't touch the highly polished banister for fear of annoying Dottie. How she does what she does at her age is remarkable – though saying that, she's always nipping in, apart from Mondays. Again, that's none of my business.

My gaze avoids the hard faces staring at me from the generations of portraits, casting doubt upon my enterprise. 'Shouldn't the likes of her be confined to the scullery?' I'd happily return there, rather than venture upstairs.

Finally, I reach the third-floor landing; the costly decoration hasn't dwindled with the climb, this floor is as luxurious as the previous two. I'm greeted by a long corridor, brightly lit by glass skylights above, and a row of eight dark wooden doors.

Now, where? I could do with a dog lolloping out to investigate the intruder, signalling which room is Ned's office. My only option is to listen at each door for any signs of life.

Door one: nothing.

Door two: silence.

Door three: stillness.

What if I listen at a door, hear a noise, knock and a woman's voice asks me to enter? I will die if I come face to face with some beauty whilst dressed like this, in muddy combats, a gilet and a headscarf. I freeze on the landing, afraid to go forward.

I can just imagine it! Her looking sultry and stunning, as if she's just stepped out of the front cover of *Vogue*.

I quickly straighten up, seeing Ned stride out from a doorway further along the corridor. Has he seen me?

'Hello, I was just about to come and find you!' he exclaims.

'Likewise, I've brought the samples for you to browse ... I wondered if you had a spare ten minutes?'

'Sure. Come through,' says Ned, turning about and re-entering his office.

I swiftly follow.

I stop as soon as I'm through the door; his office isn't anything like I was expecting. Given the age of the manor house, and the solid wood interiors throughout, I was expecting traditional. Instead, everything is high tech, modern and minimalist.

'This is nice,' I say, trying to cover my reaction.

'Not what you'd imagined, eh?'

'Not at all. I was expecting something similar to the library downstairs – heavy furniture, leather wing-back chairs and elaborate . . . oh, there it is . . . an elaborate marble mantelpiece,' I jest, pointing to the only original feature in the entire room, whilst Ned stares at my socks.

'I rarely use the fire but it would be criminal to rip that out. Do you usually walk about without shoes?' Ned settles at the conference table before the window; its polished white surface gleams. I'd expected him to settle at his desk in the neighbouring corner.

'Er, yeah, I didn't want to traipse mud through and cause Dottie more work.'

Ned snorts, obviously finding my answer humorous. 'Grab a seat and let's take a look.'

'I mentioned the gift tag I want each artist to use. I think it offers a personal touch from us at the gallery, but it also promotes Shetland. Sorry, I'm rambling,' I say, delving inside the bag. 'These are the gift tags . . . each one is printed with the gallery address on one side and the phrase "From Shetland, With Love" on the other.' I offer him the slimline tag, printed in a pale blue script on a delicate brown label, giving the effect of a parcel, with matching knotted ribbon. I hold my breath; if he doesn't like this, he won't like the other items.

Ned slowly turns the label over in his hands, carefully reading both sides, before repeating the process. He's methodical, if nothing else. I shuffle in my seat.

'Did you design this, or did they?'

'I did.'

Ned gives a repeated nod, before looking at me. 'And they're to be attached to every item that's created and sold from the gallery.'

'Yep, suggesting the item was created and dispatched with love. Hopefully, the gallery will become an integral part of Lerwick's community, supporting Shetland's tourism industry.'

'That sounds pretty neat. I like the idea of promoting Shetland as a whole, as well as our gallery.'

'Our gallery' – now there's a phrase which rubs salt into my wounds.

'It could be added to disposable drinks cups for takeaway orders too.'

'You really do think of everything, don't you?'

I give an awkward nod. Yes, sadly, I do.

'A reversal of fate regarding the tourist trust too, don't you think?'

'Certainly is. To reinforce the message, we could have paper bags . . . and tissue paper for gift wrapping. Not all items can have a label attached.' I draw each item from the bag, offering them for Ned's inspection. 'The brown paper of the label reminds me of the masonry stone in the stable yard, alongside a calm blue sky on a beautiful day.'

'Your idea too?'

'Yep, I thought about the gifts I've purchased in the past – some companies have missed a trick by not advertising themselves as a lasting memory and creating an overall brand.'

'It definitely gives an added something to a gift,' says Ned, placing all three items upon the tabletop. He sits back and stares at me. 'And your decision is?'

'I've brought them for you to decide.'

'I think not. I'm happy to go along with your vision. So what do you say, is it worth the time invested and the cost for such promotion?'

He's put me on the spot – not a place I like to be. He's waiting, and my nerves are tripling by the second.

'I believe so. I'm happy to trial it for six months and then discuss it prior to reordering.'

'Deal. Job done!' Ned gives a wide smile, before pushing the promotional items across the table towards me. 'Is there anything else?'

'No.' I quickly stand up, not wishing to waste his time.

'Are you always this jumpy?' he asks, as I repeatedly ram the chair into the table leg whilst trying to appear efficient and polite.

Must I always act like a child in his presence?

'No, only when you're . . .' I shut up, desperate to think of something to say, but fail.

Ned raises an eyebrow, which develops into a coy smile as he realises what I might have been about to say.

'Thank you, catch you later!' I exclaim, leaving the chair skewed before the table. I grab my samples and exit hastily.

What the hell must he think?

I race down the flights of stairs faster than the speed of my babbling.

Chapter Twenty-Eight

Jemima

'It is pouring down outside – you'll get soaked to your undies, lassie,' snaps Dottie impatiently, buttoning her own rain mac as we stand inside the side entrance.

'I've told you already, I'll be fine. It's a bit of rain, I won't dissolve.'

'Why bother getting wet when there are perfectly decent coats in the boot room?'

'I'm fine,' I retort, clearly not.

'You've borrowed them before.'

'Dottie. Please.'

'I don't understand you young people. You'd prefer to get soaking wet for the sake of borrowing a jacket. Ned won't mind, he never does. Clearly, you've—' Dottie stops mid-sentence, a curious expression dawning. 'You know, don't you?'

'Know what?' I say, acting nonchalant and pulling my sleeves over my hands to act as gloves.

Dottie blocks my path, beyond which the rain is bouncing off the cobbles.

'Look at me,' she demands.

'What?' I stare at her wide-eyed, in a comical fashion, purely as a deflection.

'Has he told you?' Her voice is stern and serious.

'Told me what?'

'Don't play the innocent with me. You know.'

'I don't know anything, Dottie. Now, could we please make our way across the yard?'

Dottie steps aside, allowing me to dash across the wet cobbles to the old forge. I wrench open the stable door and pick up where I left off this morning, marking out the floor with white chalk.

Within minutes, Dottie joins me.

'I'll keep asking till you tell me.'

'Tell you what, Dottie?' I say, looking up from my position on all fours on the floor, measuring and marking out the visitors' viewing area.

She looks annoyed, frustrated by my game-playing.

'Ask me no questions and I'll tell you no lies,' I mutter.

'When?'

I sit back on my heels; she's won.

'He hasn't told me anything. I found something.'

'Of hers?' Dottie's simple question cuts deeper than it should.

'Yep.'

She's waiting, so I continue.

'The last time I borrowed a wax jacket from the boot room, I found a large hairclip in the pocket. Obviously, it belongs to a woman. I haven't said anything to Ned. It's none of my business; it's his choice whether he wishes to discuss her or not.'

Dottie closes her eyes and exhales noisily. 'Why didn't you say?'

'Did you not just hear my explanation?' I retort.

'I did. But I suspect . . .' she says, trailing off. 'I knew I'd find out what was wrong that day – be it one day, week or month later. Didn't I say?'

'Dottie, please, don't go there!' I stand up, having completed the first section of floor, and move along to continue my task.

'I see more than you realise; he'd be mortified if he knew. He assumes that you think the jacket is an old one of his.'

'It's not, it's hers.' I busy myself by measuring the stable floor.

'Talk to him.'

I shake my head.

'Please.' Dottie looks upset – gutted, in fact. 'What have you got to lose?'

'My dignity?' I mutter.

'You might gain a whole lot more,' Dottie says. She lingers before leaving, adding, 'It rarely works with two queen bees in one hive, you know. Nature has a funny way of deciding which one starts afresh elsewhere.'

Old folk think everything is so simple. He's my boss; he doesn't need to explain who he's dating. Or their future plans.

I'm employed to share my ideas and do a job. He owes me nothing. The family owe me nothing, though meeting my true employers might be polite. And when the family choose to replace me – because our working relationship has become as awkward as hell and is eventually untenable, due to my developing crush – then they'll serve me my notice and away I'll go, despite all the effort and my best intentions.

'Are you OK?'

Oh no, not Dottie again.

'For the second time today, I am fine, thank you.' I look up from measuring and marking, to find a bemused Ned standing in the doorway.

'Are you sure?'

I blush intensely.

'Sorry, I misheard and thought you were Dottie. She's bugging the hell out of me, asking me if I'm fine. Nothing I say convinces her. Apologies.'

'Duly noted. But it's me asking this time, not Dottie.'

I get up from my haunches and sit down on the cool, freshly laid brickwork. 'Don't I appear fine?'

'No, you don't. It sounded like you were having a muttering rant.'

I take a deep breath. Bugger! 'A miserable morning, that's all.'

'I'm always here if you need to grumble.'

'Thank you, but I'm being stupid, really I am. I've got a "To-do" list as long as a toilet roll, and meetings booked at ridiculous times, which ruins the flow of my day. But honestly, I'm fine.'

'I'll take your word for it, so just shout if you need anything.' With that, he leaves the old forge.

Great! Now, they're both watching me. I'll kill Dottie if she tells him. 'I am employed here, and nothing more' needs to become my new workday mantra. He might be generous, kind, entertaining – whilst also being brooding and secretive – but still he's my boss. He pays my wages. He has never led me to believe otherwise. End of.

I resume measuring and making chalk marks on the brick floor.

Though I have to admit, she's a lucky woman, whoever she is. Not that I'm jealous in the slightest. I'm not! But aargh, why are all the best ones taken?

Chapter Twenty-Nine

Melissa

I eagerly follow Jemima amidst the huddle of a small crowd as we complete a tour around the newly refurbished gallery. I love what she's created in the old stable yard; you forget its history on seeing the clean interior of each rental space. A combination of aged beams and brick floors, set against the warm terracotta of fresh plaster and high-tech lighting.

I can imagine myself happily working here, selling my ceramics and textiles amongst a busy throng of artists.

I'm fearful in case anyone else in the tour produces ceramics; I can do without unnecessary competition, to be fair. I'm also a little dubious about whether I should gamble on a whole rental to myself, or await alternative options.

'And through here is our brand-new artisan coffee shop, The Orangery . . . please come through and take a seat, if you wish,' announces Jemima, leading the group inside an elaborate cast-iron framework which reaches high above our heads. 'We're very grateful that the local builders have transformed this area in a matter of weeks – thanks to their skill and dedication.'

The kitchen and serving area extends out from the bare brick of the manor house, complementing the new slate floor and providing a tasteful view of the stable yard on one side and the manicured lawns on the other.

'As you can see, we have incredible views on either side, so guests can choose whether they want to people watch or enjoy nature during their visit.' Jemima gives a tiny chuckle. 'We have plenty of seats, couches and tables to accommodate a large number of guests at any one time. We've opted for a coordinated mismatch of styles, sizes, colours and finishes – mainly because we all have a preference for a comfy chair. There's something for everyone one; highchairs are in the corner for the little ones. There'll be daily papers, periodicals in the wall rack, and our large bookcase, which is currently empty, will house our "book exchange" so guests can donate a book to the shelves, select one to take home, or simply browse, read and return whilst enjoying their visit.'

I wouldn't mind kicking off my boots and lazing on one of these colourful couches right now, they look so welcoming. This place simply oozes success; how can such a venture fail, when every element has been executed so well? This must have cost the owners a pretty penny, for sure – but still, if you want success you must plan for it.

'Take a look at the large glass cabinets along the far end wall.' We all turn to follow Jemima's gesture. 'Some arts vendors whose products are tiny have expressed a desire not to rent a complete stable to themselves; so we're suggesting that vendors of jewellery, handmade cards and small textiles can rent a shelf, or a complete cabinet, for their goods to be displayed in here. The waiting staff will be handling the cash; they'll record any sales and the artist will receive full payment for the specific items on a weekly basis. We felt monthly payments could prove difficult for some artists. Artists located in the stables will handle their own sales.'

I'm impressed. Jemima's come up with a neat idea of renting display cabinets, which solves both my problems of manning a stall on the days I teach and the sale of tiny items. My ceramic tiles and smaller textiles would have been lost in the stable setting. Though Jemima did mention the option to share a stable space and the associated rental costs – which might prove interesting for some artists.

'I can assure you that artistry will continue within The Orangery. The delights served here will be high-end and impressive; we're seeking a manager who displays a natural flare for their culinary expertise and baking craft. We hope our artisan café will become the heart of our gallery.

I'm sold. From what Dottie had said previously, I knew it was going to impress the locals, but this is out of this world. Shetland doesn't have anything like this – I'm sure the tourists and locals will be flocking here in equal measure.

'We plan to open the gallery on Sunday, the third of October. So, before we draw this tour to an end, are there any questions which you'd like me to answer?'

I simply want the paperwork, a price list for the shelf rental, and then to sign on the dotted line.

'Can I ask how the local traders in the town centre feel – do you not think you'll be pinching some of their trade?' asks a lady, at the rear of the group.

'We've had mixed reactions, to be honest. Our intention is to support all commerce and tourism within Shetland, not divide it – we all want a rosy future, but not at the cost of stifling other established businesses.'

I like her honesty, and by the contented mumbling from all sides, I think the other artists agree. There's a definite community feel being created here, a cooperative spirit enhanced by a range of diversity and talent. The loneliness and isolation experienced by many artists certainly won't be an issue here, given the yard's horseshoe layout and the busy footfall it'll attract. I like that she's not calling them 'shoppers' or 'visitors' – it's a nice touch to talk about 'guests', which adds to the positive vibes.

I hear a handful of additional questions, including, 'Why is the gallery closed to guests on Mondays and Tuesdays?' I tune out as – surely? – it's common sense that artists need a constructed 'weekend' for a work–life balance, having been here all weekend; guests would hardly be impressed to find a hotchpotch of artists open and others closed on various days of the week. I cringe as someone raises the toilet question; surely, they don't need a tour of those facilities? Though I have no doubt they will be brand new, spick and span, like the rest of the place.

I begin listing in my head the items I could fit inside a cabinet: painted ceramic tiles, my mini-series of painted nursery rhyme tiles, the ceramic necklace pendants – I might buy a tiny mannequin bust to display those correctly. My imagination flies into overdrive; I could make some mini-scarecrows as kitchen decorations holding cute messages – or blackboards, for even cuter messages.

I watch Jemima answering; she's in her element, explaining every detail. I've got nothing but respect for her. Where her ideas have sprung from, I don't know. But her dedication is inspiring. This venture deserves to do well.

Chapter Thirty

Dottie

'Are you sure you want my honest opinion?' I ask, as Ned leads me through to the newly refurbished café, now officially christened 'The Orangery'. It might be bank holiday Monday elsewhere, but here in Shetland it's a typical Monday morning, though not so typical for me. My arrival occurs under the watchful eye of three nervous-looking ladies seated around the nearest table fiddling with their coffee cups.

'Yes, but not quite yet. Our candidates are eager to start, but I wanted to introduce you first,' explains Ned, leading me towards the trio. 'This is Dottie, a long-standing friend of Lerwick Manor and a superb baker.'

'In my younger days, not so much now. Don't let Ned's flattery put you off,' I say, settling in a vacant chair.

'This is Milly, Gabby and Isla.' Ned nods politely whilst introducing them; I receive an acknowledgement from each, in turn. By the end of the today, one of them will have been awarded the job of café manager aka chief baker. I recognise Gabby, the older of the three – I think she used to cook at the local primary school – but not the other two women.

Ned settles beside me, handing me a fresh coffee; one of our three applicants is sipping hers, one is cradling the steaming mug, and one has finished already.

I've been taken aback by the level of interest shown for the vacancy, and grateful that Ned hasn't included me in sifting through the application forms; he hauled Jemima in for that task.

'The format for the day is that each applicant will be assigned a kitchen and will need to produce three bakes – all the details are clearly labelled in the assigned kitchens. Two bakes are of our choosing, the final bake is whatever you wish to create from the ingredients supplied – I'm informed that the store cupboards are well stocked,' says Ned, which I assume is a message from Jemima. I notice his cheeks blush a little after the remark. Interesting. 'Don't worry, we aren't trying to trick you. We've chosen basic well-known bakes – we'd like you to showcase your skills and produce a bake which you're proud of.'

The three ladies simultaneously fidget or exhale as he finishes explaining. Bless, they look as nervous as hell.

'Likewise, we won't be watching over you, or judging you whilst you bake – you'll be entirely alone for the allotted time. This certainly isn't *Bake Off*. Also, there'll be no handshakes awarded, not until we offer the actual position, and then . . . well . . . upon acceptance . . . I'm rambling now.' Ned falls silent, his slight blush returns.

What's wrong with him?

Jemima enters The Orangery, a beaming smile in place. There's the answer. He must have seen her walking across the stable yard to join us.

'Ah yes, Jemima returns just in time.'

'Hello again. I hope you enjoyed the coffee – it's the speciality blend we've opted to sell to our guests,' she says, pulling up a chair and settling beside me.

The candidates murmur their approval.

'Very nice.'

'Rich taste.'

'Interesting blend.'

'Before we separate, I'd like to give you each a chance to say a little more about yourself,' says Ned, glancing at Jemima.

'There might be details you wish to elaborate upon from your application. Shall we take it in order? Milly?'

'Right, so I'm Milly, I left catering college over a decade ago and have worked in the local hotel as a pastry chef ever since,' says candidate one, her wide eyes relaxing as she continues. 'I live and breathe cakes and pastries. I'm used to working long hours and have undertaken extra study in catering management.' She falls silent, shuffles in her seat before lowering her head.

'Thank you, Milly. Gabby?' says Ned.

'I'm Gabby, I've worked in a school kitchen for nearly twenty years so am used to overseeing baking on a large scale which must conform to budgets, nutritional guidelines and also satisfy the consumer. I actually remember Dottie, from the time the school linked up with the local allotments to encourage the children to choose more vegetables and berries in the dinner queue. You and Mungo delivered the donated vegetables for a week.'

'Yes, I thought I recognised you,' I say, not wishing to sound overly familiar, keeping my focus on the task in hand.

'Lovely scheme, I hope it proved helpful to the little ones,' adds Ned, as Gabby remains silent. Obviously, she'd finished. 'And Isla?'

'I'm Isla. I left catering college quite recently. I was taught how to bake by my granny when I was a little girl . . . and I've loved it ever since. I bake most days for my friends and family. I'm happy to complete additional studies, if needs be.' Her freckled skin blushes throughout, until she falls silent. I notice that she's clutching a notebook in her lap.

'Thank you for that . . . now, the only detail remaining is to select who bakes where,' explains Ned, producing three envelopes. 'Inside is a card stating either The Orangery, modern or main kitchen. We'll ask you to select and then we'll walk you to your designated kitchen. Choose away.'

As soon as he places the envelopes on the table: two hands instantly select and remove, the third envelope remains.

'I suppose this is mine then?' says Gabby, beaming a bright smile at the three of us.

'Modern,' says Milly.

'Main,' says Isla.

'That figures,' says Gabby, showing us The Orangery card.

'All sorted then, ladies. Gabby, you're staying in here, and Jemima and I will walk the others to their kitchens. You've got ninety minutes for the first bake – we've added a little extra time, allowing you to familiarise yourself with your kitchen and locate the equipment. OK?'

Three nodding heads confirm the arrangements.

'If there are any issues or problems during your day, my mobile number is on the bottom of each instruction sheet – give me a call, and one of us will come straight to you.'

'All the best to all three of you. We'll be collecting your bakes at the allotted times. Dottie here will be blind tasting and marking, alongside Ned and myself,' offers Jemima. 'Isla, if you'd like to follow me?'

'And Milly, if you'd like to follow me?' says Ned. 'Dottie, could you show Gabby where the instructions and equipment are in this kitchen?'

'Sure,' I say.

Personally, I think there's a slight advantage in the kitchen allocation; young Isla isn't expected to use the big range. But still – the 'modern' cooker in there is older than she is.

We swiftly separate. Gabby seems impressed by the investment made in The Orangery's kitchen. We locate her instruction envelopes, each is clearly labelled: bakes one, two and three.

'The third bake is definitely a free choice?' she asks, straightening the envelopes on the stainless-steel worktop.

'Yes, I believe the instructions inside simply outline a few rules, nothing more.'

'OK, I'm raring to start. Slightly nervous, but thrilled to be using this kitchen.'

'Actually, you're the first person to bake in here,' I say, knowing how excited I'd be at the prospect of christening each shiny item. 'If there are no other questions, I'll leave you to it.'

'Thank you,' says Gabby, pulling a folded tabard from her handbag.

'And your verdict?' asks Ned, as I finish eating another spoonful of carrot cake.

'You can hardly go wrong with a carrot cake, can you?' I say, not entirely sure they've picked the right bake to showcase the bakers' talents.

'I thought that, at first, but customers will be expecting a wide selection; some folk stick by their traditional choices. If our bakers can't get this right, how can we be sure they'll be able to execute something a little more artisan?' asks Jemima, justifying their choice.

She's got a point, but even so.

I've spent the previous two and a half hours with my duster and beeswax, which felt particularly strange, given that it's Monday. I'm perfectly aware that the professional cleaning team usually arrive in their van on Mondays; I suspect they've been cancelled in view of the interviews. Seated at the dining-room table, I stare at the three plates before me: carrot cakes. We've each made notes on the sheets provided. I've been honest on each occasion.

'Can I ask whose is whose?' I say.

'I'd prefer you not to know. Which is why I've collected the bakes,' says Ned. 'We simply want the best person for the job – and since the one lady was honest enough to say she knew you, I don't want the others thinking there's any favouritism.'

He's got a point.

'Then you chose bread for their second challenge?' I ask, staring at the three loaves before me. Again, I'm disappointed with their assignment.

'We can't afford to babysit the café when the rest of the gallery is up and running. We need the right person to undertake the daily running, so we can oversee the development,' says Ned, glancing at Jemima, who nods readily.

'This venture isn't a whimsical hobby, it needs managing correctly in order to be financially successful. Otherwise, the initial investment and refurbishment will have been wasted,' she adds.

'I suggest we meet back here in just under three hours, by which time the bakers will have finished their third task – the free choice. Dottie, I'm happy for you to settle in the morning room with a cuppa and a paper,' says Ned.

I bet you are, as it'll save me bumping into the Monday cleaning team when they arrive.

'I might do, though I've noticed there are several roses that need deadheading outside – would you mind if I tidied those, instead?'

'Sure, you know where the secateurs are kept.'

'I'll be prepping the signage for the gallery. Call if you need me,' adds Jemima, gathering her belongings.

'Likewise, I'll be upstairs in the office – I'll show my face to check that all three bakers are OK, and then leave them to it.'

'They'll be well under way by now,' I say, pushing my chair under the mahogany table. I intend to deadhead, then enjoy a cuppa in the morning room, though an additional slice of cake would have been welcome.

Eventually, I locate the secateurs; not in their correct place, which I blame on Natalia trying to play *House & Garden* the last time she stayed. She wasn't all that great at micro-managing the house but she dabbled, hoping it would encourage Ned. Not that most men would need much encouragement, with shapely legs up to her armpits and cheekbones to die for. I close the boot room, an unlikely place to keep peerie gardening implements, and by habit make my way through the warren of corridors towards the side entrance. On hearing someone busy in the aged kitchen, I'm brought to my senses, igniting memories of the past. I can't go waltzing through; the lass will think I'm spying on her. I quickly divert my step, heading through the manor towards the main entrance door, which will ensure that I don't compromise my status of blind judging.

My fingers nimbly open the great locks of the oak door, which was only ever opened by the butler or a footman when guests first arrived, but those days are long gone. It makes me wonder what the future will bring – not that I'll be around to witness the changes.

It takes all my might, yanking at the brass lion's head, to draw the heavy door closed, so I don't hear the tyres crunching up the gravel driveway until the red van is sweeping past me, heading towards the stable yard.

All my days, I have such bad timing. This must be the cleaning team arriving for their shift. How embarrassing!

I've always assumed they arrived first thing, not halfway through the day, to begin their shift. Though some cleaning teams have a busy rota, with office cleaning early in the mornings. I wonder how many there are? My nosiness gene is instantly triggered – there'd be no harm in seeing them unpack their gear. They haven't a clue who I am; if I wave the secateurs about, they'll assume I'm part of the gardening posse.

As I round the corner of the building in pursuit of the cleaning team, I'm greeted by a solo occupant climbing from the driver's seat. One man – now that is a kick in the teeth for me. I'm not the jealous kind, but given the amount of work they complete each week, I had assumed it was a team. I hide behind the stone archway and peer around the edge. The man goes to the rear of the van, unlocks the doors and retrieves an object from inside – his own box of cleaning equipment, I presume. I can't snipe, we each have our preferred products. Slamming the door shut as quickly as he opened it, he walks off in the direction of The Orangery.

What the hell?

Am I seeing what I think I'm seeing? A man carrying a white cardboard box. A cake box!

I quickly rummage in my pocket for a pen; I'm not savvy when it comes to investigations, but I can note down a number plate as fast as the next person. I wait while our man lets himself in via the glass doors and disappears from view. I dart forward, knowing full well that sections of The Orangery have a full view of the stable yard – the exact reason why Ned and Jemima have chosen its final design and refurbishment.

I hate writing on the back of my hand but, without a scrap of paper, I have no choice. Surprising how many raised veins and liver spots I've gained since the last time I tried this. 'You'll get blood poisoning' was the usual warning I'd hear from my parents on such occasions.

I'm peering around the stable door of number 9, my breath catching in my throat, as the guy returns to his van: empty handed. He climbs inside, starts the engine and swiftly drives away. Such a nonchalant manner, without a care or a worry; he didn't even double check the surrounding area, and he didn't seem furtive or guilty about his actions. It was definitely a cake box. I'm not mistaken, or seeing things, despite my age. What is Gabby up to?

I've suddenly lost interest in deadheading the roses, so I return to the manor via the main door. Now, what do I do? Call an emergency meeting or quietly make my way to the morning room for a cuppa?

'Can I ask how each baker is coping in their kitchen?' I ask, unsure whether to spill the beans.

'Remarkably well, considering they're each totally new to their environment. Isla seems a little flustered, Gabby as calm as they come, and Milly is using every surface available – but all seem happy with their efforts,' says Ned.

'That's good to know.'

I look up to find both staring at me intently.

'Dottie . . . what's going on?' asks Jemima, reaching for my hand.

'I don't want to affect the success of any candidate, but honesty is my forte.' It takes all of five minutes for me to recall what I've seen with the red van. The lone male and the white cake box delivery. I omit my knowledge or presumption about the Monday cleaning squad.

'Cheating, basically,' says Ned, sitting back in his chair and eyeing us both.

'Do we confront her or leave it until the third bake is complete?' says Jemima, instantly looking deflated.

'Sorry, I don't want to cast a shadow but it's not fair on the other two. I suggest we carry on as planned. Judge what each baker presents, and take it from there.'

'If proven, it'll be embarrassing to have to call an adult out on their behaviour,' adds Jemima.

'In the meantime, do we know of a local bakery that caters for home deliveries?' asks Ned, reaching for his mobile.

'I know of several – competition is tough out there,' offers Jemima, opening her note book.

'I suggest we do some homework and see what we can find out,' says Ned.

I watch as their initial shock subsides and a flurry of activity ensues. Human nature rarely surprises me. Having spent so long nurturing the newcomers at the allotments, I've seen it all. Some folk are so desperate to achieve in life they'll sink to new depths to impress others when their first port of call should be self-respect.

Chapter Thirty-One

September

High: 13°
Low: 9°

Daylight: 13 hours
Rain: 15 days
Wind: 16 mph

Note: The days are shortening, but still, it's festival month — the best!!! My pumpkin is a monster, a whopper, the biggest I've ever grown. Or seen. I've fed her comfrey tea six times a day, got her booked in for a special bubble bath and a chamois leather, before splicing time. Old Bill's offered his squeaky barrow as transport, but it's no good — this beauty needs a ride in a horse box and a hefty lift from the MacDonald boys. Blue ribbon, here we come!

Jemima

'Seriously, I haven't lost the plot, Dottie.' Given my choice of activity, I don't blame the woman for thinking it.

It's the first of September and I'm feeling raw as the anniversary of my mother's death approaches. Having completed my tours for the day, I'm keeping busy by helping Dottie to branch out from growing her flowers for traditional bouquets.

She stares as I hold open the aged oven door, urging her to place the giant baking tray inside.

'These trays are used to holding half a pig not delicate flower petals.'

'Ned's given permission, if that's what you're worried about.'

'Me? Worried about Ned, phuh! I could throw an impromptu

party in the ballroom and he wouldn't flinch. But this, this is simply weird. Whoever heard of cooking petals?'

'You're only drying them out – it'll literally take a few minutes,' I say. 'It's hardly gas mark five for two hours – and there's no need to baste every few minutes.'

'Bugger off. You young 'uns think you're so bloody clever with your new-fangled ideas.' She carefully slides the baking trays inside.

I pray she doesn't nudge the baking parchment, causing the delphinium petals to jump from their neat rows where they are lined up and carefully separated so they don't touch.

'Hardly new-fangled, we're using an oven that's as old as the hills.' I secure the doors and drop the latch. 'There, how easy was that?'

'I'll wait and see what the results are before giving praise, thanks. Now, let's get the kettle on if we've got a spare few minutes.'

'We haven't got time. That tray will be coming out in no time. We need to separate the petals for the next batch if we're going to do this properly,' I say, indicating the bin liner of delphinium blooms, which I'd insisted we pick and bring along to Lerwick Manor.

My fingers begin separating the lavender-hued petals from the flower spear.

'I saw your friend again the other day. I wasn't sure if she'd missed you while you were working here,' says Dottie, carefully removing the first tray from the oven.

'A friend of mine?'

'Yes, a blonde-haired woman from the Far Side. I spoke to her a few weeks ago, didn't she say?'

'I don't know any of the Far Siders,' I say, puzzled.

'You do.'

I give her a smile. How come the older generation have a habit of doing that?

'Seriously, Dottie, I don't. I've seen the handful of men who come to The Cabbage Patch with their lager cans and dodgy smokes, but I've never spoken to them.' I continue to separate the petals for a second baking tray.

'No, a woman.'

'I've never seen a woman on the far side, let alone made friends with one. Given their antics, I can't imagine that crew being my type.'

'That's what I thought, but she assured me you two are friends.'

'Nope. She might have me mistaken for Melissa, maybe.'

'She mentioned your front door.'

'Well, there's no confusion there then, but I still don't know who you mean.'

'I see.' Her befuddled expression confirms that she doesn't, not truly.

It's time to take the first baking tray out of the oven, which puts an end to the conversation.

'What do you think – easy, isn't it?' I ask, carefully lifting the flutter of dried petals from the parchment paper.

'Look how beautiful it is. My blooms made into delicate confetti – unbelievable, really.'

'What's more unbelievable is that your fading blooms can be used to create a useable, sellable product that others can take delight in. It could earn you a little extra to plump up your pension. It might even mean you don't have to dust these old rooms any more.'

'Over my dead body does anyone take that job from me! I'll always do a little dusting in this manor.' Her answer is delivered rather more tersely than I'd expected. She adds a smile to soften the edges. 'But this might provide a little extra for a rainy day.'

'I'm glad you're pleased; it was hard to tell for a moment.'

'I'm surprised the edges aren't blackened or burnt – such delicate petals, yet not a scorch mark in sight.'

'That's because we gently warmed them not baked them – there's a difference, Dottie,' I say, fetching a box from the opposite side of the kitchen and returning to the central table. 'Once they've cooled, I thought you could present them in decorative boxes like these.'

I hand her a paper cone, not much bigger than an ice-cream cornet, with a doily-effect top that flips down to create a lid.

'Where did you find these?' she asks, examining the cone.

'Melissa made them. She has a gadget that creates the hole effect – other than that, it's a glue and stick job. She's happy to make more if you need them.'

'Is everyone expected to rent a stable from the gallery?'

'I'm sure you can display and sell these from the café's glass cabinets. Ned would be delighted if you decided to.'

'Would he?' she says, turning the delicate cone in her hands. 'You think of everything, don't you?'

'I try to. Though it's not easy, given the tally of tasks and roles I'm currently juggling, but it'll ease once we're open. I'm sure the local weddings would love to use your home-grown Shetland confetti, rather than purchase it from the mainland.'

'There's a range of colours growing on my allotment.'

'True, but don't run before you can walk – offer a rainbow mix first, and see how that sells. Who notices what colour the confetti actually is?'

'You've a decent head on those shoulders, more's the pity.'

'What's that supposed to mean?' I ask, put out by her remark.

'Nothing, lassie, just me thinking aloud.'

Dottie

'How did Ned handle it?' asks Mungo, pouring gravy over his midweek roast dinner. I hadn't dared to bring Mungo up to speed with gateau-gate whilst tending the allotments; you never know who's listening. I'm surprised he's waited two days before enquiring; Mungo loves a bit of gossip.

'Very well, actually, I was impressed. We started off with the three of us and their final bakes – I was surprised by their selection: a fancy gateau, a towering croquembouche, and some traditional Shetland bannocks with a large bowl of tattie soup, which we tasted and discussed. While the candidates waited in the morning room.'

Ned calculated our scores and it was obvious that Isla was the clear winner – which I was grateful for, I'd have hated it to be a close-run thing. She used her initiative by asking Ned for potatoes, creating a traditional tattie soup as well as the bannocks. Both items were based on her gran's recipe book, which she was clutching throughout our talks.

'And the other woman, did he tackle her?'

'Mmmm, now there's the clincher. He called Isla into the dining room and offered her the position, which she immediately accepted. Jumping for joy she was, it was a pleasure to watch her. Jemima led her out through the main entrance, promising to confirm it in writing. On her return, Ned brought Milly in to break the news that she hadn't been successful – I think she simply tried too hard to impress, but without conquering the basics of any of her bakes.'

'Was she disappointed?'

'Of course – she wanted the position as badly as the other two – but Ned praised her before she left by saying how impressed we were by the staggering height of her croquembouche.'

'And the final woman?'

'Tsssk, I didn't know where to look, honestly. Ned brought Gabby through to join us. The bakes were still on the table; I reckon she thought the role was hers when she observed the other bakes. Ned launched into his "I'm sorry to be the bearer of bad news" routine and I swear to God her expression fell through the floor. Anyway, Ned explained that all her bakes were well executed, but then . . . I didn't even see Jemima leave the room, but suddenly she reappears carrying an identical gateau to Gabby's, which we'd purchased from the local bakery an hour beforehand. Ned wanted her to know she couldn't pull a fast one.'

'No!' Mungo's eyes light up. He swears he hates gossip, but he bloody loves it really.

'I wanted the floor to open up and swallow me, especially when she tried to say the bakery had copied her. Ned basically explained to her that the delivery guy had been spotted, that we'd done our homework and identified the baker who owned the van. She tried to argue her case, but Ned offered to show her CCTV of the driveway, capturing the vehicle's number plate and confirming her deception. It's quite amazing how rude people can become, once they've been sussed out.'

'She must have wanted the role pretty badly.'

'She did – but how can Ned and Jemima trust her with the management of The Orangery, if she can't be honest about her skills?'

'Let's hope this young woman can step up to the task. From what you've said, she lacks life experience and catering qualifications.'

'Ned's not worried. She might be very young, but she's attended catering college. Her baking knowledge was superb – she's a natural, and she's learnt plenty of tips from observing her gran. You and I both know the old lady from years back – she was the one who used to make treacle scones and sell them from her kitchen door. Remember?'

'Tilly Henderson – I took her to a local dance, once upon a time.'

'Did you now! Well, I didn't know she'd died, but apparently Isla's a chip off the old block. Ned was most impressed when she informed him how much her bakes actually cost to create. I thought the dated kitchen would put her off, but she's used to using various kitchens, which went in her favour. She's eager to start her food hygiene training, and Ned's going to organise that and support her, so there's nothing to worry about.'

'She's got an old head on young shoulders, if she played a blinder with tattie soup and bannocks.'

'Exactly. How's your dinner?' I ask, knowing the answer, given that he's tucking in happily.

'As gorgeous as ever,' he splutters, chomping a mouthful of cabbage and gravy.

'I thought I'd check, since you're so sparing with your compliments.'

'Hey, when have I ever not complimented your cooking?'

'Aye, there's no fear of me trying to pull a fast one with a local delivery.'

'Never, I'd know your cooking anywhere.'

I continue with my own plate of food. Mungo's got a point; after forty-odd years, there's not much that he wouldn't praise me for.

Jemima

'He's getting big now, isn't he?' says Ned, watching Crispy scoot about under the glare of the security lights, busy pecking at the yard's cobbles as we linger in The Orangery finalising our rental applications.

'He is. I'm not sure if I'm doing the right thing by him. I was tempted to put him on the brook and see if he swims off or stays with me. You know what they say, if you love something set it free – if it comes back.' I glance around to see Ned's melancholy expression. 'Are you OK?'

'Me?'

'Yes, you seemed . . . meh, just then.'

He instantly perks up, the fleeting sadness gone. 'I'm fine, but thanks for asking, just busy with the estate.'

'OK, shout if there's any admin you need a hand with. I could help you out for an hour here and there.'

Ned gives a nod of appreciation.

Quack, quack! The duck interrupts our conversation by staring through the window.

'He's happy enough, I doubt you've anything to worry about long term.'

'Mmmm, he can't stay on his own for ever, can he?'

'No, but while he's happy being a bachelor duck, I wouldn't worry.'

'What if he doesn't know he's not happy until I take him to the brook and he spots the single lady ducks?'

'He's fine as he is.'

'Mungo says I should put him in with the chickens – birds of a feather, and all that – but I'm not so sure.'

'Chickens and ducks aren't birds of a feather, Jemima – that'd be like a robin coupled with an ostrich.' Ned pulls a confused expression.

We sit in silence. There's nothing else to say as Crispy duck selects a new patch of cobbled yard to peck clean. Awkward glances pass between us as our conversation takes on a strangely personal meaning between employee and employer.

'Let's run through the rental list one more time, before calling it a night,' suggests Ned, pushing the applications across the table.

'Isla Henderson as The Orangery manager, chosen earlier this week,' I say.

Ned nods eagerly.

'We've formally agreed a rental with Wednesday Smith, a local blacksmith for the old forge – it goes without saying, that's where she'll be located. Decisions need to be made about the location of Verity Kendal – the wool and knitting lady, who is relocating from England – then there's the soap making, card making, jewellery artist, candle maker, wood carving and weaving ladies to accommodate; each craft requires a rental of their own.'

Ned pencils each craft on to the large map representing the gallery layout; it's exciting seeing each stable gain an occupant.

'I can confirm each in writing tomorrow and include the opening date of Sunday, the third of October – plus, there's a request from the glass blower Isaac Jameson for a shared rental in the forge, if Wednesday Smith is prepared to share.'

'Mmmm, as you said, birds of a feather flock together,' says Ned, quickly adding the details to our plan. 'Come on, it's very late – we should have clocked off by now, and you should have gone home hours ago.'

We collect our plans and tidy our coffee mugs before leaving.

As Ned locks The Orangery door, we're startled by the distant crowing of a cockerel.

'A cockerel crowing at night!' I say, shocked at such an occurrence. 'Superstition deems that bad luck.'

'Bad luck for the Far Siders, if the committee evict them for breaking site rules,' says Ned, shaking his head.

Chapter Thirty-Two

Jemima

I arrive at work bright and early with a renewed spring in my step. Last night's planning session with Ned has settled my nerves and created my 'To-do' list for the coming days. It's been a busy week already and with the allotment festival fast approaching, I'll need my wits about me to sustain this level of organisation.

'Morning, Ned!'

'Morning, Jemima. I forgot to say last night, there's no point you working at the manor without seeing how we actually look after our tenants,' calls Ned, across the cobbled yard gesturing towards his Range Rover. 'Jump in, we'll come back via the Town Hall; killing two birds with one stone.'

'Have they approved our application for highway signage already?' I ask, unsure if I should be taking such liberties by joining him.

'They sure have. There's no messing around, once the wheels are in motion,' says Ned, unlocking the vehicle.

I clamber into the passenger seat, as the engine bursts into life; we're away before I can have second thoughts.

Ned sweeps the vehicle through the yard's stone archway on to the gravel driveway. Within seconds, we're passing Dottie; she's walking towards her 'light dusting' duties, wrapped in a warm tweed coat and clutching her large handbag. On seeing the Range Rover, she waves, but on seeing us inside waving back at her, her face breaks into a broad beaming smile.

'What's up with Dottie today?' says Ned, once we've passed her.

'She's a sweetie,' I say, suspecting it was the sight of us, side by side.

'She's a minx, that's what she is. She's got fingers in so many pies, she can hardly juggle her own doings.'

Within minutes, we leave Lerwick Manor behind, cut through the town and are soon surrounded by open landscape, dotted with clusters of low-lying cottages amidst squat hedgerows. We don't speak, and yet our silence is comfortable, like the pleasing warmth of familiarity. Ned indicates and turns the vehicle on to a dirt track leading to a huge farmhouse and outbuildings surrounded by sloping fields of grazing sheep.

'The Sinclairs have been tenants for three generations. They rent a fair amount of land from us and have been pretty successful with their breeding programme for Shetland sheep. Magnus, their son, runs the farm largely single handed but he's managing to create a decent revenue, plus improve the fleece and meat quality of the breed.'

'I used to play around here when I was little,' I confess, blushing that I was trespassing on the Campbell's land, even back then.

'You did? Do you know Magnus then?'

'No. I rarely hung out with that crowd – not after my mum found out we'd been smoking in the secret dens we'd made in the far field.' I gesture across the land. 'She grounded me, severing numerous friendships ... which never really recovered, despite our connections since primary school. I knew she was disappointed, and concerned that I was going off the rails.'

'Home bird then, were we?'

'I suppose so; less hassle that way. Probably still am, if the truth be told,' I say, more to myself than Ned.

He glances in my direction before killing the engine, and our conversation dies with it.

'Out we get,' he instructs. 'Though mind the sheep dog. Floss is friendly enough but tends to jump up. She's better behaved with sheep than humans,' he adds, throwing open the driver's door and climbing down. 'Hello, Floss. Yes, I know you like a bit of fuss.'

I jump down from the vehicle, joining Ned, to find him consumed in scrunching the ears of a blue merle sheltie dog, who is lapping up the attention.

'Ah, she's gorgeous.'

'She is, though she's a bugger. She takes herself for walks along the coastal path most days . . . have you never seen her?'

'Now you mention it, I have seen a lone dog walking the fields.'

'Keeping an inventory of your grazing flocks, aren't you, Floss?'

'Morning, Ned!' hollers a male voice.

I look up to view a male in a beige fisherman's jumper and wellingtons, striding towards us from an outbuilding.

'Morning, Magnus, this one never misses a visitor, does she?' calls Ned, standing tall and shaking the newcomer's hand. 'Magnus, this is Jemima.'

'Nice to meet you, Jemima.' His hand extends, warmly shaking mine, before he casually adds, 'Ned, I didn't realise that you'd . . . well, nice to finally meet you, Jemima.'

'Hello,' I say, before his comment registers as a misunderstanding of sorts. Ned and I exchange a fleeting glance. I instantly blush, preparing for a moment of explanation, but Ned doesn't say a word.

'I thought we'd drop by to discuss the flooding you mentioned, back end of last week. It'll only get worse; what with global warming and the environmental agencies' predictions about climate change,' says Ned, as my brain lingers on the guy's misunderstanding.

Magnus thinks we're together. He said 'finally', which confirms he thinks I've been around for some time. Does he think I'm the girlfriend? That Ned has introduced me because the tenants might be dealing with me, sometime in the future?

'Jemima, are you coming?'

I'm drawn from my inner world, to find the two men have walked a fair way ahead; only the sheltie dog waits by my side, as if I'm a lone sheep separated from the flock.

'Yes, of course.' I scurry to catch them up.

Floss instantly plods to join her master's side: job done.

As we head across the fields to inspect the flooding, their conversation is a blur; my mind is fixed on the guy's initial misunderstanding and Ned's lack of correction. Why didn't Ned say something? Was he expecting me to speak up? A simple error to make – but to leave it uncorrected is only asking for trouble at a later date, especially for his true girlfriend.

Melissa

'What you're saying is that, come Saturday, I can only show orange carrots at the festival?'

'Correct. Read your rule book. I gave each allotment holder a copy, along with their entry form. There's a spare copy hanging from the notice board in The Cabbage Patch,' says Old Bill, shovelling manure into his wheelbarrow.

'That's bloody ridiculous!' I'm fuming.

'Those are the rules,' mutters Old Bill, adjusting his tartan cap. 'Anyway, I thought you were entering parsnips.'

Here we go again, bloody parsnips! I can't deny that I'm impressed by the growth of my dustbin crop, but still, that's not the point. And I haven't lifted them yet, purely on principle.

'Have you got orange carrots?' says Dottie, offering a weak smile.

'Well, yes – but as you predicted, they're going to be tiny.'

'As a newborn's winky,' adds Dottie, with a chuckle.

'Yes, I believe you warned me of that fact, weeks ago. Bill, is there any chance that I . . .?'

'Oh no. No, you don't. The rules are the rules. There's no switching, changing or bending of the rules.'

On cue, a cockerel crows, loud and proud, from the direction of the Far Siders.

We all turn and listen until it ceases.

'Well, if rules aren't to be broken, I suggest someone on the committee nails the mystery of that bird!' I say, storming from Bill's plot back to my own. 'As there's no switching, changing or bending of the rules – not on these allotments!'

I turn about at the gate, to witness their reaction to my comment. Old Bill does not look best pleased.

Jemima

Within the hour, we're nipping into the Town Hall on our return journey to the manor. Ned seems happy; he's devised a plan to tackle the increased flooding that has claimed the lives of several of the Sinclairs' ewes in recent weeks. I simply stood by and listened, knowing nothing of either flooding or flocks. Whereas here, I'm intrigued by our Town Hall.

The Victorian building houses many council departments, yet there's a hushed silence upon entering. It's as if the solemnity of authority is etched into the elaborate stonework. I linger in the entrance lobby while Ned climbs the grand wooden staircase to locate and retrieve his paperwork from the relevant department. It's not as grand as the staircase at Lerwick Manor, but nevertheless, it's impressive for a civic building where the general public are encouraged to stroll.

Whilst working at the tourist office, I'd regularly advised

visitors to nip inside and view the Main Hall on the second floor. It seemed strange, directing them to what's officially the council hub, but it's such a quaint venue, steeped in history and housing a spectacular display of stained-glass windows. I was frequently disappointed when some visitors snubbed my suggestion, as if it wasn't worth their time. My co-workers rarely mentioned the glories of the Town Hall – or circled it on the tiny map, provided free of charge – but what's not to like in seeing Shetland's history depicted in traditional glass.

I stand aside as a young couple enter with a baby carrier, heading for the registrar's office. I don't get a glimpse of the newborn; no doubt it's sleeping, swaddled beneath the pale blue blanket. How strange to attend one building from cradle to grave, and almost everything in between. I was registered here, Ned was probably registered here too. Two childhoods in the same Shetland town, yet worlds apart. How weird is that? Earlier, I'd been tempted to ask how many acres of the land around Lerwick the Campbell family own, but I chickened out. Their kind rarely talk money; they see it as vulgar, apparently.

I check my watch. Ned's been gone for a few minutes; he's probably explaining a specific detail or quickly signing a document.

I glance up the wooden staircase, viewing its steady climb. How many visitors followed my advice? I'll just nip up and be back down in less than two minutes. I'm literally following my own tourist advice.

'There you are.'

His voice makes me jump, not that I'm doing anything wrong. I am simply lost within the beauty of the Main Hall.

'Ned . . . look,' I say, standing in the middle of the empty hall, pointing at the rainbow effect upon the wooden floor created by the stained-glass windows. I'm quite choked to think that while I was standing downstairs a magical illusion was silently occurring up here, without a witness. 'Isn't it amazing?'

'Quite amazing,' agrees Ned, entering the hall and gently closing the double doors behind him.

'You don't seem impressed,' I say, slightly embarrassed by my full-on enthusiasm.

'I am. It's quite magnificent.' Ned slowly walks around the room, eyeing the colourful windows and the portrait of the Queen.

'But?'

'But what?' He turns around to face me.

'I just sensed a "but" – that's all.'

'Sensing. Is that the name of the game?' His voice has lowered a touch, and he sounds somewhat guarded.

'You know . . . gut reaction and all that.'

'And earlier, I sensed you wanted me to correct Magnus, but my gut reaction told me otherwise.' He's watching me intently.

'You should have. He totally misread the situation, he now thinks he's met your . . .' I falter on her title. 'Girlfriend' seems immature at our age, 'life partner' and 'fiancée' both sound like official commitments, but I have no idea of Ned's personal life. I wish Dottie had given me some indication.

'My partner?' says Ned, raising his eyebrows in a flickering motion.

I'm out of my depth answering him. He's waiting, staring intently, yet there's something more in his expression. There's a wanton look behind his dark gaze, a flicker of temptation or maybe curiosity.

The silence grows between us. This time it doesn't feel comfortable, like earlier, or on previous occasions – it feels prickly, weighted, almost dangerous.

The vibrancy of the rainbow upon the floor slowly intensifies, portraying each colour to its maximum depth. I know it's purely science and the refraction of light but it instantly feels like a giant mood ring.

'Ned, you can't look at me like that!' I mutter, blushing. What the hell is he playing at?

'Can't I? I believe Magnus sensed whatever it is that's developing between us. I'm surprised to hear you wish I'd corrected his assumption.' There's no stuttering, no hesitation as he delivers each word; a simple declaration between us.

'Ned!' My utterance is hardly audible. My mind is spinning whilst my stomach knots. Neither his stance nor gaze falter; we're locked in a private moment. The atmosphere is suddenly electrified, raising goose bumps. Clearly, he's joking with me, but he looks so serious. And still he's not retracting or making excuses. Not a hint of an apology. What's his game, when he already has a partner?

Ned takes a sideways step, as if viewing me in a new light, changing the blue-green tones upon his temples to a haze of purple. I gesture towards myself and then to him. 'You've got a film of colour . . . you might want to move.'

He gestures across his face. 'So have you. Yours is red and orange – not a good look.'

I take a quick succession of steps, to avoid the hues. Ned remains static.

'Anyway . . .' I say, walking around the room, sidestepping our conversation too.

'Yeah, right . . . anyway.' His tone is lighter.

The rainbow begins to fade; its muted colours become transparent, restoring the dull brown of the wooden flooring beneath, revealing the cracks and joins.

The spell is broken.

I stare at the rose window positioned high within the wall. My back is turned towards Ned, but I know he hasn't moved an inch. His stance isn't faltering. I suddenly have a notion that his suggestion isn't wavering either.

How has this happened? One minute, I'm enjoying a magical rainbow; and the next, something has shifted, altering our behaviour and understanding of each other.

'Are you ready to go – or are you yet to make a wish?'

'A wish?'

'On the rainbow.'

I grimace, indicating I'm unsure what he's on about.

'I thought you were supposed to make a wish on spotting a rainbow,' he says, looking puzzled.

'That's a shooting star. A rainbow is a covenant from God to Noah, promising never to flood the land again.'

'Ah, right, Magnus Sinclair can rest assured then ... maybe you should have mentioned that earlier; saved us a task regarding his drainage issue.'

Chapter Thirty-Three

Dottie

'Morning, Dottie, the old bugger's in a strop again,' mutters Melissa, approaching along my rows.

I stand tall, lifting my hat brim to view her properly. 'What's he up to?'

'Sitting on his bench.'

'Still sitting?'

'Yeah, I called out on passing, but he didn't answer me. He's probably still smarting about me arguing with him over the festival rules.'

'That's not the Bill I know.'

'Phuh! Between him and Mungo, with their constant chuntering, moaning and silent treatment, they aren't a great advertisement for the older man. They need to lighten up.'

Without a word, I lay my trug and secateurs on the ground.

'Dottie?' calls Melissa, as I head towards my gate. 'Dottie, what's up?'

I don't answer. I need to check. I wouldn't forgive myself if I didn't.

Melissa continues to call my name, thankfully following my lead too.

I leave my plot, make my way past Jemima's – I can see she is busy in her chicken enclosure – and head towards Bill's plot. He's sitting on his bench, his tartan cap pulled down low to the bridge of his nose.

I open his gate and enter.

He likes a quick forty winks every now and then. Likes to dream and picture the growing season ahead whilst resting his eyes.

'Bill!' I call as I traipse along his path.

No answer. His hands are clasped in his lap, his legs crossed at the ankle – a stance that I've seen a million times.

'Bill, I was wondering what you and Mungo were thinking about . . .' I waffle, not wanting to look stupid if he suddenly wakes to find me peering at him.

Nothing.

'Dottie, what are you doing?' asks Melissa, trailing behind.

'Shhhh.'

By the time I'm within two steps of him, I know.

But I continue. 'Are you playing games with me, you old bugger? Stop acting the goat and talk to me.'

Silence.

'Dottie.'

I turn about to view Melissa's panic-stricken features, her hand outstretched towards my shoulders.

'I've a good mind to play you at your own game, if this is how you treat your dearest friend.'

'Oh Dottie,' whimpers Melissa. 'Dottie, please come away – let me fetch Mungo or call Levi.'

I sit down alongside him, like we've done so many times over the years. I gently touch his shoulder. His frame doesn't give; the only thing that moves is his tartan cap, which topples into his lap. Bill's eyes are open, glazed and staring at his beautiful allotment.

'Oh, Bill. My dearest friend, always joking around – you've gone and done it this time.'

'Mungo!' cries Melissa.

Her shrill tone shatters the serenity in which Bill sits, as upright and as proud in death as he ever was in life, enjoying his allotment.

When there's no response from Mungo, Melissa dashes back along the path – to find someone, anyone, I guess. I stay beside my friend, silent in the knowledge that he wouldn't have wanted this moment to have occurred anywhere else but here.

What a perfectly peaceful way to slip away, sitting on your bench dreaming of your favourite patch of earth.

I shouldn't touch him, but I do; as a loving gesture, my hand gently glides across his eyelids.

'Dottie, oh, Dottie.' Mungo shuffles along the brick paving. He wraps his outstretched arms about my shoulders in an attempt to move me aside.

'Levi's on his way,' calls Melissa, a pace or two behind him.

'Mungo, please let me be,' I say, easing into his giant hug without a tear.

Here is our friend who has cajoled, supported and advised us for a lifetime – I'm not about to leave his side now.

'He looks so peaceful,' whispers Mungo.

'He's done himself proud this season, hasn't he?' I say, admiring the view from the bench.

'He has – though he didn't finish moving that pile of manure from one end to the other,' quips Mungo, nodding towards the stationary wheelbarrow parked a short distance away.

'I can't stand here, it's too upsetting,' sobs Melissa, failing to control her tears.

'That's OK, lovey. Mungo, can you walk her to The Cabbage Patch – someone will make her a brew.'

There isn't much we can do whilst others attend to Old Bill, so we busy ourselves with 'the bit' he's left. I wield a peerie shovel while Mungo manoeuvres the wheelbarrow back and forth.

'Don't mind us,' I say, on receiving quizzical stares from various professionals.

'He'd have wanted the job finished properly,' adds Mungo, returning the empty wheelbarrow for another load.

It doesn't take long for the word to spread about the allotments. A hushed silence descends, even the mannequin heads have opted for a mournful expression. In no time, the young woman from the undertakers interrupts our solace: they're leaving now.

On the wooden bench sits Bill's tartan cap. I collect it before it goes missing; his family will cherish it. Despite my calmness earlier, the shock is subsiding and realisation is dawning. Never again will he call out on seeing me – giving constant advice, whether required or not – and his tartan cap won't move back and forth along the top of the fence.

Allotmenteers from across the site, including the far side, form a line along each side of the dirt track as Bill leaves for the last time. Their heads are respectfully bowed in silence, recognising the loss of a man who always offered a word of encouragement and took delight in all things bright and beautiful. The very sight brings tears to my eyes; Bill would have been touched by their respect.

Neither Mungo nor I know what to do, so we do what seems appropriate: we slowly follow the procession. We're halfway along the dirt track when I hear a familiar noise: a rhythmical squeak. Turning around, I want to laugh out loud as Levi trundles behind, pushing Bill's damned wheelbarrow.

'I couldn't not, could I?' says Levi, grinning from ear to ear.

As the entrance gate is unlocked and held open, we stand in a group. Levi, still clutching the wheelbarrow handles, stands beside a doleful Ned. Melissa and Jemima are wrapped in each other's arms, weeping.

'Cheerio, old boy,' mutters Mungo, raising his hand while I hug the tartan cap to my chest.

I say the only thing that comes to mind, 'Goodbye Bill, "You've gotta do a bit and leave a bit," now sleep tight.'

The undertakers' vehicle accelerates upon reaching the road. Old Bill is gone.

Our allotments have lost one of the best.

Chapter Thirty-Four

Jemima

I stare at my giant pumpkin, through tear-filled eyes; I have never seen anything so beautiful. Or so large.

'How am I supposed to move it?' I ask, not daring to blink in case Mungo spies my emotional state.

'Move her? You're a long way off moving her, my gal. This here pumpkin needs some loving care beforehand.'

'Her?' I groan, rendered slightly queasy by Mungo's drooling tones. 'I believe she's had plenty of loving, as you put it. Far more than I'd planned.'

'She'll need a gentle wash, a scrub and a chamois leather dry-off, then we'll assess the situation.'

'Mungo, have you lost your mind?'

His stern gaze ensures I don't question his authority any further.

'Fetch a bucket of clean water, a soft clean rag and I'll collect the secret ingredient from my potting shed,' says Mungo, his bushy eyebrows lowering as if allotment skulduggery is occurring.

'Dare I ask?'

'Nope. It's my secret.'

I fight the urge to roll my eyes for the umpteenth time. I realise he's helping me all he can, given his committee status.

'Don't just stand there, girl! Fetch the rest of the equipment – there's no time to waste.'

Girl? Who does he think he's talking to? In defiance of his chauvinistic attitude, I take my time swilling the bucket clean, purely to make him wait.

'Here.' I plop the water bucket and rags beside his crouched figure.

'Thank you. You'll need a clean rag, not a soiled one.' He stares in disgust at my offering.

'Give me strength, Mungo. We're not bathing a baby, you know!'

'It's best to apply the same gentle care – it'll take you an hour, if you do if properly.'

I don't think so.

I saunter off in search of a cleaner cloth that meets Mungo's exacting requirements, which I doubt I have in my potting shed.

I return, having found a roll of blue catering kitchen paper.

'Can I smell bubble bath?' I gripe, as Mungo gently rubs the rind of the pumpkin.

'No.'

'I can. Have you used baby bubble bath on my pumpkin?'

'No! I haven't!' he rudely retorts, stuffing a small bottle back into his pocket.

'I'll pour water over it then, shall I?' I say, holding the bucket aloft and pretending to pour, knowing soap suds will instantly appear.

'Don't!'

'You are such a snap dragon, Mungo. Ahhh, because I'm right.' I replace the bucket on the ground. 'A tried and trusted trick used for over thirty years, is it?'

'Thirty-six, actually – and my pa's for twenty years before me, so don't knock it.'

I offer him the blue catering roll. He winds a large amount around his hand, scrunches it several times to soften the texture, before dunking it in the water bucket. I notice he glances inside before dipping the paper.

'Clean enough for you?'

'You can never be too sure. If you damage the skin at this stage, then its game over, so cut the remarks and watch carefully.'

'Watch and learn,' I mimic.

I study him as he tenderly wipes the pumpkin with circular motions. His hand is barely skimming the knobbly outer peel. For ten minutes, I stand and watch as he tenderly removes all the dirt and manure splatter from the giant pumpkin. I feel like a child being made to 'wait'.

I go to speak several times, before refraining; in the end, I can't help myself. 'When do we cut it from the stalk?'

Mungo answers my question with a disgruntled stare, adding, 'What's the obsession with cutting it from its lifeline? Be patient!'

'Am I supposed to be doing something?'

'Yes, learning. You've got to repeat this process, as gentle and as consistent as me, another three times. OK?'

'Three times!'

'Do you want to win this competition or not?' says Mungo, standing up and discarding his damp tissue.

I don't answer but kneel on the soil.

'Allow her to dry naturally each time, before starting again with fresh water and gentle circular motions. And Jemima, don't bruise or snag the skin. Final time, use a chamois leather to dry her off.' Mungo starts to shuffle back to his own patch.

'You're leaving me?'

'This festival doesn't revolve around you, you know? I've got my prize leeks to select, clean and dry.'

'Mmmm, don't forget your baby bubbles,' I mutter, narked that I'm being left with this ridiculous task.

'I won't.'

Melissa

I bide my time before approaching Mungo. I might get myself into trouble, but he ought to be informed.

I check the coast is clear before nipping across to his plot; he's had a stream of visitors already today. I find him, bent double, his ear pressed to the side of an aluminium bin whilst beating it with a wooden stick.

'Mungo, are you OK?'

'Just checking my leeks before I start pulling them up.' He bashes the side of each of the three large bins. 'Bang! Bang! Bang! Listen to that!'

I have no idea what I'm listening for.

His beaming smile implies I should be impressed.

'Fantastic, sounds great!' I have no intention of upsetting the old folk, especially after yesterday's sadness. 'Can I have a word?'

Mungo's expression alters to deadpan serious.

I'm embarrassed to relay the details, but need to be honest. I simply couldn't sleep. I was eager to see what my orange carrots were like so I nipped up just after midnight to harvest the row. How was I to know there would be others here?

The explanation has hardly left my mouth before Mungo is charging off along the pathway, gesturing his annoyance that security is being breeched, left, right and centre. I have no choice but to follow him to Jemima's allotment. I hope she won't be upset when my quiet word becomes common knowledge – in approximately ten seconds.

'Jemima!'

'Now what?' sighs Jemima, as Mungo shuffles towards her. She is crouched on the bare soil, rubbing a giant pumpkin like Aladdin. 'Am I circling clockwise when anti-clockwise is more favourable? Morning, Melissa!'

'Hi,' I say meekly, wishing I'd shown restraint by informing Dottie, or even Levi, first.

'Less of the cheek, please.' Mungo steps around Jemima's frame, much to her surprise, and begins delving in amongst the foliage, causing the leaves to flap about like crazy. His brow is tightly knitted; he is feeling and vigorously inspecting the sturdy tendrils.

'What the hell are you doing?' exclaims Jemima.

'Oooo!' Mungo gasps, his hands frozen in position near the surface of the soil, peering down amongst the foliage. 'Sabotage!'

I gulp so deeply, it's surely heard across every allotment plot.

'What?' Jemima ceases her polishing.

'Dottie!' shouts Mungo, holding the pumpkin as if it were a severed artery.

'Yes, Mungo,' calls Dottie, her straw hat appearing from the forest of her blooms.

'Assistance, if you please!' cries Mungo, ignoring Jemima's protests.

Should I stay or should I go? I feel wholly responsible, despite being merely the eyewitness. If I wasn't so chicken, I'd have confronted the culprit last night.

Within seconds, she joins Mungo to stare and tut at the sight amongst the pumpkin foliage.

'How disgusting!' declares Dottie. 'Have you identified the culprit?'

'Not yet, but I will. I won't let this lie.'

'Can I ask what you are staring at?' I appeal to them.

Mungo separates the foliage . . . to reveal a deep cut, all but severing the pumpkin from the main vine.

'Clear sabotage! Performed purely to affect the hydration in the coming hours, before judging.'

'Can everyone stop with the sabotage word . . . wasn't I cutting it off the stalk anyway, today?' asks Jemima, looking between their stern expressions and mine.

'You are – but surely that's your decision ... not someone else's choice!'

'I don't really mind ...'

I cringe as Jemima receives a barrage of remarks about her naïvety.

'I'd better go, and leave you good folks to it. Jemima, I'm so sorry if there was more I could or should have done. Bye.' I swiftly exit. After my disastrous harvest of tiny orange carrots, which went straight on to my compost heap, I have parsnips to prepare.

Chapter Thirty-Five

Dottie

'My eyes are getting worse, or these cameras aren't worth having,' I complain, as Mungo presses play on the CCTV footage.

'It's no worse than last time. Folk would complain if the image was crystal clear – they'd feel they were being scrutinised.'

'What an excuse to use,' I chide.

'Here we go,' says Mungo, tapping the screen.

Our shady visitor, clad in dark colours, wearing a jacket and a bobble hat pulled low over their pale haunting face, appears at the main entrance.

'The screen clock reads half past midnight.'

We watch as they use a key to open the main padlock, then slide the bolt which snags and judders upon moving.

'We need to grease that bolt,' I say, knowing my previous requests have fallen upon deaf ears.

'It's a visiting saboteur not a royal visit,' retorts Mungo, his gaze honed upon the flickering screen.

'We don't know that until we've witnessed their handiwork.'

They close the gate and replace the padlock. It's nice to see how conscientious they are, despite their alleged actions. We switch camera views to ensure continuity as they sneak along the dirt track. I'd be mortified if we skipped a section and wrongly accused someone.

'It's a female, isn't it?' I say. 'If you focus on the manner of walking, the hip movement, and even the length of stride.'

'I'd say so, but we've several short males whose stride would match.'

We fall silent as the camera tracks the route towards the front door of plot number 15, where the visitor lets themselves in with a key.

'They've got a key!' I exclaim, my hands covering my mouth in disbelief.

'Are you sure that isn't Jemima?'

'I'm damned sure. I'm not going to sit here and have you accuse Tommy's granddaughter, when she's been an asset to this allotment site. Tommy would be proud of her. The old bugger should have encouraged her earlier in life, he'd have benefitted from her company in many ways.'

'I'm just saying, because of the key. Who else has a key to that front door?'

'You!'

'That obviously isn't me!' bickers Mungo, getting narkier by the minute.

We continue to stare at the screen, though nothing is visible upon the allotment.

'Well, that's that then,' says Mungo, sitting back in his seat and scratching his head. 'I'll visit Jemima, explain what we've seen, and see if the description of the female jogs her memory.'

'It's your memory that needs jogging – who else has a key to that plot?'

'Nobody.'

'I dare to disagree.'

Jemima

'Cheeky beggars who push their luck further than they should,' snaps Mungo, after delivering his detailed description. 'So, any ideas?'

'You're asking me?'

'You don't think attacks such as this are random, do you? This was personal, aimed squarely at you. The captured footage clearly shows yours was the only plot they visited before leaving.'

'I have no idea – but it's not surprising, given the daily footfall through my plot,' I say, purely for effect.

'This isn't chance; you've been targeted. Who have you upset in recent months?'

'The whole community, in various ways – but mainly you, Mungo.'

Mungo has the decency to cough and allow my confession to pass, without attempting to challenge the notion.

'Look, I don't know anyone who fits the description: short, slim, padded jacket and a bobble hat.'

Mungo shrugs at me. 'It might be the very same person who robbed The Veggie Rack . . . does that help any?'

I fire him a quizzical glare. 'How does that help? We never identified that person either.'

'Just checking. I'd hate for you to suffer an embarrassment . . . any chance you own a bobble hat?'

My mouth falls open. 'Are you actually accusing me of sabotaging my own entry in the festival? That is sodding madness in its entirety, right there! Mungo, this conversation is over.'

'I've got a job to do on this committee. I take my role seriously.'

I didn't know my feet could carry me away to my potting shed so quickly. I bite my lip to stop myself from crying; his opinion is not worth it.

I can't bear to join the huddle, so I remain settled on the step of my potting shed and watch. Five men stand, then crouch, only to pace around, switching their positions, while assessing my pumpkin from every angle.

It's a pumpkin. It needs to be lifted carefully and delivered to the marquee before 2 p.m. What more is there to discuss?

'Jemima, what time did you last water her?' calls Mungo.

'Her last feed was nine o'clock last night – when you told me to,' I holler back, unsure if I'm about to be praised or chastised for feeding this baby on a scheduled routine, rather than on demand. I certainly feel like a new mum – out of my depth, entirely naïve, and winging my way through each day under the watchful glare of experts.

Mungo gives a curt nod in my direction, before turning back to his discussions. I imagine the team at NASA looks much the same, creating plans for the launch of their latest probe navigating the solar system. Though on second thoughts, maybe that requires less analysis.

Suddenly, there is a round of back slapping amongst the younger men, and Mungo shuffles my way.

'What did they say?' I ask.

'No worries. The MacDonald lads will help Levi to lift it, then he'll move it up to the marquee within the next hour. Happy?'

'Er, yeah.'

'Good, now where's your wheelbarrow?'

'I haven't got a wheelbarrow.'

Mungo's expression drops. Here we go, it was too good to last.

'What the hell . . . Tommy had a sturdy barrow . . . what have you done with that then?'

'Oi, I haven't done anything with it. There's no wheelbarrow on this plot – I should know.'

Mungo chunters to himself – something about stolen equipment.

'Sorry, what was that?' I say, narked beyond belief that even on festival day he's grumpy with me.

'We'd best borrow Old Bill's then, hadn't we?'

'Mmmm, maybe, or I could roll the pumpkin up the hill.'

An image of me attempting to tyre-flip it, like a competitor in a Strong Man event, comes to mind.

'And ruin her beautiful skin! Haven't you learnt anything?'

'Believe me, I've learnt plenty.'

I remain in situ, while the MacDonald trio and Levi continue to assess the situation. Mungo rejoins them after fetching Old Bill's barrow, complete with its wonky wheel, yet now lined with a folded duvet which I imagine is the highest tog available.

I wait for a further twenty minutes; the scene before me remains unchanged. Someone needs to take control and act as the foreman. As I stand to enter my potting shed, my analysis is easy: it's orange, it's large, it's pumped to bursting with water and everyone's secret growing mixture. What more do the guys need to assess? Thanks to my organised shed system, I find what I need straight away and exit within seconds. They don't notice my swift approach. They don't acknowledge my presence when I'm alongside their broad shoulders. They don't even react when I kneel, separate the mass of foliage and sweep my blade through the remaining section of vine, cutting her free.

'There now, wasn't that simple?' I triumphantly declare, turning to observe five horrified expressions staring down at me.

'Whoa, whoa, whoa! What are you doing?' cries Mungo, as the vine and tendrils spring back after the release.

'Can you please get a move on and trundle this beauty up to the manor?' I demand.

I leave the guys to it; I can't watch the brawn for a minute longer, so I take comfort in reading Grandpop's weather journal.

Dottie

I'm always up bright and early on festival day, but not this year. We've spent half the night discussing whether we should cancel the event or not, given Bill's sudden passing. With our prestig- ious judges on their way from the mainland, fliers and leaflets circulating the local area, and the majority of the allotment site participating, it felt like the only option was to plough on. As Mungo said, 'It's what Bill would have wanted,' and he's right – though sadly, I can't muster my usual vigour given the circumstances.

'Morning, Dottie.' Levi's voice brings me back from my morose thoughts.

'Morning, Levi. We took it well past my bedtime, last night, don't you think?'

'Certainly did, but it's the right decision. Could you imagine this morning's task list if you'd cancelled? Be grateful for small mercies!'

He's so right. Sometimes it's easier to continue going forward than to begin unpicking and reversing a process – does more harm than good.

'I thought you were helping with Jemima's pumpkin.'

'I am, but I thought I'd nip round to see how you are.'

'I haven't the heart to even examine my blooms,' I say, gesturing towards my row of what I hope will be prize-winning flowers. Not my first choice, sadly. But last year's row of prize-winning blooms are disfigured and scorched by Jemima's naïve chemical spraying.

'That's a pity, especially after the drama you've endured – and all the effort you've put into growing them, Dottie.'

'I can't be bothered, if I'm honest. They're bloody flowers at the end of the day, nothing more, nothing less. There are more important things in this world to focus on.'

'Such as?'

I don't answer him. He hasn't got there yet, so doesn't under- stand.

'Life's like an allotment, Levi. You have to chance your luck with the plot you're awarded. Discover and cut your own pathway through the jungle, much like Melissa did. Sometimes friends help and support, sometimes things hinder you. But once you've got a clear aim and purpose, you need to remove the weeds, plant the seeds and, hopefully, surround yourself with the prettiest blooms. Some are tender and need extra care and attention. Others wilt and die, despite everything you do for them. Occasionally, you get an unexpected delivery of manure, whether you want it or not. Again, sometimes friends will help to lighten the load. But regardless of the weather, the growing conditions, the constant threat of pests and disease, or the actions of others, you plod on: weeding, planting and nurturing. And, over time, you turn a bleak, barren landscape into a beautiful, thriving garden.

Levi listens.

My gaze blurs as my watery eyes fill with more tears. 'I'm afraid to say, Levi, I've neglected one precious bloom for far too long.'

'How many of us youngsters have you nurtured over the decades?'

He's right. Whenever there's a new face, I'm there; a little nurturing can go a long way.

'This old bugger's not a youngster any more, Levi, but a gnarly, woody specimen that I've neglected to care for properly. He's like a rambling rose I always appreciated but forgot to stake and prune at regular intervals.'

'I'm sure with a good pruning there's still life in the old bugger yet,' teases Levi, wrapping his arm about my shoulder and giving me a squeeze.

'You cheeky bugger,' I quip, my mood instantly lifted by his manner. 'Come on, help me choose which blooms to select and cut for my festival bouquet.'

Chapter Thirty-Six

Jemima

I pedal my bike along the driveway of Lerwick Manor, passing the festival marquees and the throngs of chattering people on either side of the driveway.

I can't believe how stressful entering a pumpkin has been. My breath calms as I pitch my bike inside a stable for safe keeping and go in search of Levi. Having witnessed the hair-raising moment when five grown men struggled to lift a pumpkin into Old Bill's wheelbarrow was enough for my anxiety levels. If my pumpkin makes it in one piece, I'll eat my hat.

The judging marquee resembles a wedding reception, thanks to the garlands of ivy and swathes of fresh white linen dressing the trestle tables. Allotment holders are bustling around, carefully unpacking their festival offerings from foam-lined storage boxes, blanket-laden pushchairs and classic wooden crates filled with carefully stashed produce.

I eventually locate the four wooden pallets assigned to the pumpkin category; my place card with my entry number is prominently displayed. I'm hoping my definition of giant doesn't prove to be a tiddler alongside a true giant. Thankfully, mine's the only entry delivered so far.

'We've got a problem!' says Levi, peeling back the duvet to reveal the tiniest blemish on the pumpkin skin. 'Some woman sped past in a posh car, throwing a stone up – it must have found the smallest chink in the duvet folds.'

'We're for it when Mungo finds out,' I mutter, knowing how annoyed he'll be.

'The MacDonald lads are on their way to give me a lift from the barrow on to the pallet. I'll ensure the blemish is turned towards the back,' says Levi, scouring the marquee for his assistants.

'How are we?' says Dottie, her spritely step seeming light and summery on such an autumnal day.

'I'm slightly bewildered, if I'm honest. I don't know what to do or expect . . . I feel like a spare part.'

'There's nothing more for you to do, lassie. Why not head straight to the drinks marquee for a wee dram. It'll steady your nerves, if nothing else,' chuckles Dottie, patting my forearm.

I welcome her advice; Mungo hasn't been so obliging with his advice.

'I could certainly do with a dram right now, they've just found a mark caused in transit.'

Dottie peers at the imperfection. 'Phuh! A blind man would be glad to see it!' she says. Then adds, 'It won't stop Mungo raging, but the judges won't mind one iota.'

'Don't say that, I'm shaking as it is.'

'No need, my girl. Tommy would be as proud as Punch if he were here; she's as big as any he produced, I can tell you,' says Dottie, rubbing my forearm tenderly.

'Do me a favour, if you see Mungo, tell him you left me giving her a final polish.' I chuckle at my own joke, only to be met with two deadpan faces.

'That's exactly what you should be doing,' says Levi, waving as he spies the MacDonald trio through the crowd.

On entering the drinks marquee, my head bobs back and forth, trying to spy familiar faces amongst the crowd; given my height disadvantage, my line of vision is filled with chests and upper backs. If I catch Ned's or Melissa's eye, then great – a bonus, if I manage to avoid Mungo.

I sidestep through the crowd towards the makeshift bar, arriving to find a precarious stack of metal barrels, a selection of cardboard cups and a mismatch of allotment folk pretending to be bar staff.

'A dram of whisky please,' I say, knowing my stomach couldn't handle a larger volume. Whilst waiting, I browse the passing crowd. There are plenty I recognise but very few who I'm on speaking terms with. Suddenly, the crowd parts and there's my cousin.

'Pippa!' I yell, waving and hollering until she has little choice but to notice me.

'Hiya, I thought I'd find you in here,' she pants, on reaching me through the bustle. 'Busy or what?'

'It's a great turnout – and they haven't officially opened the festival yet,' I say, before staring at my whisky shot, delivered in a Maximo-sized cardboard cup.

'Sorry, we haven't got any smaller cups,' mutters the barman, adding, 'I can't locate the ice bucket at the moment either.'

Great, warm whisky lost inside a supersized cup.

'Can I get you a drink, Pippa?' I ask, before handing my money over.

'No. I'm not stopping, just passing through. I used to attend every year, alongside Granddad – it was our little tradition.'

'Was it? Grandpop never said.'

'Oh yeah, every year, just me and him. He usually entered a huge pumpkin – and most years, he won the blue ribbon.'

'I'll have to remind Dottie of that, she remembers everything.'

'There's no need, you'll upset the old dear by reminding her.'

I suppress a wry smile. What is it with my family? What do they achieve by lying? The satisfaction of hurting others – and momentarily inflating their flagging egos? Or does it simply drip from the tongue, without much care or thought?

'I've entered a pumpkin this year, she's a big bugger.'

'Mmmm, I thought you might. Ciao!'

'Ciao!' The word dies on my lips.

I can't carry off such a cool departure, unlike Pippa. Her svelte figure quickly slips through the crowd and is lost from view. Why she hangs her belongings from her rear pockets like a teenage skater boy eludes me. Maybe it's an attempt to highlight her shapely arse. Absent-mindedly, I bring the cardboard cup to my lips and gulp, forgetting its contents, causing myself to choke when the whisky burns the back of my throat. I'm spluttering, coughing and drooling unattractively when Ned approaches from my left.

'Hi, Jemima . . . are you OK?'

I peer through watering eyes and wave my cup in his direction as an explanation.

'You really should take more water with it,' he teases, on seeing my whisky dregs.

'I forgot what it was . . . my brain . . . thought it was coffee . . . given the takeaway cup.'

'Woah! A poor excuse if ever I've heard one,' says Ned.

I glance in Pippa's departing direction; pity she didn't linger for a moment longer.

'How are we feeling? Nervous?'

'Why else would I be on whisky at this time of day?' I grimace, fighting a second bout of schoolgirl nerves. 'No way, I'm hiding from Mungo. There's a blemish on the pumpkin due to some maniac driver spraying Levi with stones and grit. I don't intend to be around when he finds out.'

'I see. In that case, you'd best dash – because here he comes.' Ned's expression moulds itself into a fixed grin, as he thrusts me forward.

I fall into the midst of a chattering group of men, who stare at their new addition.

'Oops, so sorry, I slipped.' I peer between their shoulders, observing Mungo ranting at Ned. He's definitely found out about the blemish. I hear Ned mumble a series of remarks before Mungo dashes off.

'Sorry, that was utterly rude of me.'

'I gather he's seen it?' I ask.

'He says you and Levi were irresponsible with your delivery duties.'

'I give up. The man needs to get a life. It's not even his pumpkin, it's mine!'

'I hear you – but think about the dedication shown by others during their midnight prowls. Anyway, he's probably bricking it because the judges are due. I'll catch you later, OK?'

'Ciao.'

Ned frowns at my response, does a double take and walks off, smiling. I vow never to use that phrase again; the likes of Pippa sound ultra-cool, I simply sound old. I swig back the remains of the whisky and choke a little more.

Melissa

I stand at the back of the crowd, trying to claim a space by elbowing my way forward, but the big buggers won't let me pass. Wobbling on tiptoes, I attempt to see what's going on. Surely a stage or a small platform would have been a better idea! But no, the three judges, who've been escorted from the beer marquee by Mungo, are on the same level as the crowd, so I don't stand a chance of seeing them properly. Thankfully, a microphone is in use so I can hear each prize-winning announcement. This isn't what I was expecting. I thought I'd be able to dash inside the judging marquee, to discover a card announcement or a little blue ribbon beside my parsnips. But no such luck – the committee are dragging out this section. Based on my experience, I bet this is Mungo's idea.

'We'd like to thank every participant – in our eyes, they are all winners,' announces Mungo, looking particularly comfortable clasping the mic.

A part of me wants him to burst into song, like a pub singer crooning about a carrot, but I can't think of any suitable lyrics.

'Anyway, could we have some quiet, please, so our judges can be heard clearly by everyone. If the prize winners would approach the awards table upon hearing their names announced, we'd appreciate it. Don't be shy now. Mr Brown, our head judge . . . over to you.'

Mr Brown taps the top of his microphone like all the best people do.

'Can I start by saying what a fabulous day we've had – there are some very talented gardeners and allotment holders here in Shetland. We're very impressed by the standard of produce presented today . . . but I'll hesitate no longer. It hasn't been easy choosing some of the category winners, others not so much . . .' A titter of laughter ripples through the crowd. 'Sorry, I couldn't resist! Without further ado, let's start with our largest entries. The third prize in the pumpkin entry goes to Kaspar . . . Kaspar . . .' The judge is stuck, mouthing the beginning of the unfamiliar surname, as the crowd convey their sympathy – we all struggle a bit with it.

'Yes, I'm here!' shouts Kaspar, dashing through the crowd to save the judge from performing his goldfish impression for a moment longer.

'Congratulations,' says each judge as they warmly shake hands and hand over a certificate and green ribbon.

Kaspar beams while Ned readily snaps a photo of his celebratory moment.

'Second place is awarded to Henry Jones,' announces the head judge.

There's total silence as we await an excited shout from the Far Sider ... but nothing.

'Oh, is Henry not present?' Mungo asks the crowd. A wry smile is dawning upon his features.

I slowly shake my head; let's keep that grudge alive and burning bright, Mungo.

'Never mind, Henry obviously had other things to do this afternoon,' Mungo announces. 'Thank you to the judging panel, I shall take those. We'll make sure that Henry is aware of his achievement, his second-place certificate and ribbon. Please continue.'

'And we're delighted to announce that the first prize for the giant pumpkin category is ...' Unexpectedly, the crowd begin to stamp their feet in a thunderous manner. 'Jemima Button!'

'Woo hoo!' I scream, as the volume surrounding me increases to a deafening pitch: whistles, applause and chanting, which I know she'll hate. I scan the crowd and see her tiny frame reluctantly edge forward, thanks to a gentle nudge and encouragement from the crowd. She's blushing profusely. Bless her.

'The winning pumpkin weighed a staggering four hundred and twenty-seven pounds! Quite an amazing achievement there, Jemima. The farm machinery we used to weigh it struggled for a moment, but was OK after a few adjustments.'

The noise quietens as Jemima stumbles along the line of judges, shaking hands and thanking them, before collecting her certificate, prize voucher and blue ribbon. Ned captures the moment, regardless of her awkward expression. She won't thank him for snapping that image, that's for sure. I'm thrilled for her. Like me, she wanted to grow one thing purely for fun, yet she's been pelted with advice, moaning and criticism by the barrowload. She'll be delighted that her prize-winning specimen will provide bowls of soup for the crowds at tonight's mash-up bash. Mungo is ecstatically happy before he realises that the entire crowd can see his beaming smile – totally unprofessional for a committee member – and reverts to his default expression: a poker face.

'Well done, Jemima, Old Tommy would be dead proud of you, girl!' utters Mungo over his microphone as Jemima walks back through the crowd, attempting to hide her blushing features. Instantly, on hearing her granddad mentioned, she dissolves into uncontrollable tears before the entire audience.

Silly arse, why did he have to say that? She's a gibbering wreck. I dash forward, ready to scoop her up and deliver her to the safety and anonymity of the crowd.

I burst through the throng of people, only to find Ned has got there before me.

Ah, bless.

I stop in my tracks; I'm not needed. I stare as Ned gently steers her aside, cradling her juddering shoulders within protective arms, drawing her so close it causes her face to mush against his chest. I swiftly turn about to see if anyone else is seeing what I'm witnessing. No one else is reacting with surprise, other than me. Can't anyone see what this woman means to this guy? Isn't it bloody obvious? Look at him – deflecting any advance from onlookers who dare to get near her. His physical presence has grown in stature: back broad, arms wrapped around her, head bent and whispering into her ear.

Oh my, I never saw that one on the horizon! Bloody hell, when did that happen? Does Jemima know?

I stand and stare as Ned leads Jemima towards the other marquee – she's obviously in need of a stiff drink.

'Melissa, would you do the honours and take photos with your mobile, please?' asks Mungo, over the public address system.

'Sure.' I'm in shock; I'll agree to anything right now. I take my position before the awards table and await the next category.

Chapter Thirty-Seven

Dottie

I see her before she spies me, her mane of blonde hair gently dancing in the autumn breeze. She's beautiful, I'll give her that, but not inside and out – unlike some I could name. I slow my pace to observe her true self, instead of the polished public persona she conjures – the one she frequently uses with me. I see the inquisitive, sly, slightly morose features which she frequently hid from Ned. The pinched, taut expression portraying the inner workings of a woman on a mission. A woman, possibly in love, but not with the man himself – more his heritage, assets and status. A woman who wasted the best part of five years leading him a merry dance with her 'do I, don't I?' routine, only to cause untold hurt with her final lack of commitment. A woman I don't particularly like, or wish to warm to, but who nearly became mistress of all that she surveys. Natalia. Lean, leggy and lucratively obsessed with collecting hearts, regardless of the aftermath.

Firstly, who invited her?

Secondly, can I get rid of the woman before Ned lays eyes upon her?

'Dottie, there you are! I was looking for you!' she squeals.

I mask my disgust with an extra-value smile and approach, ready to receive her Judas greeting. I have no qualms about it; she likes me a fraction less than I like her.

'Still pottering around, I see.'

'Yes, always pottering, me – always have, always will. What

brings you back to our tiny corner of the world?' I'm not impressed that she's here. I now have a game and a half, making sure Ned doesn't get wind of her presence. My hopes for Jemima will be squashed in one afternoon, if Natalia attempts to wind him around her little finger again.

'The tradition is always to have the festival in September, isn't that so? A little browse on the web and I found the details. I'd have thought Ned would have been around.'

'No, he's busy. Very busy. Did you see the awards ceremony?'

'Phhh! No. I've only just arrived – one tiny blue ribbon looks much like another, don't you think?' says Natalia, looking over my shoulder in search of him.

'I find such rewards fairly insignificant but encouraging for others.'

'Did you win the flower posy ribbon again? I'm sure Ned has run out of charming remarks to make as he hands over your annual trinket.'

'Ned always has a kind word for others.'

Her expression snaps back in my direction. 'I noticed the reno-vated stables – that's where I parked. It's about time he ploughed some money into this place, before it falls down around his ears. It'll be worth seeing how he handles riding again.'

'Actually, he's not stabling horses; he's got bigger plans. You know Ned, a man of few words – but he never stops planning, despite what others may believe.'

'His idea?'

'Yeah.' I hate lying, but needs must.

'Wow! That's not the Ned I know. My Ned was more con-tent plodding about his estate busying himself with tenants and repairing drystone walls.'

I raise a suggestive eyebrow.

'Still single then?'

'Natalia, it really isn't my place to speculate or gossip.'

'I remember – a trusted servant, and as silent as the grave, where Ned boy is concerned. Still dusting, are we?'

'A methodical regime works for me.' I attempt to rise above her level, but she always jangles my nerves. 'And you, still modelling?'

'Pah! Certain products, certain days – you know how it is ... it depends if your face fits the promo ad, and who's in charge of the budgets.'

'Congratulations, I didn't realise you'd moved on from being a hand model in nail polish adverts – well done!'

Her expression drops. Meow, but necessary – touché. I appreciate why I can't hold my tongue against this woman; it's her invisible draw on Ned's attentions. She seems to put him under a spell whenever she visits. Though her unexpected arrivals usually coincide with her lack of work and her need of money. The last twice, she's wheedled her way back into his heart only to stay for a matter of months before disappearing faster than she'd arrived.

'Still at his beck and call then?'

'Mmmm, maybe – maybe not so much.' I sound idiotic; bordering on jealous.

What wouldn't I give for him to settle down with a hardworking young woman, who treated him right, toiled alongside him and provided the comfort he needs in life? I just pray Jemima doesn't walk this way while I'm attempting to remove this beauty from the festival.

'It's been lovely chatting, but I should find Ned for a proper update. See you soon.' With a sugary sweet wave, waggling just her fingertips, she strides across the lawns, her blonde mane swinging left to right, in search of her target. Possibly a reenactment of her shopping strut along Prince's Street, at home in Edinburgh. I can't help but notice how many men, young and old, perform an involuntary double take; they can't help glancing in her direction, their gaze following in her wake. She's a real-life stunner, exuding sex appeal and class, but deep down she's as deadly as Medusa. She might shimmy her wares across the lawn, to be admired by all and sundry. But she won't find him; Ned's squirrelled himself away in his office.

Melissa

'And so we arrive at the final award of the day. Which is traditionally awarded by the allotment committee here in Lerwick. We've decided that the prize of the festival's wooden spoon goes to . . . Melissa Robins,' announces Mungo.

'Cheeky bastards,' I mutter, a fake smile dressing my lips as the crowd begin to cheer. I'm centre stage, kneeling on the grass, having taken all the photos since Ned's swift departure with Jemima. I stand up as Mungo continues to waffle on.

'I have to say, I warned her not to, but this woman does what she wants – she's that sort of allotment holder, aren't you, Melissa?'

'What the hell?' My parsnips were not bad – and he sodding well encouraged me every step of the way, from planting to pulling.

'So, a big round of applause for Melissa, please. The judges agree with us and feel that her carrots are possibly the worst ever grown upon this earth, let alone our allotment site.'

Carrots? I didn't enter those pathetic specimens!

'Please look out for how they'll be incorporated into tonight's mash-up bash – possibly as the garnish. Here . . . look.' He holds aloft a minuscule bunch of carrots which I threw on to my compost heap during the early hours of the morning.

I slowly approach the awards table. 'Who the bloody hell entered those on my behalf?' I mutter, collecting my prize spoon.

'You did!' whispers Mungo. He adds, over the microphone, so everyone can hear, 'Please don't be embarrassed, we all suffer failures in this game at one time or another, Melissa.'

'Thank you so much, I promise to put it to good use!' I say, gallantly waving the spoon while people on the front row capture a memento photo for me.

'I suppose you'll be able to explain yourself?' I say, brandishing my wooden spoon once I locate Levi in the bar, some ten minutes after my moment of glory.

'Congratulations, you truly deserve it,' he says, tipping his half-empty cup in my direction, acknowledging my success.

'I was so embarrassed when he held aloft my tiny-weenie carrots.'

'Don't worry, I doubt those at the back could even see them!'

'I thought you were my friend.'

'You're not blaming me, are you?'

'Yep, this prize reeks of you from beginning to end. You shared Mungo's mishap with me – and thought you'd offer up my efforts to grow carrots, just as a laugh.'

'No, I didn't. I swear to you.'

'Then who?'

'Well, take a guess.'

'Are you serious?'

Levi swigs his pint and pulls a comical expression.

'Did you tell Mungo you'd told me?'

Levi shakes his head and swallows. 'Yeah, he'd relish that conversation. Hey, Mungo, Melissa now knows of your moment of public humiliation.'

'Right, we'll see about this!' I didn't know I could be so het up by a high-jinks trick.

I'm in search of Mungo before Levi can stop me.

'Mungo – a word, if I may!' I call, spying him coming round the corner of the stable yard, cradling a large glass of his home-made beetroot wine. He attempts a swift turnabout but fails miserably.

'Melissa, how are we?' he chortles. 'Have you sampled a glass?' he asks. 'Very good, if I say so myself. It's taken years to perfect the recipe, but this is definitely the best I've—'

'You git! You stole those mini carrots from my compost heap, purely to embarrass me in front of everyone.'

'Me? Never!'

'You've let yourself and the committee down with your behaviour.'

Mungo begins to cough and splutter.

I continue whilst I still have the chance and the rage. 'I don't know how, but you know that I know of your festival embarrassment, and you thought you'd teach me a lesson. I get that you don't want the allotment gossips reviving old news, given your position, but your actions were below the belt.'

'Maybe someone else is aware and taught you a lesson, instead,' he says, staring beyond my right shoulder.

'Ah, so you do know what I'm talking about.'

'Not at all, young lady. I have better things to do than steal from allotments. I'm head of security; I take my duties very seriously.'

'We all know that, you say it enough times. Wouldn't it be funny if everyone knew about your midnight prowling? Some of us have seen you taking care of other people's compost heaps.'

He nearly drops his wine glass on hearing my final words.

'And your secret trips to "feed" a certain prize-winning plant. Now, how funny would it be if that slipped out, after I'd guzzled a few glasses of your beetroot wine!'

Mungo's face is darkening, going slightly beetroot in colour, like his wine. His mouth is working furiously but no words are coming out.

'Sorry, Mungo, what was that? You're sorry for snooping about my plot with your extensive collection of spare keys? Well, thank you for the apology, Mungo – I do appreciate it.'

'Everything OK, folks?' asks Dottie, appearing at my right shoulder.

'It is now. And so, having cleared up that little matter – I think I deserve a large glass of your home brew.' I gently ease his wine glass from his podgy fingers, taking a sip from the opposite side of the glass. 'Thank you, Mungo. I'll leave you two lovebirds to chat.' I head off towards the marquees, leaving behind a bemused Dottie and a stunned Mungo.

My actions were extreme, but necessary, if I'm to hold my own amongst the allotment holders and the committee. I'm sure I'll pay for taking Mungo's drink – a pretty decent home-made plonk – but no doubt I'll know about it tomorrow.

Chapter Thirty-Eight

Dottie

I stand before the beer tent watching the throng of merry people milling about, chattering and eating. It feels like the end of an era, not having Old Bill about, checking and rechecking his timings and agenda. There was many a year we'd end up not speaking until the majority of the festival was over and the crowd were enjoying the mash-up; then we'd celebrate with a wee tipple and give ourselves a pat on the back for having organised another wonderful event. A wave of sadness washes over me, much like the North Sea upon the rocky west coast.

Old Bill gone.

Tommy gone too.

There's no getting away from the fact that we're getting older, if not wiser, though in Mungo's case grumpier, by the season. As if by magic, the crowd parts and there is Mungo, whisky in hand, gesturing how big something was with one outstretched hand. I bet a pound to a penny he's talking about Jemima's pumpkin. He won't admit it to anyone, but he's as proud as a peacock with her gaining first prize. Something tells me he's a little too proud for someone who has only given advice.

I wouldn't put it past him. Though whether it was for Jemima's benefit, or to preserve the legacy left by Old Tommy, I wouldn't like to hazard a guess. The crowd swarms back together, blocking my view of Mungo and co, but revealing the rear view of a woman in jeans and a jacket. A sense of déjà vu swims around my brain. I know her. I can't recall her name but she's the lady I spoke to one morning, wandering around on our side of the allotments, who claimed to be friends with Jemima – though Jemima adamantly refused to admit she knew her. The woman turns sideways; from her rear pocket hangs a bobble hat, similar to the one worn by our secret saboteur. I take a step or two sideways to see who she's chatting with: Jemima.

My word!

How many times did she deny knowing that woman, yet here she is, as bold as brass, yapping away. I've got a good mind to . . . in fact, I will.

I march through the crowd as if my life depends upon it.

'Hello, how lovely to see you again,' I say, interrupting their conversation.

Jemima looks surprised as I address her friend directly.

'And to think when I mentioned you to Jemima here, she claimed not to know you. Yet here you both are – like true buddies.'

'Dottie, this is my cousin Pippa . . . Pippa, this is Dottie. She's one of the committee members who has kindly organised this—'

I cut her short. 'We've met before. This is the Far Sider woman who said she knew you – said yours was the plot with the front door – but when I asked, you claimed never to have spoken to her.' I glance between them expectantly. If I uncover some twisted scandal or dodgy dealings in relation to this pair, I swear I'll have no involvement with organising the festival next year.

'Mm-hm,' says Pippa, nonchalantly.

'She's not even an allotment person!' exclaims Jemima.

'She is.'

Jemima glances between us indignantly.

I stare at her outfit. Again, it seems familiar: a padded jacket, jeans and . . .

'That bobble hat,' I exclaim, pointing at the woman's pocket.

'I'd like you to meet a friend of mine, called Mungo, who believes you sabotaged Jemima's pumpkin.'

'Me?' says Pippa, gesturing towards her own chest. 'I don't think so.'

'You've got a key.'

'I haven't,' says Pippa.

'We've got CCTV images that prove otherwise.'

Jemima's mouth is widening by the second.

'Jemima, it's been great catching up, but this . . .' She rudely gestures towards me. 'Potty old ladies acting gaga in public, accusing folk, isn't my thing. I'll catch you another time, sweet.'

'Would you care to view the footage?' I say, getting slightly above myself.

'Lady, you keep it and watch it with a nice mug of cocoa and your slippers on.'

'How dare you!' seethes Jemima, her hand snatching at Pippa's forearm, holding her in situ. 'Our grandpop admired this woman immensely. If she says that you were caught prowling, then I believe her. How dare you be so unkind towards me! We're cousins.'

'Phuh, cousins! How belittled did Callie and I feel at the solicitor's office? I hope he left you a decent inheritance, because the likes of me aren't interested in staying in touch with you!'

'Is that what's bothering you?'

Pippa shrugs nonchalantly.

'I turned up with the intention of handing the keys back, but I changed my mind when I saw what a lovely space he'd created – I was on sabbatical, remember?'

'Prove it.' Pippa snatches her forearm from Jemima's hold. 'I know what I know.'

'And so do we!' I add venomously. 'You owe her an apology.'

'Hardly! I don't think so. I'll see you around, Mima, some-time . . . maybe.'

Pippa turns to leave our company. I move faster than I have in years, sidestepping to block her path.

'I think Jemima needs her keys back, if you don't mind.'

'What kinds of friends did Granddad keep? Call your Rottweiler to heel, Mima,' snarls Pippa, thrusting her hand into her jeans pockets and producing a key ring with two keys attached. 'With pleasure.' She slaps the key ring into Jemima's outstretched palm and stomps off, her hair bouncing with each step.

'Are you OK?' I ask, as Jemima bites her lip, her eyes glistening. 'Don't get upset about the likes of her, lassie.'

'You're right.'

'Come on, you need a dram of the strong stuff,' I say, quickly linking arms and guiding her towards the beer tent. 'They always say you can choose your friends but not your family.'

'Isn't that the truth? Except for Grandpop – I wouldn't have changed him for the world.'

Jemima

'Mungo, can I have a quick word?' I ask, tapping him on the shoulder. I spy him in the beer marquee, enjoying a glass of beetroot wine and chatting in a group with the three judges. I hate to interrupt his conversation; he rarely has the chance to talk to such prestigious gardening folk from the mainland.

'Certainly, certainly,' he says, gesturing to the group that he'll be back, before turning his full attention to me. 'What's the issue?'

'There's no issue ... except ... I want to return these.' I pull the certificate, prize voucher and blue ribbon from my jacket pocket; its silky satin texture glistens within my outstretched hand. 'I can't keep it. I didn't truly earn it. I know that other people were feeding my pumpkin during midnight expeditions.'

Mungo frowns, glances over his shoulder at the judges and

hastily moves me aside, out of their earshot. He doesn't look happy as he takes a slurp of his wine.

'I don't think so, young lady,' he retorts in a gruff voice.

'I think so. And I think you know so too, Mungo.'

'Talk like that is absurd nonsense and gossip, Jemima,' says Mungo, his voice suddenly increasing in volume. 'You won it fair and square, well done! Tommy would be proud of you.'

'Mungo, they aren't listening – they're busy talking to Kaspar,' I report, pushing the blue ribbon into his hand. 'Here, take it.'

'No. Keep it.' He pushes it back into my palm.

'I can't. It would be a lie!' I thrust the blue ribbon back at him.

We tussle back and forth, the blue ribbon creasing and folding between our grasp.

'No!' I say adamantly, stepping backwards, away from our strange little game.

On hearing my outcry, several people near us turn about and stare. My final objection had been voiced a little louder than I intended. Mungo quickly stuffs the blue ribbon into his pocket, politely smiles at our audience and keeps his pocketed hand in place.

'You're making a scene, Jemima,' he says, through his fake smile, half hidden by his wiry beard.

'No. You're making the scene. You and I, and Levi – probably Dottie too, and definitely Ned – we all know that various males have been secretly tending to my pumpkin. And my compost heap,' I add, for good measure, purely to witness his reaction.

'What do you know about compost heaps?'

'I know you allotment guys have been watering mine, that's what. I won't be touching it without gardening gloves.'

Mungo takes another large swig of his wine.

I hastily continue. 'Grandpop earned each of his blue ribbons. I didn't, so I can't keep it. I suggest you reverse the judging decision and award first prize to the guy who gained second place.'

'I don't think so,' says Mungo, choking on his beetroot wine.

'Mungo, who cares if Henry's a Far Sider? This is precisely why I don't want the blue ribbon. It's not mine, Mungo. I can't proudly display it alongside Grandpop's ribbons. I don't want decades of deceit, regret or bad feeling hanging over me because of a sodding pumpkin. You need to forget that festival from aeons ago; move on with your carrot aversion and the Far Sider vendetta.'

Mungo's stubborn gaze clears, like June clouds drifting aside to reveal sunshine. Gone are his grumpy stare and his furrowed brow.

A moment of clarity occurs. 'Is that why you're handing it back?'

I nod.

There's silence as we both digest what's been said and accept the true winner of this year's blue ribbon.

'Thank you, Mungo. I'll let you get back to your group.' I rub his forearm, as if thanking him for hearing me out and understanding my predicament.

I head towards the marquee's exit. I feel lighter; being truthful is always the right thing to do.

'Jemima!' I turn as Mungo calls my name. 'You're more like your granddad than you realise – a chip off the old block.'

I smile, acknowledging his compliment. A wave of pride knots at my throat. Mungo's right; me and Grandpop were like two peas in a pod. Maybe next year, this 'Little Pumpkin' will nurture her own pumpkin patch and earn a ribbon of her very own.

Melissa

I cradle my wine glass and stare across the manicured lawn towards the small wooded copse in the distance. This is the life. To be content and simply enjoying the view, beneath the stars. If asked, I wouldn't know what to choose from a 'wish list' – there's nothing I could buy which would improve my life at this given moment. Not a new car, a bigger house or a luxury holiday. Maturity certainly enlightens and changes your perspective on life.

I take a sip of the home-made wine, to find Levi staring at me from his position a few feet away.

'A penny for them!' he says, cradling his beer bottle. 'Or is your beetroot wine as bad as it sounds?'

I smile. 'Actually, it's very nice. My thoughts aren't worth deciphering.'

'Try me.' He skooshes his chair across, gaining distance from his jovial crowd.

'Where do I even start?' I say, exhaling deeply.

'I hear the beginning's a fair point to work from.' He leans forward, resting his elbows on his splayed knees.

'That's so long ago, I can hardly remember it.'

'Once upon a time there was . . . now, finish the sentence.'

I laugh. My eyes meet his and neither one of us looks away.

He's lovely. And he knows it; bloody cocky with it too.

'Nah, I can't pretend to know the opening line to my story. And you, what follows "once upon a time"?'

'Once upon a time, there was a young lad who was the wise-cracking joker all through school, who then acted the fool at college and failed his exams. He totally messed up the route for continuing his education, so he did the one thing he knew he could do around Shetland.'

I can hear his honesty.

'He reckoned he was the big shot around here, and slowly, over time, he's been corrected. He once thought he'd have women swooning around him, would be driving a flash car and living the dream life by the time he was this age. But he's not. He's simply plodding along, muddling through each day and looking out for the decent woman who he probably should have snapped up at least a decade ago.'

'And the ending?'

Levi shrugs. 'I have no idea. He doesn't seem to be getting any nearer to the prize, despite how hard he tries.'

'That's a sad story.'

'Mmmm, I reckon so too.'

'What's he planning to do?'

'Phuh!' Levi turns, looking off into the distance, towards the copse on the other side of the lawn. 'He knows what he should do – or wishes to do – but the reality of actually having the guts to chase what he wants may hurt others . . . and that isn't what he's about. That's the thing about being the class clown; he can't handle the crowd when their laughter stops and true emotions have to be faced.' Levi stares back at me. 'I suppose it depends what the leading lady does.'

'She has a choice, does she?'

'She does . . . though I doubt she knows how important her choice is.'

I sip my beetroot wine. My brain daren't ask a question, for fear of hearing there's another younger, fitter model.

'Levi, what's going on?' I muster the courage to ask, after a few minutes of staring at the top of his lowered head. 'You've kept your distance for weeks . . . and now this.'

'Come on, let's walk and talk,' he says, standing up and indicating the vast lawns before us.

'I don't think we're supposed to venture further than this,' I say, glancing at the others seated along the patio.

'If Lord or Lady Muck wish to object, they can come and have a quiet word. Bring your drink,' he says, as I stand up to join him.

We scurry down the nearest stone steps. My heels sink into the turf as we dash into the shadows lingering about the edges. Our hands are clamped together as he drags me along, my wine sloshing over the rim of my glass. I haven't run like this in years. Where the hell is he taking me?

We stop amongst the trees. His hand snakes about my waist, pulling me closer into his body, connecting us at various points, from shin to shoulder. His lips are passionately seeking mine, our noses occasionally bumping. My fingers stroke the nape of his neck, a gentle rhythmical touch, playing with the fine, close cut of his hair.

Can I do this? Is this what I truly want or need?

I want to be soothed. I need to belong.

My thoughts swirl and work upon my brain, much as my touch does upon his body.

His hands stay firm about my waist, playing it safe; he's too frightened of offending me. I will his hands to move, to explore, to play, to tease and dissolve the loneliness that dwells deep within me. I want skin on skin.

'Melissa, let's take this back to mine.'

His words are balm to my lonesome heart. He wants me, I want him. Hamish doesn't want me; he'd be here, if he did.

'We can't both walk out together.'

'We can if we want to advertise it to the entire allotment association,' he teases, releasing my waist to tenderly stroke my cheek.

'Not my intention.'

'I suggest you go first. I'll linger for a moment and then make my way back to mine.'

I nod. My heart is thumping with such passion – this is what I want.

Others will think it underhand, sly, even cheating, but it's different. It's not some long lonely stretch, week after week, waiting for your man to fly home for a short break, or even to get back to you with a feasible date for a holiday week.

Levi is here, now.

And so am I.

'I'll see you in a short while,' I say, pecking his cheek.

Chapter Thirty-Nine

Dottie

'Excuse me, I'm looking for Melissa ... any chance you've seen her about?'

Turning around, I'm greeted by the polite manners and rugged features of a man who is expectantly awaiting an answer. I don't recognise him as a local, but he's obviously made the effort to attend our allotment festival.

'Actually, I was looking for someone myself, so I know exactly where Melissa is. Come with me, I'll show you.' His knotted brow eases and he thanks me. I pause in my search for Jemima. Where she's got to is anybody's guess; maybe she's taken herself off in search of Ned, before Natalia wheedles her way back in.

'I've searched each of the marquees,' he says. 'Someone sent me on a wild goose chase through the stable yard – and now, I don't know where else to look.'

'That's fine, we've used various areas of the manor grounds today. The evening's mash-up is being served from the terrace area – she was there no more than fifteen minutes ago. This way.' I take the lead, my tiny feet scurrying from the grassy area and along the driveway's gravel, unsure who this nice young man is. But if he's seeking Melissa, I'm not going to disappoint him, or her. 'Have you enjoyed the day so far?'

'I've only just arrived. I missed the actual festival, as such.'

'So you don't know that she was awarded the booby prize for her mini carrots – diddy, but still delicious.'

'Did she really? She's been joking all week about parsnips.'

'I'm afraid she didn't win any prizes for those – but still, she tried.'

'That's Melissa, always a trier.'

In no time, we've cut through the stable yard and The Orangery, stepping out on to the terrace, where merry groups are finishing off their mash-up or milling about with drinks.

'Now, she was seated over here, nearer the steps,' I say, cutting through the various chattering huddles.

The man's smile is growing by the second.

'She can't have gone far.'

As the words leave my lips we both turn towards the expanse of lawn, to witness a couple dashing gleefully along the edge. Their outline is almost hidden by the shadows, but I still recognise the man leading the way, his arm outstretched behind him, and the woman, her head thrown back like a gleeful child: Melissa.

Think fast, Dottie.

'Well, would you believe it? She was here a second ago. She must have headed back out to the driveway, at the same time as we were walking through the stable yard.' I speak in a rush, in a poor attempt to divert his attention from the lawn.

'Mmmm, maybe. But I doubt it, somehow,' he says, inhaling deeply, his gaze fixed upon the dusky shadows of the now empty lawn. 'Thanks for looking, anyway. I'll get going, I think.'

'Don't do that. Join in and enjoy a wee dram whilst you're here – more, if you're not driving,' I say, trying to cover up the awkwardness.

'Thanks for the offer, but I'd best be off. Enjoy your evening.'

I watch as he hurriedly strides from the terrace, retracing our steps through The Orangery. I sense there's a storm brewing on the horizon for Melissa. How much of Mungo's beetroot wine has she had?

'Dottie, have you seen Ned?'

At last, Jemima pops up.

'How are you enjoying yourself, sweetheart?' I reign in my excitement at the thought that she's searching for him.

'Loving it. It's much better than I was expecting. Though I just wanted a quick word with Ned – to thank him for earlier.'

'I haven't seen him for a while. You might want to check inside – you know what he's like, hiding away in his office most of the time,' I whisper, not wanting others to overhear us.

Jemima gives me a swift peck on the cheek, before dashing off towards the side entrance. It'll be locked but she'll have her keys, as always. I pray that she finds Ned in need of her company; it'll give them some time alone together.

Jemima

I check the coast is clear before nipping through the side entrance, quietly locking the door behind me. I have keys, so technically I'm not trespassing. I'm simply in search of my friend, to thank him for hosting a wonderful day, and I'm excited to share the positive comments received about our ... *his* new venture. I should also thank him for comforting me earlier, when I got upset about Grandpop.

The manor is silent and virtually in darkness as I tiptoe through the corridors, crossing the threshold to enter the main house, before nipping up the grand staircase.

I'm slightly tipsy, thanks to the numerous glasses of Mungo's beetroot wine and the several whiskies I've consumed throughout my day.

The third-floor landing is in darkness, except for a glimmer of moonlight shining through the skylights above. This time, I have no qualms about heading straight for Ned's office, where a thin strip of orange light seeps under the door, confirming his occupancy.

I take a deep breath, purely to counteract the effects of my final whisky, then rap a strange but novel tune upon his office door and enter, without waiting to be asked.

'Ned, I just wanted to say—' I stop dead. My heart plummets to the pit of my stomach.

Ned swiftly turns in his desk chair, an expression of surprise etched upon his features as I, wide-eyed and open-mouthed, take in the beautiful creature perched upon the edge of his desk, a tad too close to his seated body. She's wearing the skimpiest silk two-piece top and shorts, displaying perfect alabaster skin and lean, long limbs. Her shoulders are bare and she has a midriff as taut as a stretched canvas. I'm unsure if she's wearing expensive lingerie or inappropriate summer wear, given she's in Shetland in September. Either way, this queen bee is a definite distraction from his late-night session of estate paperwork. The accounting books, piled high on the desk, provide a suitably vanilla backdrop to her model pose and their two empty brandy glasses.

'Sorry, I didn't realise,' I mutter, my gaze repeatedly retracing the length of her body.

Likewise, she does the same to me. Suddenly, I morph into a pumpkin wearing bad clothes, my hair a dishevelled mess, and my mascara ruined by the tears I shed earlier for Grandpop.

I need another whisky, preferably a double. No ice. No water. And no sipping.

'Jemima, I was just talking about you,' says Ned, turning to the goddess at his side. 'Didn't I just mention her?'

The goddess nonchalantly raises an arched eyebrow in reply; her gaze remains fixed upon me. Her flowing locks cascade about her shoulders like a waterfall. I can imagine the enamelled butterfly clip nestled within her tresses, perfectly complementing their glossy colour.

'Ignore me. It wasn't important ... I'll catch you another time, Ned.'

'I'm Natalia, nice to meet you.' She remains seated, extending one delicate hand in my direction. There's a definite two-foot gap between the location of her fingertips and my grubby mitt, so I shuffle forward in a semi-bent, curtseying style to grasp the proffered hand of Ned's beautiful girlfriend. I knew she'd be drop-dead gorgeous, just bloody knew it!

'How rude of me. Natalia, Jemima ... Jemima, this is Natalia,' says Ned, gesturing between us.

Natalia smiles; I repeat her name for good measure. I doubt I'll forget this moment: her stunning body, sophisticated name and delicate debutante handshake.

'No worries,' Ned reassures me. 'What did you need?'

Natalia smiles demurely, before picking a stray hair from Ned's shirt collar, her perfectly manicured fingers allowing it to drop to the carpet. I note the gesture – her suggestion of boredom alongside defined intimacy – but attempt to ignore it by continuing my speech.

'Thank you for hosting such a fabulous day ... I'm not sure you've seen much ... I know how busy you are with work, but it's gone swimmingly well. And Isla, our new catering manager, has excelled at cooking produce for the mash-up bash ...' I hesitate, seeing Natalia roll her lips, probably suppressing a chuckle. 'I wanted to thank you for the support you've shown me in recent weeks.'

'My pleasure. Though I don't believe my support compares to the cooperative efforts of others nurturing your prize-winning pumpkin.'

'Pumpkin?' sniggers Natalia.

Ned throws her a sideways glance, before turning his attention back to me.

'Anyway, I just wanted to say thank you. I'll be off ... and leave you two to . . .' I don't know how to end my own sentence; I have no idea what they were up to, before I gatecrashed the party. I rapidly shuffle back towards the office door, hoping I don't bump my ass on the doorjamb. 'Nice meeting you, Natalia. Bye, Ned.'

I escape his office as swiftly as my stubby legs can manage, distancing myself from Ned and his beautiful girlfriend. What's that old saying? I need the serenity to accept the things I cannot change, the courage to change the things I can, and the wisdom to know the difference between me and the likes of Natalia. It's like comparing Kew Gardens to an overgrown allotment plot, complete with stinking compost and a huge water butt.

I have every intention of grabbing my bike and heading home. But once I've blindly navigated my route out to the stable yard, I instinctively take a left turn, edging The Orangery, and find myself on the paved terrace before descending the stone steps. Heading who knows where, for who knows what reason.

Breathe, breathe.

My controlled breathing isn't working; my mind is racing, my chest is tightening and my palms are tacky. My feet carry me along the border of the lawn as my hands frantically waft at my neckline, trying to cool my skin, preventing my anxiety from building. Distraction, distraction: I need to focus my mind elsewhere.

Ned must be delighted that we've finally met; he's finally got to show her off, got to observe us side by side. My mind replays her 'pumpkin?' query along with her eyebrow gesture, igniting a further tightness deep within my chest. It was the only moment when her manners slipped, but who can blame her? He's probably shared with her numerous anecdotes about my daily chores and rookie errors. I'd laugh, if I saw me entering centre stage in that cosy scenario.

The clammy sensation spreads from the nape of my neck down the length of my back.

This isn't good. I'll walk it off in the fresh air. Hopefully, it'll pass as quickly as it arrived.

Breathe, breathe.

What the hell was I thinking? Why would any man look at the likes of me when they can enjoy the likes of Natalia?

Breathe, breathe.

I've done so well in recent months, yet this feels awful. I've been kidding myself for weeks that I'm coping, getting better and handling my anxiety, when all the time it's been simply lingering in the background waiting to pounce.

Much like Natalia, appearing out of the blue.

The fountain is turned off as I approach. The centrepiece looks out of place, protruding from the water, without the attractive vigour of the waterfall: an object without point or purpose. The sound of trickling water might have helped distract my thoughts.

Breathe, breathe.

I circle the edge of the pond, trailing my fingers along the shimmering surface as the koi carp writhe and glide like ghosts below. The coolness of the water brings a sense of relief to my skin and helps to calm my disordered thoughts. I continue to stare into the dark waters, admiring the fusion of colour, before being snagged back into reality.

'Ned! What's the point?'

I'm startled at hearing her voice cut through the darkness.

'Seriously, she'll find her way home. She'll probably collect the bike tomorrow.'

'Natalia, she never leaves it overnight. Ever.'

I squint into the darkness, peering in the direction of the copse, and catch their movement fast approaching. I dart from the pond's edge across the shale, heading towards the abandoned orchard on the far side, swiftly nipping in amongst the stunted trees as Ned appears. I press myself flat against the nearest tree;

its shortened trunk ensures I have to cower as the lower branches graze my temples.

'For fuck's sake, Ned. What does it matter?'

Ned appears at the koi pond, his head twisting back and forth, scanning the area.

'Ned, are you even listening to me? Ned!'

'What?' he calls, looking over his shoulder towards the figure emerging from the copse, still inappropriately dressed in skimpy silk shorts, with a jacket clutched about her shoulders.

'Why can't we go back inside and pick up from where we left off last Christmas? All this drama – and for what? A pathetic allotment holder who can't even string a few coherent sentences together. What's the bloody point?'

Chapter Forty

Melissa

'Melissa, wait a minute!' calls Dottie.

I'm walking along the manor's driveway. I pause, as she hobbles towards me, out of breath and waving her hands.

'A word, if I may,' she says, holding my forearm to steady herself.

'Dottie, I haven't seen you all evening.'

'Likewise . . . you've had a man looking for you.'

'When?'

'I thought you were sitting on the terrace, but you were nowhere to be seen – if you get my meaning.'

Oh Lord, please don't continue.

'I felt ill – too much beetroot wine,' I say. 'I took a walk to clear my head.' No doubt, the gossip will be circulating the allotments before the sun has chance to rise.

'Well, as I told him, "She was here a moment ago . . ." And then he left. You might want to get yourself away home.'

How embarrassing that she's covering for me whilst reading my guilty conscience, despite the darkness.

'And he left the terrace or left-left?'

'He definitely left the festival – he didn't linger about, lovey.'

'Thanks, Dottie, I'll get off home and see what's what.'

'I would, pet; he seems a decent sort – nice manners and an auburn beard.'

That confirms it: Hamish always has beautiful manners towards strangers, though the beard is usually stubble.

I feel the panic rise in my chest. I need to be home, and quickly. 'Good night, Melissa.'

'Night, Dottie, and thank you.' I set off at a quickened pace.

I need to get back. I need to be home alongside Hamish and face whatever questioning he has. I can't pretend I'm not flattered by Levi's attentions, his gentle warmth, his open desire to know me better. But right now, I must focus on us. The 'us' who stick to our vows, despite the surrounding temptation.

The key snags in the front-door lock as I eagerly insert it, twist and turn.

'Hamish, are you in?' I call, dropping my keys upon the hall table and dashing through to the lounge, without flicking a light on.

Nothing has changed; the carpet's vacuum lines remain untouched. I head for the kitchen to repeat the same routine; my solitary glass is upturned upon the draining board alongside my breakfast bowl.

I hear a creak in the floorboards of my bedroom.

He's here!

Taking the stairs two at a time, I see his outline standing in the doorway of my room – our bedroom.

'Hi,' I whisper, unsure how to proceed. I wish to forget the previous hour and react on instinct.

'Hey, babe, I thought I'd surprise you.' His tone is even, not a hint of anger, suspicion or argument.

'Why didn't you say? I'd have been here to greet you.' I remain at the top of the staircase, knowing each sentence will pave the way towards our future: good or bad.

'I wanted to surprise you. You sounded so fed up. I wanted to do something nice for you, for us.'

'I'd have cooked something special, picked you up from the airport – changed the sheets.' I giggle, hoping he follows suit.

'Stuff the sheets – who needs clean sheets?' he says, peeling his T-shirt over his head and throwing it into the darkness.

Cue my move.

I dash across the landing and plant impatient, wanton kisses upon his jaw, neck and finally his mouth. His arms wrap about me without hesitation, giant hands spanning my back to pull me in close as I inhale his scent. Hot, passionate kisses rain down upon my cheeks and neck as my head tilts back, encouraging him. I lift myself high, wrapping my legs about his waist and back, as he stumbles backwards into the bedroom and deposits us upon the mattress.

It's as if he's never been away.

All thoughts of the festival are gone. The walk of temptation in the orchard with Levi, my friend, is a distant memory.

I have no idea what Hamish witnessed from the terrace, but he's happy in the knowledge that I am here, he is here, and we are together.

I lie half covered by the duvet and listen to his breathing as Hamish dozes beside me. I can't sleep; my mind is racing, churning over the events of the night. My hand felt right in Levi's, we'd giggled like children dashing along the edging of the lawn. Lord knows what we were thinking, hoping or planning – but it's no laughing matter, when it comes to love and life.

I glance at Hamish as his breathing stalls and he snuffles in his sleep. Our love and the two of us – that's all I need or want. How stupid to chance my past, present and future in a fleeting embrace with a friend. Regardless of our circumstances, careers or confusion along the way, it's what Hamish and I have when we're together that matters. So what if my patience is stretched by his lengthy absences, or my bed empty and cold on certain nights? One day, whether it goes to plan or not, this will be our Monday to Sunday routine, two heartbeats filling the silence of our home.

Dottie

'Are you ready for the off, Dottie?' asks Mungo, offering me his arm at the end of a long evening.

'Oh yes. It's nearing my bedtime, and I for one have had enough for today. You?'

'I'm fit for nothing after the past few days we've had.'

I gratefully link my arm in his and we begin our shuffling walk along the driveway. It'll take us far longer than it should, given that we've both been drinking his beetroot wine.

'We've done Old Bill proud, haven't we?' I say, gazing up at the stars as we plod along.

'Phuh! He's probably up there pencilling his list of tasks and instructions for next year's festival.'

'As if! That would take him all of six minutes, with his head screwed on and a mug of tea in his hand,' I say, recalling this year's committee meeting.

'It'll be easier next year. We'll have Jemima on the committee, and she can organise it on our behalf.'

'That's a bit of a cheek; she's only just arrived at the allotments. Who says she'll want to join our committee?'

'She'll join, trust me.'

'And Levi? Won't he be expecting an invite to join the committee?'

'He'll understand. We'll explain that it's easier when we have the manor family on our side.'

'Mungo, the gal's the project manager – nothing else. Anyway, come the morning, Levi might find himself stuck between a rock and a hard place, after what I saw tonight.'

'Eh-eh, any news?'

'Not quite . . . you?'

'Only that I caught up with Henry from the Far Side after

Jemima refused the blue ribbon for her prize pumpkin. By default, it belongs to him. I congratulated him and added a little extra detail relating to possible evictions occurring if they don't clean their act up. He assures me the cockerel will be gone by tomorrow, and he'll be having a quiet word about the wacky baccy smoking.'

'A job well done, Mungo,' I say, as we approach my garden gate.

'I try my best. Thank you for a good day, Dottie. Old Bill would have been proud of us. I'll see you up the allotment tomorrow morning.'

I pause, without releasing his supporting arm. 'Are you not coming in for a night cap?'

'Dottie Nesbit, in all these years, you've never once invited me in when I've walked you home.'

'It's a lady's prerogative.'

Mungo falls silent, glancing between my house and the route towards his own. He has his moments; some days, he can be mean towards others, and his ego regularly surfaces when his knowledge is challenged, but towards me, I couldn't ask for a kinder, more caring companion. There's nothing he wouldn't do for me, in sickness or in health. Maybe, after all this time, Mungo's one of those men who might not bring more trouble than they're worth?

'Come on, you old bugger! I haven't got all night to wait for an answer.'

'In which case, count me in.'

Jemima

Ned circles the pond edge, just as I had minutes before, staring at his beloved carp. He settles on the stone edge, as is his habit, his legs swinging wide, shoulders rounded, head bent.

Natalia saunters up and boldly stands between his knees,

edging herself closer to his frame; his bowed head doesn't allow her to connect with him.

'Ned. Please.' Both her hands rest upon his shoulders.

His posture remains unaltered – unlike mine, which is suddenly tense and alert.

'I was pleasant. I love meeting the locals. But seriously, I'm hardly going to agree to the likes of her joining us, am I?'

Ouch! I've got a good mind to step out from the shadows in dramatic fashion and correct her, but I don't. I remain behind a tree, peering at the drama unfolding before me.

'I give up!' says Natalia, stepping back from Ned's dejected frame. 'I'm done, Ned. I can't keep doing this with you.'

His face lifts to address her; his features appear hauntingly blanched, devoid of emotion.

'Natalia, apart from partaking in a brandy, I haven't asked you for anything this evening.'

Her pretty mouth is wide, hands outstretched at her sides. 'Exactly. You are something else, you know that, don't you?'

Ned doesn't respond but simply stares up at her fine features, as she battles to control her mane of hair, fighting against a gentle breeze. Obviously, in need of her pretty butterfly clip.

'Anyway, I've got a funny feeling about little Cinderella and her prize pumpkin,' she sneers. 'So I'm going to head off home. As if . . . the likes of you and the likes of her . . . well, well.'

Inwardly, I beg Ned to remain silent and not reach for her hand.

'See ya, Ned,' Natalia shouts over her shoulder, striding towards the path leading through the wooded copse.

Peering through the bare branches, I watch his actions. Ned remains motionless, staring ahead across the lawn. He looks tired, lost actually, sitting alone in the darkness.

He's probably regretting letting her leave; she's been drinking brandy, after all.

Ned stands and crosses the lawn to linger beside the walled gate, before twisting the iron ring. But the gate doesn't open. Instantly, his hand reaches for the bolt. He immediately turns and stares, scanning the open area stretching between us: he by the gate, me amongst the stunted apple trees.

The secure bolt confirms I haven't nipped through from this side.

He knows I'm still here! My parked bike is a reliable sign, but Crispy duck wandering about the yard is a dead cert that I'm close by.

If he spots me, my behaviour will appear foolish and jealous.

He leans his back against the stone wall, his expression hidden by the shadow, his hands sunk deep into his pockets.

'Jemima?' His hesitant whisper is barely audible; it registers a chill along my spine.

I refrain from answering, by holding my breath.

'Jemima, come here.'

To refuse would seem churlish.

I step out from behind the tree, and stand before him. I'm angry that he knows, frustrated that he sensed my presence, yet relieved that he's called me out from my hiding place.

'Did you see her leave?' His voice is soft, yet deep.

'Yes. She didn't seem happy.'

'I suppose not.'

'What did she mean by "the likes of you and the likes of her"? I assume she means me.'

'Mmmm, so you heard.'

I wait, not trusting myself to speak, for fear of interrupting his explanation or revealing my true thoughts.

'Ah, well, there's the thing. For you to understand, I need to come clean. I've let you believe that I'm the estate manager around here, working on behalf of the family, my relatives. Well, the truth is, I *am* the family, with no other relatives. Jemima, I lied. It was easier than having you know the truth, easier than allotment folk knowing the truth, when all is said and done. I enjoy a level of privacy, I like the comforts which life has delivered, but I don't want some of the responsibilities which come with this territory. I'm content dealing with the tenant farmers, their businesses and managing the land – just not the social stuff which comes with the manor.'

I remain quiet, listening. I want to understand. To appreciate his viewpoint and position in life, but the only words swimming about my mind are 'you lied'.

He falls silent, his shadowed features stare at me: waiting.

'I've had a smashing day. I enjoyed prepping the pumpkin, the judging was nerve-wracking, and Mungo sent me over the emotional edge by mentioning my grandpop. But do you know the worst part of my day?' I ask, pausing in case he wishes to answer.

'Right now?'

'No. It was begging Mungo to retract and reverse the judges' decision, because I didn't deserve to receive first prize. Henry did. Henry planted, nurtured and prepped his pumpkin alone. He didn't have midnight prowlers helping out with secret potions. And the best part of today?'

Ned shrugs.

'It was Mungo accepting the blue ribbon and promising to deliver it to Henry in the morning, despite him being a Far Sider. See, that's the difference, I don't lie. I can't accept a prize, knowing that it isn't rightfully mine. How could I pin that alongside Grandpop's genuine ribbons?'

'I don't get what you're saying. How does this relate to what I've just told you about me?'

'Because now you're showing your true colours. You lied about your position and status, you've lied about me working for a non-existent family, you've forced Dottie to lie in her interactions with me, and you've even lied by hiding your girlfriend, fearing my reaction towards her might affect our working relationship.'

'Woah, woah, woah!' stutters Ned. 'Girlfriend? Now, hang on a minute.'

'It's OK. You don't have to pretend, Ned. I found her hair clip in the wax jacket you allowed me to borrow. It's fine, I'm at fault. I get it, I need to reign back and create boundaries within which we can both work to ensure the success of the gallery.'

'Jemima, now listen. You said you heard what she'd said ... well, didn't you hear her mention last Christmas? For us to pick up where we left off?'

I fall silent, trying to recall Natalia's actual words.

'I swear, there is nothing going on between us. Whether she mislaid a hair clip, I don't know. I knew the jacket was hers, but where was the harm in you borrowing it? Hell, Dottie borrows it sometimes. I haven't hidden a girlfriend, I haven't lied about that.'

It's now my turn to shrug.

'Look, I don't know how much Dottie has said, if anything. But this is it, right here. Me and the manor. Trying to live the best I can, given the situation and environment in which I find myself.' He gives a snort, before continuing and gesturing past me. 'Christ, Jemima, I'm no different to the bloody carp in the pond – plunging to unknown depths in order to survive, knowing perfectly well there's little chance that I'll thrive as I am.'

His words hit home, acting like balm upon my vehement outburst. Is Ned as alone as I am? Am I barely surviving too? Or am I diving to unseen depths in order to thrive? My emotions begin to surface, overwhelming me.

'Dottie said that I should talk to you about finding the butterfly clip.' Tears spill from my lashes, as I repeat her advice.

'Did she, now? Well, Dottie was right. Some might say you lied by not being honest and telling me,' he says, his thumb gently brushing my cheek and removing a tear.

'Are you going to come clean to everyone?'

'Maybe. Dottie was sure you'd twigged, the night of the CCTV. She warned me there was no way I could feign it much longer. You're too sharp, too diligent, and would never believe in an estate manager taking liberties by accessing the forbidden gateway.'

'She's not wrong. I now realise that your name was missing from my compiled list. As were Melissa's and Levi's, as they'd taken a day trip. Dottie was upset with you for using the walled gateway, which nearly compromised the secret she'd so diligently kept. After which, she made an error in naming Melissa as the woman we'd witnessed unlocking the entrance gate. It was my cousin Pippa, all along, using keys taken from our grandpop. So, now what?' I say, sniffing back more tears as he lowers my hand, leading me across the lawn towards the pond.

We stand beside the carp pond, the ghostly forms dipping and diving, creating ripples.

'Jemima, think of the moments we've shared in recent weeks . . . do you seriously think those moments came about by chance? Or was I watching and waiting for any opportunity to be near to you?'

I look up earnestly into his face, my gaze questioning him to clarify.

'Bloody hell, Jemima, I might not be the most forthright bloke around here, but I know what I want when I see it. I even dashed into town amidst weekend shoppers and tourists to get a sodding haircut.' He reaches for my hand, raising it to gently brush against his lips; his words linger in the night sky. 'Yes, I lied about my role, I've been lying about it for years. How on earth could I be honest with you, when others never twigged I was the rich boy from over the bloody wall? Dottie convinced them, and that suited me. I knew, the moment I saw you dithering and wobbling about on top of that piled-up skip, that we would be together. I was smitten at first sight.'

I can barely see his dark eyes, just a slight glimmer in the night, as I search his features for the truth.

Slowly, he wraps his arms about my shoulders, a welcome gesture as we stand in the darkness with a sliver of moon and a smattering of stars above. He leans closer to me, his strong jawline and gentle lips drawing nearer; I can't resist lifting my chin, my eyelids close, and I'm lost within his kiss. It's a kiss filled with truth, passion and desire. I don't want it to end, but slowly it does, with gentle nuzzling and contented sighs. We gaze inanely at each other, intoxicated by emotion and relief, as a shooting star flits across the night sky; we both react instantly and point towards the magical sight overhead, which has already faded.

'Did you make a wish?' I ask, excited to share.

'Of course.' He pulls me closer, softly planting a kiss upon my upturned forehead. 'I wished that you might be as honest with me as I am about to be with you.'

'Honest?' I say, pulling away from his body to view him clearly. I'm bemused that his shooting star wish doesn't make sense. Why waste a wish?

'Despite everything that has happened tonight, it's time to be totally honest and tell you how I've been feeling these past few months. Now hear me out, please.'

My mouth opens wide in astonishment, as he continues.

'I didn't lie simply to hurt you. It was a poor attempt to protect myself, and possibly you, but it turns out my efforts were pointless, given that I've fallen deeply in love with the young woman on the neighbouring allotment. The very same one I saw crying inside her potting shed, who made numerous errors and yet still had the heart and soul to help others, create new enterprises and show resilience when it all appeared too much for her to handle. I never expected someone like you to simply walk into my life while I tended my honey bees.'

I want to burst with joy. My wish had been simpler; to feel his arms wrapping themselves around me and holding me close.

Ned's dark eyebrows lift, in an expectant manner. 'Jemima . . . I'm waiting for a reply.'

'Ned Campbell, despite only knowing you for a short time and experiencing the precious moments we've shared . . . it would be rude of me not to be as honest and say, I've fallen for you too. I forget whether it was your apology which secured my heart, your brooding looks during our silent glances, or your prowess when lifting me down from the edge of a skip – I don't know, but I too have definite feelings for you.'

We passionately embrace, his arms wrap tightly about my body as I nestle into his chest, happy in the knowledge that neither of us will continue to struggle alone. Without a word, Ned gently takes my hand, leading me across the lawn towards the paved terrace, returning us to the warmth and security of Lerwick Manor.

Epilogue

Thursday 30 September

Note: Pumpkin soup for three meals a day. I can't give it away for love nor money. Pumpkin chutney, pumpkin jam, pumpkin pie, roasted, sliced, diced pumpkin — even the local bairns wouldn't take the remaining ones to hollow out and carve for Halloween. I'll store these last few in my potting shed, they'll keep until next year if I'm lucky.

Jemima

Having consumed several glasses of wine, I feel incredibly tipsy as I make my way through the happy gathering mingling within The Orangery. I'm searching for a particular group; not necessarily a specific face that I recognise, but a social group who I truly hope have accepted Ned's invite. Smiling faces surround and greet me from all sides as I pass by; I'm noting those I've chatted to and those I must catch up with in a few moments' time. After I've spoken to the Happy Days residents, if I ever find them.

It's such a relief that Ned agreed to me organising a last-minute celebration ahead of the gallery's grand opening. It seems a fitting way of thanking those who have kindly contributed, and a means of introducing new friends. As Ned joked, 'If you can't do it, then nobody can.' And he was right.

There was no going back, once I'd set the wheels in motion. With the refurbished facilities at hand, the right friends awarded the right task, and our newly appointed catering manager – it was a cinch. Though I have some misgivings about the music system Kaspar and Levi have borrowed from a local pub; the volume seems unreliable, the disco lights are slightly retro, and the blaring tunes appear to leap and lurch between various decades and genres without any logical mixing.

I spy my sought-after group, happily sitting at the back of the room, away from the music system; Grandpop would have hated the continual drum and bass thud. Thankfully, someone has kindly rearranged a selection of comfy armchairs around a coffee table or two, providing a suitable area. I don't suppose the folk at Happy Days sheltered housing get out and about much for raves and partying.

'Hello, I'm Jemima . . . Tommy's granddaughter,' I say, giving a little wave and raising my voice in case anyone is hard of hearing. 'Thank you for coming, I really do appreciate it. I never got to thank you for your kindness towards my grandpop – he loved being part of your community and various social groups. Arrangements for a final farewell proved difficult, without upsetting the rest of the family,' I explain, praying they understand my predicament.

'Oooo, don't you worry, we had a cheeky toast within our social hub, didn't we?' says a spritely lady within the group, her sequined dress sparkling wildly under the flashing lights. 'Our little whip-round managed to stretch to a fine bottle of Jameson's – we each enjoyed a dram or two, that night.'

I make my way around to her chair and crouch down between her seat and the neighbouring wing-back chair.

'We miss him terribly,' adds a frail gent, wearing thick spectacles, his finger swiftly wiping beneath the rim. 'He was a laugh and a half, was Tommy. He'd do aught for anyone.'

It feels strange, knowing this select group kept Grandpop happily entertained, outside of his allotment posse, with their tales of scooter mishaps, addiction to daytime TV and daily quiz programmes.

'I hope you've all had plenty of buffet food – I don't want anything left over,' I say, knowing the mountain of food prepared earlier.

'Jemima, there you are!' cries Dottie, appearing amidst the crowd, beckoning me urgently.

She looks radiant in a turquoise evening gown, minus her usual wide-brimmed hat, though the additional twinkle to her eye in recent weeks has been noted by everyone.

'Quick, quick, quick!'

I duly excuse myself from the Happy Days guests and hastily make my way over to Dottie, who doesn't give me chance to speak before she does.

'Your cousin Pippa's here. What do you want us to do? Mungo said to throw her out, I said to watch her like a hawk, and Levi said it really isn't our place to decide.'

'Wow! You three certainly have my back, if nothing else,' I say, absorbing the details, knowing Pippa didn't reply to the invite. 'Has Ned seen her?'

'Nope. Why? Do you want him to deal with her?' asks Dottie, peering through the crowd.

'Not exactly. It's hardly his duty to deal with my family issues, now is it?'

Given how close we've become since the festival night, some might say otherwise – but for now, I'm playing my cards close to my chest. We've barely been apart for longer than an evening, both blissfully content in the knowledge that our 'courting' is getting serious. Modern dating seems so haphazard, courting more intentional. It might sound old-fashioned in some respects, but we've maintained a decorum whilst growing closer with each passing day. There's been no flighty behaviour or game-playing. Instead, we've truly got to know each other through meaningful conversations, childhood memories and shared values. Ned's even joked about me designing my own tartan, though I'm tempted to formally adopt the newly created 'Spirit of Shetland' tartan; its colours represent our landscape so beautifully. Every day has felt special, unlike anything I've experienced before; I'm more in tune with Ned than any previous beau. A whirlwind romance, you might say, born from working alongside each other whilst carefully balancing our growing affections, but one I wouldn't change. From one partnership to another.

'All my days! Jemima, be quick, otherwise she'll have nabbed the spare set of manor keys and be off with the Campbells' best silver before you know it. There's no time for faffing about.'

'Does she know?' pants Mungo, having scurried through the bodies to join us.

I notice his hand snakes about Dottie's shoulder, his eyes are ablaze with sparkles too, and his wiry beard seems somewhat tamed since festival day.

'Look at you pair, the new Bonnie and Clyde of Lerwick, eh?' I tease, noticing a flirty blush to Dottie's cheek upon his arrival.

Mungo ignores my remark. 'The likes of her can't be trusted amongst decent folks. What if she chances her hand at swiping the keys from the Happy Days group? You'd be mortified if she stole their pensions like she did our honesty boxes!'

'Our honesty boxes, is it? I do remember a certain someone claiming he had no interest in our Veggie Rack project – wanted to close it down, I believe he once said.' I make eyes at Dottie, drilling home my point.

'Stuff and nonsense, I wouldn't dream of saying . . . anyway, what is it you're doing about this cousin of yours?'

I glance around the room of guests, in search of an answer. My aunt and uncle are sitting po-faced on the far side of The Orangery; neither relative seems inclined to enjoy their party invite. 'My cousin Callie hasn't bothered to attend even though she RSVP'd, so what's the harm in Pippa staying?'

Dottie's mouth opens wide in astonishment. Mungo begins to splutter, having just regained his breath.

'I really can't be bothered with it all. I'm on the brink of starting a new venture, so I might as well . . .' I cease talking as a new face, much loved and much missed, appears amongst the crowd of guests. 'Dad!'

I scurry off, leaving Dottie in Mungo's safe hands, whilst I fling myself into my father's open arms.

'Congratulations! My little girl managing a gallery – who'd have thought it. And looking so well too. Are you all ready for the grand opening?'

'I certainly am. I'm so glad you made it, Dad. I honestly wasn't sure you'd get a flight in time from the mainland. What with the short notice and . . . forget it, I'm wasting time yapping nonsense. You need to come and meet Ned, owner of the gallery and . . . the new man in my life,' I say, beaming with pride.

It feels good, saying it aloud to my dad. Instantly, he's intrigued – especially given the rarity of such introductions. I hastily steer my father through the crowd; I suspect they will get on like a house on fire, which might prove to be a true blessing or a curse, in due time.

On introducing Dad to Ned, I tentatively stand back admiring the two men I love. As predicted, their connection is instant. Like sowing seeds at the allotment; there's no chance of skimping on the basic groundwork if you desire a fruitful harvest in the future.

'I'll leave you two guys to chat some more,' I say, conscious of lingering more than is necessary.

I dash about amongst the chattering guests, my eyes peeled for one person. A man who probably won't want to disclose anything but his upbeat spirit, but someone who deserves to know that true friendship is never forgotten, despite our busy lives. Be it catching an AWOL chicken, or attempting to recycle and then reassemble a polytunnel, or simply giving advice about an orphaned duck. Friendship counts for a lot in my book, especially when you have family such as mine – who I can't rely upon.

'Levi, a quick word, if I may,' I holler, over the noise of the large music speaker behind which he is stationed. I grab his jacket sleeve pulling, him towards the exit door.

We leave the noise behind. The cobbled courtyard is chilly and silent, apart from the thud of the bass and the sporadic quack of a solitary duck.

'Anything up?' asks Levi, eager to assist, as always.

'Not with me, no, but I was wondering how you've been since . . . well, since the festival.' I'm pretty certain something occurred on festival night. Dottie's been dropping some very heavy hints.

Levi shrugs.

I feel guilty for not making time in recent weeks to check on him. 'Nah, I'm not accepting that. You and I spent the summer months working alongside Melissa – we both know that there has been a certain spark flickering between you two. Now, out with it. How are you, really?'

Levi exhales deeply. His eyes are partly covered by the shadow cast from the stables, but I can see the hurt; their doleful expression tells all.

'That bad, eh?'

'I'm gutted, Jemima. I would have loved her to the ends of the earth and back, if she'd given me half a chance. I thought she felt the same, but obviously not.'

'Levi, I'm so sorry. Have you spoken to her?'

'Oh yeah, we're still good friends, but it won't . . . it can't be the same, not now. It'll take a while to get my head around it, but I'll get there. I'll be fine.'

I watch as his chin lowers and he averts his gaze from mine.

'Levi, please shout if you want to chat. You've helped me no end since my arrival at the allotments. It's time for me to repay that kindness, OK?'

Levi gives a weak smile. 'Thank you, I appreciate that, Jemima.'

'Come on, back in we go. I've still got so many guests to speak to.'

We re-enter the throng of merriment.

'Jemima, are you happy with how it's going?'

I turn to find our newly appointed catering manager, Isla,

freckle-faced and bright-eyed, doing the rounds with a huge platter of warm buttered bannocks.

'I'm thrilled, but what are you doing waiting on folk? You should be enjoying yourself after the amount of effort you've put into preparing the party food – and at such short notice!' I take the silver platter from her grasp.

'Honest, it's fine. I love helping out at parties,' she says, retrieving the platter.

'I assume you've met the other artists who've taken a residency in the gallery?'

'Yeah. There's a group over there . . . and another bunch in the far corner. I've met Wednesday Smith, the blacksmith – she's the live wire, with her shocking-pink hair. And the weaving ladies, the glassblower guy and the candle man. But I haven't met the wool lady who's starting up The Yarn Barn – Verity, I think her name is.'

'She's not officially arriving from the mainland until Friday night,' I say, which is cutting it a tad fine for Sunday's opening, in my opinion. 'Hopefully, you'll find there's a lot in common, given that you're all creative types. I'm not sure it matters what the crafted material is – iron, wool or dough – birds of a feather seem to flock together.'

'They certainly do, Jemima,' says Isla, nodding vehemently.

I spy Melissa and Dottie standing nearby; now's my chance to catch them together for a private word, so I hastily excuse myself and watch Isla drift off amongst the guests.

'Ladies, can I say how glad I am that I didn't hand my keys back to the council on that first morning, back in the spring?' I link my arms through theirs. 'I've thrived since becoming part of your allotment and Friday gin club.'

'I knew this day would come,' teases Dottie, nipping my cheek with her thumb and forefinger. 'The moment I laid eyes on you, I thought, "She's Tommy's girl, through and through – she'll stay put." You've blossomed since joining us, as if reaching your full potential – like one of my beautiful delphiniums.'

I beam with pride; Dottie's got the magic touch, be it with flowers or people.

'I'm still miffed, I can't lie. Your decision lumbered me with the jungle that was plot eighteen. I'd have been in heaven with Tommy's neat borders and chicken run,' teases Melissa, squeezing my arm. 'I'll try to forgive you, as you're so damned lovely – plus you've agreed to my request for a display case for my ceramics.' We turn to glance at the wall of display cabinets which, I am trustily assured by vendors, will be overflowing with beautiful objects by Saturday evening.

'I can't believe so much has happened in a few short months. But really, I wanted to say thank you to both of you. You've been such great friends to me, helping me out with endless tasks, guiding me, chivvying me along when it was going wrong. Even forgiving me when I caused damage and mayhem with chemicals, or unwisely relayed gossipy conversations. It feels like a dream come true to find myself here – and to think, I originally viewed it simply as something to do during my sabbatical.'

'And your anxiety attacks . . . they've buggered off,' says Dottie kindly, her watery blue eyes glistening.

'Pretty much, Dottie. I'm coping better, and yes, they've definitely subsided. I suspect those resulted from the shock of bereavement and the grief caused by my mum's sudden passing, and then Grandpop's, within such a short space of time. I felt so alone, yet you two were unknowingly waiting to support me, like tiny seeds waiting to burst through the soil with vigour and life. It's amazing, really, the impact we have when we truly connect with others.' My voice cracks as my eyes well up.

'Our pleasure, Jemima. And likewise, you've done the same for us,' says Melissa, giving me a warm smile to ease my moment. 'I was filling time whilst Hamish was working away. But now, we've settled on some serious plans for the future, during his recent holiday break. He's promised me just six more months working away and then he'll be home for good, which means we can start planning for the patter of tiny feet.'

'Oh, you've done so much for me, lassie! You've put my heart and mind at rest. I was beginning to get a bit worried about a certain someone, but not any more,' says Dottie, tapping her nose repeatedly and looking in my direction, before adding, 'mum's the word.'

'And you and Mungo?' I ask, huddling closer to Melissa, intrigued to hear more good news. 'There's a rumour that some committee members are planning more than next year's festival arrangements over their nightly cocoa.'

'Or should that be over their beetroot wine?' corrects Melissa.

'Oh, stop it! You troublesome two,' giggles Dottie, blushing for Scotland. 'I could spill the beans too, you know. I've witnessed my fair share whilst doing my dusting duties here at the manor – I think there's a new queen bee emerging.'

Melissa is open-mouthed, turning her attention to me.

'Melissa, I haven't any secrets . . . I've had a wonderful month getting to know Ned, I won't deny it. I just wish Grandpop was here to share in my newfound happiness. It's literally been my dream come true and the sparkle of every Hollywood movie since—'

The sound system's mic buzzes into life, causing everyone to cringe and shudder at the ear-piercing noise.

'Sorry to interrupt, folks, but can anyone see Jemima?' comes Ned's deep voice, loud and clear over the tannoy.

'Here! Here!' shout numerous people in my vicinity, duly pointing at me.

'Jemima, would you care to join me, please?' instructs Ned.

I'm not sure I like the sound of this but I refrain from complaining, leave my two dearest friends and squeeze back through the crowd, as requested.

'Ah, there you are!'

I whisper a quick apology before standing beside him, facing the party guests: mainly friends, some family and our newly acquainted artists. It feels right to have organised such a gathering, even if it was very last minute. I haven't felt this happy and content in a long time.

'Ladies and gentleman, can I thank each and every one of you for joining us to celebrate the opening of the new gallery in the coming days. A venture brought about thanks to Jemima's savvy thinking and intuition – whilst weeding, I believe,' says Ned, as the crowd chuckle at my knowing expression. Ned glances at my reaction before continuing. 'It goes without saying that, despite my newly revealed status as the hereditary owner of Lerwick Manor, Jemima is the heart and mind behind this new project . . .'

A ripple of applause begins and steadily grows. Much to my embarrassment, Ned waits for it to subside, before continuing.

'She definitely offered up the solution to a huge issue, just in the nick of time. As you now know, I was on the cusp of calling in a tourist trust for serious discussions. You know this young woman, she doesn't accept public praise too kindly – shirks it at every opportunity, actually – so, to save her blushes, I hope you'll join me in a suitable toast, one befitting the new venture, which I . . . *we* hope brings good fortune to every artist, craftsperson and customer who takes delight in the fabulous wares on display. Be it locally or thousands of miles away, each item will bear a discrete yet decorative label, clearly stating our intentions: I give you "From Shetland, With Love".'

'From Shetland, With Love,' chorus the guests, raising their glasses in our direction.

I swiftly sip my drink as a distraction from their collective gaze, before mouthing, 'Thank you.' I've never been one for public demonstrations and am eager to return to my mingling.

'Excuse me, one final thing before we return to enjoying what remains of our evening,' says Ned into the mic, turning towards me as he speaks.

I politely smile, knowing I'll be safely back amongst the crowd within minutes.

Ned gently takes my hand in his. 'Jemima, it can't have escaped the attention of everyone who knows us, that in recent weeks something very special has occurred . . . blossomed almost, right before their eyes. I sensed my bachelor days were drawing to an end the very first moment I saw you, balancing precariously on top of a skip.' He turns aside to speak to the party. 'I won't go into detail – but I'm sure Dottie will, after a few more sherries.'

There's a ripple of laughter from the allotment posse, before Ned continues speaking to me. My eyes are drawn to his, as his fingers squeeze mine a little more tightly. It might only have been a matter of weeks since the festival, but this moment feels surreal. Our feelings are so true. So natural.

'You and I both know that, despite ours being a rather short acquaintance and courtship, we fell in love . . . undeniably, head over heels and very quickly. There seems to be a belief in the Campbell family that "when you know, you know" and, Jemima, I definitely know. I know that I couldn't have achieved this . . . without you. I know that all my future plans include you by my side. Jemima, I believe you know it too. And so, I wish to ask one simple question: will you marry me and agree to be my wife?'

I know my answer, without hesitation.

Every eye is upon me. Every breath is held a fraction longer than necessary. Every heart skips a beat.

'Yes.' The word barely has the chance to escape my lips, before Ned wraps me tightly in his arms. We passionately kiss, amidst a deafening round of applause filling The Orangery.

'Thank you,' whispers Ned, his eyes glistening as he pulls back from our embrace to view my smiling face. 'Birds of a feather do flock together, always.'

'Mmmm, I'm thinking more along the lines of Old Bill's motto, "You've gotta do a bit and leave a bit," for the future generations of Lerwick Manor.'

Acknowledgements

Thank you to my editor, Kate Byrne, and everyone at Headline Publishing Group for believing in my imagination and giving me the opportunity to become part of your team.

To David Headley and the crew at DHH Literary Agency – thank you for your continued support. I couldn't ask for a more experienced or dedicated team to champion my career.

Thank you to my fellow authors/friends within the Romantic Novelists' Association – you continue to support and encourage me every step of the way. I promise to repay the generosity and kindness received in recent years.

A heartfelt 'thank you' to the Shetlanders for providing such a warm welcome whilst I holidayed in Lerwick, Shetland – who would have thought that this little girl's dream of visiting the top of the weather map would result in a story!

Thank you to Steven Cooper of The Workshop, Old Finstown Road, St Ola, Orkney, Scotland (info@aurora-jewellery.co.uk) for kindly granting permission for me to include the newly created tartan 'Spirit of Shetland' – its colours are truly beautiful in representing the Shetland landscape.

Thank you to my family, for always loving and supporting my adventures.

And finally, thank you to my wonderful readers. You continue to thrill me each day with your fabulous reviews and supportive emails. I'm truly humbled that you invest precious time from your busy lives to read my books. Without you guys, my characters, stories and happy-ever-afters would simply be daydreams.

from Shetland, with love

Bonus Material

Kaspar's Condensed Milk Cookies

Kondenspiimaküpsised
Makes 24 biscuits

Ingredients
250g plain flour
1 tsp baking powder
150g butter, cubed
175g sweetened condensed milk
1 tsp vanilla extract
2 tsp water
1 small beaten egg
Pinch of salt
Utensils
Cookie cutters (a diamond shape is traditionally preferred)

Method
Preheat the oven to 200°C/Fan 180°C/Gas 6.
Place the dry ingredients into a mixing bowl and add a pinch of salt. Rub the cubed butter into the dry mix until it resembles a crumbly mixture. Add the vanilla extract. Add the condensed milk to form a dough-like texture. Add the water, if required. Refrigerate the dough for 30 minutes, allowing it to rest.

On a lightly floured surface, roll out the dough to a thickness of approximately 5mm. Cut into the desired shapes, using the cookie cutters. A diamond is the traditional shape for these cookies. Brush with the beaten egg and bake for 8–10 minutes, until golden brown.

Spend the holiday season in glorious Lerwick!

Look out for

from Shetland, with love at Christmas

New Beginnings at Rose Cottage

Don't miss this perfect feel-good read
of friendship and fresh starts from Erin Green,
guaranteed to make you smile!

Available now from

Taking a Chance on Love

The perfect feel-good, romantic and uplifting
read – another book from Erin Green
sure to warm your heart!

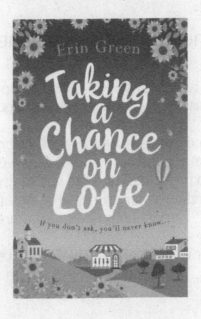

Bookends

When one book ends, another begins...

Bookends is a vibrant new reading community to help you ensure you're never without a good book.

You'll find exclusive previews of the brilliant new books from your favourite authors as well as exciting debuts and past classics. Read our blog, check out our recommendations for your reading group, enter great competitions and much more!

Visit our website to see which great books we're recommending this month.

Join the Bookends community:
www.welcometobookends.co.uk

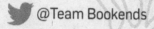 @Team Bookends   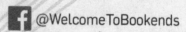 @WelcomeToBookends

C017010669

Erin Green was born and raised in Warwickshire. An avid reader since childhood, her imagination was instinctively drawn to creative writing as she grew older. Erin has two Hons degrees: BA English literature and another BSc Psychology – her previous careers have ranged from part-time waitress, the retail industry, fitness industry and education.

She has an obsession about time, owns several tortoises and an infectious laugh! Erin writes contemporary novels focusing on love, life and laughter. Erin is an active member of the Romantic Novelists' Association and was delighted to be awarded The Katie Fforde Bursary in 2017. An ideal day for Erin involves writing, people watching and drinking copious amounts of tea.

For more information about Erin, visit her website: **www.ErinGreenAuthor.co.uk**, find her on Facebook **www.facebook.com/ErinGreenAuthor** or follow her on Twitter **@ErinGreenAuthor**.

By Erin Green

A Christmas Wish
The Single Girl's Calendar
The Magic of Christmas Tree Farm
New Beginnings at Rose Cottage
Taking a Chance on Love
From Shetland, With Love